Praise for the Nov
Susan Holloway S

The Countess and

"If witty Nell Gwyn was 'the King's Protestant whore,' equally witty Katherine Sedley was 'the King's plain whore.' In this well-researched novel of the racy Stuart court, Susan Holloway Scott introduces readers to a spirited mistress of the unfortunate James II. You will come to love Katherine, as the notoriously stubborn and hard-to-please James himself did."

—Margaret George, author of *Helen of Troy*

"Susan Holloway Scott masterfully recounts the destiny of the Countess of Dorchester, from the joys and trials of a privileged childhood to the intrigues of the court of James II. Restoration England springs to life in this witty, utterly engaging heroine."

—Catherine Delors, author of *For the King*

The French Mistress

An *Historical Novel Society Review* Editor's Choice

"Delicious! . . . Ms. Scott has an incredible talent not only for re-creating . . . Restoration England, but also for bringing these historic characters, caught in a web of their own making, to life. Compulsively readable, this wonderful novel will keep you turning the pages, unable to stop, until the bittersweet end."

—Dish Magazine

"Scott's grasp of period detail is impressive and colorful. She fleshes out these well-known historical figures' psyches so they become alive and human, and her words evoke the senses—one can feel silk and wool against skin, experience the discomfort from long hours of standing in an overheated ballroom, and witness the first shocking view of London from a Frenchwoman's perspective. She expertly weaves the complex political events of the time into the flow of the story, which makes for a thoroughly entertaining, enjoyable, and intellectually stimulating read. Highly recommended."

—*The Historical Novels Review*

"Scott returns to the bawdy court of Charles II to bring another of his mistresses' lives to light, Louise de Keroualle, who caught his roving eye and rose to power. Scott follows Louise through the labyrinth of court intrigue, painting a rich portrait of Charles' decadent reign. . . . Scott's feminist approach to history is refreshing."

—*Romantic Times*

continued . . .

The King's Favorite

An *Historical Novel Society Review* Editor's Choice

"This is a wild joy ride through Restoration England, with Nell firmly gripping the reins. Susan Holloway Scott is so intuitive with period language and so involved in the psyches of her characters that you are at all times *there* with them, seeing what they're seeing, feeling what they're feeling—and always, *always* rooting for the petite whirlwind of a heroine."

—Robin Maxwell, author of *O, Juliette*

"This is an entertaining fictionalized memoir that brings alive from an 'insider's' perspective a transformation period in English history as Cromwell is out and the Stuarts are back in. Nell comes across as intelligent and witty as she uses double entendres to get the better of hypocrites who claim to know what is morally best for others (sounds so contemporarily familiar). Genre fans will appreciate the life and times of *The King's Favorite*, as the 'Duchess' of biographical fiction Susan Holloway Scott provides an insightful seventeenth-century tale."

—*Midwest Book Review*

"The story of the Oxford-born barmaid turned prostitute turned orange seller turned renowned actress—and, ultimately, the mistress and closest companion to Charles II—is one of legend. Scott takes this well-worn story and breathes life and spirit into it. . . . Scott does such a marvelous job of imbuing Nell with innate intelligence and a love of life that the reader just can't help falling in love with her too. A joyous and highly recommended novel."

—*The Historical Novels Review*

Royal Harlot

An *Historical Novels Review* Editor's Choice

"As in her popular *Duchess*, Scott captures in her latest historical novel the brilliance and hard beauty of Barbara Palmer (Lady Castlemaine), the Merry Monarch's most famous and enduring mistress. . . . Scott finds a careful balance in Barbara, not salvaging her as a sinner, but giving her something of a heart under all that reputation."

—*Publishers Weekly*

"Having previously provided a fictional memoir of Sarah, first Duchess of Marlborough, Scott brings to vivid life another of the seventeenth century's most notorious, brazen, and powerful females. If anything, *Royal Harlot* is an even more assured, nuanced, and colorful portrait of a woman and her age.... In her intriguing portrayal, Scott tempers Barbara's rapacious sexuality while presenting a Charles who seems far less frustrated with her tempestuousness than the historical record indicates. And although the real Barbara was better known for her ambition and avarice than her maternal devotion, the novelist incorporates her motherhood to good effect. Among this novel's many strengths are Scott's impressive depiction of time and place, her evocation of the Restoration-era mind-set, the exuberance of the period, and her sure, succinct presentation of complex historical events. The reader can well believe that this is a memoir penned by a woman who—in reality—was clearly too busy living to ever write one!" —*The Historical Novels Review*

"The Countess of Castlemaine, labeled the Great Harlot of Charles II, never denies or regrets her nature in this fascinating rendering of an outrageous love affair that defies convention and public outrage in Restoration England. . . . Relating the details of Barbara's fictionalized life, the author takes into account the historical events and unusual influence of a powerful woman in the Restoration court, fleshing out the countess's adventures with gusto, her flaws all the more glaring in the waning years of her power. All in all, this is a thorough and imaginative re-creation of Palmer's long career and her extraordinary talent for manipulating circumstances to her own advantage, an informative and plausible treatment of the controversial life of a successful woman in a man's world." —Curled Up with a Good Book

Duchess

Named a Booksense Notable Book by the American Booksellers Association

"Wonderful... whisks the reader into a period rife with intrigue, love, sex, war, and religious strife." —*The Historical Novels Review* (editor's choice pick)

"All the trappings of supermarket tabloids: intrigue, treachery, deceit, and sexual scandals." —*Publishers Weekly*

"Susan Holloway Scott has brought to life the racy world of post-Restoration England in her richly researched and beautifully written *Duchess*."
—Karen Harper, author of *Mistress Shakespeare*

"No dry dust of history here, but a vivid portrait of an intriguing woman with all her flaws and strengths. Rich in period detail, the novel also has all the ingredients necessary for a compelling read, conflict, suspense, intrigue, and the romance between Sarah and John Churchill, one of history's great love stories."

—Susan Carroll, author of *Twilight of a Queen*

"Compelling; it grips the reader from the very first sentence and never lets go. Scott does a wonderful job of bringing Lady Sarah and her world to life."

—Jeanne Kalogridis, author of *The Devil's Queen*

• Also by Susan Holloway Scott •

The King's Favorite

A Novel of Nell Gwyn and King Charles II

Royal Harlot

A Novel of the Countess of Castlemaine and King Charles II

Duchess

A Novel of Sarah Churchill

The French Mistress

A Novel of the Duchess of Portsmouth and King Charles II

The Countess and the King

A NOVEL OF

THE COUNTESS OF DORCHESTER AND KING JAMES II

SUSAN HOLLOWAY SCOTT

NEW AMERICAN LIBRARY

NEW AMERICAN LIBRARY
Published by New American Library, a division of
Penguin Group (USA) Inc., 375 Hudson Street,
New York, New York 10014, USA
Penguin Group (Canada), 90 Eglinton Avenue East, Suite 700, Toronto,
Ontario M4P 2Y3, Canada (a division of Pearson Penguin Canada Inc.)
Penguin Books Ltd., 80 Strand, London WC2R 0RL, England
Penguin Ireland, 25 St. Stephen's Green, Dublin 2,
Ireland (a division of Penguin Books Ltd.)
Penguin Group (Australia), 250 Camberwell Road, Camberwell, Victoria 3124,
Australia (a division of Pearson Australia Group Pty. Ltd.)
Penguin Books India Pvt. Ltd., 11 Community Centre, Panchsheel Park,
New Delhi - 110 017, India
Penguin Group (NZ), 67 Apollo Drive, Rosedale, North Shore 0632,
New Zealand (a division of Pearson New Zealand Ltd.)
Penguin Books (South Africa) (Pty.) Ltd., 24 Sturdee Avenue,
Rosebank, Johannesburg 2196, South Africa

Penguin Books Ltd., Registered Offices:
80 Strand, London WC2R 0RL, England

First published by New American Library,
a division of Penguin Group (USA) Inc.

First Printing, September 2010
1 3 5 7 9 10 8 6 4 2

Cover painting: *Ludlow Castle*, William Marlow (1740–1813)/Bridgeman Art Library
Cover painting: *Barbara Villiers*, Peter Lely (1618–80)/The Trustees of the Goodwood Collection/
Bridgeman Art Library

LIBRARY OF CONGRESS CATALOGING-IN-PUBLICATION DATA:

Scott, Susan Holloway.
The countess and the king: a novel of the Countess of Dorchester and King James II/
Susan Holloway Scott.
p. cm.
ISBN 978-0-451-23115-4
1. Dorchester, Catherine Sedley, Countess of, 1657–1717—Fiction. 2. James II, King of England, 1633–1701—Fiction. 3. Great Britain—History—James II, 1685–1688—Fiction. 4. Great Britain—Kings and rulers—Paramours—Fiction. 5. Mistresses—Great Britain—Fiction. I. Title.
PS3560.A549C68 2010
813'.54—dc22 2010016683

Set in Minion
Designed by Ginger Legato

Printed in the United States of America

The Countess and the King

Prologue

BUCKINGHAM HOUSE, LONDON
June 1708

It is true. I have committed my share of sins, both large and small, and who in this mortal world hasn't? Yet surely the gravest of my faults was not my doing, and that was to have been born plain into a world of great beauty.

Ah, there you see how I was likewise blessed. For if I was granted neither pleasing sweetness in my face nor languid grace in my form, I did receive a love of truth and a joyful abundance of cleverness. Indeed, those who've had the misfortune to feel my barbs might peevishly claim I'd been given more wit than was my rightful share. I disagree. All ladies are vulnerable amidst the prowling lions at Court. Pretty, silly fools will always have their place, but not for long. The luscious, dewy petals of the rose soon wither and fall away, yet it is the thorns that remain ever sharp.

I've found no fault with my life as a thorn. I have been well loved by both a king and a commoner, one who was a most excellent and honorable man and one who was neither. I have seen one monarch hastened from his throne, and been among the first to welcome two more in his stead. I have been a mistress because it amused me, a wife because I wished it, and a countess in my own right, without the weary encumbrance of an earl to hamper me. How many ladies of mere idle ornament can claim the same?

But then, I was always different from the others. I *am* different. And where, I ask you, is the sin in that?

Chapter One

Bloomsbury Square, London
July 1667

With my cloak tied beneath my chin and new yellow kidskin gloves on my hands, I was ready to join Father for our journey. The footman had taken away the traveling trunk with my belongings, and when I'd last looked down from my window, I'd seen him and a groom struggling to lash it atop Father's own trunk on the back of our coach while my maid Danvers scolded them both. I knew I should go below now and not keep Father waiting, yet still I lingered in the center of my bedchamber, torn by anxious indecision.

Was nine years too old an age for dolls? Danvers had assured me it was, and she'd know better. I would be ten at my next birthday, in December, which meant I'd only five more years after that before I would be considered old enough for a place at the royal Court of King Charles. I was quite sure there'd be no dolls in the palace lodgings for the maids of honor, nor, for that matter, would there likely be any among Father's grand noble friends in Epsom now. Better I should act as the young lady I intended to be than to cling like a babe to childish playthings.

Yet still I looked with longing at my doll Cassandra, propped against the pillow biers on my bed where Danvers had arranged her. Her tiny wood feet pointed straight from beneath her silk skirts, her hands carved like white mittens folded one over the other in her lap, her hair only a little frizzed beneath her lace cap. The sternly quizzical expression on her painted face remained as unchanging as the fashionable black patches that dotted her ever-rosy cheeks.

I had loved Cassandra from the moment Father had brought her to me from Paris three years before, and since then she had been my constant, almost desperate, confidante. I was the lone child to bless my parents' union, and in our grand mansion house near Lincoln's Inn Fields, I'd neither sisters nor brothers to share my play, my secrets, my fears. I'd only Cassandra.

I clambered across my bed and grabbed the doll, tucking her familiarly into the crook of my arm. I couldn't bear to leave her alone, here where she'd have no company for the fortnight I'd be away with Father at Epsom. My toes had scarcely slid back to the floor when I heard footsteps behind me, and I swiftly turned about with guilty haste.

"Ah, so Lady Cass is to travel with us after all," Father said. "How honored I am to have two such handsome ladies in my party."

He smiled fondly, not at all perturbed by my attachment to the doll. Truth to tell, I doubted there would've been much I could have done that would vex him that day. He'd vowed that he'd anticipated this little junket of ours (our first such) almost as much as I, and I could scarcely wait to have his company to myself in the coach. I seldom did, for Father had much to occupy him. In addition to being a baronet with properties and estates to oversee, he also wrote poems and plays, real ones that were bound in leather in his library downstairs. More impressive, my father was a great favorite at Court, and everyone knew he was considered among the closest and dearest of friends by His Majesty himself.

But while I was very proud of my father, I saw very little of him. He was often gone for weeks at a time when the king tired of Whitehall and moved the Court to one of his other palaces or the estate of a favorite lord. Even when Father was at home there were many nights when he'd remain at Whitehall Palace or return home so late that the first dawn had already begun to glimmer over the rooftops. I'd peek from my window to watch him, so spent that he'd need the help of two servants to climb down from his carriage and up the steps to our house. I wasn't exactly sure what was done at Court at such an hour, but I was certain it must be important, as was everything to do with King Charles.

"Come now, my beauteous Miss Sedley, let us depart." Father made a sweeping bow and held his hand out for me to take. "High time we quit this place for the delights of the country."

I grinned and curtsied, for I loved these rare times when Father played the gallant with me. He *was* a gallant, too, as he was most particular about his dress. His coats were cut long and of silken, plush velvet in the French fashion, his breeches extravagantly wide and cuffed with rosettes of ribbons, and his periwigs tall and full and often tied with a lovelock or two. He was especially careful of his neckcloths, snowy tumbles of *point d'Espagne* or *point de Venice* that were never besmirched by a single crumb or drop of wine, let alone my grubby infant fingers. Yet Father was also blessed with a gallant's wit, a clever way with a jest or story, and he could make anyone laugh aloud, whether a costard monger in the park or the king himself. Was there any wonder that I believed Father the most handsome, most amusing, most perfect gentleman in all London, or that I loved him with a fervent devotion more suitable to a distant deity than a mere mortal parent?

"Your servant, Sir Charles," I said grandly, eager to continue the game. I shifted my doll from one arm to the other and slipped my little fingers into his hand, raising my chin high the way I'd seen the great ladies do while riding in St. James's Park. "We must away, my good lord, away, away!"

He laughed. "Where the devil did you learn that phrase, poppet?"

"One of the plays you took me to," I said eagerly, for he'd only just decided me of an age to attend the theater with him. "I disremember the title, but I thought that turn was most fine."

"So it is." He raised my hand and kissed the air above it. "Then let's away, away, little Katherine. I wish to be in Epsom by supper."

Humming some merry scrap of a tune, he led me down the staircase as if I were in truth a great lady. But on the last landing, I stopped and would go no farther.

"Stay, Father, please," I said softly. "I must bid farewell to Mama."

"Your mother." In an instant all the merriment drained from his round-cheeked face. "Do you wish me to come with you, Katherine?"

"I'll be well enough by myself." He always volunteered, and I always refused.

"You are sure, Katherine?" he asked with worry, and that, too, was a constant.

"I'm not afraid," I said at once, more to convince myself than Father.

I often *was* afraid when I went to Mama's rooms—not of her, but of what I might see or hear that I'd later wish I hadn't. "I won't be long."

"Do what you must, poppet." He tried to smile, too, as sad an effort as my own. "Mind you, don't say where you and I are going. It would only distress her further."

"I won't. I vow." My mama wasn't like other mothers. I had to take special care with my behavior in her presence, and consider well what I said to her. "Why should I wish to upset her?"

"Good lass." He bent to kiss me on my forehead, a paternal benediction. We were bound together in a thousand little conspiracies like this, Father and I, and together we understood what the rest of the world could not. Without another word, I hurried away with Cassandra in my arms, and left him to stand alone on the landing.

Mama's suite of rooms was at the back of the house, where she'd have only the healthiest air from our gardens, and where, too, she'd not be overheard by those passing in the street. The footman who was always stationed at her door opened it for me and stepped forward to announce me to my mother.

"Your Majesty," he said, bowing deeply. "Her Royal Highness the Princess Katherine."

"Your Majesty," I echoed, and sank into a deep curtsy before Mama, who was seated in a tall-backed armchair before her bedchamber window.

Now, this chair was not a throne, any more than I was a royal princess or my mother the queen. But through a sad disordering of her mind, my poor mama had forgotten that she'd been born Lady Catherine Savage, daughter of His Lordship Earl Rivers, or that she was now the wife of Sir Charles Sedley. Instead she thought herself to be the Queen of England, Catherine of Braganza, and likewise believed my father King Charles Stuart, and nothing any physician or surgeon had attempted had been able to persuade her otherwise. She *was* the queen, and all our household was obliged to treat her thus, or risk her illness worsening. No doubt she believed the others around her—her physician and his assistant, and her confessor, too—were members of her royal household. It was just as well if she did, for by Father's orders, she was never left alone, from fear she'd harm herself.

"You may rise," Mama now said to me, and leaned forward to present her cheek to me to kiss. She wore a white brocade dressing gown and every jewel that Father had given her in happier days: precious rubies and sapphires and pearls jumbled together on her person, and topped by a player's false crown of brass and colored glass. Strung among the jewels were many rosaries and crucifixes and other dangling Romish trinkets, for even in madness she had remained a fervent Papist. She'd had her hair dressed in the Portuguese manner that the true queen had affected when she'd first come to England, with stiffened curls across her forehead and over her ears.

She smiled as I kissed her cheek, the dangling pearls of her earrings tapping gently against my face.

"My sweet, dear Katherine," she said to me, stroking my face lightly with her fingertips. "How do you fare this day?"

"I'm well, ma'am." I took comfort in the gentleness of her touch. Mad or not, she was still my mother. "How did you sleep?"

"Sleep, sleep!" she exclaimed darkly. "I never sleep, child. Ask your father the king the reason why, and ask him, too, why he leaves my bed for another!"

With concern Dr. Mertonne bent over my mother, the curls of his long periwig blocking her face from my sight. Father had chosen him to attend Mama specifically because the doctor was a Papist, too. Though I didn't believe the whispers of my Rivers cousins that Dr. Mertonne had only made my mother more ill with his treatments and draughts (for surely Father would have dismissed him if that were so), I still did not like him, nor the way he hovered about Mama. Besides, he smelled foul, of stale herbs and decay.

"Pray be easy, ma'am, and calm yourself," he cautioned my mother, taking her wrist in his long fingers. "It's unwise for you to become distraught over matters you cannot control."

"That is true, ma'am, very true," murmured Father Bede, one of the numerous Romish priests who visited her regularly. "God's will cannot be questioned."

Restlessly Mama sighed, and brushed aside the doctor so she could again see me. "You're dressed for a journey, Katherine. Is His Majesty your father carrying you away from me?"

The question took me by surprise. "Not for long, ma'am," I said, hedging. "Only for a little while."

"Then he *is* taking you away," she crowed with triumph. "Where will you go, Katherine? Our palace at Richmond? Our castle at Windsor?"

"No, ma'am," I said, forgetting my promise to Father. "To Epsom Wells, to join his friends and see the horses race."

She sank back into her chair, wilting like a flower with a broken stem. "Epsom," she repeated softly, forlornly. "Epsom. Your father once took me there, too."

I expected her to speak of the king again, but instead her expression gentled, and for a rare moment the strident mask of her illness slipped from her features. Instead she once again became young and beautiful, and I smiled with wonder, dazzled by the change.

"We were newly wed, Katherine, and your father loved me still," she said, her voice light with the coaxing sweetness I could just remember. "He bought me a nosegay of white roses to hold, and he laughed when I picked my horses to win by the colors of their manes. I was only seventeen, yet I believed myself to be the most fortunate lady born, and your father and I the finest couple of fashion in England. Lah, lah, Sir Charles and Lady Sedley!"

She smiled at the memory, and I smiled, too, eager to hear more. Yet as suddenly as that happy moment had come, it scattered and vanished like petals before the wind. Instead of pleasure in Mama's eyes, I now saw only fear, a fear I could not comprehend, and one that frightened me so much that I shrank from her, clutching my doll tight against my chest.

My mother pressed her fingertips to her temples and grimaced as she struggled to keep her torments at bay.

"Take care, my angel," she warned me, her words now coming in harsh, ragged gulps. Her fingers became agitated, sliding from her temples to pluck restlessly at her hair. "Be wary of those men who would harm you, and who would order your life to suit their own, and—and—oh, Holy Mother, preserve me!"

With a keening wail, she buried her face in her hands, sending her tawdry crown clattering to the floor.

"What a wicked child," Dr. Mertonne snapped at me as his servant hurried to snatch up the fallen crown. "See the misery you have brought to Her Majesty! See how she suffers because of you!"

"I didn't harm Mama!" I cried. "I did nothing!"

"Your appearance alone was sufficient to unsettle Her Majesty," he said sternly over my mother's wails. "For her sake, I must ask you to leave this room at once."

I refused to obey him and remained, as if my trembling defiance would somehow serve my poor mother.

"You've no right to order me about," I said, daring greatly. "You're only a doctor."

Imperiously he stared down his crooked nose at me. "And what are you but a false, wicked daughter? How can you care more for your own insolent pride than for Her Majesty's welfare?"

"I am not wicked!" I cried, horrified. "She is my *mother*!"

"She is Her Majesty the Queen of England, Scotland, and Ireland," he said sharply. "You would do well to remember that."

Again he seized my sobbing mother by the wrist, and with his other hand drew a small lancet from his pocket. I knew what would come next. Mama's pale arms were already crossed over with the scars from being bled. Father had explained that this was done to bring her ease, but what I'd noticed for myself was how my mother insisted on ever more bracelets, shining silver and gold, to cover the shame of those scars.

"Courage, Your Majesty, courage," murmured Father Bede as he pressed a jeweled rosary into my mother's trembling fingers. "Know that faith in our Heavenly Father brings the only real solace from earthly suffering."

Lost in her confusion, my mother stared at him through the tangle she'd wrought of her hair. Something in his promise touched her, for as soon as he began to speak a Latin prayer, she followed, repeating his words with whispered reverence. She did not cry out as the doctor's narrow blade sliced into her white skin, or flinch as he pressed her arm to make her maddened blood flow, drop by scarlet drop, into the silver cup held by his servant.

I watched, my heart racing with distress. I cannot say which I found the more wrenching: the gore of my mother's bloodletting, the teasing sweet glimpse of what she'd once been, or the way she'd been so swiftly seduced by the priest's prayers while I'd been left forgotten before her. Most likely it was all those things together, an unhappy brew for any child to swallow.

I lingered for another moment, hesitating between my impulse to flee and my duty toward my mother, and the fluttering hope that she'd spare one more gentle word or glance for me. But she did not; she could not. I turned and ran from the room with Cassandra, and back to the parent whose love I didn't question.

Father must have guessed from my face what had happened. In wordless empathy, he held me close and led me away from the unhappiness that hung about our house like a midnight shroud of deepest mourning. Not trusting me to a servant, Father himself lifted me into the coach, and as we drew away from our house, I curled on the seat beside him, pressed as close to his side as I could manage.

Our coach was a splendid one, elegant enough to make others point and stare as we passed them by. Yet though our family's arms were picked out in gold on the door and the cushions on which we sat were of softest Spanish leather well stuffed with fleece, our ride was still dusty, lumbering, and jostling, and I felt every bump and rut of the road we traveled. I was thankful for the sturdy security of my father beside me and for his shoulder beneath my cheek, and as London's houses and churches gave way to the green trees and fields of the country, I found my melancholy sorrow began slowly to jumble away. From excitement I'd not slept much the night before, and as the afternoon sun gilded the inside of the coach, I drowsed, stroking Cassandra's flaxen hair and dreaming of the racing white horses I'd see in Epsom.

"Was she unkind to you, poppet?" Father asked softly, waiting until we were well into the country to interrupt my pretty dreams.

"No," I said, the word muffled against his shoulder. I concentrated instead on pressing Cassandra's painted hands together as if she were at prayer.

He sighed. "Your mother means you no harm, Katherine. She does love you, after her own fashion. But she's other affairs on her mind at present. I don't believe she'll be with us much longer."

At once I feared the worst, and twisted around on the seat to face him. "Mama?" I cried. "She's not going to die, is she?"

"Oh, no, no, her body's perfectly sound," he said quickly. "I meant that her Romish priests have proposed a fresh course for her, and she is tempted to agree."

I frowned. "Dr. Mertonne wouldn't permit it."

Father grunted, his obvious displeasure with the doctor most agreeable to me. "This will be your mother's decision, not Dr. Mertonne's."

"She would make such a decision?" I asked, astonished that he considered her capable of any decision at all.

"She will," he said solemnly. "I have always permitted your mother to follow the faith of her choice, no matter that it differs from yours and mine. If now she wishes to travel with Father Bede to a convent in Ghent, then I'll not stop her."

"But why would she wish to leave us?" Troubled, I remembered what Mama herself had told me earlier, and how she'd warned me against the will of men. But had she meant Father, or her priest, or some other ignoble fancy of her afflicted mind?

"She'll be away for a time, poppet, only for a time," Father said without answering the question I'd asked. He frowned, concentrating on brushing away some stray dust of the road from his sleeve. "Most likely she'll already be gone when we return."

"While we are away?" I asked, bewildered. "So soon?"

"It is for the best, Katherine," he said firmly, so I wouldn't doubt. "Nor do I wish you to believe any of this is your doing. If your mother feels a purpose to be among these other pious English ladies and the Benedictines, if she feels it will help her regain her peace, then we must oblige her. God willing, she could return to us much improved."

I nodded, unable to think of a suitable reply as tears stung my eyes. Because I couldn't recall a time when Mama had not been mad, I could not imagine a future where she'd be well, either. All I knew for certain was that she'd been too beguiled by her priest and his prayers to say farewell to me.

"Don't fret, Katherine," Father said, smoothing a stray lock away from my forehead. "It's not such grievous news. This change in your mother's situation has made me consider yours as well, and the sorry truth is that I've rather neglected you."

No child wishes to hear such a confession, though in my heart, I'd often suspected the same. Worse and worse, I thought miserably, worse and worse. My distress must have shown on my face, for Father began to make little *tut-tut* noises that were, I supposed, intended to soothe me.

"It's entirely my fault, poppet, and none of yours," he said contritely. "I've been a sorry sort of father to you. I've left you to be raised by servants and a madwoman. You would have been better treated if I'd tucked you in a basket and sold you to a pack of Gypsies for a few shillings."

"You wouldn't have done that," I said, shocked he'd say such a thing, even in jest. "I'm a Sedley. I'm your daughter. If you had sold me to the Gypsies, why, then I'd have welcomed it, for I vow they'd not be so careless with me."

At once I regretted my words, spoken as they'd been from my distress rather than with filial disrespect, but Father didn't care. Instead he laughed aloud, his eyes widening with amusement.

"Oh, aye, you're my daughter," he said proudly. "I've only to look in the glass to see the likeness between us, and listen to the prickle in your voice now to hear it. You'd have made a fine Gypsy wench, ready to lead your band back to my house to rob me as I'd deserve."

I did favor Father, with the same pale skin and quizzical brows, and eyes so dark as to be black—a Gypsy face indeed, for us both. But I'd never thought that my impertinence (for so my governesses had always deemed it) could have come from him, nor that Father would find it desirable, either.

"I *would* make a prize Gypsy," I declared, emboldened, and hoping to please him further by following his lead in this foolishness. "I'd bring my fellows to our house, too, and show them the scullery window that Cook's maid only pretends to latch at night, so the footman from Fanshawe House who's her sweetheart can come to her after the others have gone to their beds."

"Is that so?" Father asked, laughing still. "Lah, but you've a ready wit for so young a creature!"

I nodded vigorously, and though his laughter lingered, he seemed to be studying me with a new thoughtfulness.

"You surprise me, Katherine," he said. "Not about the servants, of course, for they do but ape their betters, but on account of this gift for saucy chatter. I can well imagine how you'll make His Majesty laugh, and find favor for us both because of it."

I gasped. "Truly?"

"Truly," he said. "There are two sure ways to please His Majesty. One is to make him laugh, and the other—the other is not for you to know yet, poppet. But you'll see. A little polish by way of education, a little experience, and we'll make a pretty courtier of you yet. How old are you, eh?"

"Ten," I said, wishing he'd remembered such an important fact himself. "Or nearly so."

"Oh, aye, I recall it now," he said, and sighed with gloomy remorse. "I was only eighteen myself when you were born, of an age when I'd no right to be siring any children. I'll never consent to your marrying so young, sweet. Mark it now and do not forget, for I mean to keep my word."

"Yes, Father," I said, my heart racing with anticipation. I cared not a fig for my unknown bridegroom, floating somewhere in the misty future. I'd more immediate desires. "Do you mean for me to begin at Court now?"

"Eager to be on with your life, are you?" he asked, his voice still heavy with melancholy. "What do you know of Court?"

"What you have told me," I answered promptly. "That it's all the most beautiful and clever persons in England gathered about His Majesty at the palace, and that it's the most wondrous place on earth for amusement and entertainments, like the playhouse, only everything's real."

He raised his dark brows. "I reveal such secrets?"

"You have," I said, sure he wouldn't deny it. "Why couldn't I become a maid of honor?"

"Who the devil put that notion into you head?"

"Grandmother Rivers," I said. "She vowed that to be of service to the queen or to the Duchess of York should be the desire of any young lady who wishes to show her loyalty to the Crown."

"Your grandmother is thinking of the Court when she was a girl, a hundred years ago," Father said. "There's little honor to being a maid like that now, and the only girls who seek the post are so poor that they need the pitiful dowry that the Crown provides. You, thank God, will not be in that groveling position."

This was sobering news to me, yet still I wouldn't give up. "But why couldn't I come to Court with you, as your daughter?"

"Because you're still too tender for that world," he said bluntly. "Not all of the king's Court is wondrous, not by half. The place is ripe with temptation and scandal, and filled with rogues who'd like nothing more than to ravish and debauch you simply from spite toward me."

I blushed scarlet. Not all the gossip I'd overheard from servants involved footmen and maids. I'd also listened to enough whispered tattle of our handsome king and his many mistresses that I understood Father's worries.

"I'm not a fool, Father," I insisted. "I'll not let any rogue debauch me, I swear it."

He winced. "I'd rather not hear such words from you just yet, Katherine," he cautioned. "A maid as young as you—ah, you'll need more years and seasoning before I'd toss you into those cruel waters, and more time to grow into your beauty before I'll expect that of you."

That was a hopeful kindness. I was painfully aware that I wasn't the most lovely of children. Beneath my costly gowns I was as thin as a bundle of sticks, and though I was seldom ill, I'd a sallow pallor to my cheeks that made my dark eyes seem too large for my face and my mouth too wide. But I believed Father when he said I'd blossom, and loved him all the more for it. With him to watch over me, why couldn't I begin my life at Court now?

"But you said yourself I'd been too long alone in our house, and if Mama leaves, too, I'd—"

"Katherine, no." He tipped his head back against the squabs and closed his eyes with a groan. "Merciful God, is there a greater punishment for an old libertine than to have a daughter of his own?"

"Please, Father, please," I pleaded softly, resting my hand on his sleeve. "Let me be with you."

He sighed again and slowly opened his eyes, regarding me as if he'd never seen me before. In a way, perhaps he hadn't. As we gazed at each other there in the rocking coach, I realized that I knew as little of him as he did of me.

"Don't beg, Katherine," he said at last. "It's demeaning in one of your rank, and it permits others to take untoward advantage of you. Let that be your first lesson in the world, yes?"

"Yes, Father," I said quickly, not daring to say more from fear I'd displease him further. "That is, no, I shall not beg. Not to you, not to anyone."

"I am glad of it," he said, and cleared his throat. "Are you still in the nursery, or are you with a governess?"

"Mrs. Robin is my present governess." I felt it unnecessary to remind Father that he'd employed her himself. Besides, she was only the latest of several such creatures I'd endured, none of them choosing to remain for long in a household with a mad mistress.

"Is she now?" he said. "Has this Mrs. Robin taught you to read and to write as you should? By my lights that's all a lady truly requires, for minding her Scripture and her *billets-doux*. Can you cipher well enough not to be cheated by tradesmen?"

"Oh, yes," I assured him, though I likely would have sworn I'd been taught how to fly to the tops of the trees if I'd sensed he'd wished it so. "Mrs. Robin has taught me French, too. But she is not kind, Father. If I do not make my stitchery so neat as to please her, she pricks my fingers with her needle by way of punishment."

He frowned and shook his head, and I knew that Mrs. Robin's time was done. "What need do you have of stitchery, eh? I'm not planning to set you out as apprentice to a seamstress."

"Thank you, Father," I murmured meekly. "That is not my wish, either."

"I'll vow it's not, my clever little Kattypillar," he said, laughing. "My daughter a seamstress!"

His eyes still bright with merriment, he tapped his fingers on the coach's window, considering, and I held my breath for his judgment. He always wore a heavy gold ring with a carnelian intaglio, and now that stone caught the sun, glinting bright as the gay life I hoped for.

"Very well, Katherine," he said at last. "We'll give this Mrs. Robin her notice, and I'll play your tutor instead. Does that please you?"

I nodded eagerly, my palms pressed together with purest joy. Now that he'd made up his mind on this course, his fancy for it seemed to grow, as if my future were some other frolic for him.

"I'll take you to Epsom for this fortnight," he continued, "and other places as it pleases me, and teach you what you'll need for success in company. If you prove as quick as I expect, then in time we'll go to Whitehall as well. Here now, what's this?"

With a grunt, he bent down to retrieve my doll from where she'd slipped from the seat to the floor of the coach.

"Poor Lady Cassandra, cast away without a thought!" he said, brushing the doll with the back of his fingers. "I'd sooner expect the moon to drop from the heavens than for you to neglect your dear Lady Cass."

Swiftly I reclaimed my doll, smoothing her ruffled skirts and returning her to her place of honor on my lap with my hands linked around her. But Lady Cassandra's spell over me had been broken. Father was to be my new companion, and I was dazzled by the kind of education he was offering to me. It wasn't the prospect of a career at Whitehall—for in truth I'd no more notion then of the politics and intrigues that made the royal Court at once both so amusing and so dangerous—but the simpler promise to be more in my father's company. And for so lonely a child as I, that was more than enough.

Chapter Two

Epsom Wells, Surrey
July 1667

Father and I reached Epsom late that afternoon. I'd been so intent on the horses that I was surprised to find that Epsom itself was not simply a racecourse, but a small town, and a fashionable one at that. Though the buildings were humble, the streets seemed as filled with elegant folk walking about as if we were still in St. James's Park. This, Father explained, was due to the healthful waters for which the place was famous, and for which people were willing to travel great distances to drink. From the coach window, I saw the wells where the waters were drawn, and the long lines of men and women waiting to take their pints. The water was reputed to cure most any ailment or complaint by way of a thorough purge, which Father described in such gleeful detail that I giggled, exactly as he'd intended.

Fortunately such miraculous (if noisome) cures were not for us, at least not on this day. Instead of the public inn I'd been expecting, our coach stopped before a neat small house surrounded by a tall hedgerow and spreading trees whose shade was particularly inviting after our dusty journey. The afternoon had grown very warm. Sweat trickled down my back between my smock and my stays, my fashionable leather gloves clung damply to my hands, and my petticoats seemed heavier than a winter coverlet across my legs.

"We'll be lodging here as the guests of Lord Buckhurst, who has hired this house for the summer." Father blotted his forehead along the front of his periwig before settling his beaver hat atop; being stout, he sorely felt the heat of the day. "Lord Buckhurst is an important gentleman at

Court and a favorite of the king, from being heir to the Earl of Dorset. A lord you will do well to please, Katherine. He is also an especial friend of mine, and I'll thank you to show him your very best manners."

At once I imagined this Lord Buckhurst as a stiff-backed peer, old enough to have served the former king. It was easy; my mother's family was rife with such gentlemen. As Father and I stepped past the footman who held the door, I shrugged away my weariness and composed myself to act as I did before my more ancient Rivers relations.

"His Lordship is in the garden, Sir Charles," the footman said, bowing as he took my father's stick and hat. "He asked that you join him."

Father seemed to have no need of the footman to show him the way, leading me himself through the house's twisting, old-fashioned halls to the chamber that overlooked the garden. The back door was thrown open to catch the summer breezes, and I could hear voices and laughter coming from beyond its threshold. The venerable Lord Buckhurst wasn't alone. Suddenly shy, I shrank back behind the flaring skirts of Father's coat, and belatedly I wished I'd not left Cassandra behind in the coach for the servants to bring to my chamber.

"Faith, Sedley, for once you have kept your word, and about a woman, too," a gentleman said in an affected drawl. "Even if she is a very small woman, and your daughter at that."

"Present her to us, Sid, if you please," said a second gentleman. "Coax the little dear from her hiding."

"Come, pet." Father set his hand upon my shoulder and gently pushed me forward. "You've my word these gentlemen won't bite. Lord Rochester, Lord Buckhurst, my daughter, Katherine. Make your curtsy, child, though these two sorry rogues scarce deserve the honor."

Obediently I seized the sides of my petticoats to spread them as I'd been taught and sank into a deep, respectful curtsy. As a child (and to my relief), I wasn't expected to speak, not even after Lord Buckhurst languidly gestured for me to rise. Instead I stood on the garden step, stunned into wide-eyed silence by the scene laid out before me.

A dining table and cushioned armchairs had been brought out under the trees and set upon a large Turkey carpet spread over the grass. Whether the table had been laid for a late dinner or an early supper, I could not tell, but from the number of cast-off dishes and empty bottles—and the jollity of the company—I'd venture that they'd been at it for a good long time, and planned to remain longer still.

Closest to us was Lord Rochester: astonishingly handsome, with a straight nose and jaw, heavy-lidded eyes, and a sly mouth meant for mockery. Lord Buckhurst's mien was more coarsely fashioned though also comely, with a longer nose and straight, dark brows. Because of the heat, they'd both shed their periwigs and bared their close-cropped heads in the garden's privacy, and they'd likewise doffed their jackets, neckcloths, and waistcoats, shoes, and stockings, lolling comfortably with their shirts open at the throat and their sleeves shoved back to their elbows. I'd never before witnessed gentlemen in such indolent, familiar disarray, and it shocked me as thoroughly as if they'd both been naked as Adam in another garden.

But they weren't alone. There was an Eve, too, in their lordly garden. Wearing only a smock, a half-laced bodice, and a single petticoat, a small young woman with red-gold curls sprawled across Lord Buckhurst's lap, her bare legs and feet dangling over his much longer shins. A popular actress named Nell Gwyn, she had been featured in one of the last plays I'd seen with Father, and it startled me to find her here now, without costume or paint. Several flop-eared spaniels lay in the table's shade, dozing or gnawing on the discards from the table in a manner not far removed from their masters above.

Lord Rochester waved with an expansive flourish. "Welcome, Mistress Sedley," he said, his voice thick with wine. "We're *most* honored by your presence among us."

"Indeed," Lord Buckhurst said, raising his glass toward me. Copper-haired Mrs. Gwyn slid from his lap and took up the bottle from the table to refill his glass, the red wine cheery in the sunshine.

"To our fine, fat friend, Little Sid, and his kid," he said grandly. "Or rather, to Little Sid and his littler kid."

This was not the welcome I'd expected, though I curtsied again. I was hot and tired and hungry, and worst of all, I was ill at ease and unsure of where I fit into this peculiar party.

Father had always been the supreme figure in my life, and I'd never considered him small in size, nor had I heard anyone address him by anything other than Sir Charles. But these gentlemen were not only much taller, even whilst sitting down, but also of a far superior rank to a mere baronet. Were lords permitted rudeness without rebuke? Was that why Father only smiled happily when they spoke to him with such disrespect? If that were so, I could scarce imagine how His Majesty must address his acquaintance. Or was this just another of my lessons toward becoming a courtier?

"You've always threatened to bring your daughter to us, Sid," Lord Buckhurst said as he considered me, "but I never believed you'd actually act upon it."

"You know I never make idle threats," Father said, shrugging his arms free of his jacket to join them in *dishabille*. "It was time Katherine began to see more company to ready her for Court, and besides, I couldn't abandon her any longer at that house."

"What, your private madhouse with the lunatic queen?" Lord Buckhurst peered at me as if searching for signs of disorder in my visage. "At least there's no doubt the girl is yours, and not some Bedlam doctor's byblow. Lord, how she favors you, or she would if you hadn't starved her to her bones. That must come from her mad mother, eh?"

I could keep mute no longer, not when he spoke so of Mama. I'd be the most disloyal of daughters if I had, and that I couldn't bear.

"If you please, my lord, my mother cannot help being mad," I said, ready to be Mama's champion. "That's why she's going to Ghent with the priests, to see if they can cure her, and it's barbarous unkind of you, my lord, to mock her for it."

Lord Buckhurst heaved an enormous gasp and struck his fist to his heart with such affected surprise that the others all laughed—including, to my relief, my father.

"God's blood, Sid," the earl exclaimed, "but you've raised a sharp-tongued little chit!"

"I do not wish to be a sharp-tongued chit, my lord," I said, the justness of my cause giving me courage. "I only defend my mother, just as I would defend my father, if he did needs me to do so."

Father bent down to kiss me on the forehead, his eyes full of delight. "There now, Buckhurst, how can you fault that?" he fair crowed. "That's rare spirit, especially in so young a lady."

"We mean no harm, little miss, despite what this blustering blowhard might say," Lord Rochester said with another world-weary sigh. "We are all mad ourselves to some degree, anyway, as you'll soon learn for yourself."

"What she'll learn is that you're a pack of bullying drunkards," Mrs. Gwyn declared. She gave Lord Buckhurst's arm a poke and he in turn swatted her bottom, which only caused her to laugh. With a couple of graceful little hops, she came to me and made an artfully sweeping curtsy. "I'm Nell Gwyn, sweet, though your father didn't see fit to introduce us proper for all that we're the *oldest* of friends."

"I know who you are, Mrs. Gwyn," I said eagerly. "I've seen you at the King's Theatre, on the stage."

"I look different here, don't I, without all the paint?" She winked broadly at me. She *did* look different from the actress I'd remembered, the one who'd made whole audiences hang breathless on her next word. She was younger than I'd realized, not more than six or seven years older than I was myself, yet so small that we were nearly the same height. She was as merry as the first of May, her round face rosy and her eyes full of mischief, and she seemed incapable of standing still, ever dancing lightly on her bare feet. "You must call me Nelly like everyone else does, and I'll call you Katherine, as friends will."

I smiled, liking the idea of such a friend. I knew from my father that she was common-born, and she was an actress, which was as much to say she was a whore, and not suitable company for a lady like me. Grandmother Rivers would have been most grievously distressed. But I did not care, and it pleased me endlessly that Father didn't, either.

"Thank you, Nelly," I said, at once shy and proud of this new acquaintance.

"Thank *you*, Katherine." She laughed, and pulled me over to the table. "Now take your fill of whatever you please. There's no ceremony among us here in the country."

She piled a plate high with sliced chicken, pickled eggs, strawberries, and buttered buns, and when I politely protested that it was too much, she added more, and ordered me to eat it. When she poured wine in a glass for me, I looked anxiously to Father for guidance. I'd drunk cider and small beer, as every child did, and a sip of the blessed wine at the rail for Holy Communion, but I'd not been permitted French wine before this.

"You have my leave to test it, pet," Father said with a beneficent nod. He'd settled comfortably in the armchair beside Lord Rochester's, and had already half emptied his own glass of the same wine. "It's better you learn the flavor and effect of wine here, among friends, than later with those who'll take advantage of your befuddlement. Nelly'll attest to that."

Nell nodded vigorously. "There's more women ruined by strong waters than false lovers, and that's God's honest truth. This glass and no more for a little mite like you."

I took the glass from her, holding the bowl cupped in my hands, and sipped it tentatively. Though I knew this was another lesson for me, I couldn't keep from puckering my face and sputtering at the unfamiliar taste, sending the gentlemen to roar with laughter.

"Pay them no heed," Nell said kindly. "They'd swim in the stuff if they could, the sots. Have a nibble of that chicken, then try it again."

I did as she bid, and the second swallow was tolerable, and the third more agreeable still. By the time I'd finished my supper and the wine with it, I'd decided there was no pleasanter place in Creation than this garden, and no pleasanter people than my father's friends. The afternoon faded into dusk, and servants came to light the lanterns hanging from the branches of the trees. To my delight, glowworms appeared along the edges of the garden, tiny, festive specks of light. Nell offered to teach me the newest dances, and I happily shed my shoes and stockings like the others and giggled and hopped through every jig she knew there on the grass as the new moon rose over the hedgerows.

"Will you be staying here, too, Nelly?" I asked when we paused between jigs and ate strawberries in cream, sitting cross-legged on large cushions like heathen sultanas. "Or must you go back to your own lodgings?"

She laughed, and licked her tongue across the curving bowl of the silver spoon. "Course I'll be here. I'm to stay the whole of the summer, or so long as His Lordship wishes my company."

If I'd not drunk the wine, I doubt I would've had the courage to ask what I next did—though that in itself was another lesson learned of the power of spirits, and a most valuable one at that.

"Are you Lord Buckhurst's mistress?" My voice had dropped to a fearful whisper. "Does he keep you?"

Unashamed, Nell grinned and coyly tapped her cheek with the spoon. "His Lordship and I are friends, good friends. I amuse him, and he rewards me for the amusement. Is that answer enough?"

"You called my father a friend, too."

"Your father?" she repeated, and her smile softened. "Nay, Katherine, your father's safe from me, and so's your mother."

I flushed, shamed that she'd read me with such ease.

"Don't ever pity me or my kind, Katherine," she continued gently. "Where is Lady Buckhurst on this fine summer eve, I ask you? Where is Lady Rochester? Yet here am I, jolly as can be, eating strawberries and dancing in the moonlight. I choose the gentlemen I love, for so long or so short as I wish. I'm as free as those stars in the sky. What proper lady-wife can say the same?"

There was much in this blithe little speech for me to ponder, countering as it did everything I'd been taught in my own short life. My confusion must have shown, for Nell kissed me lightly on the cheek by way of commiseration, and looped her arm familiarly into mine.

"What would you wish to do now, love?" she asked. "Perhaps it's time to see you put to bed."

Swiftly I shook my head, for what child ever longs for bed? "I'm not weary," I said, willfully stifling the yawn inspired by her query. "I should much rather pet the dogs."

She laughed and led me back to the table and the dogs beneath it. Before long I was in much the same state as they, curled on a cushion upon the grass to doze contentedly while the conversations of my elders rolled over my head.

"So tell us true, Sid," Lord Buckhurst asked. "Are you already trolling for a worthy husband for your little kid? Is that why you're priming her for Court?"

"Sweet God, no," Father said with comforting haste. "There's no hurry for that."

"No matter, no matter," Lord Rochester said. "She'll have her share of suitors, that's for certain."

"That girl?" Lord Buckhurst asked with a scornful incredulity that wounded me to the quick. "Forgive me, Sid, but she bears such an unfortunate likeness to you that unless the graces themselves conspire to work a miracle—"

"The miracle is her papa's money," Lord Rochester said. "She's Sid's lone heir, you know. How much will the little darling be worth?"

Father sighed. "Twenty thousand a year by last reckoning."

Forgotten on my cushion, I pressed both my hands across my mouth to stifle my amazement. Father was famously fortunate, and had prospered well during the late wars while other gentlemen had lost their entire estates, but I'd given no thought to the extent of his wealth, nor its relationship to me beyond my own daily security. Twenty thousand a year was a sum exceeding my comprehension. My maidservant Danvers was paid five pounds per annum, and she considered that a fair wage, much above the cook maids in the kitchen who received but three. To learn that I'd receive four thousand times that for no more than the luck of being my father's daughter was so bewildering that I wondered if I were in fact dreaming a fancy.

Lord Buckhurst echoed my own amazement and whistled low in appreciation. "Twenty thousand! What's beauty to that, eh? She'll have swains hovering about her like bees to the sweetest blossom."

"It means freedom for her," Father said firmly, with such conviction that I felt a rush of pride that he'd speak so on my behalf. "Katherine won't be required to take whichever rogue offers the most for her hand, but instead may choose her spouse with care. No one, man or woman, should be forced to wed where there's no love."

Lord Rochester made a derisive snort. "No one should be forced to send his spouse clear to Ghent to be rid of her, either."

"I recall you were in such a fever to wed your lady, Rochester, that you stole her away like a thief in the night," Lord Buckhurst said, "yet now you abandon her at Adderbury as completely as if she were in China."

Curled up with a snoring dog in my lap, I'd no interest at all in Lady Rochester at Adderbury. Why didn't Father defend himself to his friends?

Why didn't he explain to them, as he had to me, that it was Mama's own desire to go to Ghent?

Yet what Father did say next pleased me even more, for he defended neither himself nor Mama, but me.

"I've faith in my little Katherine," he said with such tender fondness that tears filled my sleepy eyes. "You'll see. My Katherine will make a great mark in the world, as grand as any lady can be."

As grand as any lady can be. How I did relish the sound of that! A fine prediction, yes, but the finest part was how it proved Father's love for and confidence in me. With that to warm me, I must soon after have finally fallen asleep and later been carried to rest in my chamber, for I recall nothing more until I awoke in an unfamiliar bed.

It was still night, with the same moonlight that I'd shared with Nell and the glowworms now lighting my small bedchamber almost as bright as day. I found Cassandra on the pillow beside me, and with her in my arm, I slipped from the bed and went to gaze from the window. The garden was quiet now, the lanterns doused and the table cleared by the servants, and my elders and the dogs alike gone off to their own beds.

From boredom, I leaned farther from the window, my long plait falling forward over my shoulder. The house was shaped like a lopsided L, and idly I wondered which of the other darkened rooms belonged to Father, and which to Lord Rochester and Lord Buckhurst and Nell. As if my wondering was answered, I heard Nell's unmistakable laughter ripple from the window across the yard from mine.

If she were awake, then likely she was as in need of company as I. I abandoned Cassandra on my bed and eagerly scurried into the shadowy hall, my bare feet padding over the floorboards.

As I'd already observed, this was a house of considerable freedom and little formality. Some of the chamber doors had been left ajar, and as I made my way, I passed the bedchamber where I glimpsed my father's ample silhouette sprawled on his back beneath the sheet, rising and falling with his snores. I hurried on past, toward the door that I guessed was Nell's. This, too, stood open, and I slipped inside, my heart beating with anticipation at meeting my new friend again. But the chamber was only a kind of parlor or dressing room, empty except for the ghostly pale petticoats and stockings carelessly strewn about. Disappointed, I'd begun to retreat when Nell laughed again, the sound coming from the chamber adjoining the one in which I stood. Eagerly I hurried to this door, and stopped.

Nell was there, yes, but not alone. Instead she sat astride Lord Buckhurst in the center of his bed, her smock billowing over them both and his bare shins and long feet poking out awkwardly beyond the end of the sheets. His head was supported by a small mountain of pillows, and he held his hands outward to grasp Nell around the waist, as if to make certain she'd not topple from his lap. I thought this was rather nice of His Lordship to secure her that way, as if she were riding a horse instead of him.

Now I know better, of course, and realize that the only animal being emulated was that of a lascivious two-backed beast. But at that time, in my childish innocence, I took their posture as no more than a convenience for conversation—a conversation that I, standing in the dressing room, could not help but overhear.

"Sedley told me the king was asking after you to Hart," Lord Buckhurst said, his gaze intent upon Nell before him. "He wondered aloud when little Nelly would return to his playhouse. All there in the tiring room heard him, and by now likely a good many beyond it, too."

Nell shrugged extravagantly, one round, pearly shoulder slipping free of her lace-edged smock. "Hah, I'd wager Hart had a sour enough answer for him. Poor man, you and I must have quite broken his heart between us."

"I don't give a damn about Hart or the sourness of his reply," His Lordship said, sounding rather sour himself. "Your past is no concern to me, Nelly. What I wish to know from you now is whether you have designs on the king."

" 'Designs'!" Nell tossed her unpinned hair back over her shoulders and laughed raucously. "Hey, ho, that's a pretty fancy! That Nelly Gwyn should have designs upon His Majesty!"

But Lord Buckhurst did not share her amusement. "I don't care where you love, Nell, so long as you don't play me for a fool. And if you're already scheming to jump like a flea from me to the king—"

"Oh, my lord, you know I'd never do that to you." Gently Nell rocked forward, just enough to make His Lordship groan. She smiled, and languidly pressed her hand across his lips to keep him quiet. "I've told you before, my darling. Hart was my Charles the first, and you're my Charles the second. What need do I have for a Charles the third?"

"You've reasons beyond counting when your Charles the third is already Charles the Second, King of England." He seized her little hand and nipped roughly at her fingers, more like a large and unruly dog than a lover true.

But Nell only laughed again, albeit more softly. "The summer and no more beyond," she said. "That was what we agreed between us, wasn't it?"

"Damn you, Nelly, why won't you answer?"

"Because I have," she said, leaning forward to kiss him. "It's only your pride that makes you unable to hear me. But be easy, my wicked, jealous lord. It's never been my way to dandle two men at the same time, and I'll not begin now. Whilst we're here, I belong only to you. Could ever I dare ask the same of you? I wonder. Could I be enough to keep you happy?"

"You know you are," he did not say so much as growl, again like that ill-mannered dog. To my shock, he reached up and ripped the front of her smock, rending the Holland linen so that her breasts spilled forward, to his obvious delight. "You know you rule me, Nell, my heart and my soul."

"More like your cods and your cock," she said with a teasing low chuckle, unperturbed at having her clothing torn away. Instead she grinned, and guided his greedy hand to her now-naked breasts. "But I'll happily be your queen, my lord, so long as you'll share your scepter."

Chuckling still, she lowered herself more fully into his embrace, and I shrank back farther into the shadows. Nell would have no use for my company now, that was certain. With my heart strangely racing from all that I'd witnessed, I withdrew as silently as I'd come.

Back again in my own little bed, I stared at the top of my bedstead with Cassandra in my arms, my thoughts too busy for sleep. In one short day, I'd learned that my mother preferred her priests and a foreign convent to me and London and that my father didn't care that she did. I'd likewise learned I was an heiress to a considerable fortune and that I'd not be pressed to share it with any husband. I'd observed that much of what I'd been taught by my governesses seemed to bear no kinship to the world beyond my nursery; that a good woman such as my mother suffered and lost her wits even as she said her prayers, whilst a bad woman such as Nell prospered and laughed and enjoyed herself as she chose. I'd my first true glimpse of Father's friends, known infamously to the rest of London as the Merry Gang. Most of all, I'd learned that Father himself was a cheerful inhabitant of this giddy world of pleasure and amusement and debauchery, and that he was happy, even eager, to guide me to my own place in it, too.

In short, my second education had begun, and I scarce could wait to prove myself a prize scholar.

Chapter Three

THE KING'S HOUSE, DRURY LANE, LONDON
May 1668

"Do you wish an orange, Katherine?" Father asked as soon as we'd found our places on the first bench before the stage. He wasn't looking at me, but at the rest of the playhouse, eager to see who among his acquaintance (and his enemies) might already be there. "Here's a girl if you do."

The orange girl smiled slyly at my father and plucked one of the fruits from the beribboned basket on her hip. As she offered the golden fruit in her hand, she leaned forward to grant him a better glimpse of her ample breasts, tempting him more than me. Everyone in the playhouse knew Father, from the greenest orange girl to the manager, Master Killigrew, and on this day everyone sought to please him, too.

"For th' little lady," the girl said, finally deigning to smile at me with considerable condescension. I was ten, not much younger than she must have been herself, but she was so far below me in station that I could afford to be gracious as I took the orange.

"Thank you, dear," I said, and smiled sweetly in return. She might have breasts, which to my impatience I'd yet to sprout, but at least I'd all my teeth, which she did not. "And thank *you*, Father."

"Yes, yes, you're welcome," he said, his gaze still busily roaming over the house. "Damnation, the king's still not here."

"He'll come." I dug my thumb into the orange's dimpled peel. "You know His Majesty's never prompt."

"Kings don't need to be prompt, pet." He stood, too restless to sit, and anxiously stroked his fingers across the lace on his neckcloth. "Killigrew will just have to keep those infernal fiddles scraping away until the royal party shows itself. We can't begin until he does."

"No, you can't," I agreed, slipping the first sweet segment of orange into my mouth. "It would be inexpressibly rude."

"Oh, I'm certain His Majesty would find the words for expressing his displeasure." He sighed, tugging on one of the long curls on his periwig. "Perhaps I should send you to sit up in the boxes with some of the other ladies."

"No!" I exclaimed, horrified he'd so much as suggest such a thing. In all the times he'd brought me to the playhouse, this was the first we'd not sat in the boxes, but down here in the pit, close to the stage. Already the pit was far more exciting, filled with Father's raucous friends and other foppish gentlemen and mysterious beautiful women who hid their true selves behind black vizard-masks. I liked being the only girl of rank in the pit, bright and proud as an elegant little bird in scarlet silk trimmed with green lacing, and I'd no wish to be banished back to respectability, especially not today.

"I belong here with you, Father," I said. "You said yourself I'd bring you luck."

"That is true," he admitted, and at last he smiled wanly at me. "Here, Katherine, give me a kiss for that luck."

I clambered up on the bench to reach his offered cheek.

"There," I said, granting him a great smack from my orange-sticky lips while around us others laughed and applauded my filial display. "That's luck for you, not that you shall need it."

"Not with you by my side, sweet," Father said, and kissed my forehead in return, as pretty a show as the one that would soon commence before us. I was so often with Father now about the town that I'd become nearly as known as he himself, and though I was not entirely pleased by being dubbed Little Sid's Kid (for what lady, however young, wishes to be called after an infant goat?), I'd come to love the attention and my father's approval with it. Yet this afternoon felt different, with Father too ill at his ease to find joy in the notice of others. Hoping to coax him to better cheer, I pirouetted on my toes as Nell had taught me, balancing on the bench with the half-eaten orange in my hand.

"You shall see, Father," I promised. "By nightfall, everyone will be shouting your name with praise."

Father made a wry grimace. "So long as they're not shouting *at* me, Katherine. What more can a lowly playwright wish?"

"A full house and a long run, and the devil take the critics," I answered with rare relish for one my age. "Or hang them till their necks stretch and their breeches fill. I don't care which, so long as it makes them kind to you."

"Hah, that's a pretty sentiment." He could not help but smile at that, for there were few things that amused him more than to hear me parrot the style of fine, vulgar wit I heard amongst his friends. "'A full house and a long run.' Would that it comes true."

To be sure, I wasn't being particularly original. They'd spoken of nothing else but unfortunate ends for cruel critics since Father had announced he meant to try his hand at writing a new play.

But then, a play was a considerable undertaking for a gentleman, and for many weeks he'd huffed and labored in his library to produce the work we'd come to see fair launched. The play was called *The Mulberry-Garden*, after the section of St. James's Park given over to midnight foolery and illicit trysts. That was also a fair description of the play's content, and from what I'd seen myself of the rehearsals, it was a merry romp indeed, sure to find as much favor with audiences as it had with me.

But Father would not be soothed, still looking anxiously at the empty royal box. There had been a great crush to enter when the doors had been opened at noon, with finer folk paying poor men to hold their seats whilst they dined elsewhere. Now that it was after three, the true audience was in their places, restless and impatient for the royal party to appear and the play to start.

"We shall see, pet, we shall see," Father murmured, dabbing his lace-bordered handkerchief to the gathering sweat on his forehead. Suddenly he smiled, sunny with relief. "Look, Katherine. Huzzah! Reinforcements at last!"

I turned to see three of his closest acquaintances coming to join us: Lord Rochester, Lord Buckhurst, and His Grace the Duke of Buckingham. These three noble rogues sauntered down the center aisle to our bench, as fine as strutting peacocks in their laced coats and silk cloaks, heeled boots, curled periwigs, and swords slung from shoulder belts, and aware, too, of the fuss so much male splendor caused. As self-styled wits, the poems and satires they penned about others could be just as sharp as the swords they wore, and far more amusing to all but their targets. They were not only Father's friends, but friends to His Majesty as well, under his special protection. They'd often found need of it, too, when their infamous amusements went too far and caused injury to others.

Ignoring me, Lord Buckingham pushed past to embrace Father, whispering something into his ear that made Father laugh uproariously. I was wary of His Grace. He was older than the other gentlemen in Father's circle, with a cunning fox's face I found impossible to trust. I could scarce imagine how he'd become both a politician and a diplomat in the king's service. He'd a quick temper over nothing, and I'd seen him draw his sword in a tavern over a chicken not cooked to his liking. All these gentlemen had a taste for dueling, no matter that it was against the law, but Lord Buckingham was the one who'd killed several opponents on the field of honor, including the husband of his current mistress. Yet the king had permitted him to escape justice, and still favored him like another brother.

"Good day, Katherine," Lord Rochester said solemnly, bending down for me to kiss his cheek, as was now my custom with him. His handsome eyes were red-rimmed, and he smelled of wine, a scent I'd come to recognize with ease. "You've seen enough of Sid's play to judge it. Will it find favor with this rabble?"

"It will," I declared, and repeated my wish for Father. "A full house, a long run, and the devil take the critics."

"That, and make the king laugh," Lord Rochester agreed. "His Majesty will send your poor father to the Tower if he doesn't laugh aloud at least three times."

Innocently I believed him and gasped with dismay, until the others laughed, excepting Lord Buckhurst.

"Oh, the king *will* laugh," he said sourly, his suety face more unpleasant than usual. "He'll laugh at any rubbish so long as it has a part for Nell to show her legs, the little whore."

Rochester tipped his head to one side with sly disdain. "Our dear king has seen so many whores' legs and so much of what lies between them, that I doubt even Nelly would make him laugh if he didn't wish to. If he laughs, it's because he's amused, and if he's amused, it will be because of the words of Sid and the talents—the *stage* talents—of Nell."

"She fills the benches, Buckhurst," Father said. His black eyes were bright as jet, a sure sign of mischief to come at Lord Buckhurst's expense. "London loves her. Why, the world loves her! Why shouldn't the king as well?"

"To hell with the fat asses on the benches, Sedley." Lord Buckhurst's expression grew even more dour. "Rather it's the king who fills *her*, with love or without."

Lord Buckingham smirked, and shoved his gloved fist into Lord Buckhurst's shoulder in mocking play.

"Give dear Nelly her due, Buckhurst," he said. "The lass can scarce be faulted for showing the good taste to shed you for the king, like any respectable whore would. We all know you'd only bought her for that one summer."

"Five hundred for nothing," Lord Buckhurst muttered bitterly. "For nothing but to be humiliated."

"But that's not true," I piped up, determined to defend my friend. "Nelly gave you everything you wanted, fair as can be, and a pox upon your lies for saying she didn't."

The gentlemen swung about toward me, as if they'd forgotten I stood on the bench in their midst. For an instant I feared I'd overstepped and spoken more boldly than was wise, no matter my good intentions. But Father grinned, and clapped his hands with bemused approval.

"Act as our judge, Katherine," he said. "You'll be fair, I know, for you've nothing to gain from being otherwise. Where should Nelly by rights cast her favors? To Lord Buckhurst or to His Majesty?"

"His Majesty," I said without hesitation.

Lord Buckhurst groaned with exasperation, and cast his gaze upward to appeal to the heavens. "What the devil did you expect her to say? The king is the *king*!"

"No, Your Lordship," I answered. I'd not forgotten how he'd been the first to liken me to a baby goat, and had called me plain as well. "I said that because the king is more agreeable as a man."

That made Lord Rochester and Lord Buckingham roar with laughter as did many others around us besides. Father caught me in his arms and swung me, shrieking happily, from the bench, my petticoats flying about my ankles.

"There, did I not say she'd speak only the truth?" Father demanded proudly. "A veritable Oracle of Delphi in our midst!'

"The devil take your truth, Sedley," Lord Buckhurst said, the stormiest clouds of discontent gathered on his brow. "You said she was to act as judge, not for spouting nonsense like that."

"She spoke the truth, Buckhurst, and the rest is of no account," Father said, and kissed me again. "You've earned syllabub for supper, dearest, if that is your desire."

But my desires were soon forgotten, for His Majesty arrived, and at once we all rose and curtsied or bowed in respect until the royal party had settled. Immediately after, the play at last began. I curled close beside Father, and listened as the first player stepped forward to speak the prologue. Like Father, I also listened for laughter and other signs of a happy audience. While he did not need the play to prosper for the sake of his bread, as did the true playwrights like Mr. Dryden, I knew Father's pride was bound up in his work so that much was at stake this night.

Yet soon I forgot the others and lost myself in the witty words. I'd attended rehearsals with Father, and without trying I had learned the parts so well myself that unconsciously I whispered them along with the players, beginning with the first speech by Sir John Everyoung:

Let's every one
Govern his own Family as he has a mind to't;
I never vex my self that your Daughters
Live shut up as if they were in Spain or Italy;
Nor pray don't you trouble your self that mine
See Plays, Balls, and take their innocent Diversion,
As the Custom of the Country, and their Age requires. . . .
I think those Women who have been least
Us'd to Liberty, most apt to abuse it, when
They come to it.

How that made me smile with delight, and wonder whether the others realized what I did: that Sir Everyoung spouted Father's own beliefs, and that the daughters in the play were encouraged to take their "innocent diversions" much as was I. When I watched Nell prance merrily as the youngest daughter, Olivia, I imagined myself as Olivia, with the charming rogue Jack Wildish as my own sweetheart. Most of all, I glowed with happy pride, content that my Father could love me so much that he'd show it for the world to see in this play, and thought myself the most fortunate of young ladies to be blessed with such a parent.

Now I am sure that others (like my grandmother Rivers) were appalled by this selfsame freedom. Since Mama had left us, I'd given myself entirely to Father's tutelage. From him and his circle I'd learned such skills as playing cards for stakes, singing bawdy songs with full knowledge of their meanings, and instructing the drawers at taverns like the Dog and Partridge exactly how much sweet wine to whip into my syllabub. I seldom found my bed before midnight and thereafter did not leave it until noon the following day. I'd been given free reign of the books in Father's library, and my reading now consisted entirely of plays and romances that I consumed with a breathless fervor. For all that we professed to be Anglicans, we seldom rose on Sunday morn in time for service, nor was there a single volume of sermons or other thoughtful religious guidance to be found beneath our roof.

To have me stand on a bench in the pit of the King's House, as I just had, and judge between a lord and a whore was exactly the sort of antic amusement that delighted Father most. He often treated me more like a clever small pet than a daughter, and I was in no position to understand the difference, nor worry about the consequences that might arise for me later. How could I at so tender an age? On that afternoon, all that mattered was the orange in my hand, the humorous play before me, and Father's arm around my shoulder; I wanted nothing more.

At last Olivia and Wildish were wed and every other conflict well resolved, the epilogue spoken, and the final dance danced. The players took their bows, and Father rose from the bench, his arms raised to acknowledge the applause around him. To me the play seemed a roaring success, and I hopped up and down with excitement beside him. But Father seemed to me to be more relieved than joyful, and as he led me through the well-wishers to join the players backstage, he paused outside the tiring room to confide his newest concern to me.

"I failed, my own little Kattypillar," he said mournfully over the jostling din around us. "The king did not laugh."

"Faith, he must have!" I exclaimed with disbelief. "You couldn't have watched him every moment, unless your head could twist about like an owl's."

"I didn't need to look, sweet," he said, his round face gloomy with disappointment. "I would have known if he had. I cannot fault him if he didn't. It was a poor enough performance. Not even the players knew their lines."

"Just one forgot his line in the second act," I said, "and no one noticed."

"Killigrew should have rehearsed them further, so that they might have wrung more wit from my sorry words. Merciful God, why ever did I aspire to be a poet?"

"You *are* a poet, Father," I insisted. "And everyone *did* so laugh, just as they should have."

Dolefully he shook his head. "I do not know, pet, I do not—"

"Sir Charles!"

The woman seemed to burst through the narrow passage, past two other gentlemen crowding there for admission. She was small and plump, with glossy golden hair and dimpled pink shoulders shamelessly displayed with much of her bosom. She wore only her stays and a petticoat over her smock, having already shed her costume from the play. But her face still wore the gaudy paint of her craft, her eyes lined round with lampblack and her cheeks patched with bright pink. As she threw her arms around Father to kiss him, the white powder on her bare arms and chest dusted his velvet coat like a baker's apron with flour.

"It's a triumph, Sir Charles, a complete triumph," she crooned, kissing him wantonly. "*You* are a triumph!"

"Stay awhile, you pretty hussy, and tell me more," Father said, willingly sacrificing his waistcoat for her embrace. "A triumph, eh?"

"Oh, in every, every way," she cooed, and he pushed her against the wall and grabbed a fistful of her skirts.

I watched impatiently. She was Mrs. Mary Knapp, a close friend of Nelly's, and another actress in the King's Company, though neither as talented nor as popular as Nell. She'd also a husband somewhere, a jockey. Father didn't care, and neither did she. I'd long ago realized that she kept company with my father in the same way that Nell had done last summer with Lord Buckhurst. I should not have been surprised, I suppose, for Father was still a youngish man, not yet thirty.

To be sure, Mrs. Knapp never dared appear in Great Queen Street, but I didn't doubt that Father experienced her favors elsewhere. In his circle, every gentleman kept at least one mistress, and I knew visiting brothels to dandle with whores was an accepted sport. His Majesty himself led this merry pack of hounds, with the Countess of Castlemaine living in Whitehall Palace for his convenience, Nelly here at the playhouse, and numerous others scattered about London.

Father was only following the fashion with Mrs. Knapp. It had distressed me when I'd first become aware of his attachment to her, and further when I found she was far from the first actress to attract his attentions. I'd thought unhappily of Mama and the sad things Father had hinted at concerning their marriage, but in time that had faded, as had many of my memories of Mama. Besides, I liked Mrs. Knapp just as I liked Nelly. She jested boisterously with me and gave me honey biscuits and bid me sit at her looking glass while she dressed my hair, having once aspired to be a lady's maid before she'd gone on the stage.

But because Mrs. Knapp possessed far more gifts for coaxing Father from his black mood than I, I soon tired of their cooing and cuddling, and decided to look for Nelly on my own. She was easy enough to find. Still in Olivia's costume, she stood on a tall stool in the center of the crowded tiring room, a tankard in her hand. She spotted me at once, waving to me over so many taller heads.

"Here, Katherine, here!" she called. "Let the little lady pass, if you please!"

Like the Red Sea for Moses, the crowd of well-wishers parted for me to join her, and I eagerly skipped across the room. But I'd only taken a few steps before I realized the king himself stood on the other side of Nelly's stool, and I came to a skidding halt to sink to my curtsy before him.

"Rise, my dear," the king said, his voice rumbling deep with amusement. If a monarch should be instantly recognized by his subjects, then Charles II was meant to be king. He was swarthy-complected with heavy-lidded eyes and an air of melancholy at odds with a near-constant half smile, and it was clear that from his great height—he was by far the tallest gentleman in the room—he missed nothing. Though the gentlemen closest to him preened in bright silks, his own dress was dark and plain, almost somber, though of the finest quality, and the wide brim of his black hat was uncocked and unadorned save for a single curling white plume. Yet he was not a monarch who kept himself aloof on his throne. He went freely about London and among his people, and finding him here, laughing and jesting among the players, was proof enough of his informality.

Even so I was awed to stand before him, and more than a little afraid. It did not matter that Father played tennis with him, nor that Nelly warmed his bed, nor that beside him stood his bastard son, Lord Monmouth, who was not so very much older than I (though, sadly, far prettier). He was still the King of England, and I only a ten-year-old girl, albeit one who'd been encouraged to speak freely.

"Tell me, little Katherine," he said, smiling as he bent toward me from his lofty height. "What did you make of your father's play?"

I raised my chin and prayed I did not tremble or shake. "I thought it most fine, Your Majesty."

His smile widened. "That's a fine, loyal sentiment for a daughter."

"Thank you, sir," I said. "But I spoke from truth as well as loyalty."

He chuckled, and those around him did as well, the way it always is with kings. "Is it also true that you find me more agreeable than Buckhurst?"

I flushed, and wished the floor would open and swallow me up. Belatedly I noticed the Duke of Buckingham at his side, his smile smug and sly, and knew at once who'd borne the tale of my "judgment" so swiftly to the royal ears. It taught me a worthy lesson, too: that tattle concerning kings flies ten times as fast as the ordinary kind.

And loudest of all among those finding amusement at my discomfiture was the duke himself.

"Do not expect an immediate reply, sir," Lord Buckingham said to the king. "The truth is a difficult notion for the female mind to conceive. It goes against a lady's very nature."

"Forgive me, sir, but that's not so," I said, once again speaking in haste rather than with caution. "Rather if I hesitate, it's because I'm too young to be a courtier, and have yet to learn how to bend the truth to suit my needs."

The king might not have laughed at Father's play, but he laughed aloud now at my impertinence.

"Well said, little one, well said," he said, doting upon me. "Though I don't wonder Sid keeps you from Whitehall."

"Thank you, sir," I said, feeling more brave. "And I do believe you're more agreeable than Lord Buckhurst. Nelly does, too."

"Oh, aye, Nelly does!" cried Nell herself, laughing heartily. "Where's your rascally father, Katherine? He should be with us to hear your pretty speeches."

"I am here, Nell, so you needn't chide me," Father said behind me, all jovial good humor now after Mrs. Knapp's cheering. "I heard every pretty word Katherine said, and proud I am of her, too."

With grateful relief, I started to turn to join him, only to recall that I must wait upon the king's pleasure before I could retreat. I turned back, so plaintively beseeching in my posture, if not my words, that His Majesty laughed again.

"Go to your father, child," he said indulgently. "Sedley, that girl is a prize. Clearly you've sired a lady-wit after your own model."

"I try to oblige, sir," Father said, winking even as he bowed.

The king nodded, his gaze absently sliding back to Nelly's ankles in yellow stockings, close before him on the tall stool, even while he spoke to my father. "An excellent play, Sedley. Her Majesty in particular enjoyed the dances. Most amusing. Have we lost you to the playhouse forever now?"

Father grimaced dramatically. "Faith, no," he said. "There's far too much work in it for me."

"A good thing, too," the king said. "I'd hate to give you over to these wicked rascals. I've much more need of your wit at Whitehall than they do."

Everyone laughed politely. Somehow that seemed to mark the end of my father and me as entertainment, and as the king returned to his conversation with Nell, the rest of the company returned to their own convivial diversions as well. There is nothing like a group of players and their supporters for finding a reason for celebration in most anything or nothing, and a full house for Father's play was more than reason enough for noisy, well-meant revelry. The sport continued long after the king had left (and Nell soon followed, in the carriage he'd sent back for her), and shifted to Rose's Tavern in Russell Street, not far from Drury Lane.

It was past midnight by the time Father and I stood at the door of the tavern, waiting for our coach to bear us home. Or rather, I sat dozing in an armchair near the door with Father's coat across me, done in by too much of my syllabub-reward, while Father bandied with Master Long, the Rose's keeper, who would laugh at most anything after Father had settled the large reckoning for our entire party. Despite the hour, the house was still bustling with company and servants rushing back and forth to the various rooms with ale, beer, and wine as well as dishes for late suppers.

Once again the front door opened, and Mr. Long excused himself from Father to greet the newcomers, three gentlemen together. As soon as they stepped into the candlelight, Father realized he knew them as well, and hurried to join Mr. Long, bowing deeply. This was not surprising, for sometimes it seemed as if Father knew every man, high and low, in London, and sleepily I began to close my eyes again.

"Wake, Katherine," Father said, gently shaking my shoulder. "You must wake, and pay your respects."

I grumbled crossly and rolled my head, and reluctantly roused myself only enough to stand and make a fumbling, rumpled curtsy before the gentlemen.

"Your Highness, my daughter, Katherine," Father said with more pride than I certainly warranted at that moment. "Katherine, His Royal Highness the Duke of York."

The Duke of York was the king's surviving brother, and since the queen was barren, he was the heir to the throne as well. He also served as the Lord Admiral of the King's Navy, and was often away from London tending to the fleet and the war with the Dutch, which was why I'd never yet seen him in passing. Even in my fuddled state, I knew I must address him with respect, and swiftly I improved my curtsy with more grace and regard, so as not to shame Father.

"So this is the lady that's spurred so much talk this day," the duke said, his voice soft and full of warm kindness. "Rise, sweetheart, if you please, so I might have a proper look at you by the lights."

I stood as I was bid, and turned my face toward the branch of candles overhead. I expected the duke to mirror his brother by being dark and melancholy and exceptionally tall. He was as tall as the king, yes, but there the resemblance came to an end. The Duke of York seemed to me as dazzling as Apollo himself, with skin bronzed and ruddy from the sun and a gold-blond periwig to match, his face shaven clean and his jaw as square and manly as could ever be imagined.

And lah, his eyes! I'd never seen such eyes before, a blue so brilliant it was as if all the seas he ruled as admiral had been gathered into his gaze. I was so intrigued that I wondered if he were only a fancy and I dreamed still, or perhaps the wine in the syllabub had stolen my wits completely away. What other explanation could there be?

"So you are the bold lady who trumpeted the truth to my brother?" he said, smiling down at me. "That you believed he was the more agreeable man compared to Buckhurst?"

"I did, Your Highness," I said, feeling a good deal more shy now before him than I had earlier at the playhouse. "Father asked me to judge between them, and I did."

"But how brave of you to speak your judgment!"

"It was the truth, Your Highness," I said. "That made it easy to say."

"Nonsense," he said soundly. "The truth can be the most difficult thing in the world to say. I like brave women. Sedley, why have you not brought this charming dear creature to us before?"

"She is only ten, Your Highness," Father said, and I heard an unexpected warning in his voice, even if His Highness did not. "Far too young for the intrigues of Court."

"Not at all," the duke said. "If she knows truth from falsehood, why, then she's more advanced than most of the pretty fools at Whitehall." He loomed over me, his voice coaxing. "I've two daughters of my own, you know. The Lady Mary and the Lady Anne. You could play with them as often as you pleased if you were at Court. The duchess would watch over you as if you were her own."

I caught my breath. To be welcomed into the duke's household as easily as this, to join the heady world of Court so soon—

"If you please, Your Highness." Father came to slip his arm around my shoulder as if to keep me safe, an uncommon gesture for him. "Katherine is my only child, and as a father I must beg to keep her with me a little longer."

I knew better than to whine or plead, but my disappointment was sharp. Father had always said he wouldn't let me go to Court until I was older, but to be able to attach myself to the family of the Duke of York would have been a rare opportunity indeed.

"You are certain?" the duke asked. "My daughters would be pleased by Katherine's company."

Father shook his head and opened his hands, as if to say the decision could somehow not be helped, though faith, I could not see why.

The duke sighed, and shrugged. "Ah, well, you are her father, Sedley. It's your choice. But if in time you have a change of heart—"

"In time, Your Highness, I will be most honored, and so shall my daughter." He smiled graciously, and made his familiar elegant bow. "How could we not, with the favor of a lord as esteemed as you are?"

But in our coach, Father was uncharacteristically silent, staring from the window into the night streets.

"Did His Highness truly mean to offer me a place in his household?" I asked wistfully.

"Oh, he meant it," Father said. "The duke is not a man given to empty words. If he wanted you to live with the young ladies at their palace in Richmond, then it would have been done."

Sadly I considered the prize offered by the handsome duke, a prize I'd now perhaps lost forever. "I could have gone, Father. I'm almost ten, old enough to—"

"No, you're not, Kattypillar," he said gently. "Not for that."

"But I could—"

"In time, Katherine," he said, and I knew there'd be no more arguing. "In time."

Chapter Four

Great Queen Street, London
March 1671

It is said that the habits established in youth are the hardest to break as the years pass, and certainly that was the case with me. My father's indulgence gave me much freedom and little guidance, and like the fledging bird that tries to fly too soon to flutter unformed wings, my first attempts to act beyond my tender years were often not sweet. I told unseemly jests, I swore when I lost at cards, I laughed too loudly, and my ever-sharpening wit was much more suited to one of Father's libertine friends than a brash, ungainly girl of thirteen.

Yet precisely at the time in my young life when I needed to be more restrained by my father, he offered even less than before. His stock as a royal favorite rose again, and not long after his play's performance, he was included along with Lords Buckingham and Buckhurst as a member in the king's autumn progress, and I was left behind in London. Ostensibly this leisurely royal journey was a chance for the king to view the eastern counties of his kingdom and meet with his noble supporters. In reality, it was only an excuse for the gentlemen to continue their usual amusements, save in different locations. By day they attended the race meetings at Newmarket, they hunted the hare and they hawked, and they coursed at a furious pace with the royal greyhounds (the young Duke of Monmouth was known to keep a particularly well-bred pack) across the wide countryside. By night it was the usual fare: hard drinking, gambling for high stakes, and dallying with low women.

Father's absences continued in the following year, when he likewise followed the Court to Dover for a month of revelry with the king's youngest sister, Henriette. Soon after, he was appointed part of the diplomatic mission led by the Duke of Buckingham that traveled to Paris and Versailles for a lengthy visit at the palace of Louis XIV in honor of the signing of a new treaty between the two countries.

Because I was not a true member of the Court, I wasn't included on any of these journeys, which was, as I look back to it, likely just as well. Tales of scandalous behavior made their way to London, including one particular night in Newmarket when Father and Lord Buckhurst had drunk so much that they decided it would be a fine thing to run noisily up and down the town's streets in a complete state of nature, a sight that, truly, I'd rather not have witnessed.

Still and all, I was unhappy at being left behind in London with only servants to watch over me, rootless and lonely. I'd become accustomed to the excitement of life with my jovial father, and I missed it almost as much as I missed him. Each time he returned, we fell into the same old ways about London, and because I was older, he also began to take me to balls and other entertainments at the palace. Yet even that wasn't enough to occupy me entirely. By my thirteenth birthday in December, with the new year of 1671 before me, I'd begun to find friends of my own.

Now, it might well be asked how a young lady of that age would acquire her own acquaintances in a city so vast as London. Some of my new friends were in positions similar to my own, with parents who were too occupied as courtiers or in following their own pleasures to supervise their children with any diligence. Others came from families whose fortunes had yet to recover from the wars, and thus led a haphazard existence on the edges of fashionable London. Yet others were more dubious still, young persons well beneath me in rank that I'd met while in Father's company in playhouses, taverns, or at Nell's grand new house, bought for her by the king.

Most were older than I, too. On account of my worldly manner and having reached my full height, I was often now taken for an age beyond my true one, sometimes even sixteen, when many girls were wed, the same age that was proclaimed by Lord Rochester and other libertines at Court to be the perfect apogee for a woman's beauty.

Alas, no matter my age, I'd not much of that particular quality.

Venus thus far had quite ignored me. In my size, I followed more my Rivers blood than my Sedley. I remained as thin and angular as a weedy, underfed apprentice, and though my mantua-maker did strive to correct nature's deficiencies with buckram and sheep's wool, my bosom was sadly more bone than breast, and nothing to inspire a gentleman. I was the same height as Father now, he small and round for a man, and I tall and thin for a lady. The sight of us together often occasioned foolish jests about how opposite we were. No wonder, then, that I found it endlessly flattering to be mistaken for older, and saw little reason to correct the error.

But however I met my new companions, they were as pleased with me as I was with them, perhaps even more so. Why shouldn't they be? I was amusing and bold, yes, but more important, I'd a large, richly appointed house at my disposal and it contained not a hint of a disapproving elder.

All of which is a roundabout explanation of how, on one of the first spring days of May, I came to be walking in St. James's Park with one of these very companions. Jane Holcomb was one of my dearest friends at the time, a distant niece of the Earl of Abercorn. She was the most beautiful of my acquaintances as well, tall and elegantly formed, with wide blue eyes and a lovely smile that she often employed to hide her lack of any real cleverness. If she had no wit to the point of silliness, then I had no beauty, so between us we did well enough.

The sun was pleasingly warm, filtering through the new green leaves that had just begun to appear in the top branches of the trees. The canal shone bright as new-polished silver, and the light breezes were as gentle as a caress. People of every rank filled the park, parading across the paths and lawns to enjoy both the day and each other, and Jane and I were no different. Happy to be finally rid of our winter cloaks, we wore bright new gowns and broad-brimmed lace hats as if it were summer already, and I took care to bid my watchful footman (he accompanied me at Father's insistence, not my own) to keep a respectful distance, so as not to distract from our fashionable appearance.

"Those two ensigns are watching us," Jane whispered, raising her ribbon-trimmed muff to shield her words. "There, those two."

"What do we care if they watch us?" I made a sweeping show of scattering a handful of bread crumbs into the canal for the ducks, who cackled and quacked in a furious frenzy. "That is why we're here, isn't it?"

Jane frowned, perplexed. "I thought we'd come to feed the ducks."

"To feed the ducks," I explained patiently, "and to be seen by gentlemen. That's what we ladies *do*, Janie."

"Very well, Katherine," she said, "because they are coming here to us."

They were an excellent pair of young gentlemen, perhaps eighteen at most, with glossy polished boots, swords at their waists, and curled plumes in their gold-laced hats. There is something so delightsome about a gentleman-soldier, from the bright silken sash of his regiment to the whiff of valor that make them irresistible to ladies, or at any rate to ladies as young and as impressionable as Jane and I were. The taller fellow made us a neat bow by way of catching our interest, and I caught my breath, feigning that I'd only just noticed him. He was the more handsome of the pair, with a fine sparkish air, and I was determined that he should be mine.

"Forgive me, ladies," he said most gallantly with his friend grinning beside him, "but I am new arrived to the city and in need of some advice."

I smiled archly, striving to attract him by subtlety, while Jane giggled beside me.

"I am sure ladies such as yourselves will know the answer," he continued, appealing entirely to fair Jane while seeming not to see me, though we stood side by side. "Can you tell me if the water in the canal is wet?"

Jane only giggled all the more at this idle foolishness, which was likely what the ensign desired.

"No, sir, it is not," I said, determined to be noticed, too. "That water is not wet. That is His Majesty's own canal, and by royal decree the water within burns as hot as the devil's own flames."

Startled by my reply, he looked at me for the first time, and I blushed.

"'Od's blood!" he exclaimed, and flashed a quick glance to his friend. "Is that so, mistress?"

"It is, sir," I said, grinning wickedly. "Like the most licking flames of hell around the fat ass of a sinner."

"Indeed!" he said, astonished, and laughed.

I laughed with him, to show I knew my speech was daring nonsense, and offered him my most languishing look (well practiced in my looking glass).

After that, it seemed most natural to invite both the ensigns to join Jane and me in our coach, and repair back to Queen Street for further conversation and light refreshment. We four sat in the back parlor with the doors to the garden thrown open and ate buttered bread and jam and shared two bottles of Father's French sillery that I ordered brought up from the cellar. With our humor much and merrily improved, Thomas (for so my soldier was called) proposed a game of ombre, and I quickly brought out the cards. Our stakes were just as swiftly agreed, with kisses for forfeits. I was a good hand at cards, having been well trained by Father's friends, but it took all my considerable skill to play worse than Jane so I might be the first to lose.

"Come, Mistress Katherine," Thomas said with mock severity, turning in his chair to face me and patting his thigh as if to summon me. "Time to cover your losses."

My heart racing with eager anticipation, I went to stand between his legs. It would be most pleasing to be kissed by him, for he was very comely, and the sulky disappointment on Jane's face (for all that she was my friend) was extra spice.

"Mind you, I'll cover my losses and no more," I teased him as I bent to offer my lips, "for the only rogue who'll cover *me* will be the one I wed."

"Such empty oaths are made to break," he said, and before I realized it he'd seized me around the waist and hauled me across his thighs. I'd hoped he would do this, and after a slight show of maidenly resistance, I gave myself over to his attentions. From the corner of my eye I could see that Jane, too, had succumbed to her gallant, the two kissing with furious passion.

True, I was only thirteen, and not half so worldly as I believed, but having been a witness for so long to the behavior of my father and his friends, I was now eager for my own share of experience. Already I'd learned that while men often were first attracted to prettier faces than mine, there were ways to make them forget my deficiencies. I opened my lips as a signal to Thomas that I'd welcome a deeper kiss, and he happily obliged with an ardor I matched. Even through my petticoats, I relished the feel of his well-muscled thighs beneath me and his arm around my waist, holding me there with perfect, delicious ease. I was as eager to pay back my debt as he was in claiming it, and when he dared to creep his hand beneath my kerchief to the negligible prize of my breast, I only sighed with delight.

Until, that is, I heard the door to the room open and my father come in.

"Release my daughter, you damned thieving dog!" he thundered, charging toward us as he drew his sword from its scabbard. "Free her at once, else I cut your prick from your ballocks, as you deserve!"

"No, Father, don't!" I shrieked, rolling free of the ensign. I threw myself against my furious parent to stay his sword, knowing he'd not dare harm me.

My erstwhile gallant had already flown from his chair, and he and his comrade were retreating with an unseemly haste that would have incensed their officers.

"Forgive me, sir," he stammered as he grabbed his hat. "I did not intend—"

"I know exactly what you intended, you damned whoreson!" Father shouted, too tangled with me to employ the sword in his hand. "Leave my house at once, all of you!"

"Farewell, Katherine," Jane called, likewise fleeing. She waggled her fingers at me in sympathy and farewell, and smiled to show she'd no hard feelings. "I'll write anon."

"Your letters won't be welcome here, madam," Father said curtly. "Go, away with you, back to whatever filthy bagnio that spawned you!"

"Father, please," I exclaimed. "She's my friend, and a lady, a Holcomb, and niece to the Earl of Abercorn."

"She could be His Majesty's own daughter," countered Father with palpable disgust, "and I'd still damn her as a whore and toss her from my house."

From the hall, we heard the servant close the front door after my friends, and with relief I stepped clear of Father. My fear for everyone's safety had not been an empty one. Like the Duke of Buckingham and the rest, Father wasn't afraid of brawling and bloodshed. Even now, with my friends gone, his face remained flushed with his fury, the veins in his temples pulsing at an ominous rate. They might have escaped; I'd not be so fortunate.

But being Father's daughter, I likewise knew the wisdom of attacking first. Besides, my own temper was already simmering, both from embarrassment at having been so shamed before those I'd wished to impress, and from being interrupted at my pleasurable play.

"You'd no right to dismiss my friends like that, Father," I began warmly. "What manner of hostess does that make me, that I cannot—"

"An empty-headed hostess who invites the worst young jackals into her father's house." He shoved his sword emphatically back into the scabbard, and peered inside the nearer sillery bottle. Frowning, he took it by the neck and turned it upside down to demonstrate how thoroughly we'd emptied the contents. "Must you serve my best sillery? I have to pay the devil himself to have it smuggled from France away from the navy ships. You might have poured piss into the glasses, and those dogs would have not known the difference."

"The sillery is *my* favorite wine," I said indignantly. "If you'd not wished me to acquire a taste for it, then you shouldn't have given it to me in the first place."

He growled, too outraged for lowly words, and thumped the empty bottle on the table. "Where are your wits, Katherine? What should I make of this, to find my house made into a brothel full of drunken soldiers? What if I'd not returned when I had? Where would this have led?"

"Oh, yes, Father, and where were you?" I demanded, setting my arms akimbo. It did not take much observation to see that he wore the same clothes from the day before, the once-impeccable lace neckcloth now spotted with last night's wine and his stockings drooping about his ankles, though somewhere he'd met with a barber to shave his jaw clean. "I haven't seen you since yesterday noon. What brothel were you attending all the night long, that you might recognize another here?"

"That is none of your affair, Katherine," he said, warning enough in his voice if I'd but paused to hear it.

"Is Mrs. Knapp still in your favor?" I demanded, my voice rising shrill. "Or was it Mrs. Hewes again? Faith, Father, there have been so many that I cannot recall them all."

He took a deep breath, and to my surprise replied with far more calm than I was showing. "I have been with Mrs. Ayscough."

"Mrs. Ayscough?" This was a name new to me. "Which playhouse does she frequent? Is she with the King's Company, or the duke's?"

"Neither," he said curtly. "She is a most respectable lady, sister to a barrister in Gray's Inn, and given your behavior here this day, you are not fit so much as to speak her name."

I gasped, as shocked as if he'd struck me. In all our frolics together since Mama had left, he had never once taken the part of another woman against me like this. I stepped back from him and folded my arms over my chest, striving to recover. Father would never dally with any sister to a barrister. Surely this must be some jest of his, some perverse contrivance to increase my own guilt. Even the name he'd concocted for this woman—Ayscough—sounded like a prank.

"If she is so respectable, Father," I said, raising my chin, "then I do not understand what you see in her."

"That is between the lady and me, Katherine." Though I'd backed from him, he now followed, unwilling to make this any easier for me. "What concerns me now is you, and this scene here today. How did you come to know those two soldiers?"

"Jane and I met them in the park," I said, a perfectly harmless explanation. "Feeding ducks by the canal. They seemed agreeable, and—"

"Have you learned nothing of the world by now?" he asked, incredulous. "Every man is base at heart, whether he is highborn or lowborn, a beggar or a prince, or even an agreeable rascal near the canal."

"But you have always told me that I am to be free to find love where I choose, just as you have," I protested. "You've said no one should go against their hearts for love."

His expression hardened, which I'd not expected. "I meant that you should wed a gentleman of your own rank or better as you pleased, not give yourself to any snorting young buck who paws the ground before you. Are you still a virgin, or is your maidenhead a memory?"

I flushed, shamed to be asked such a thing by my own father. In truth I was the most skittish maid imaginable, for all my bold and brazen talk. Among the actresses in the playhouse, I'd seen the consequences of a big belly and a faithless lover who'd fled, and I could not fathom how a moment's pleasure could possibly be great enough in the balance against so much ruin and suffering. Besides, with my large marriage portion, I knew I was a considerable prize, and I'd no wish to squander my maidenhead for nothing in return.

"You know me, Father," I said. "I would never have granted that last favor."

"If you grant everything else, Katherine," he said bluntly, "then most men will think it their right to claim the rest whether you wish it or not, and you will be the one left with a brat in your belly."

"I am not such a fool as that!"

"What woman is?" He grunted. "Perhaps I should just make a match for you now with some dull, honest lordling and be done with it, and give you over to a husband's keeping."

"No, Father, please!" I cried. To be wed to some stranger and taken away off to breed in the country was the sorry fate of most girls of my rank. I'd always smugly believed that, because of Father and my fortune, I'd be saved from such gloomy respectability. "You cannot mean to do that!"

"What, to make a modest, respectable woman of you? Is that the greatest curse I can cast at my daughter?" He sighed deeply, and I wonder if in that moment he'd any regret for how I had been raised. "I wish you to be happy, Katherine, and I wish you to find the love that will make you so. But I ask that you be a little nicer in your hunting, and take care after your own safety. I have little desire to return home to find you murdered or worse. No more soldiers in my parlor, mind?"

"No, Father," I said meekly, kissing his cheek by way of apology. "No soldiers, I vow."

"No soldiers," he repeated with a mournful air. "How neatly you parse that, Daughter! No soldiers, no, which is to say you'll not give up sailors, jugglers, cutpurses, or rat catchers."

For the first time since he'd returned, I smiled, and slyly, too. "You forget all the rogues to be found at Southwark Fair. I could be like Lady Castlemaine, and pluck up another Jacob Hall."

"Lady Castlemaine!" he exclaimed, arching his brows with mock horror. Despite her role as a royal mistress, the beautiful Countess of Castlemaine was notorious for her wide taste in lovers beyond the king, and had most recently taken the celebrated ropedancer Jacob Hall into her bed. "Why not choose Messalina herself as your patroness? Lady Castlemaine, indeed."

"You must grant that she's done very well for herself and her children," I said, teasing yet telling the truth as well. Lady Castlemaine had prospered as a royal favorite, receiving titles, jewels, rich livings, and power from the king in return for her wantonness. I slipped my arm around Father's waist. "By comparison I am not so very wicked at all, am I?"

"No, but then, you are still very young, with years to achieve the same degree of infamy, though please God I will not live to see it if you do." Gently he patted my back as he'd done when I'd been a little child. "Now come, call your maidservant and make yourself ready. We'll leave in an hour."

"Leave, Father?" I asked, surprised. "For where?"

"Why, for Whitehall, of course," he said, and winked. "I can't very well leave you here alone to make more mischief, can I, Kattypillar?"

There was no better way to describe my Father's influence upon my life than this. He had begun by chiding me for behaving too wantonly, then had ended with making jests about the most infamous harlot of our time. Finally, by way of a punishment, he was taking me with him to the Court where Lady Castlemaine reigned like another queen. His anger had melted as swiftly as frost before the sun of his indulgent affection for me. I'd been forgiven with the ease of one friend to another, rather than with the severity a parent should on occasion show toward a wayward child. Was it any wonder that, as contrite as I'd been, I'd no real intention of heeding his warning?

But so it was between Father and me, and as I ran off happily to dress, I considered only how much he must love me, and gave not a thought to the disasters that his indulgence might bring to us both.

AMONG ALL THE PALACES OWNED BY the royal family, there was no other hall so grand as the Banqueting House in Whitehall. It had been conceived fifty years before as a tribute to the glorious buildings of Imperial Rome, and King James I had sent his architect, Inigo Jones, clear to Italy for inspiration. The hall he'd created was an imposing display of snowy pilasters and gilded volutes, all crowned by three glorious paintings in the ceiling overhead by Sir Peter Paul Rubens. There had been nothing like it at the time in England, and when filled with bejeweled courtiers beneath scores of candles, it remained imposing enough to steal the breath away from even the most jaded visiting Frenchmen.

At least it did for me. I stood beside Father against the east wall of this grand room and stared upward at its lavish carved walls picked in gold and a ceiling painted to look as if the very heavens had opened overhead. Surely this was the most beautiful place I'd ever seen, made more beautiful by the company gathered beneath the dozens of candles.

The king prized beauty and youth among his courtiers, and though he would be forty himself this year, most of those closest to him, like Father and his friends, were a good deal younger. Though tonight's entertainment was nothing so special as a ball or masque, all the ladies in attendance wore costly dress, with plumes in their hair and as many jewels as could be draped over their person. The gentlemen followed their lead, with ribbons tied into their elaborately curled wigs, silken suits of every possible color, and gaudy jewels on their fingers, on the scabbards of their swords, on the ornaments on their doublets, or even as a single dangling earring, after the fashion of the old king.

I was as elegantly dressed as any of them, especially for a lady my age. The rose-colored silk of my gown brought the same pleasant color to my cheeks, and the full sleeves with their cunningly pinked edges and loops of gold ribbon gave grace to my angular form. Once my heavy dark hair had been drawn back from my face to better show my eyes (my best feature), the locks had been curled with an iron and made to stay with sugar water. I'd fat pearls hanging from my ears and more about my throat, and on my finger was the matching pearl and garnet ring that Father had given me on my last birthday. Fluttering my fan, I felt every bit a part of the Court, a place I was sure I'd been born to be.

The performers were a small chorus of Frenchmen with several musicians besides, all recently come from Versailles. I'll grant that their voices were sweet as holy angels', and on another day perhaps I would have enjoyed their music no end. But it had been months since I'd been inside Whitehall, and I was far too excited to pay heed to mere music, however sweetly sung. What I wished to know was the latest scandal regarding all the grand folk before me, and Father, being Father, was happy enough to oblige.

"Who is that black-haired lady beside the king?" I asked softly, using my painted fan to shield my words. While most of us stood or sat on benches, the king and queen had armchairs to represent their thrones, set squarely before the musicians. The queen, Catherine of Braganza (how disappointing it was to me that we bore the same saint's name!), was as always dull-looking and ill at ease, her hands resting awkwardly outstretched on the arms of the chair. With her as queen, it was easy to understand why this was not a court where wedded wives held sway, however highborn they might be. Around the royal couple sat several other favored friends and attendants in chairs, but it was the lady sitting on a cushioned stool to the right of His Majesty that had caught my eye.

"There," I said, tipping my chin in her direction. "The lady who's captured the king's attention. Who is that?"

"Ahh, that's his newest infatuation," Father said with unabashed relish. "Louise de Keroualle is her name."

"What of Nelly?" I asked with surprise. When last I'd seen the actress, not a fortnight before, she'd been basking still in the royal affection, with the king's curly-haired babe on her knee in the fine new house that His Majesty had leased for her, at the east end of Pall Mall.

"Oh, Nelly still has her charms for him, there's no doubt of that," Father assured me, "but she's too lowborn to hold his interest forever. The mademoiselle, however, is the daughter of a French nobleman, and the king has always had a taste for French fare."

He gathered the fingers on one hand and kissed the tips in a French salute. "The lady was in Madame's household when he first spied her, and with Madame's death, Louis himself decided she'd make a pretty gift to Charles. She's on the palace rolls now as a maid of honor to Her Majesty, but no one is fooled, except perhaps the lady herself, who plays that she's too fine to do what she must, and that is to be fucked by the king in the name of France."

I listened, carefully sorting through so much information. I knew the lady Father referred to only as "Madame" was the king's youngest sister, the royal princess Henriette, who had been wed to Louis's brother, Monsieur. Madame had died last summer in Paris, and may or may not have been poisoned; the scandal had been very great, and the king had been devastated by his sister's death. If this French mademoiselle could console him, why, then this might be the most clever gift that Louis had ever sent.

"She is very pretty," I admitted, unable to keep the wistfulness from my voice. The young Frenchwoman's beauty was perfectly in fashion: she was plump and pale, with round rosy cheeks and lips and sleepy wanton's eyes. Beneath the king's hungry gaze, her tight-laced breasts quivered like snowy offerings, her black hair trailing in natural ringlets over her shoulders. "I don't wonder that His Majesty desires her."

"Along with every gentleman in this hall," Father said, unconsciously smiling himself as he studied the lady. "It was Buckingham's chore to bring her from France last autumn, and he claims it took a bottle of brandy every night to make him contain his lust for her, or else he would have despoiled the royal gift before it had even crossed the Channel."

While the queen steadfastly listened to the musicians, I watched the king take Mademoiselle de Keroualle's dimpled hand and raise it to his lips, his dark gaze fair smoldering with desire. She in turn did no more than grant him the most tremulous of smiles. It was a pretty sight to see him strive to woo her with such elegance, romantic enough to make me sigh with sympathetic longing. Would that some gentleman would gaze at me like that!

"Why doesn't she permit His Majesty to be her lover?" I asked my father, mystified. "He is the king. He is most charming and agreeable. He'll grant her everything she could ever want."

Father shrugged. "The king wishes he knew that answer, too, considering that's the only reason she's here. Perhaps she's frightened of Castlemaine's wrath. God knows I'd be."

I searched about for the infamous countess. "There she is, Father, beneath the window. She doesn't look very wrathful to me."

"You've never seen her in a rage, throwing crockery and shrieking like a harpy." Father shuddered dramatically. "It only proves how gifted she must be in other areas that the king's put up with her for over ten years."

I thought it was easy enough to see why. Tall and voluptuous, Lady

Castlemaine had a presence that the Frenchwoman never would, and that much enhanced by the ransom of sapphires around her elegant throat. Though the countess was no longer alone in the king's affections nor was her beauty the freshest, being nearly thirty and having borne a half dozen children, she still maintained her place at Court and in the king's heart. She was secure enough that even now she did not cling to the king's side, but wandered freely about the room. Yet as fascinated as I was by her, it wasn't her jewels that had caught my eye.

"Why, Father, look," I murmured with studied amazement. "She's with a soldier."

She was, too, a young ensign not much different in age or appearance from my own gallant from the canal. This one had golden hair, made more startling by how darkly browned he'd been made by some distant sun. His conversation with the countess appeared both animated and flirtatious, and pleasing to them both.

"A soldier," Father repeated in disbelief, though when he glanced my way I saw that he was trying not to laugh. "Oh, Katherine, Katherine. When I warned you not to follow after her, I'd no notion she'd be the one to copy you instead."

I smiled, but not quite so merrily as Father himself did. To be sure, it was only a jest, yet I understood the bitter irony at its core. Lady Castlemaine would never follow me. My inheritance would grant me more independence than most women would ever have, but in our world of the Court, the only real fortune for a lady was her beauty. The queen was unlovely, and sat alone. Louise de Keroualle was lush perfection, and the king worshiped her. By such reckoning, Lady Castlemaine was as rich as Croesus, whilst I would always be no more than a beggar rattling the poor box.

Though Father loved me dearly, he was but a man, and as thickheaded and callous about such matters as every other of his sex.

"It would seem Her Ladyship is tired of him already," he blithely continued as we watched the young officer part with the countess. "I vow he must not have been deemed sufficient to worship at her altar. Poor young pup! He must learn that a goddess like that can choose whomever she pleases. Ahh, but here's real choice, Katherine. That fellow in green, addressing her now: that's the French ambassador, doubtless ready to produce another sizable bauble in return for her influence over the king. They say she's still the most powerful woman at Court, perhaps in England, and there's the proof."

If Lady Castlemaine's rare beauty was the proof of power and success for women at Court, then I'd no wish to watch any further. Instead I let my gaze follow the gold-haired ensign as he made his way through the crowd, his hair glinting in the candlelight. Suddenly he stopped before an equally fair-haired lady, each smiling at the other in happy greeting.

"Who is that, Father?" The mean and grudging part of me hoped the officer had slighted the countess for this other lady, who had a long nose and longer face, and none of the countess's beauty. "Do you know her? The lady in silver, there, with the ensign."

"There? That's Mrs. Arabella Churchill," Father said with a weary disdain to show he didn't believe Mrs. Churchill was quite worth his time for gossip. "As plain as turned dirt, that one, yet she's still the duke's favorite."

"The duke?" I asked. "Which duke?"

"His Royal Highness the Duke of York," Father said. "The king's brother. Mrs. Churchill has been his mistress for years and years now, since she first came to Court as maid of honor to Her Highness. Now he keeps her in a house in St. James's Square, so she's done well enough for herself. She's borne the duke two bastards, including a son last summer, which is more than Her Highness seems able to do. But then, it's never the Stuart seed that's at fault, is it?"

I studied Mrs. Churchill with fresh interest. Of course I'd heard of her. Who in London hadn't? She had succeeded in holding the duke's interest far longer than any of the others, including his wife. Still, it wasn't surprising that I'd not seen her before. The two royal brothers each maintained separate courts—the king at Whitehall Palace, and the duke at St. James's Palace, on the far side of St. James's Park—with entirely separate households, chapels, and staffs, down to their own treasurers, secretaries, and attorney-generals. Because Father was attached to His Majesty, we were naturally more often at Whitehall than St. James's. The St. James's Court was quiet now, Her Highness having only recently given birth to another daughter, to the disappointment of all who'd hoped for a male heir. That would explain Mrs. Churchill's presence here instead.

As for the Duke of York's having seduced her when she was his wife's maid of honor, that I knew, too. His Highness was infamous for poaching among the younger female attendants (Mrs. Churchill had been fifteen when he'd first seduced her), and I'd come to realize that that had likely been Father's unspoken reason for forbidding me to join the Yorks' household long ago. Yet even with so much of this knowing-knowledge, I remained fascinated by how homely Arabella Churchill had succeeded in an arena without any of the womanly arsenal possessed by beauties like Lady Castlemaine.

"As plain as dirt," Father repeated. He took two glasses of wine from a passing servant's tray and handed one to me. "No, to liken her to dirt is to do disservice to the great mother earth. Rather Mrs. Churchill is plain as sand, without color or form or moisture to her."

"Has she a pleasing wit?" I asked. "Can she make him laugh?"

Father drank deep of the wine. "Faith, I wouldn't know. How could I, when confronted by the horror of that face?"

"Then His Highness must love her," I said, the only explanation I could conceive. I had myself spoken to His Highness just the once, but I recalled him as having blue eyes and a deep voice that had spoken to me in a kindly manner. "Love. That's why he's kept her so long, Father. He loves her. The poets say that love is blind, and so it must be with the duke."

Father screwed up his mouth as if he'd swallowed a foul-tasting draught. "If the poets say that of Mrs. Churchill, then they're not only blind, but piss-poor at their craft as well. A true poet dedicates himself to beauty, Katherine, beauty and nothing else."

I sighed, and resigned myself to abandoning this particular battle. I'd get no further answer from Father now, not when he'd seized upon a subject so thoroughly that he couldn't let truth interfere with his declarations. Besides, there was no denying that Arabella Churchill *was* plain, far more plain than I, which, being thirteen, I found selfishly heartening.

"Then tell me, Father," I said, beginning anew. "If that is Mrs. Churchill, then who is the officer who is making her smile?"

Father frowned and drank more as he studied the pair, likely offended that any gentleman could bring himself to speak to the lady. Then suddenly he brightened, his whole face lighting with revelation.

"I know who he must be, Katherine," he exclaimed. "Mark the likeness, though in him it is far the more comely. He must be her brother John, new returned from defending Tangiers against the corsairs. A pretty, brave fellow, and a good friend to Lord Monmouth as well. Surely he's one who should be able to defend himself from Lady Castlemaine."

I watched as Ensign Churchill kissed his sister's cheek and then departed, slipping out through one of the several doorways. With a sister who was the duke's mistress and a friend who was the king's bastard son, he was bound to do well at Court. I was sorry to see him go. He was, as Father said, a pretty, brave fellow, and if he'd remained, I would surely have contrived somehow to meet him.

"No soldiers, Katherine," Father cautioned, following my gaze. "If for no other reason than because their lives are notoriously short. That fellow will likely be posted off to some distant war or other, and be dead before Christmas."

I sighed with melancholy. Father was right about soldiers, but it seemed such a waste that one as handsome as Ensign Churchill would be doomed to perish so soon.

"Hah, those yowling Frenchmen are done at last." Father set his empty glass on a nearby volute and offered me his arm. "Come along, pet. There'll be proper music for dancing now. Show me what I've paid that dancing master to teach you."

I danced with Father and several other older gentlemen besides. With good intentions, Father forced several young whelps close to my own age to dance with me as well, doubtless hoping I'd find one to my liking. I did not. They might have been the sons of peers and most suitable candidates for a respectable match, but one had a face covered with raging pustules, another was so shy he could scarce raise his gaze from his shambling feet, and the last was half a head shorter than me, and wiped his nose on his velvet sleeve.

"You're very quiet, sweet," Father said later, as we rode in our coach through the quiet streets for home. "You must be ready for your bed."

"I am," I said, and yawned mightily for emphasis. I wasn't tired, not really, but all that I'd seen that evening had given me much to ponder about my future and what I wished from my life, and I wasn't in the humor for more conversation.

"Then I'll leave you at the door," he said, "so you might go upstairs directly."

"Why?" I asked, sitting upright. "Where will you be going instead?"

"I promised I'd call on Mrs. Ayscough," he said. "I won't be long."

Though it was dark in the coach, I didn't need to see his face to know he was lying and when I rose tomorrow morn, he'd not yet be home.

"I must introduce you to her," he continued, his voice too full of cheerfulness for the hour past midnight. "You will like her, I think."

I would not lie in return, and we passed the rest of the way in silence.

Chapter Five

GREAT QUEEN STREET, LONDON
September 1671

While I had already observed how the great gentlemen at Court were far more devoted to their mistresses than to their wives, there was one area in which the royal wives always attracted their husbands' attentions. Queens had but one true purpose in their lives, and that was to produce a male heir to secure her husband's throne. An additional son or two was preferable, as a guard against the perils of sudden illness or accidents. Such misfortunes were common enough; my own father, born a younger son, had only come into his title and fortune because he had survived a virulent dose of the measles, while his older brother had not.

But while the king had sired numerous sturdy bastards with numerous mistresses, his homely Portuguese queen had given birth to nothing but empty hopes, and after seven years of marriage, her womb was considered inhospitable and barren. Thus the importance of the Duke of York had increased: not only was he himself next in the line of succession, but his two young daughters, the Lady Mary and the Lady Anne, were next after him. Yet despite the famous rule of old Queen Bess, daughters were no one's choice for a monarch. Sons were what was required, strong, healthy sons. In ten years of marriage, the Duchess of York had suffered through eight pregnancies and had produced several sons, but they had been mean and sickly babes, and none but the two daughters and one weakling infant son, the pitiful Duke of Clarence, had survived.

In February, the duchess had been delivered of yet another unwanted daughter, to the discouragement and disappointment of both the king and the duke. But Her Highness was done with disappointing. Soon after

Father and I had seen Mrs. Churchill at Whitehall, the Duchess of York died of a cancer of the breast, a cruel, wasting illness that plagued her for many months before killing her.

Because of the foul nature of her corpse (leastways that was the reason given by the palace, even though no one believed it), her body was not mourned in public state, as was the custom for royalty. Instead, within three days of her death she had been interred in Westminster Abbey with next to no ceremony, attended by neither her husband nor her brother-in-law. Her Highness's death was no more than a passing inconvenience to the king, who callously decreed that her mourning must not interfere with the celebrations for his own birthday on 29 May. Thus it was not considered worthwhile to bother draping the palace in black, or even putting the households into mourning. No one grieved or missed her, because, poor lady, no one had loved her.

Even before she was buried, the talk of the Court was not her death so much as the rumor that on her deathbed she had converted to the Romish faith. That she had done so with the duke beside her was more scandalous still, for there were already whispers that His Highness was being seduced by the Papists away from the Anglican Church. Protestant England would never tolerate a Catholic king, and the duke's unsettling inclinations were blamed on his dead duchess, one more failure to accompany her to her grave.

It was imperative that the duke remarry. Both the last daughter and the sad little Duke of Clarence had perished soon after their mother, and the question of the succession was more pressing than ever. All agreed that His Highness must wed a fertile Protestant princess who would lead him away from Rome, and with unseemly haste the search was begun across the Continent for a suitable bride. In the meantime, the St. James's household was left in disarray without a mistress. The former duchess's attendants were either pensioned off or found new places with the queen while the two surviving princesses returned to their nursery in Richmond, with the freshly widowed duke said to be quite happily wallowing with his dogs in his unkempt bachelor quarters.

Yet even a death that brings little sorrow can cast a somber pall, and the spring and summer that followed the duchess's death were quieter seasons than usual. Father took me with him to Kent to see to his properties there and to escape the heat of London. As was customary, the king took much of the Court with him first to Windsor Castle, and then to Newmarket for the fall races. That he also took Louise de Keroualle with him with the intention of finally claiming her elusive maidenhead was also widely discussed to considerable amusement, a far more pleasing subject than the sordid circumstances of the Duchess of York's death.

While I continued to entertain myself with my own friends and Father with his, I couldn't deny that he'd changed. When he was in London, we went about together to many of the same taverns and playhouses and entertainments at Court as before, but there was an undeniable difference to him that made me uneasy for being unexpected.

It wasn't just Father. Many of his favorite companions had altered their ways as well. Nelly Gwyn had quit the playhouse for good, and was huge with another bastard by the king. Lord Buckhurst was said to be willingly entangled with the beautiful, widowed Countess of Falmouth, and unwillingly mired in legal battles with his own parents regarding his inheritance. Lord Rochester had likewise buried himself in the country with his wife and children, attempting another of his frequent (and unsuccessful) cures for too much wine and, it was whispered, the pox.

I wondered if Father had likewise made a similar vow. Oh, he was outwardly as merry and witty as ever, particularly in the presence of the king, but he didn't drink as deeply as he once had, or behave with the old abandon. I doubted there'd be any more debauched escapades with Lord Rochester or Lord Buckhurst that involved drunkenness, actresses, and public nakedness. Instead Father spent more time attending to his seat in the House of Commons and at his desk in his library, reading and writing. Whenever we went out together, he now pushed me toward callow young gentlemen of his choosing, not mine, striving to point out the merits of each with embarrassing enthusiasm. Though he was scarcely thirty, Father had begun to seem old to me, and rather dull.

I was convinced the fault (or the reason, if I were to be less pessimistic) was to be laid at the feet of the mysterious Mrs. Ayscough. Once or twice more, Father had raised her name to me in conversation, and each time I had refused to discuss her. I'd never had such qualms about his other mistresses. He'd always shown a fondness for actresses that were cut from the same cloth as Nelly—jolly and vulgar and kind. There hadn't been a one that I'd disliked.

But Mrs. Ann Ayscough seemed different. To begin with, she'd lasted longer than the others. She never seemed to accompany him out among his friends, or, for that matter, with me. Instead she and Father seemed to spend quiet evenings in each other's company and no more, a most curious circumstance for a gentleman as gregarious as my father. From what little I could surmise without asking outright (which I'd no intention of doing, unwilling as I was to show any interest in her), she truly was that most rare and fearsome of creatures among our Court-bound society: a respectable, sober, modest lady. In short, she must be as unlike me as was possible, and I did not trust her at all. For the first time, I was relieved when Father was off to join the king at Newmarket or on an autumn progress, because it meant he was not being beguiled by the (surely!) cunning Mrs. Ayscough.

If I had been older, or more experienced, or less blinded by my own attachment to Father, perhaps I would have realized the foolishness of ignoring the lady's very existence in the hope that she would simply fade away, like smoke above a chimney.

But she did not. And to my sorrow, that drifting smoke was nothing compared to the hot flames that would rise up from beneath it to scorch me forever.

"You pick where we're to dine, Father," I said as we climbed into the coach. "I don't care, so long as I'm with you."

Father smiled, reaching down to pull the hem of my petticoat from being caught in the coach's door by the servant. It was the kind of small, watchful service he'd done for me when I was younger and in his care, and the gentleness of it touched me. I was nearly fifteen and no longer the child I'd been; there was something about the hazy September afternoon that made such changes seem both inevitable, and poignant, too. The sun still had the golden warmth of summer, but the days were shorter now and the nights had the first chill of autumn. The blooms of July had wizened and turned brittle in our garden, and the leaves in the trees were beginning to trade their green for shades of yellow and red.

"I thought we'd visit the Folly one last time before summer's done," Father suggested, as if to read my thoughts. "There won't be many more days like this before they shut for the season."

"Oh, the Folly!" I exclaimed with happy anticipation. "You could not choose better."

The Folly had always been one of my favorite resorts in all of London, made all the more special because it was only open during the warmer months. Half playhouse, half eating-house, the Folly was a low wooden building that stretched across three barges floating in the river. It was of course well moored, so as not to suddenly drift away downriver with a hall full of outraged diners clutching their spoons and tankards.

"I thought you'd agree," Father said, smiling at my response. He settled his hat lower over his brow to shade his eyes against the slanting afternoon sun. "And what better place to tell you all the latest news from Euston Hall? Surely there can be no greater foolishness in all of the Maker's Creation than what was contrived for His Majesty and the French mademoiselle."

I gasped and caught at his sleeve. "Oh, you must tell me at once!"

Father had returned only that morning, riding into town with the king himself. If anyone knew what had occurred at Euston Hall—the country seat of Lord Arlington, situated near the racecourses at Newmarket, and offered to His Majesty as a place of assignation—then it would be Father, and in the most luscious detail, too. "Tell me *everything*."

He laughed at my eagerness. "We've all afternoon, Kattypillar," he said easily, lolling back against the leather cushions. "I'm not about to spill everything before we've even reached the river. To be honest, I'd rather hear of how you passed your days than how many false tears a French harlot wept."

"Mademoiselle always weeps." Louise de Keroualle was already renowned for her tears, so much so that Nell mockingly called her "The Weeping Willow." "That's nothing new. You'll have to tell me more than that."

"Oh, I will," he promised. "But you must go first."

I sighed wearily, certain my idle little amusements could scarce compare with a royal deflowering. But dutifully I began, telling how this friend's bitch had a new litter of pups and that one had lost twenty guineas in a wager over the number of China oranges piled in a particular basket, and I was chattering still when at last the coach stopped not far from the Somerset Steps. It had been a long time since I'd had Father's complete attention, and I hadn't realized how much I'd missed it. He could be an excellent listener when he chose, offering the exact degree of exclamations, agreements, and questions to make a conversation sail along, which was doubtless one of the reasons he'd had such success at Court.

With my hand in the crook of his arm, we made the short, pleasing walk to the river, past the pale stone facade of Somerset House (once the dower house to the king's mother, Queen Henriette Marie), through the formal gardens, and down the steps to the water. The Folly was tied close to the steps, there at the bend in the river.

Given its very nature, the Folly was an odd sort of dining-house, low and flat and built of wood that had been gaudily painted. The windows were wide and without glass, but with shutters that were lashed open to catch the breezes from the river. Every table had an excellent view of the water, with a small stage for performers in the center. On this day, there were four fiddlers playing spritely jigs and other airs that blended agreeably with the voices and laughter of the patrons.

We were not the only ones who'd decided to take dinner here today, and the house was crowded, for all that the Folly was known as a costly place. The keeper recognized Father at once, however, and we were swiftly shown to a private table near a window. Father bespoke us wine and, to start, a dish of the eels for which the Folly was known.

I drew my chair closer to the window, leaning my arms on the sill to better see the water. All variety of craft plied the river before us, from low skiffs with a single waterman at the oars to the rich barges and yachts of noblemen, with gaily colored pennants flying from their masts.

"Look there, Father, at that boat," I exclaimed, pointing. "That man has a huge white dog sitting with him, proud in the stern as if he were the lord mayor himself."

"Katherine." To my surprise, Father reached across the table to take my hand from the sill, covering it with his own. "Know that I love you, Daughter. Whatever else, that will always be true."

I stared at him, pleased but wary, for pronouncements like that were not his usual custom.

"What manner of palaver is that, Father?" I asked with a small nervous laugh. "Faith, you sound as deadly solemn as one of Mr. Dryden's wooden heroes."

"Pray not that!" he exclaimed. Yet still he regarded me with great fondness, his expression so soft and doting I felt tears sting my eyes. "It is the truth, Katherine, that is all, and I fear I've not spoken it enough to you, as a father should to his only daughter."

"You do," I said, my words failing to explain what I felt for him at that moment. "You—you do."

"Then I am glad," he said softly, "and honored. Ahh, here are the eels."

The serving maid set the dish on the table and we fell upon them with hearty delight; not that we truly were so ravenous, but because the rare tenderness of that last moment had been almost too much for either of us to bear.

But we'd scarcely begun before the keeper came to our table. He bowed before Father, and whispered something to him that I was clearly not meant to hear. Immediately Father rose, crumpling his napkin at his place on the table.

"What has happened?" I asked with concern. "What is wrong?"

"Nothing at all," he said, and smiled in a fashion that did little to reassure me. "I'll be away only a short while."

I watched him hurry off with the keeper, my pleasure in the dish of eels gone. I wondered if Father had received some grievous news from the palace, or had been summoned by a royal messenger, as had happened before. That would explain his haste; no one dawdled with a request from the king. Sipping my wine, I disconsolately stared out at the river, and as I sat alone for a quarter hour or so, I hoped that I'd not be abandoned entirely.

"Katherine," Father called with sweet eagerness, and I turned swiftly, smiling with relief.

And in that same instant, my smile stopped cold, and so did my breath.

Father was not alone. At his side was a woman, his hand linked as familiarly to hers as it had been with mine such a short time before. This lady was small of stature, yet agreeably round in her figure, and near to the same age as my father. She was dressed in a blue moiré jacket and petticoat trimmed in Flemish lace, a quiet, modest taste that was several years behind the fashion. She'd light brown hair and blue eyes and a small pink mouth, and under other circumstances, I would have declared her a comely, respectable lady. She did in fact appear as a barrister's sister from the City, not another lighthearted actress. But because my father held her hand, I could think of nothing more beyond that and what that little sign of affection would mean to me.

"Katherine, this is Mrs. Ayscough," he said. "You know I've spoken of her to you before. Ann, this is my daughter, Katherine."

He needn't have bothered with his introductions. I'd already guessed who she was.

She smiled warmly and held her hand out to me. "Katherine, I am so happy to meet you at last," she said. "Your father speaks of you constantly, you know. But I vow, sir, you've not done her justice. Your Katherine is far more pretty than I'd been led to expect."

"Are you disappointed, madam?" I said, my bitterness welling over. "Were you expecting a loathsome mongrel bitch, fit only to be kicked? Is that what you wished for me?"

"Katherine!" Father said sharply. "Be agreeable, I beg you, and mind what you say."

"Why should I, Father, when agreeability seems to have been entirely forgotten by you?" If I'd been carved from wood, I could not have felt more stiff and awkward as I did then; though if I'd truly been fashioned of wood, then at least I would not have suffered the pain that I did. "Why did you bring her here? Wasn't this to be a day for us together?"

"And would I have been able to make you attend me if I'd told you my purpose?" His face was flushed with anger and embarrassment, as, no doubt, was mine. "This lady has become most dear to me, Katherine, and I'll thank you to regard her with the respect she deserves."

"Respect, Father?" I rose, not from regard, but because I was preparing to escape this miserable conversation. "Why should I show her any more respect than I have for the rest of your whores?"

Father raised his hand—the hand not holding Mrs. Ayscough's—

and for one awful instant I feared he would strike me. He meant to, I knew; I could see it in his eyes, though he'd never once struck me before. But at the last, it was the table that bore his anger, as he thumped his fist hard onto its edge before me.

"You will apologize, Daughter," he demanded, and I realized that it was the first time that he'd not called me "Daughter" as an endearment. "You will apologize at once for—"

"That's not necessary, Charles," Mrs. Ayscough said with a gentleness that served only to vex me all the more. "The girl's distraught, that is all. She did not intend it."

"But I did," I said, adding a quick shake of my head to prove my seriousness. "Do you not know my father is already wed, madam? Has he told you that? My mother is not dead, and she is still my father's wife. Thus you *are* his whore."

With a wordless growl, Father lunged toward me, sending a chair between us crashing to the floor, and I scuttled backward from his path. The others around us craned their necks to watch, and I could see the keeper hurrying toward us with a pair of large menservants.

"No, Charles, please don't!" Mrs. Ayscough pleaded, seizing my father by the arm to hold him back. "She only needs time to accept it!"

But I'd no wish to accept anything, not from either of them. My sight blurred with tears, I bowed my head and ran through the room, stumbling my way around the other tables and chairs and astonished diners.

Mrs. Ayscough must have made a move to follow after me, though all I heard was Father's reply.

"Leave her, Ann," he thundered. "As she is now, she can go straight to the devil for all I care."

Sobbing, I pushed my way past the keeper's wife and the servant holding the door. On trembling legs, I staggered up the steps to the small landing overlooking the river. With my hands clutching tight to the wooden rail, I retched up everything that was in my belly and perhaps beyond. Finally exhausted, I sank to my knees and buried my face in my hands in abject misery.

Straight to the devil. First I'd lost my mother's love to a church I didn't understand. Now my father, too, had forsaken me. For five golden years, I'd been Father's favorite, and now—now I wasn't.

I was nothing.

For the next three days, I stayed with my friend Mary Holcomb, crowded into the lodgings she shared over a tavern with her widowed mother. I could not bring myself to see Father at home, or risk finding him again with Mrs. Ayscough. He must have felt the same regarding me, for though I sent a message regarding my whereabouts to my maidservant so the household would not worry or search for me, I received nary a word from Father in return. If I'd the tiniest hope that he'd come seek me out to apologize, which I did not, then with his silence that hope was dashed. Clearly he'd put his new whore before me, and the sooner I hardened myself to the wretched truth, then the less his scorn could hurt me. That was what I told myself, over and over again, but try as I did to believe it, I could not. The image of him so tenderly shepherding Mrs. Ayscough would not leave me, nor would the wound the sight of it had caused me.

Finally I crept home, carefully choosing to return in the early afternoon when Father would surely be out to dine. Yet I'd scarcely placed one weary foot on the stair when I heard him call my name from his library.

"Katherine?" he called again, and before I could run up the stairs and escape, he'd come into the hall.

He wore a quilted cap in place of his wig and a quilted scarlet silk dressing gown over his shirt and breeches, as he often did whilst working among his papers.

"Katherine," he said. "I would like to speak with you in my chamber."

Though his expression was stern, not angry (and the best I could expect), I hesitated still, my hand on the stair's rail.

He held my gaze evenly. "If you please, Katherine. I will not keep you long."

He said nothing of how I'd been away, nothing of how I wore the same clothes that I'd worn to the Folly, nothing of concern or that he'd missed me. But he likewise said nothing of Mrs. Ayscough, and with that as a slender comfort, I slowly stepped from the stairs and walked before him into his library.

I had always liked this room, reflecting as it did my father's tastes. The shelves overflowing with books, the leather armchair drawn close before the fire, the desk with the draft of another play stacked to one side, the carved bust of Aristotle between the windows and the bronze clock fashioned like a crouching panther on the chimneypiece—all of these belongings were so of a piece with Father that I felt my throat tighten.

"You will sit?" he asked, motioning toward the chair across from his.

I shook my head. I still wore my cloak, my hands folded tightly within.

"Very well, Katherine." He dropped heavily into the armchair. "If that is how you wish it, then so it shall be. But mark that it's by your desire, not mine."

He sighed, tapping his thumb on the carved arm of the chair as the panther clock ticked and the fire in the hearth below crackled and popped. This was not right; we seldom were lost for words between us.

At last he began. "I will not insist that you apologize to Mrs. Ayscough, because she, in her mercy, has forgiven you. God knows that was not my decision."

"No," I said. "I should guess it wasn't."

With his chin lowered, he looked up at me from beneath his dark brows, an unspoken warning that I'd do well to heed. "She is a part of my life now, Katherine. I love her as I have never loved another woman, and she has honored and blessed me by returning that love."

"Did you never love Mama?" I asked sadly. "Not even when you wed her?"

He winced. "We were too young to know what true love was, pet. I have explained that to you before. Your mother and I were pushed together by those who wished to see us settled, and in our innocence we obliged and did as we were bid. What affection there was between us was not binding, nor long-lasting."

"You are still wed to her," I insisted. "She is your wife."

"My wife by law, but not by heart," he said firmly. "The ties that men contrive can never be so strong as those wrought by love alone."

"Then what of me, Father?" My voice rose plaintively. "If you would so easily disavow my mother, then will you cast me aside, too, as a careless by-blow, a bastard of no consequence?"

"You are my daughter, Katherine," he said firmly. "You may try me and test me, but before God, I will always love you."

I looked down, more troubled than I could express. He had likewise once sworn before God to cherish my mother, to no lasting purpose. I'd long since guessed that he'd had more of a hand in that poor lady's departure from our lives than he'd admitted to me, and here, I thought unhappily, was the proof.

"What I wish beyond all things is for you to find a gentleman who will love you as you deserve," he continued, unaware of my thoughts. "I'd hoped you would have found him by now, to begin your own life properly."

"Why should I wish a husband for that?" I protested, and I didn't, especially not one chosen from the wretched creatures Father had urged upon me. "Once you promised me the freedom to love as I chose—"

"And I still do," he said, as if he were making perfect sense instead of twisting everything around to suit his own desires. "I wish you to love the man you wed."

"As his *wife*," I said, thinking of the ill treatment afforded most every wife around me, including his own of my mother. "Where's the freedom in that?"

"But you see, Katherine, that's exactly where I believe Mrs. Ayscough will be of benefit to you." He leaned forward with an unsettling eagerness. "She's a good woman, a fine woman, if you'll but give her a chance. She can guide you in a way I can't, with a woman's wisdom, to learn your proper place—"

"Faith, Father, that is better than any play," I said bitterly. "That you should have your whore counsel your daughter in how to be a proper wife!"

I saw him struggle with his temper, yet finally rein it in, another way he'd changed. "Do not be so flippant with me, Katherine. It does not become you."

"Oh, yes, and who taught me to be so?" I cried, overwhelmed by the unfairness of what he said. "Who once thought I was the most amusing daughter possible? Who would praise me for telling the truth?"

"Katherine, please—"

"No, Father, please listen to *me*," I said, my voice breaking like my heart. "Or have I become so inconvenient that I'll be sent away to some distant convent, too, to leave you free to live exactly as you please?"

Abruptly he rose from his chair, and I felt fiercely satisfied, knowing I'd goaded him so far. But instead of confronting me, he turned away and went to stand before the window with his back to me. The only sign of displeasure he allowed me to see were his hands, furiously clasping and unclasping behind his back. The carnelian stone of his ring caught the light from the window as he did, red as the blood we shared.

"This is decided, Katherine," he said, curt and oddly distant. "Nothing you say now will change me. You can choose to play the harpy, and make matters difficult for all of us, or you can see reason and agree that this is best for you as well, and welcome Mrs. Ayscough as she deserves."

I could think of a thousand other things that Mrs. Ayscough deserved. But Father was right. I'd no recourse. He was by law my master until I gave myself over to a husband, and he could control every detail of my life and my fortune for me. My only choice now was as he said, to be a shrill harpy or an obedient lamb.

I chose the harpy.

But exactly as Father had warned, my refusal to embrace Mrs. Ayscough as a false mother did not change his mind. There are few things in the world more fearsome, nor more stubborn, than a libertine who has reformed for the sake of a virtuous woman, and that was exactly what Father had become.

Thus, in April 1672, I was a most unwilling witness to the "wedding" of my father to Mrs. Ayscough at our family's church in Southfleet, Kent. I alone seemed to care that Father's wife still lived, and that this service was a travesty. By law it was bigamy, punishable by death to both parties, though I suppose because Father was still in so much favor with His Majesty, the law did not pertain to him. Yet even the lady's barrister brother-in-law seemed well content with the match, and the rest of the small party gathered there cheered and wished them happiness as if they were lawfully wed. My father beamed, his round face wreathed with rosy joy, and his new lady blushed as she modestly rested her hands on the rounded belly of their coming child, another reason for this shamming false service. Even the spring sun came from the clouds to shine on them as they stepped from the church and into a carriage gaily decked with ribbons and greenery.

Hanging back, I could feel no such balmy content, and hurled aside the daffodils I'd been forced to carry. My gloomy dread was justified, too. Soon after this wedding, Father decided that our old house in Great Queen Street was too near to my mother's family for comfort, and likely it was, considering his illicit new arrangement with a so-called wife. With great fanfare and bustle, we removed to a grander house in Bloomsbury Square overlooking the piazza, a more fashionable address where our neighbors included many peers and other persons of note.

Other changes to our situation were less agreeable. Lady Sedley (for so I must ever after call her, even though she urged me to call her "Mother"; I refused, for the sake of my true mother's memory) took full control of our household and my father's affairs.

The transformation was immediate, and unpleasant. She released most of our familiar old servants for being lazy and indifferent, and replaced them with others of her choosing. She set Father on a new regimen of economy, where he and I both must account for our every expenditure, which she would tally herself in a book like some mean clerk. She judged him too portly for his health, and insisted he forgo the taverns and eating-houses in favor of eating every dinner and supper at home, where she could supervise each morsel that passed his lips. She took possession of the keys to Father's cellar, and limited the wine that was served at table. The fine old hours that Father and I had kept, tumbling into our beds after midnight and rising at noon, were declared a heathen habit, and forbidden. If I did lie abed too late to suit her, she'd come in herself, beating a kettle with a spoon to rouse me in the most loathsome manner possible.

Worst of all, she determined to reform me, and make of me a modest young maid fit for marriage. She forbade me to swear, to sing bawdy songs, to wager at cards. She took away my romances and plays and replaced them with sermons and dry tracts on housekeeping. My old friends were banned from our house, and I could not use the coach or leave the house without her permission. Worst of all, I was no longer allowed to accompany Father to Court, for fear I'd be further polluted by the lascivious company to be found there.

To my dismay, Father agreed to every one of these odious measures, even applauding them as wise and timely. I could not fathom how, in the name of love, he so willingly agreed to be gelded by this woman, and it saddened me no end to see his bright spirit broken and bent to her yoke.

I was not so obliging. Her endless petty laws didn't make me more obedient, but only more cunning in my circumvention. I learned how to bribe her servants, slip through windows, and falsify my accounts. I lied to her so often and with such ease that she could never be sure of what I said. I exhausted her with my recklessness, especially as she came closer to the time she'd bear her bastard. Because she foolishly hoped to win my favor (which I would never grant), she kept her complaints about me from Father, which only made me bolder yet.

But as resourceful as I'd become, I still was shocked by Father's actions when at last she was brought to bed in July 1672. The bastard was a boy, the son that every gentleman so longs for as a replica of himself. Father proved this by giving the babe his own name, Charles, at the christening, and just as his so-called wife was addressed as Lady Sedley, so now this brat was granted the right to the family name as well.

Most appalling of all, Father chose to treat the bastard as his lawful heir, and rewrote his will in the babe's favor. There was, I suppose, much precedent for this around us, for even the king was said to be considering making the base-born Lord Monmouth his rightful heir because the queen was barren. Yet that was of no comfort to me. Like a jewel in a shop window that has not been sold in a timely manner, my value as some unknown gentleman's wife was instantly reduced in the market. To be sure, I was still considered a prize heiress, only not quite so grand as before, and the sting of this humiliation added further to my dislike of Lady Sedley. How, really, could it not?

Thus I squandered the better part of a year of my young life, as good as a prisoner in the home where I'd been born. Also like a prisoner, I dreamed and planned and plotted my eventual escape.

And when at last my opportunity came, I was ready to seize it as my own, and flee.

St. James's Park, London
October 1673

Surely there are few things more tormenting to a young lady of fifteen than to be within sight and hearing of pleasant company, yet still denied to join it.

So it was for me on a cool afternoon in October. My stepmother, Lady Sedley, was determined to take her young son, Charles, to St. James's Park to let him toddle across the grass and gawk and coo at the deer. Although of course she would take a nursemaid for the baby, her own lady's maid, and a footman as attendants (for she never would scrimp on herself), she still requested me to join her. I'd no wish to hear her prattle for the afternoon, but the chance to walk in the park was too tempting to miss.

We embarked after dinner with enough coverlets, cloths, biscuits, caps, and clouts to support a regiment of infants, but Lady Sedley would fuss as if her son were wrought of spun glass, rather than being a small model of Father, stout and ruddy in his petticoats. We left our coach at the street, and walked into the park and toward the animals, with little Charles babbling and waving in happy anticipation. Not only were there ducks of every variety on the canal, but also fancy goats and deer on the grass, so tame they'd come close from curiosity, then dance nimbly away, a pretty sight indeed.

Lady Sedley chose a spot for the footman to spread our coverlet, and set her precious bundle on the grass. Immediately he put his unsteady legs to the test, lurching and lumbering against his leading strings as he made his way across the uneven grass toward the nearest deer. To no one's surprise but his own, the deer was frighted by this small and noisy apparition, and took care to keep its distance. The baby wailed with frustration, Lady Sedley and the nurse rushed to comfort him, and as soon as he'd been petted and soothed into silence, he'd spy another beast nearby, and the whole foolishness began again.

As can be imagined, I wanted none of this. Instead I sat on the coverlet, my skirts arranged as prettily as I could make them, and pretended not to watch the gentlemen who in turn were ogling me as they strolled the paths. We were not far from the Horseguards' Parade, and the delicious, robust spectacle of broad shoulders and scarlet coats. As much as I longed to walk among them, and if I were fortunate perhaps engage in amusing flirtation, I knew that if I dared, Lady Sedley would at once send her footman to fetch me back. I felt as if I were bound by my own pair of leading strings, to keep me from venturing too far.

I sighed with frustration, and made myself look instead toward the facade of Whitehall Palace for less distraction. Yet even that pile of brick and turrets could offer me no peace. One glance at the square, pillared front of the Banqueting House, and memories of all the balls and other entertainments I'd attended there filled my thoughts. Ah, ah, what I'd give to be included in those revels again!

"Katherine!" Short of breath, Lady Sedley came slowly toward me; she'd yet to regain her former girth, though her babe was more than a year old, and smugly I knew my own slenderness irritated her in comparison. "Katherine, I wish you to go buy me an apple. They are at their peak at this season, you know. There's a costard monger selling them there, on the edge of the parade."

I lolled indolently back on the coverlet, taking my time in obliging her. "You know, my lady, that the man has most likely filched them from the Royal Orchards in the far end of Hyde Park. Do you truly wish me to purchase for you property stolen from His Majesty?"

"Katherine, please." Lady Sedley sighed impatiently, one hand pressed to her side. "It is only an apple. I don't know why you must turn even the most simple request from me into a disagreement."

"I wasn't disagreeing, my lady," I said, stretching languidly before at last I stood. "I only wished you to realize the risk of your desires, and the consequences you might face."

"How kind." She drew two coins from her purse and handed them to me. "Take care you choose one without any bruises, and pray don't dawdle."

"Yes, my lady," I said, and sauntered away, tossing the coins lightly in my gloved palm.

It felt good to stretch those leading strings, if only for a few minutes. The wind had increased since we'd come to the park, with gusts tugging and tossing my petticoats around my legs. As I walked, I held my hand flat on the crown of my hat to keep it from lifting away; the hat was new, black beaver with a red plume and a wide brim that caught the breezes like a sail. I accepted the first apple the old man drew from his basket, and when he winked at me, I winked slyly in return, to make him cackle with delight. But as soon as I paid him and took the apple, a stray gust tore my new hat from my head, and sent it rolling and bouncing like a black cartwheel across the parade.

With no thought beyond retrieving my hat, I raced after it with the apple clutched in my fingers. My hair began to pull free from its pins and blew across my face, and as I ran I ducked my head to shake the hair away from my eyes. I did not see the horses and riders coming toward me, or realize that I'd run directly into their path, until the first horse reared before me as the rider drew up short. I staggered backward in fear and confusion, and as my heel caught in my petticoat, I tumbled backward and sat ingloriously in the dust.

The first rider had already dismounted and was hurrying toward me as I struggled to work my heel free from the hem of my petticoat without tearing it.

"Damned infernal shoe," I muttered, painfully aware of the spectacle I'd made of myself. "Damned, damned, *damned* infernal shoe!"

"Are you hurt?" the gentleman said with concern, bending down beside me. "If I've harmed you—"

"No, no, sir. I am entirely fine," I said, finally losing patience and ripping the petticoat's hem to free my heel. "It's not your fault at all that I caught my wretched shoe—oh, *oh*!"

At last I looked up, and realized to my horror that I was sprawled in the dust of the Horseguards' Parade with His Royal Highness the Duke of York standing over me.

At once I began to scramble to my feet to make a proper curtsy, but he rested his hand on my arm to still me.

"Be easy, be easy," he said gently. "Better to make sure you're unharmed."

He smiled, and I smiled in return. He was as I remembered, his face lean and brown from a life out of doors, his eyes a rare brilliant blue with small lines radiating from them like rays from the sun. His smile was unbalanced, his lip curling upward almost as if sneering, though I knew he wasn't. Yet I liked the unexpected air it gave to his expression, a spark of danger that to me, who'd never known real danger in my life, was fascinating. He wasn't anything like the callow boys my own age. He was older than Father, true, but I sensed a restless vitality about him even as he crouched beside me; it had been no mean feat of strength or horsemanship to draw his mount up as swiftly as he had. He wore a dark blue coat with narrow gold braid, yellow breeches, and tall, polished boots with spurs, such as any other gentleman of breeding might wear for riding, and there was nothing to mark him outwardly as a royal prince—except, of course, the way that the others around us were curtsying or bowing with their hats in their hands.

"It was entirely my fault, Your Royal Highness," I said, full of contrition. "I lost my hat to the wind, and I was chasing it without heed to where I was going."

"It's never the lady's fault." The duke motioned to one of the men who'd been riding with him, who at once went off after my wayward hat. "You're sure you're not hurt?"

"Only my petticoat," I confessed, "and that's easily mended."

"Oh, yes, the petticoat." He looked down at my feet, or more accurately, at my ankles and the good deal of my calves that were still exposed. True, they would have been difficult to overlook, clad in bright emerald with orange embroidery; I always wore fancy stockings in the hopes that they'd distract from the thinness of my legs. Apparently the ruse worked with the duke, for he seemed to study them with open fascination.

Suddenly I recalled the old scandal of how he'd first noticed Arabella Churchill: an indifferent rider, she'd insisted on going hunting with the Court, and been thrown at the first fence. Knocked senseless with her skirts tossed high, she unwittingly offered the duke a heady glimpse of her thighs and beyond, enough to beguile him into her bed. The story was enough to make me blush now, though not enough to make me adjust my own skirts quite yet.

"You're Sedley's girl, aren't you?" he asked. "The one who speaks plain?"

I grinned, pleased at being recalled after so long a time. "I am, Your Highness, though no longer the child you once met."

"Not at all," he agreed, gruff with approval. "What of that apple, eh? Did you bring it to tempt me, like Eve in the Garden?"

I'd forgotten Lady Sedley's apple entirely, somehow still in my hand. Now I held it up to him, hoping it hadn't in truth been stolen from the Royal Orchard.

"Better that it be Eve's tempting fruit, Your Highness," I said, "than Hermes' discordant apple."

He frowned, and to my mortification I realized my clever classical jest had gone beyond him.

"Temptation's always better," he said, taking the sure course.

"Always, Your Highness," I said, nodding with eager relief. "That is, so long as one does not immediately succumb."

"True enough," he said. "There's no temptation without tempting, yes?"

He laughed heartily as if this leaden remark were the greatest of witticisms, which it most definitely wasn't. But he was the Duke of York, and I was so flattered he'd taken any notice of me that I would have forgiven him far worse than that.

The man who'd been sent for my hat appeared with it, bowing as he held it out to me. I thanked him, and scrambled to my feet to accept it. The duke insisted on helping me rise, which made me blush again.

"Thank you, Your Highness," I said, and held the apple up to him. I hadn't realized before how much taller he was than I; no wonder I'd long ago likened him to the sun, rising high above me. "For you, in gratitude."

"Or temptation." He smiled as he took the apple. "Do not be so shy, Miss Sedley. We should like to see more of you at Court."

"Yes, Your Highness," I said, and at last I curtsied. "I am honored."

"As I am tempted. Good day, Miss Sedley." He smiled one last time, and returned to his horse, held by a servant. He swung up into the saddle with perfect manly grace and ease, and gathered his reins in one hand. With his gaze still intent upon me, he bit into the apple, spraying sweet juice and flecks of skin across his jaw.

The significance of that juicy bite was not lost upon me.

"What was that about, Katherine?" Lady Sedley demanded as soon as I returned to her. "What did His Highness say to you?"

"Nothing of importance, my lady," I said, purposefully vague. "I stumbled and fell, and His Highness asked after my welfare."

"That was gallant of him," she said, her eyes narrowed with suspicion.

"It was," I said. "I gave him your apple by way of thanks."

Her mouth opened with a silent gasp of disappointment, though I think in truth my little adventure had made her forget entirely about the fruit. At least that night at supper, she could speak of nothing else to Father without mentioning that she'd been the one who'd sent me off on her errand.

"She fell at His Highness's very feet, Charles," she said. "There on the Horseguards' Parade, for all the world to see. She *fell* at his feet! There can be no other way to describe it."

"The other, more accurate way to describe it would be to say I sat down on my ass," I said, idly pushing my spoon in circles through my soup. "That's what happened."

Fortunately Father laughed, for sometimes not even Lady Sedley could tamp down his old taste for bawdry. "You did, did you? And what did His Highness make of that?"

Lady Sedley answered before I could. "What the duke made of it was a great deal of conversation."

I glanced at her askance. I couldn't tell if she was scandalized by my accidental encounter with the duke, or impressed by it.

"If the duke made a great deal of conversation with Katherine," Father observed dryly, "then it was a great deal more than he has ever made before in his entire life. The man has not a drop of wit in his entire being."

"It's true, Father," I said. "I was holding an apple, and I made a jest about it being the Apple of Discord from the Judgment of Paris, and His Highness clearly had no notion of what I meant. Instead he could not proceed beyond Eve in the Garden, and that apple, and temptation. It was very dull."

Father laughed again, waving his spoon in my direction for emphasis. "No classical allusions for the Duke of York, if you please. It taxes his limited facilities, and pains his head. His Majesty, yes, for he is a wicked clever man, but not the duke. I am in perfect wonder that he'd even venture to jest about Adam and Eve."

"He shouldn't be making jests about the Fall and temptation to Katherine," Lady Sedley said primly. "It's not appropriate for him to speak to a lady her age regarding original sin."

Father snorted. "Oh, I doubt any of it was particularly original, considering what is said of His Highness's forthright manner of sinning. Bitchery, that's I've heard it called."

Lady Sedley's expression grew pained, but I only laughed, and longed for the days when Father had always spoken thus. The royal brothers were always ripe targets for infamy and slander. In his bedchamber His Highness might well behave like a lustful, slavering hound covering a bitch in heat. How would I know otherwise? The two times he'd addressed me, he'd been kind and direct, and no less respectful than any other gentleman at Court.

Of course, there had also been the way the duke had ogled my legs, and how I'd liked his attention and not bothered to shield my limbs with any decorous haste, but Father and Lady Sedley need not hear of that. Nor need they hear of how he'd looked at me when he'd bitten my apple, or how it had been enough to make my heart race and my knees weaken beneath me.

No, they need know none of that.

Father must have finally realized his wife's unhappiness, for his laughter faded to a smile, and with a sigh he settled back in his chair.

"Ah, no matter, no matter," he said, patting the sides of his waistcoated belly contentedly as he always did after enjoying a meal. "His Highness will soon be a bridegroom again, with another young creature leading him through his paces to get an heir."

"Has the bride been decided, then?" Lady Sedley asked, clearly relieved that the conversation had shifted to a more suitable subject. "Have you learned that?"

"Not only decided, but wed," Father said. "There was talk of nothing else at Whitehall this day. The Italian Princess Mary Beatrice d'Este is the bride. Lord Peterborough himself stood in place for the duke as the vows were said in the lady's palace in Modena."

Still in the glow of the duke's earlier attention to me, this talk of his new bride did not concern me. I'd seen how it was with royal weddings, how they were affairs of state, not the heart, or even desire.

"They say she has already begun her passage to England and, with favorable weather, should arrive by Christmas," Father continued. "Mary Beatrice; that's our new duchess."

"An Italian, and a Papist, from the very lap of Rome." Lady Sedley shook her head in disgust. "She is niece to the Pope himself, and you know she will take her orders directly from him. That is not what the duke needed, nor England, either. Why not a good Protestant princess?"

"You forget, my dear, that much of the Continent does follow Rome," Father said mildly. "Protestant princesses don't grow on vines, you know. Peterborough did his best, but there were simply none to be had."

Lady Sedley shook her head. "But consider the Court as it stands, Charles. The queen is Romish, her ladies are Romish, the duke's first wife made her conversion before she died, and there's plenty who think His Highness has done the same."

"You've no proof of that." Father had always been tolerant of Papists, seeing no harm in them, despite their silly trappings and rigmarole. I was not so certain. I hadn't forgotten how the Romish priests had seduced my mother away from Father and me, and perhaps even from her natural wits.

"I've heard the duke now wears a rosary hidden beneath his waistcoat," my stepmother said with righteous Protestant fervor. "I've heard he fingers it whenever he thinks no one is looking."

"I didn't see any rosary about His Highness's person today," I said, hoping the conversation would return to more interesting subjects, such as me. "He wore spurs on his boots, but no rosary."

But Lady Sedley ignored me as if I'd not spoken at all. "I've heard His Highness has had a confessional built within St. James's. You know as well as anyone that His Highness refused to swear he wasn't a Papist when the Test Act was passed."

"He hasn't yet," Father said. Even I knew of the Test Act, passed earlier in the year by Parliament. Designed to sniff out Papists in the military and the government, the Test Act required all who held a position of trust to swear that they were Anglicans, or resign their place. Already scores of Catholics had been forced to give up their posts, including Lady Castlemaine and Lord Clifford, and, of course, the duke himself, who'd been forced to step down from his leadership of the Admiralty—a considerable sacrifice for him who loved the navy and the sea.

"He hasn't yet, no, nor will he ever pledge himself as he should to the rightful church," Lady Sedley said. "He won't, because he can't, having given his soul away to Rome. When was the last time he attended services with the king, instead of skulking off among his priests? I can only imagine what plots they're contriving together."

"Oh, Ann, please," Father said. "Next you'll be waving the warming pan beneath our bedstead each night to scare away the lurking Jesuits."

"Not beneath our bedstead, no," she admitted reluctantly. "But it's wise to be watchful when even the king's latest harlot is a Papist, and a French one at that. And now we're to have an Italian for our new duchess. Parliament will be in a frenzy. Whatever was His Majesty thinking, to permit such a match?"

"He was thinking that the lady is young, strong, and healthy enough for breeding any number of princelings," Father said wearily, motioning for the manservant to refill our glasses. "Poor young miss, to be taken from her home and her family and carried across the sea to wed a man she's never met! The difference between our customs and her own will be difficult for her, to be sure, but she is only fifteen, and I suppose will soon adapt to English ways."

Fifteen, I thought with astonishment, the same age as I. Perhaps that was why Father was showing such sympathy toward the princess, and why, too, he was gazing at me with indulgent tenderness across the table.

For myself, I'd not paid much heed to the talk of a new duchess, though it had been everywhere in Londoners' mouths this past summer. The rumors had carried the marks of an old ballad tale: the Earl of Peterborough traipsing about from one royal court to another with his casket of royal jewels (valued, it was whispered, at more than £20,000, the bait for a princess being extravagant) as he tried to find a suitable bride for His Highness. The chance to become Queen of England was not thought to be a sufficient lure alone. Most of the other, more ancient royal families on the Continent considered England to be a mean, poor, uncivilized country, and unworthy of their daughters. Everyone at Court knew that Lord Peterborough had found few prospects, and that his reports to the king had been discouraging; this princess was too old, that one too homely, while another refused to risk her Catholic soul for life in a Protestant land.

But Mary Beatrice d'Este of the Duchy of Modena had been agreeable, and had agreed. Or rather, most likely her brother had agreed for her. If I'd thought I had too many rules to my life, what must it be like for an Italian princess? Was she truly bound to the Pope, as my stepmother feared, and many other Englishmen with her? It was hard to conceive of so young a lady capable of all the dangerous mischief ascribed to her. Was she in fact beautiful, or had Lord Peterborough exaggerated, as was expected? Before Catherine of Braganza had arrived from Portugal to wed His Majesty, she, too, had been lauded as a beauty, while the truth had proved quite otherwise. Would this Mary Beatrice have rabbit's teeth, or thin, greasy hair, or be stooped or bent or limping?

"To the health of Her Royal Highness, the Duchess of York," Father said, standing as he raised his glass, and Lady Sedley and I did the same. "May she prosper and find happiness here in England, and enjoy the love and loyalty of her people."

Solemnly I drank to the new duchess. Through good times and ill, the Sedleys had always been loyal to the royal family, and I'd be no different. I emptied my glass, the wine sweet on my tongue, and thought of how odd it seemed to pledge myself to a lady my own age.

And even as I did, I wondered if the princess would wear emerald-colored stockings that would catch the duke's admiring eye.

"AT LAST YOU'VE COME, KATHERINE," Jane Holcomb said as I climbed into the hackney. "You're so late, I was sure you'd turned coward and kept away."

"It wasn't my fault," I said, squeezing next to her while the two gentlemen across from us grinned at me through the murky light of the hackney's lantern. "One of our maidservants had the toothache and had come down to the kitchen. I had to wait until she returned to her bed."

"I'm glad you escaped, Katherine," said George, Jane's older brother. "It would have been a sin not to have you with us, tonight of all nights."

I smiled, more from excitement than for his sake. Poor George Holcomb; while he professed a great passion for me, I'd found it impossible to return his affection. He was every bit his sister's equal in empty heads, despite being a student at Oxford. Besides, I suspected much of his ardor was more for my fortune than my person.

"It's Guy Fawkes Night, George, and I vow I wouldn't miss it for anything," I declared, tightening the ribbons on the velvet mask that covered most of my face. Jane was masked, too. It was safer for ladies at night, and besides, it was much more exciting to be mysterious. "The glorious Fifth of November! Lady Sedley would have had to chain me to my bed to keep me from coming out tonight."

I felt a small pang of guilt. Tonight it hadn't been only my stepmother who'd ordered me to remain at home, but Father, too. Guy Fawkes Night ostensibly honored the anniversary of the thwarting of a long-ago plot to murder King James I, his family, and the entire House of Lords with a sizable charge of gunpowder placed beneath it. A rogue named Guy Fawkes had led the plot, with much assistance from foreign-born Catholics. Though Fawkes hadn't succeeded in igniting anything, the celebration remained an excuse for fireworks and bonfires and burning straw effigies of Fawkes and the Pope, and general drinking and frolic.

It was a noisy and thoroughly English holiday, and in past years Father and I had gone together to see some of the most elaborate bonfires. One year he'd even taken me to stand on the roof of Whitehall with the king and queen, the better to view the bonfires scattered at various street crossings around the city, and then we'd gone to watch another, enormous bonfire before Nell Gwyn's house in Pall Mall.

But this year would be different. Ever since the marriage of the Duke of York to Mary Beatrice of Modena had been announced, London had been an unsettled place. That unsettlement had ranged from mild disgust with the royal match, to a fearsome hatred for all things and people related to the Catholic faith. All foreigners had been at risk for their very lives, and there were many rumors both of menacing Jesuits infiltrating the city through the bride's wedding party, and of innocent people chased and beaten in the streets because of their faith.

The burning of pope effigies that were a customary part of Guy Fawkes Night now held a more ominous edge to them, and some of the bonfire builders were already promising to toss effigies of the Italian princess into the flames as well. Privately His Majesty himself had said that it was just as well the lady had not yet reached England, or he must fear for her safety. That had been enough for Father. If the king (who was famously trusting and indulgent of his people) was concerned that the celebrations might grow out of hand, then Father was certain I'd no place in the middle of it.

Yet here I was, doing exactly as he'd forbidden. With the blind confidence—and arrogance—of youth, I was sure no ill would befall me so long as I was with my friends. Wasn't he doing much the same, watching the bonfires with the king and the rest of the Court? I was counting on returning to my bed before either he returned or Mrs. Sedley awoke. It was my usual trick, and one that had worked for me many times before. If they didn't know I'd disobeyed, then I really hadn't, had I?

" 'Chained to your bed'; now, that's a tempting diversion, Katherine," teased Ralph Walker, George's friend from school, and the fourth of our party. Another younger son, his family had him marked for the ministry, though I could scarce imagine one less suited to such a calling. "How I should like to watch that!"

"Watching's all the diversion you'll ever have, you dog," I said, shoving his knee away from mine. "That, and your own five-fingered servant. What lady would have you?"

"You would, my darling," he said, sighing as he pretended to be lovesick for my sake, "if you'd but come to your senses. What pretty times we could have in your bed together, my dear Miss Sedley!"

The others laughed, while I didn't deign to answer his foolishness. Instead I only rolled my eyes with disgust behind my mask as I took the bottle of wine Jane had passed to me. The wine was smuggled Spanish and rough to the taste, but its heat was welcome on the chilly November night.

"You know Katherine's resolved not to take any lover, Ralph, especially not so loathsome a toad as you," Jane said. "Her maidenhead's reserved for a husband, and no other."

"To have a husband, Janie, I must first be a wife," I said wearily, for she and I had shared this same conversation a hundred times before, "and I've yet to understand the merit in that sorry state. Everything for the man, and nothing left for the lady. An English wife's little better than a pitiful black African, bound in slavery to the master that's bought her."

"Then why waste your life without the pleasures of love?" Ralph asked, leering at me in the half-light of the hackney. "Bid me sweetly, and I'll be happy to rid you of that troublesome maidenhead."

"Oh, yes, and your own in the bargain," I scoffed. Jane and I often jested like this, talking bold as if we were jaded courtiers ourselves. "It's only that I've yet to find a gentleman worth the bothering."

Now, I'll grant I was dissembling a bit. In truth I'd begun to dream I'd indeed found such a man, but not that I'd ever confess it to my friends.

"There's always a convent," George said, taking his own turn with the wine. "You could go become a nun like your mother."

I went very still, shocked he'd dare say such a thing, even with his tongue loosened by wine. Swiftly I looked to Janie, who was concentrating on something in her lap to avoid my gaze. It had been long into our friendship before I'd confided the truth about my mother, a confidence I now mightily regretted.

"A plague on your ignorance, George," I said defensively. "My mother was raised in the Romish faith and follows it still, but she is not a nun."

"But she is a Papist." There was a cruel edge to his voice that I'd never heard before from him. "You can't claim she's not, living in a convent as she does. And you're at least half a Papist yourself, coming from such a mother."

"I am my mother's daughter, yes," I said warmly, "but I am not a Papist."

No one spoke, and worse, they were all looking from the coach's windows as if the most fascinating sights imaginable lay just outside.

"I'm not a Papist," I said again, wishing I didn't sound quite so desperate. "And to the devil with you all if you believe otherwise."

"Oh, be easy, Katherine," Jane said at last. "It's of no account."

Before I could answer, George softly began to sing the little rhyme we'd all learned as children.

Remember, remember the Fifth of November,
Gunpowder, Treason, and Plot,
I know of no reason

Why gunpowder Treason
Should ever be forgot.

The others began to sing with him, over and over and more and more raucously, until I, too, joined the singing, as the easiest way to restore the good humor to our little party.

But as we stopped by first one bonfire and then another, I realized my joy in the night was gone. Oh, I drank and sang and laughed with the others, but I couldn't give myself over to the revelry. I felt different; I felt vulnerable and helpless to defend myself. This year *was* different, and the suspicion of all things Catholic that I'd glimpsed in my friends seemed a thousand times worse around the bonfires.

The last fire we stopped to view was by far the largest, staged at the wide end of the Strand where a Maypole was usually raised. By the time we arrived, the crowd of celebrants was already too thick for us to draw close in a carriage, forcing us to climb down and go the rest of the way to the crossing by foot.

The pyramid-shaped pyre was nearly as tall as the rooftops of the surrounding houses, and those who'd built it must have been collecting wood and other rubbish for weeks beforehand. Pitch-soaked knots of wood and sticks daubed with tar had been planted deep within, so as to make the fire burn long and bright. Those who'd set the fire still brandished their torches as they danced around the edges, black, devilish silhouettes before the bright flames. The great heat from so large a fire cut through the chill November night, flushing my face with its glow.

The crowd rumbled with an ominous excitement, made up as it was of mostly men and low women who were likewise mostly drunk. Nor was it a happy, jovial drunkenness, but a mean one, full of vicious oaths and slanders against Papists and the Pope, and how they should be served. Father had been right: this was no place for me, or for any lady. Even masked as I was, I clung close to George and Ralph, as did Jane, and prayed they'd tire of the spectacle soon so we might leave. Not that such good judgment seemed likely. By the dancing light of the flames, the faces of our two gentlemen were as twisted and as ravenous as any of the sailors and apprentices around us.

Suddenly a great roar rose from the crowd. From one of the side streets, the first of the straw figures was carried forward: a life-sized creation of Guy Fawkes himself in his tall-crowned hat, his straw neck stretched grotesquely as he dangled from his gallows. With more cheers, he was tossed into the flames, the figure quickly falling to pieces as the dry straw was consumed.

Next, and of far more interest, came the Pope's effigy, his figure hunched and squat on his throne and his painted face made more grotesque with an enormous red wax nose. He, too, was quickly hurled into the flames, the figure breaking free of the throne to tumble apart with a burst of scattering sparks that drew a fresh roar, the shouts of hundreds combined into one inhuman exclamation of ferocity.

"Straight to the devil where he belongs!" George shouted beside me, shaking both his fists toward the fire. "Burn in hell, you Italian bastard!"

His words were only an echo of those around us, hatred made palpable in a way that made me tremble. What would become of me if they learned I'd a Catholic mother? The straw pope was gone now, the remains dropping deep into the bonfire. That is done, I thought with relief, yearning now for the safety of my home. Now we'd be able to leave.

But another straw effigy had appeared, and was being passed hand over willing hand across the top of the crowd toward the fire. This figure was a woman, with oversized breasts and frizzled rope for hair and a wax nose nearly as large as the Pope's had been. She'd a clumsy crucifix stuffed into her mouth and a ducal coronet of straw on her head, and if anyone were so empty-headed as to mistake her identity, she'd a placard of her own tied over her jutting breasts:

MARY D'ESTE
WHORE TO POPES & DUKES

Sickened, I listened to the vulgar taunts and chants and crude boasts of how these good Anglicans would serve the new Catholic bride if they'd but have the chance. I remembered, too, how Father had said the king was glad the lady had yet to arrive in our country, and as I watched these dogs paw at the straw breasts of the effigy even as they spat upon it, I couldn't help but agree. My belly churned with disgust and fear, and I was almost relieved when they finally ended their sport and tossed the loathsome thing into the flames. A yowling scream of terror and pain came from the fire, but beside me George only laughed.

"That's the cat they tied inside Her Highness," George said, grinning like a madman. "It makes a fine racket, doesn't it? How I'd like to make the Italian bitch scream like that!"

I was sickened beyond measure both by the cruelty and his response to it.

"Take me home," I demanded. "I cannot bear this any longer. Take me home *now*."

I do not know if my unhappiness sounded so strongly in my voice that he could not ignore it, or, more likely, the others were simply tired of this amusement as well. No matter the reason, we soon after wandered off to find our hackney, and I was the first to be left off before my darkened house.

I hurried through the alley to the back door and let myself into the kitchen. With my shoes in my hand, I crept up the familiar staircase, not needing a candlestick to light my way. Without thinking I hopped over the third tread, knowing from long practice that it was the one in the flight that squeaked loudly. The only other sound in our house came from the looming case clock in the front parlor, its measured, rocking tick-tock following me up the stairs.

It was long past midnight, and my father's bedchamber was dark and silent. While I'd made this furtive return so many times that I gave it no real thought, tonight I was even more distracted than usual. Inside my cloak, I was shivering still, and not just from the cold. I could not put the memory of everything I'd seen and heard this night from my head, the distrust of those I'd believed were my friends and the danger I'd willfully, heedlessly, plunged into, and that combined with the poor wine I'd drunk made me long for the refuge of my own bed. At last I came to the door of my own rooms, and with my head bowed, I gently pushed it open.

And there, to my sorrow, was my father.

Chapter Seven

Bloomsbury Square, London
November 1673

"Good evening, Katherine." Father was sitting in the armchair before my fire, the book that he'd been reading open across his knee. I couldn't tell how long he'd been waiting there for me; he was still dressed for the palace, the gold embroidery on the cuff of his coat glinting by the fire's embers.

"I'm sorry, Father, please," I began, plunging at once into my apology. "I didn't intend to—"

He held his hand up to stop me. "Don't lie, Katherine," he said softly. "I know you too well for that. You'd every intention of doing whatever it was that you did, else you'd be asleep in your bed."

He didn't fly into the rage I expected. He didn't seem to be angry at all, leaving me to stand in confused silence before him.

"You weren't alone, of course," he continued. "Who was your company?"

I dropped the shoes I still held with a thump; no need for quiet now. "Jane Holcomb and her brother."

"Those two," he said with disgust. "They are beneath you."

For the first time, I didn't defend them, not after tonight. It is almost impossible for someone my age to admit that a parent's judgment is wise and correct; the words will stick in the throat unspoken, and so it was with me now.

He studied me, his eyes narrowing a fraction. "At least you have returned safe. Did you find the excitement, the pleasure, you sought? Was it worth the deceit?"

I pushed my hood back, considering how best to answer. If it had been Lady Sedley asking, I would have blithely said whatever I thought would save me from punishment. But to Father, as he was before me now, I could only speak the truth.

"No," I said, my voice so low I wondered that he heard me. "It was not."

"No?" he asked, almost pleasantly, as if he were asking after my dinner. "You've always enjoyed watching the bonfires in the past."

I squeezed my eyes shut for a moment, wishing that were enough to make me forget the princess's effigy. "This year was different. I saw things I—I wish I hadn't."

"Kattypillar." He rose, holding his arms out to me, and I ran to the solace of his embrace. "London is not always a pretty place, is it?"

"It was *ugly*," I said, my words muffled against his shoulder. "What I saw, what they did—I'll never forget that, Father. How can I?"

"You can't," he said softly. "But in a way, it's better you don't. Perhaps it will remind you to take care of who you choose as friends and recall where your true loyalties must lie."

"Loyalties, Father?" Confused, I pushed away from his chest to study his face. He tried to smile, confusing me more, for he'd always been a man for whom smiling came as easy as breathing.

"Oh, yes, Katherine," he said. "I learned tonight that you will be called to Court."

I shook my head, not understanding. "But I've been going to the palace with you for years."

"Not like that with me," he said. "For yourself. The king wishes you to be among those supporting the new duchess at St. James's. You won't be a maid of honor, mind you—I told him you'd no place among those beggarly bitches—but as a follower, a supporter, even a friend. His Majesty thought that because you were of an age with Her Royal Highness, you might please her with your wit."

"The king asked for me?" I asked, now shocked as well as confused. I stepped away from him, pressing my hands over my fluttering heart. "To be asked to St. James's, I'd have thought the duke—"

"It was His Majesty's suggestion," he said firmly. "Not His Highness's."

He smiled quickly, bitterly. Father had been a favorite at Court since the king had returned to his throne, and he knew exactly what manner of men the royal brothers were. He wasn't blinded by the Crown. He had shared in their debaucheries, doubtless with greater intimacy than I could ever imagine, or wish to. But he likewise knew how things were arranged in palaces, how one thing was said to cover another. I had caught the duke's eye, but it was to bring comfort to his duchess that the king would invite me to join them. Thoughtfully, as a considerate brother welcoming his wife's new sister to the family.

Neither Father, nor I, believed any of it. Nor would there be any question of refusing such an invitation, not from the king.

"This is not what I wanted for you, Katherine." Father turned away from me, staring down into the fire with his hands clasped behind his back. "You still seem so young, and not ready for—for this. You deserve more. I'd hoped instead you'd wed a man who pleased you."

I gave a nervous little shrug to my shoulders. "I still might," I said to please him. "There will be many more gentlemen to choose from at Court."

"If you are fortunate, yes." Fortunate, but unlikely, and we both knew that, too. No honorable suitor would wish royalty for a rival.

"Perhaps it is just as well that you'll be spending less time here," Father continued with resignation. "We could not have continued much longer as we have been in this house. You have made yourself so disagreeable to Lady Sedley that she weeps in our bed from despair."

"I do not see how I can be blamed for her tears, Father," I said, unable to resist one more jibe. "If doing her wifely duty to you makes her weep, why, then, that is not my fault."

"Katherine." He glanced over his shoulder at me, his expression pained. "That is precisely what I mean. You have never tried to be a proper daughter to her. I can only pray that you will be better able to mind your tongue at Court."

"I know that." Now that the first shock of the invitation had worn away, I could think only of all the excitement before me. "Court will be different."

"Court *will* be different," he agreed, "because there your words will have far more consequence, and more peril, than they ever had beneath this roof. You'll find few true friends and many false ones at Whitehall, and everywhere will be those eager to push you aside to take your place. Choose your allies with care, sweet, and make as few enemies as you can. And be chary with your loyalty, so it keeps its value."

"I will, Father," I promised promptly, though I'd no real notion then of the wisdom in his words. "I will."

He sighed again, this time with impatience. "Do not expect the duke to take immediate notice of you. Thank God, this is not a guarantee of anything. I'd worry more if you were in Her Highness's household, a constant temptation to him."

I nodded, impatient myself with his warnings. Whether the duke honored me with his favor or not, I was still determined to make my gaudy mark on this gaudy Court and claim as much glory from it as any lady could. *That* was what I wished for myself, and in my head I brushed aside all his fussing about allies and enemies.

"The duke has been living as a gallant bachelor since his first duchess died," Father continued. "Things will change for him now. Not only is he still entangled with Arabella Churchill, but he'll also have a new wife for his amusement. She is said to be most beautiful."

"As I am not," I said tartly. "I know my gifts, Father, such as they are."

"Your gifts are considerable, Katherine," he said, "so do not play that card with me. You'll need them all for yourself, anyway. Because the duke has chosen to lean so far toward Rome, his position here in England is precarious. The king may have kept Parliament at bay by not permitting them to meet, but there are still plenty of members calling for this Catholic marriage to be dissolved before it can be consummated, and even more who wish the king to send his brother from the country entirely on account of his beliefs. St. James's Palace will not be an easy house for anyone."

To my shame, I'll admit that I'd heretofore concerned myself more with plays and gowns and other idle amusements than thoughts of politics. Father's stern talk was as new to me as the murderous hatred of all things Romish that I'd witnessed earlier in the evening. But I could see now how this must be the other side of being a courtier, and at once I resolved to make myself more aware.

"Parliament cannot stop the duke's marriage, can they?" I asked, thinking how the princess's long journey might be for naught. "If the king has given his consent, then they can't override him, can they?"

Father sighed. "Not if they cannot meet, no," he admitted. "The king is gambling that the lady will arrive before they do. Then His Highness's duty will be to get his duchess with child as soon as is possible, to secure both the succession and his own place at the Court. It will be to your advantage that he'll have no time for you at present. You won't be forced to choose loyalties, or bind yourself too closely to him. If His Highness were banished to another country, I would hate to have to lose you with him."

I nodded, my thoughts tumbling. "Then what am I to do, Father?"

"You go to St. James's, as you've been bid," he said evenly. "Look about you, and consider well every possibility that may present itself. Keep yourself free of His Highness for as long as you can. There's no real glory in being a whore, Katherine, no matter her title or wealth. I would much rather have you wedded to a gentleman I could respect and who could give me grandchildren who are not bastards."

"Faith, Father," I exclaimed, overwhelmed by so much serious advice. "You would speak of grandchildren with me still a maid!"

"I cannot help it." With his thumb he gently wiped something from my cheek, then held his finger up for me to see the black smudge on it. "A bit of soot, no doubt from the fire. We cannot have you less than perfect, can we?"

"No, Father." He was regarding me with such tenderness, such affection, that I felt tears sting my eyes.

"You're my daughter, Kattypillar," he said softly. "You're my daughter."

WHILE THE DUKE AND DUCHESS OF YORK had been officially wed on the last day of September 1673, the two did not meet each other until late November, when at last the bride arrived in England. By all reports, the princess's journey had been an arduous one, filled with bad weather and worse roads. The bride's party had traveled not by sea, but by land, from Italy through France, at the insistence of Louis XIV, who had strongly encouraged the match between the English duke and the

Catholic princess; there were whispers that Louis had even supplied the bride's dowry. But while Mary Beatrice had been lavishly feted by the French nobility along the way, she'd also fallen victim to a severe bout of the bloody flux, and had been forced to slow her journey to recover her strength.

His Highness the duke made a brave show of playing the gallant bridegroom, sending a yacht (named the *Catherine*, much to my amusement) to France to fetch Mary Beatrice across the Channel on the last leg of her journey. On that cold and blustery morning, he didn't wait before the hearth in Dover Castle, but stood with a handful of shivering attendants on the stony beach to welcome her. Only his most devoted friends had accompanied him from London; with the members of Parliament raging against His Highness, not many courtiers wished to risk being connected too closely with the duke or his unpopular marriage.

Nor was the bride cheered by the sight of her eager groom. Weak and pale after a rough November crossing from France, Mary Beatrice required the support of her ladies to climb from the boat and make her way across the beach. There she gazed up at the smiling duke and collapsed with tears into her mother's arms. While the Italians were chagrined, His Highness was undaunted, and painfully aware of the urgency of their situation. After repairing to a private house near the shore, the Bishop of Oxford quickly read the marriage contract over them to reaffirm the vows made by proxy months before at the ducal palace in Modena.

The duke was so enchanted with his duchess—who proved to be as beautiful as claimed—that every witness remarked it, while the lady herself continued to cry, even as His Highness slipped the wedding ring on her finger, three rubies set in golden chain. She'd scarce time to admire it there before her new husband swept her off to bed, to confound Parliament and consummate the marriage. There, it was assumed, the bride likely wept even more.

In a way it was surprising that we heard no more details of the wedding night. Through Father, I'd long ago learned that there were few secrets and less privacy at Court, whether for the youngest maid of honor or the king himself, and there was so much interest in this new bride that no detail about her was considered too small for speculation. While she and the duke shared their first three days together in Dover, these details of the wedding and a few more raced back to us at Court in London. We discussed her unfortunate propensity for weeping, her inability to meet her husband's gaze, the copious amount of blood left with her maidenhead on the sheets after her wedding night. Even the king himself was wild with curiosity about the lady, and ordered the royal barge to carry him down to Greenwich so that he might be the first to greet her and escort her himself into London.

A great number of courtiers had gathered in the gallery at Whitehall to be in attendance when she finally arrived by the river stairs. The gallery was a long passage connecting the public rooms of the palace with the more private lodgings of the royal families, and we were to stand on either side as Mary Beatrice and her party passed before us to her new quarters. We were crowded thick together by order of the king, so that we might offer a proper English welcome and outdo whatever the French king had ventured. No one was openly supporting the duke, not against Parliament and popular opinion; last night some London churches had pealed their bells in honor of the wedding, but there'd been far more interest in the burning of yet another effigy of the Pope, this one so elaborate as to have been valued at £50.

I stood with Father, Lord Rochester, Lord Buckhurst, and several others of their acquaintance. Lady Sedley was ill and had remained at home, so our little group had much the irreverent feel of the old days, except that I was now fifteen and grown and no longer their pet.

"I've heard there's already a wager between the king and duke over how long we must wait before we have an heir," Lord Buckhurst said. "The duke swears his bride will slip his son nine months to the instant from their wedding night."

"Nine months, hah," Lord Rochester said. "If she wept as much as they say, then she likely washed away his seed before it could take."

Father held up a coin between two fingers. "I'll wager that Her Highness will produce a child in exactly nine months. Italian women are reputed to be notoriously fecund, the reason she was chosen. Thus I say nine months to the day, but a daughter, not a son."

"There's nothing wrong with a daughter, Father," I protested, swatting aside his offered coin. Having a son by Lady Sedley had made my father as proud as a strutting rooster (or at least a strutting bantam), as if the production of another male was enough to make him a petty king in his own right. "There'd be no sons at all if it weren't for daughters, too."

Father smiled fondly. "I do not include you, sweet, for the duke would never sire so superior a daughter as you. But then, there was no crown hovering over your birth, either."

"You know we'd never slander *you*, dear Katherine," Lord Rochester said, winking at me. "We wouldn't dare, knowing how quick you'd be to repay us in kind."

"In kind, my lord, and in plenty," I said, smiling slyly over my fan at him. "I believe in returning such a loan with interest, as any good friend would another."

"Don't test her, Rochester," Father warned. "She's only begging for an excuse to launch her attack."

I grinned proudly. Still, I knew better than to engage Lord Rochester in such a battle, even in jest. Precocious though I might be for a lady of my age, I still knew that the earl's wit was as sharp as his sword, and I was wary of becoming his target.

"Much safer to speak of the king," Lord Buckhurst said, looking back toward the doors to the river as if expecting His Majesty at any moment. "The worst he can do is send us to the Tower."

"Ahh, but I've fresh slander of a more interesting variety." Lord Rochester leaned between Father and me with a conspirator's gleam to his eye. "I've had it on most excellent and irrefutable authority that the Italian ladies have brought with them a certain special friend as a comfort against our chill northern land."

Father began to laugh, and I guessed this must be an old jest between them.

"I believe I know this friend of theirs," he said. "A modest fellow for an Italian, and despite all the places he has traveled, as silent as the grave itself. Not at all like you, Rochester."

"Who is it, my lord?" I begged, for I hated to be left out of their foolery. "Tell me, if you please. If he's part of Her Highness's household, then I must know him. What is the gentleman's name?"

The earl made a long, woeful face and sighed. "Oh, my cherub, I doubt Her Highness will introduce you to him. He is so wicked dear to her, so—so *essential*, that I warrant she'd rather give up her priests than share him with other ladies."

"You torment my poor daughter, Rochester," Father said, laughing harder. "Go on, tell her the name of this shy Italian-made gallant."

His Lordship leaned closer to me, pressing his hand over his heart. "You must vow never to confess that you learned this from me," he said solemnly. "The gentleman's name is Signior Dildo."

Signior Dildo. I flushed scarlet, yet couldn't help but laugh heartily, too. It showed the shameless company in which I'd been raised that at sixteen I knew enough of these lascivious playthings (though I vow I'd never employed one myself) to understand the earl's jest in all its meanings.

Somehow His Lordship kept from laughing himself, and instead screwed his face up with mock distress. "Oh, Miss Katherine, Miss Katherine, pray do not laugh at the poor signior's plight!" he chided dramatically. "If His Highness learns of the signior's very existence in his bride's household, why, he's sure to fall into a jealous rage, or even a deep melancholy. Truly, what English husband could blame him, considering—"

But at that moment the king was announced, and even the infamous Signior Dildo was forgotten as the footmen opened the doors at the far end of the gallery. We'd expected His Majesty to come first, as was proper, but no one had thought he'd appear with the new duchess on his arm instead of his brother's. It presented an interesting challenge: we all wished to see the lady for ourselves, but at the same time protocol demanded that we sink low in a bow or curtsy with downcast eyes before the king. Like the rolling tide of the ocean before the moon, we dutifully drew back and sank as his tall figure walked between us, yet at the same time we did our best to steal a glimpse of Her Highness.

I was the same, peeking up from beneath the nodding curls on my forehead. The king had already shed his boat cloak from his little voyage from Greenwich, and it was apparent he'd dressed with more care than usual in honor of his new sister-in-law. He was dressed with rare splendor, his dark gray coat and breeches picked out with silver and trimmed with loops of scarlet ribbon, the Order of the Garter embroidered in gold thread on the breast of his coat and a curling red plume on his flat-brimmed hat. His expression was easy and pleasing as he chatted with the lady (in French, a language they shared in common), his dark eyes bright with admiration. So it always was with our king and women of every age and nation; Father swore His Majesty could charm the fleas from the back of a mongrel, so long as the fleas were female.

As an Italian princess of an ancient family, Mary Beatrice was hardly a flea. But she could not have been any more dazzled by the king than if she'd been one of those besotted fleas, her hand tucked familiarly into the crook of his arm and her lips parted in breathless fascination as she listened to whatever pretty nonsense he was casting her way.

Of course it must have been the simplest thing in the world for the king to speak pretty nonsense to Her Highness, for she did indeed possess the great beauty that everyone had predicted. She was blessed with large, expressive eyes, white skin, full lips, and masses of glossy black curls: in short, the ideal of beauty in our time. Elegantly tall and slender without being thin, she knew exactly how to sweep her fur-trimmed skirts across the black-and-white floor as she walked on the arm of a king.

"What a divinely delicious creature," Lord Rochester murmured behind me, and Father and the other gentlemen around me made happy, low sounds of agreement.

I felt the familiar pang of longing that always struck when confronted with beauty that would never be mine. It was not exactly jealousy, so much as a familiar, wistful melancholy. Gentlemen would never gaze at me with the same fervid desire, or smile at me with that kind of unthinking male approval that these gentlemen showered upon Mary Beatrice. Yet just as my melancholy was sadly familiar, it was also one I'd long ago learned to push away, a burden I didn't need. As Father often told me, I'd other gifts.

Thus I forced myself to look past her beauty. It was strange to me that she was even younger than I by four months, yet already pushed forward to play the grand role of royal breeder. There was an empty, trusting innocence to her face that must have come from being raised in a convent in ignorance of the world, as Italians did with their ladies. No wonder the gentlemen here found her so pleasing, for an unthreatening beauty will always be in favor.

I wondered idly how much—or how little—she knew of this Court and the new life she'd have here. Was Modena so far away that she wouldn't have heard of our charming king's profligacy, or how Whitehall was lately ruled by his French mistress, Louise de Keroualle, the newly created Duchess of Portsmouth? Doubtless she'd been told the unhappy tale of how neither king nor duke had yet fathered the much-desired son necessary for the succession. But had she likewise been informed of the numerous bastards that the royal brothers had sired outside their wives' beds? Did she know that at this moment, Arabella Churchill sat contentedly installed in her new house in fashionable St. James's Square, awaiting the birth of her fourth child by the duke?

I'd wager that she knew none of it, a thought that made my spirits rise. She might have beauty, but thanks to my father, I had wit. It was no mean consolation, either, for vacant beauties did not long survive or prosper at this Court. His Majesty set the precedent for that. He'd dallied with more women than he could likely recall, but the ones who'd remained in his life—Lady Cleveland, Lady Portsmouth, even my old friend Nell Gwyn—had done so by their cleverness, and their ability to amuse a gentleman who was both quick-witted and easily bored.

I was smiling as the duke walked past me, escorting his wife's mother, the Dowager Duchess of Modena. He didn't notice me, nor did I in honesty expect him to. There were so many of us in the gallery that he likely would have required one of his admiral's spyglasses to have spotted me in that crowd.

No matter. As the time had drawn closer to my actually attending the Court in St. James's Palace, I'd realized that Father was right, and that I would be wise to use this time to find my own place among so many strangers without being the scandalous center of their attention. It was, I suppose, one small advantage I had over a beautiful princess. No one would be studying me today and wondering if, after three wedded nights, I was already quickening with the heir to the throne of England.

But though the duke might not have noticed me, he was the one in that grand procession who caught and held my eye. He wore his magnificent wedding suit, a soft gray woolen fantastically embroidered with gold and silver honeysuckles and lilies and lined with bright coral silk. As splendid as any ancient god to me, he still was made to follow his brother the king, who'd claimed not only all the attention, but also his bride. For once it would have seemed more fair for the duke to have gone first, or so I thought, and felt a righteous indignation on his behalf. I knew what it was like to be overlooked, and there was no pleasure to be found in it.

"Ah, now, here's Her Majesty at last," Lord Buckhurst said softly. "If ever there were two women made to be sisters in misery, then it would be these."

The queen had entered the far end of the gallery, and stood with her ladies around her, a dour scowl on her unlovely face as she waited for the king to bring the new duchess to her to be introduced. The two seemingly had much in common: both were princesses sent away from their homelands to marry strangers in a foreign country, and both were Papists, too. But the queen's greeting to the younger lady was as chill and unwelcoming as she could make it, without so much as the hint of a smile on her ill-tempered face. Clearly this response had been planned, for every one of her ladies echoed her mistress's expression, stony and unkind. The new duchess drew back, wounded and confused, while the king frowned and tried to make a jest to ease the awkwardness. A murmur of surprise rippled through us courtiers, whispered amazement and delight that we'd witnessed such a ripe and scandalous insult.

"There you are, Katherine," Father whispered, close to my ear. "That's exactly what you needed."

"What, for the queen to be ill-mannered?" I asked, incredulous. "What need do I have for that?"

"What you need, sweet, is to be more observant, if you wish to prosper," he said, his voice low and intense as the royal procession disappeared from our view. "You've seen Her Majesty behave badly, yes, but you've also seen more than that. She's drawn her battle lines as neatly as any general, and with all of her best officers at her side, too. But given how weak her position already is at Court, and how little anyone cares for what she says or does, this was not wise. Instead of making the princess an ally she could most likely have controlled, she has chosen to view her as a rival. A foolish move, especially if the princess produces the heir that the queen has not. But then, Her Majesty has never been particularly adroit in such matters."

I sniffed with disdain. Whether from an incomplete knowledge of English, her barrenness, or simply from her native character, the queen had no gift for Court politics. "*That* is true enough."

"It is," Father agreed shrewdly, "but you'd be wise to learn from how she errs, rather than simply to mock it. The king is already disposed to like the duchess. That's clear enough. But because the queen has foolishly scorned her, he'll now become Her Highness's champion, too. Just as it has been a risk to be too closely linked to the duke, now there'll be a great rush to be among his duchess's circle. Perhaps she'll even have enough power to draw her husband back into favor, too. If she can manage to conceive, why, then perhaps she'll even be forgiven her religion."

I nodded eagerly. "So you would have me ingratiate myself with her?"

"'Ingratiate' might be a bit strong, Katherine," he cautioned. The crowd was beginning to scatter, and he offered me his arm to lead me away, too. "But it would do you well to learn what pleases her and what doesn't, so that when you are presented to her, you'll be so pleasing that she'll long for more of your company, even your friendship."

This had been Father's own successful path with the king for as long as I could remember. He had made the king laugh with his offhanded jests, had entertained him with his poetry and plays, had supported him endlessly in the House of Commons, and had been one of his most reliable partners at the royal tennis court.

"Be agreeable, and ask nothing for yourself," he advised. "That will make you stand out from all the others groveling around her."

I nodded, for this, too, was drawn from his own experience. Father often spoke proudly of how he'd never once asked a favor of the king. Given our family's fortunes, cynics might say that it was an easy vow for Father to keep. But there were plenty of other gentlemen who were higher born and far richer (most notable being the Duke of Buckingham), who hounded the king with endless requests for boons and gifts, so I judged Father's restraint as a true and honorable one, and also one I'd do well to emulate. Besides, what could I beg from the princess that I didn't already have?

"Most of all, Katherine, you must decide what is best for yourself," Father said, giving my hand a reassuring pat. "Given the foolish, fawning young creatures who'll swarm about the duchess, I can well imagine that she'll find you the one lady of truth in the lot."

"A lady of truth is not the same as a true lady, Father." I smiled wryly. "I can only be who I am. You, of all others, must know that."

"I do, Daughter," he said, and winked at me as he'd done when I was a child. "And that is why I might fear for Her Highness, but not for you."

Chapter Eight

WHITEHALL PALACE, LONDON
January 1674

As Father had predicted, there were a great many foolish, fawning creatures clamoring to make their faces known to the new duchess. But no matter how foolish or how fawning, the irritating truth was that many of them also possessed a higher rank than mine. No matter how impoverished, a highborn lady would always take precedence over mere Miss Sedley, for my father's baronetcy was as minor a title as there could be. Thus, for the first weeks of Her Highness's residence, I dressed myself with care and rode each day to the palace in our carriage, and returned home late that evening disappointed once again in my quest to be presented.

Christmas passed and my sixteenth birthday with it, and Twelfth Night after that, with the new year of 1674 beginning as well. Most of the Italians who had accompanied Mary Beatrice made their farewells in January, and began their long journey back to their homeland. The duke showed considerable kindness in permitting his bride to keep a number of Italians in her household. (The king had shown his wife no such courtesy; when they'd wed, he'd immediately dismissed most of the queen's Portuguese attendants and all of her priests.) Countess Lucrezia Pretonari Vezzani would serve as Her Highness's lady-in-waiting and Pellegrina Turini as her woman of the bedchamber, both dear friends from her childhood, as well as several lesser servants and two cooks familiar with her foreign tastes. To considerable grumbling about London, she was also permitted two Romish priests, Father Antonio Guidici as her confessor and Dr. James Ronchi as her chaplain.

But nothing could compensate for the departure of the duchess's mother. Mary Beatrice was inconsolable, refusing to eat and keeping to her rooms to weep. This was understandable, for the duchess was only fifteen, and given the distance between Modena and London, she'd likely never see her mother again in this life. I'd never been close to my own mother, given her madness, but if I'd been told I must bid farewell to Father forever, I'd have been inconsolable, too, exactly like the princess. There were already rumors that she was with child, which would have likewise explained her tears and, perhaps, her unhappiness. But her distress made for another string of days in which I wasn't presented to her, another delay during which I fussed and fumed. How could I hope to win her trust if she'd yet to know of my very existence?

Yet I wasn't idle. Far from it. As Father had counseled, I used my time well. Since I was now freely admitted to both St. James's and Whitehall, I took the opportunity to learn my way about both palaces, sometimes with Father as my guide, but more often on my own, or in the company of a friend or two. As I did, I took care to observe as much as I could, just as Father had advised, to see such subtle messages as how one lord's palace lodgings might overlook the flowers of the Privy Garden, while another was cramped and crowded behind a staircase. I learned the names and faces of all of the ladies who'd positions with both the duchess and the queen, because such knowledge might someday have use. I even asked Lord Rochester, who had made a tour of Italy in his youth, to teach me a phrase or two in greeting in Italian, so I might salute Her Highness in her own language.

Most of all, I began to increase my acquaintance. Following the manner of the king, our English Court was an informal one, and while I might have to wait for my introduction to Her Highness, there were no such formalities among lesser courtiers. People addressed one another freely wherever they were, and because I wasn't some shy, unsure country miss, I was confident that I'd soon make the new friends that would become the allies Father swore I needed.

All of which explains how, on a January morning, I came to be waiting once again in the duchess's antechamber while I hoped to be called. Beside my seat on a window bench stood another hopeful visitor, a handsome young captain serving in the Scottish regiment of Douglas's Foot, new returned from fighting under Lord Monmouth with the French army against the Dutch. This officer wore his scarlet coat with dashing aplomb, the fat silk knot on his shoulder and his sword at his hip, and the skirts of his laced coat flaring at the exact degree to display his manly form. It was natural that we converse, we two being the youngest supplicants by many years. I soon learned from his own lips that his name was James Grahme, and he'd been born in Yorkshire twenty-three years before, and that his father was a baronet, the same as was mine.

But of far greater importance to me at that moment was that he'd a long, elegant face and merry dark eyes that seemed to hold some secret jest, that he spoke quickly and decisively in a manner that I found most attractive, and that when I in turn spoke to him, he listened as if what I said were the most fascinating words he'd ever heard. In short, I was beguiled by him, and he by me, and if the duchess chose to keep us both waiting for all eternity (or at least the rest of that particular day), then neither of us would have been displeased.

"I have come to believe Her Highness does not truly exist, Miss Sedley," he said, "and I vow it would seem to be your experience, too. Why else should she not wish to see such amusing persons as ourselves?"

"Ourselves, and all these others, too," I said, making a graceful sweep of my hand to include the good twenty or so in the antechamber who, like us, were made to wait on Her Highness's whim. "How I wish I were a duchess myself, so as not to be made to languish like this. It is not at all fair that gentlemen might rise through their own industry. Consider yourself, already made captain."

He bowed in happy acknowledgment. "Fortune smiled upon me," he said modestly. "That, and my superior officers."

"But you must also have been hugely brave, to have risen so far at so young an age," I insisted. "At such a pace, sir, you'll be a general before you are thirty."

"Only if the foolish ministers do not sue for peace," he said with a melancholy sigh. "Without war there is little chance for glory."

I nodded, for his sake willing to ignore the common popular sentiment that the current Dutch war had cost too much and accomplished too little, and the sooner it was ceased entirely and a peace made with the

Dutch, the better. "But still you must have hopes of advancement based on your record."

"There are no guarantees," he said with the melancholy that always clung to younger sons. "My father believed His Highness might help me, considering his military interests, but now the duke seems so much in disfavor that his notice might be more a hindrance than a help."

This was sadly true, and I thought of how my own father had warned me to keep myself from the unfortunate taint of the Duke of York. While Mary Beatrice's natural sweetness had earned him a small measure of forgiveness, her religion had not, and the marriage had done more to drag him lower in public esteem than otherwise. Parliament remained furious, and was determined that the duke should feel their displeasure. As the leader of those members most critical of the Court, Lord Shaftesbury in particular declared that the duke had lost his right to sit beside the king in the place reserved by custom for the Prince of Wales, but must instead be demoted to a bench with other, lesser dukes. There was even a motion before the House of Lords to debar Papists entirely from the succession.

"I judged the duchess might have more influence with the king," the captain continued. "Or she might, if she'd but see me."

"She'll see you, I'm sure of it, and thus see your qualities, too." It grieved me, having him so downcast, and I was determined to cheer him however I could. "If I were only a duchess, too, I'd be your champion, and present you myself."

He smiled. "That would be a pretty thing for us both, wouldn't it?"

"It would," I declared fervently, wishing such a favor truly were in my power to grant. "Why, I would do most anything to be made a peeress."

"Anything, Miss Sedley?" He chuckled, amused by my bold talk, as gentlemen usually were.

I dipped my chin, the better to glance up at him from beneath my lashes. "I said *most* anything, sir. I've my limits."

"What lady doesn't?" he asked. "But it cannot be so difficult as that. Truly, all you need do is to wed a duke or other grandee."

I shook my head and sighed mightily. "Believe me, Captain Grahme, I should much rather try my luck against the loathsome Dutch than marry a lordling. What would that title be worth to me once it and I were buried away together in the country by my wedded husband?"

"Then that gentleman would be an ass, Miss Sedley," he declared, sweeping his laced hat over his bent leg, "and undeserving of your company."

"But you, sir, have earned it with that pretty scrap of nonsense." I slid farther along the bench to make room for him to join me, patting the polished wood by way of invitation. "Pray, join me. There's no telling how much longer we must wait."

"Miss Sedley, I am honored." He sat close beside me, taking care to arrange the hilt of his sword so as not to tangle with my skirts, and I smiled happily up at him. Like many young soldiers, he didn't bother with a wig, but wore his own hair, dark and thick and flowing over his shoulders. If anyone were to be honored, it was I, to have such a handsome fellow for company.

I smoothed my skirts over my legs, thankful that though I'd taken care with my dress for the sake of the duchess, my splendor instead would be for the benefit of Captain Grahme. I wore a gown of green thrown silk from Florence with deep embroidered cuffs not unlike his own (the newest fashion from Paris) and trimmed with alençon lace as white and thick as the snow in the park. I'd pearls hanging from my ears and more around my throat. I carried a small fur muff on my wrist, too, for show and for warmth, for I'd learned it was often cold enough inside Whitehall for my breath to show.

"My plan is less taxing than marriage, Captain Grahme," I confided. "I intend to find such favor with Her Highness that she'll recommend me to His Majesty for a peerage on my own merits."

Skeptical, he cocked a single brow. "Forgive me, Miss Sedley, but there is only one path for a lady to win His Majesty's favor to that degree, and that is by traipsing up the back stairs to his private bedchamber."

"Captain, please." I frowned at him with mock severity. "I said I should succeed on my merits, not my back. I've planned my campaign with care, too, studying how best to please Her Highness, if only she would deign to acknowledge me."

We sighed in unison, glancing once again at the closed door to Her

Highness's rooms with the two palace guards with their halberds before it.

"I've heard the duchess is a learned lady," he suggested. "I've heard she's a rare taste for poetry."

"Poetry!" I exclaimed, and began to laugh, raising my muff to my face. Tucked in my pocket for safekeeping was a handwritten poem by Lord Rochester that he'd been circulating among trusted friends. It was, however, hardly the sort of verse to win Her Highness's favor, even though she was mentioned by name within its lines. Lord Rochester had expanded his jest about Signior Dildo into a minor epic, cataloging the good signior's employment by a number of well-satisfied ladies at Court, including those of the highest rank. It was very wicked, yet hugely amusing and neatly done.

"You laugh, Miss Sedley," the captain said, puzzled, yet clearly wishing to share my amusement. "Most ladies pine and sigh over poetry."

"Not a poem such as I'm remembering." Impulsively I drew the sheets from my pocket. "This is the work of a noble gentleman of my acquaintance, though I've sworn not to tell his name, from fear he'd be punished for his talent."

I unfolded the sheet and handed it to him.

His eyes widened. "Faith! 'Signior Dil—' "

"Hush, sir, hush. You mustn't read it aloud!" I said, giggling and glancing nervously about at the others in the room. I was already daring greatly by sharing the poem with him, and I'd face certain disaster both at Court and with Father and Lord Rochester if it became more widely known through my doing. "To speak it aloud would ruin us both."

I suppose if Captain Grahme had been an exceptionally honorable gentleman—there were a rare few of them scattered about the Court—then he might well have been outraged by the cheerfully scurrilous piece in his hands. He might have torn it in disgust, and denounced me as the wickedest jade in Christendom for having shown it to him.

He might have done all those things, and worse.

To my considerable relief, he did none of them. Instead his greedy gaze fair devoured the slandering words, while his lips curved in a delighted, incredulous smile. Reassured, I let myself share his amusement, leaning in to his shoulder to read the poem with him.

You Ladyes all of Merry England
Who have been to kiss the Dutchesse's hand,
Pray did you lately observe in the Show
A Noble Italian call'd Signior Dildo?
The Signior was one of her Highness's Train
And helpt to Conduct her over the Main,
But now she Crys out "To the Duke I will go,
I have no more need for Signior Dildo!"

He laughed heartily, then smothered that laugh behind his hand. "S'blood, Miss Sedley, how did you come by this? What gentleman is the author?"

"I told you, I'm sworn not to tell." Eagerly I leaned closer, his long hair brushing against my bare wrist. "Here we are, among all the others come to kiss the duchess's hand."

He grinned at me with charming wickedness, and I thought of how there is nothing like a shared secret to bind two people more closely together.

"We must be sure to take notice of this signior," he said. "Perhaps he's the reason you and I have seen so little of Her Highness."

I giggled, leaning closer over his arm. "There's much more. Turn to the next sheet and see the part about Lady Cleveland, and—"

"*Miss Sedley*."

I started with surprise. The duchess's chamberlain had called several other names besides mine, but mine was the only one I heard, and when I looked to the chamberlain, I was equally sure that he was staring only at me in stern disapproval.

"You've been called, Miss Sedley," Captain Grahme said. "Go, and *bonne chance*."

I smiled my thanks to him, but also was quick to take the poem from his hands, tucking it deep inside my muff for safekeeping. Composing myself as best I could, I hurried to join the other ladies.

I'd sat dawdling for so many days that it seemed my admittance through those heavy doors fair flew by, and before I'd quite realized it, I was spreading my skirts and sinking low in a curtsy before Her Highness. She held out her hand for me to kiss as a proof of my loyalty, then motioned for me to rise.

Mary Beatrice was even more beautiful than I'd realized before. Her apartments were among the most desirable in the palace, with a fine view overlooking the ice-dappled river, and the bright sunlight that streamed in through the windows flattered her clear, pale skin and quick, dark eyes. She wore no paint, nor did she need to, and her only jewels were a pair of ruby drop earrings that matched her wedding ring. Still unaccustomed to our English winter, she sat in a cushioned armchair close before the fire with rich furs wrapped over her gown for warmth. Her ladies sat around her like bright flowers, a cluster of young faces that I'd no time to sort one from the other, and frantically I tried to think of what to say that would set me apart from them. Why was it that I'd had so much time to prepare for this moment, and now that it had come, I'd neither a thought in my head nor a word on my lips?

"Miss Sedley is the daughter of Sir Charles Sedley, Your Highness," an older lady was saying behind me. "Sir Charles is an intimate friend of His Majesty. He is also a gentleman of many talents, and has written both a play and poetry that have pleased His Majesty."

"Miss Sedley." Perched on the edge of her chair, the duchess smiled shyly, and it was a surprise to realize that she might be equally eager for me to like her. "Do you like books, too?"

"Oh, yes, Your Highness," I said, relieved she spoke English, for in my excitement I'd forgotten all my carefully practiced Italian. But there was one thing I did remember Captain Grahme saying, and I used it now. "Yes, Your Highness, I do enjoy reading, most especially poetry."

"Poetry!" Mary Beatrice sighed happily, clasping her hands together over her breasts. "I love the poetry, too, Miss Sedley."

"Indeed, Your Highness." I smiled, relieved I'd succeeded this far, and already thinking of pleasant ways to thank Captain Grahme for his advice. "So do I. How could one ever weary of poetry?"

"*Per favore*, Miss Sedley," she said, again with the eagerness that was almost begging. "Please. I must learn the English poets. Would you speak a favorite English poem for me now?"

If my thoughts had fled before, now they came rushing back in a dreadful haste, and with a dreadful single-mindedness, too. The only poem I could recall was Lord Rochester's, the only lines I could remember the ones that pertained to Her Highness:

But now she Crys out "To the Duke I will go,
I have no more need for Signior Dildo!"

Unaware, Her Highness smiled at me expectantly. How fortunate that she could not read my thoughts! "You have many favorites, yes? It is hard to choose?"

"Forgive me, Your Highness," I said, my cheeks afire with my secret, growing misery. The folded pages of the poem seemed to burn like a scorching brand in my muff, ready to destroy my career at Court before it had even begun. "As you say, there are so many from which to choose."

Still she waited, as did her ladies around her, and if I could have summoned a yawning cavern to appear in the floor of Whitehall Palace to swallow me and my mortification whole, I would have gladly done so. But instead of some mythical cavern, what came to my rescue was my own dear father. Seemingly from nowhere, a scrap of one his poems came to my mind, lines I could recall and recite without fear.

But I am tied to very thee,
By every thought I have;
Thy face I only care to see,
Thy heart I only crave.

All that in woman is adored
In thy dear self I find—
For the whole sex can but afford
The handsome and the kind.

The lines had been written by Father to honor some nonexistent woman, a Celia or Chloris who was more a convention than an inspiration; at the time, he'd been contentedly wallowing among various actresses at the playhouse. But as I recited, I realized I could also turn the words into a kind of paean to Her Highness. Thus, when I came to the final lines, I held my hands outstretched before the duchess, my palms open in honor of her eminent goodness, or rather, her handsomeness and kindness. It would have made Father laugh aloud to see his idle conceit employed to such effect, but I likewise believed he would have been proud of me, too, and my quick-witted idea—and laughed uproariously when I told him the reason for it.

But best of all was how it pleased Her Highness. She sighed with pleasure at the sweet words, and her ladies around her sighed, too, in a breathy, romantic echo.

"Very pretty, Miss Sedley, very prettily spoken indeed!" she said, and I do believe there were sentimental tears brightening her eyes. "Do you know the author?"

"I am most honored, Your Highness," I said, adding a small dipping curtsy in acknowledgment. "As for the author, I know him well. Those lines were writ by my own father."

Her Highness gasped—with wonder, I suppose. "What a devoted daughter you are, Miss Sedley, to speak his poem to me, and how fortunate Sir Charles is in you! Come, come, sit here near me, and tell me how it is to have a poet for a father."

I smiled, and took the place beside her that the other ladies grudgingly made for me. Through wit and the aid of two gentlemen, I'd made a fair beginning. But I also knew that what Captain Grahme had offered me—a French wish for good luck—had likely been the most useful gift of all, and I meant to return it to him as soon as I could.

I HAD ALWAYS BELIEVED THE EARLY months of a new year to be the dullest. The festivities of Twelfth Night were done and the Yule log of Christmas nothing but a charred hulk at the back of the hearth. Farmers had little to bring to the city markets from the country, and as a result the food even at my father's table became lean and uninteresting. A deep snowfall could make the streets impassable by coaches, and there was no question of toiling along a snowy street by foot, ruining shoes in the slush and dragging petticoats and cloaks heavy with crusting ice. People tended to keep as much to their own fires as they could, and there was a marked paucity of dances and other amusements.

One read novels, wrote letters, played cards, scratched pictures into the ice on the windows, and wondered whether it was in fact possible to perish of boredom.

But none of that was the case in the winter of 1674. To be trapped by snow inside Whitehall Palace was hardly the same as being locked away with only Lady Sedley and her servants for grim company.

Because I held no true position in the Duchess of York's household—such as a maid of honor or a lady of the bedchamber—I'd no real responsibilities, either. All I was expected to do was be handsomely dressed in costly style (for even ladies without great beauty were still expected to be ornaments to the Court) and to be amusing, and to oblige and entertain Her Highness however she required. I was considered part of her train, and much like the other kind of dragging train on a gown for Court, my presence was for no real purpose than to make a grander show. It was rather like being a perpetual guest at a dinner without end. Father had served the king in this way for nearly fifteen years, whether telling jests, drinking through the night, riding to hares, or playing tennis, and thus it seemed to me to be entirely natural to spend my days and nights anticipating the whims of a lady even younger than I was myself.

Thus in Her Highness's lodgings, I wagered at cards, danced new dances, and read poems aloud that weren't by my father. I attended plays presented by the Duke's Company, and balls and other entertainments given by His Majesty. I walked in a veritable pack of ladies through St. James's Park to watch the sliders on the frozen canal, and I threw snowballs at gentlemen we knew on our way. I learned to sweeten my humor to Her Highness's convent-bred sensibilities when I made jests before her, and to laugh when she made jests in turn, whether they were truly amusing or not. It was often much more tedious than it sounds in the telling, but I'd quickly come to understand that such is the life of a courtier.

Yet there were also times when Her Highness wished no company at all beyond those closest to her, and then I was free to amuse only myself. I'd found several acquaintances among the duchess's ladies, but no firm friends; if they seemed callow and tedious to me, then I am certain they judged me vulgar and outspoken. I did not care. I'd always preferred the company of gentlemen to ladies, and so it was now.

Or rather, one specific gentleman. I saw much of Captain Grahme that winter. While I had aligned myself with Mary Beatrice, he had finally followed his father's advice and become attached to the duke's circle. In a way, he'd no choice. In February, both Houses of Parliament had voted for ending the war with the Dutch, and likewise ending England's uneasy role as an ally of France. The Peace of Westminster was signed soon after, to much relief in the country, if to no celebration. There was little reason for rejoicing, for England had as much as conceded that the Dutch, led by Prince William of Orange, were stronger and more wily at war than the immense combined forces of Charles II and Louis XIV. At Court, the Peace was discussed only in the quietest conversations, as one does with topics that are difficult or shameful. We all knew that if England swung back toward the Protestant Dutch and away from Catholic France, then the tide would likely swing that way at Court, too, and more pressure would be brought to bear upon the duke to turn his back on Rome, and instead return to the Anglican Church of his birth.

For soldiers like Captain Grahme, the Peace brought more immediate changes. There was now no war to anticipate returning to with the warmer months (for war, like farming, was an endeavor ruled by the seasons), and without it, no hope of advancement. Worse, Parliament had decided that without a war, England had no real need for a costly army, and already Lord Danby, the minister of the exchequer, was busily planning ways to disband entire regiments. Whitehall was filled with officers desperate to plead their cause and save not only their regiments, but their very careers. It was a pleasing time for us ladies, to have so many handsome uniformed gentlemen underfoot, but it was sadly taxing for the officers.

I commiserated freely with James (for so I'd swiftly come to think of him), who was often gloomy at the prospect of life without a war to fight. He still hoped to attach himself to another of Louis's French regiments, as he'd done in the past, but even that seemed a distant hope. Lord Monmouth, the king's eldest baseborn son, had for many years led the English officers fighting courageously with the French, but now even he had decided to embrace the new peace and remain home this summer. James was not in as perilous waters as some officers—he'd a serviceable income of his own from his family—but still he worried, and did his best to please the duke in the hope of securing his future.

Because James and I were in much the same situation, we shared what we learned and overheard, and what we glimpsed of those above us that might someday prove useful to our betterment. I know it must seem curious to those unfamiliar with the pattern of our Court, that the newly wed duke and duchess would lead such diverse lives, yet so it was. They'd each their own apartments, attendants, and servants, and while the duke would dutifully visit the duchess's bedchamber, he seldom remained in her bed for the entire night. The duke was also deeply embroiled in trying to preserve his own position against those in Parliament who wished him altogether removed from the succession, and he spent most of his waking hours rallying supporters rather than dancing attendance on his bride. Father had been wise in his prediction: His Highness had little time to squander on Her Highness, let alone on noticing me.

Because of this, James and I had much to exchange when the royal couple had their first public quarrel in February. From my place, I had heard of how the duchess had received an unsigned letter revealing not only the existence of Arabella Churchill as the duke's mistress, but of how she'd recently given birth to their fourth child. I'd witnessed myself how furious this unwelcome news had made the duchess, and how in her rage she'd hurled crockery and had called down endless imprecations upon her husband in Italian that must have been very bad indeed. I'd seen, too, how when her anger was spent, she'd wept bitterly with the pain of his betrayal, and shut herself away from the rest of us for most of a week.

James, however, saw only the duke's side. His Highness had rejoiced over this newest bastard, and he'd no intention of abandoning Mrs. Churchill, either. Like nearly every other gentleman, he believed there were wives and then there were mistresses, and he could see no reason in the world that he shouldn't have both. His Highness damned the anonymous informer as a wrongful meddler, and crossly wished his young wife would be less outraged and more understanding.

It all gave James and me (and everyone else at Court, from the lowest maidservant to the French ambassador) a great deal to discuss, and it also provided one more reason for us to arrange to meet. In truth, we did not need excuses; we were fast enough friends without them. We met to walk in the park where we'd not be overheard, and found each other at the evening entertainments as well. In many ways, James and I were cut from the same piece. Our families were of the same rank (though to be sure, mine was far the more wealthy), we laughed easily, and we both were quick-witted with little patience with those who weren't. He enjoyed my boldness and my bawdy jests, and with him I'd no need to pretend to be anything that I wasn't. I was silently awed that so handsome a gentleman would wish to be with me, while to my even greater wonder, he called me fair, and claimed my face and slender form pleased him above all others.

Before long what had begun as a useful acquaintance soon grew into far more, which was likely to be expected considering that I was sixteen and he twenty-three in a palace feverish with *affaires du coeur*. It wasn't exactly an intrigue, for James and I liked each other too well for the callousness of that, but it wasn't merely a friendship, either, not with so much a-simmering between us. I suppose it was a friendly dalliance, or a dallying friendship.

No matter. I was happier that spring than I ever could recall in my young life, and James Grahme was the reason.

"So tell me true, Katherine," Father asked with genteel indifference. "Should I be ordering my first letter to Netherby?"

"Netherby?" I repeated, even as a guilty flush stained my cheeks. I was traveling with Father in his coach to Windsor Castle, to join the Court in residence there for the late summer months. This was the first time I'd been included in the shifting of the Court from one palace to another, and I was beside myself with anticipation. My lodgings would be in the town of Windsor and not in the castle proper, but I'd still be included in all the sundry festivities and amusements.

James was already at Windsor, being involved with some sort of military spectacle planned by Lord Monmouth. The duke and duchess had also gone ahead to the castle with His Majesty, gliding up the river from London on the royal barge, but I'd remained a few days longer in town to have Father's company. Though we were both now at Whitehall, I seldom saw Father as often as I wished, and I'd looked forward to this journey with him now as much as when I'd been a child and too often left behind at home. What I'd expected was our usual bantering conversation and a merry exchange of tattle. I never imagined he'd begin like this.

"Yes, Netherby," he repeated, his smile deceptively benign. "In Cumberland? I believe that is where Sir George Grahme resides."

"Yes, Father," I said faintly. "That is where Captain Grahme was born, and where his father lives still."

"I was sure of it," he said, swatting away a stray bee that had flown in the coach's open window. "But you've still not given me your answer. Should I be making overtures to Sir George to arrange a match?"

"There's no match to be made, Father," I said quickly. "Captain Grahme and I are friends, nothing further."

He laughed softly. "I know you better than that, Daughter. The pair of you are the most lovesick young creatures to be found at Court this season. Even His Majesty has remarked upon it. You can deny it all you wish, but if you don't realize it for yourself, then you've suddenly lost the considerable intellect that I know you possess."

Still I did not answer, mired in confusion. James and I *were* friends, and no more. There'd never been any lover-ish talk between us, and certainly no talk of a match. We'd discussed the reasons often enough between us. I'd no wish to wed any man at my age, and James had likewise vowed that he'd never risk leaving a wife a widow so long as he remained bound to the battlefield. How could either of us think of marriage?

"You know I'd rather you didn't wed a soldier," Father continued. "But I've asked after him, and this Captain Grahme is no ordinary sword shaker, but an Oxford scholar."

I groaned at that. Father, too, could claim to be an Oxford scholar, having attended Wadham College, and there was no more certain way to win his favor than through that gloomy, ancient university.

"Do you know that after your captain matriculated from Christ's College, he was entered at the Inner Temple to learn the law?" Father continued, his enthusiasm growing by the second. "That's an intelligent gentleman, Katherine. An excellent gentleman! He possesses other qualities that will recommend him to a less bellicose career, and I've heard his agreeable manner and cleverness have drawn the approval of both the duke and the king."

"Father, please—"

"He's only the second son of a baronet," Father continued, as eagerly as if I'd not spoken, "but his mother's father is a Scottish peer, the Earl of Hartfell. Your captain has a respectable income for all that, and combined with your portion, you wouldn't want. If the fellow pleases you, and will make you happy, then I don't see why I cannot send a letter to his father and—"

"No, Father, don't, I beg you!" I cried. "If you do this, you'll spoil everything!"

He drew back with surprise. "Since when does a lady protest that marriage will spoil everything?"

"Since—since I am the lady, and James is the gentleman." I reached in my pocket for my handkerchief, my tears spilling down my cheeks. My reasons were too shameful to confess, even to Father. They showed me as miserably unsure of my own merits as I was of James's fidelity to me. The sorry truth was that I feared that if James were pressed to claim my hand, he would retreat from me entirely, and I'd be left with nothing. Behind my brave and brazen facade, I dreaded his abandonment more than anything, and that he would come to realize how much more handsome and worthy he was than I. As friends, I felt a happy security, and I could put my fear aside, but I'd not the courage to test myself as true lovers might.

"If you were to address James's father," I said, struggling to explain at least part of this wretched mess to satisfy Father, "then he would feel as if I were obligating him, and I would not wish that."

"But it wouldn't be you," Father said, mystified. "It wouldn't even be me. The first letters would come from my secretary, as is proper for any contract."

I'd no doubt that Father was acting from purest love for me, which made me cry all the more. "That's not what I want, Father, and neither does James."

"My poor Kattypillar." Lurching from one side of the coach to the other, he sat beside me, putting his arm over my shoulder to draw me close. "You know I've never denied you anything. What is it you wish me to do regarding Captain Grahme? What will give you happiness?"

"Nothing," I said. His coat smelled familiarly of tobacco and wine and silk and wool, scents I associated with my childhood, when my life truly had seemed so much less complicated. "I want you to leave everything as it is, so that we—we may continue as friends."

"As friends." He sighed with resignation, if not comprehension. "Very well. Friends it shall be, and I'll keep my spoon from stirring your kettle. If friendship is what you want with Grahme, then you shall have it."

"I do," I said with a last little sob. "I—I am content."

Yet my misery remained as our tired horses drew us up Castle Hill, and when I walked up the steps and through the old stone gateways, I felt as exhausted and spent as the tower flags that hung limp in the still summer-afternoon sun. By the time I finally met James in the lower cloisters, soon before we were all to gather for supper, I was so distraught that instead of greeting him with a sweet and cheery face, I promptly burst into more tears.

"What is wrong, Katherine?" James asked with concern. "What has happened?"

He looked so handsome to me, standing there framed by the cloister's stone arch with the fading light of evening spilling around him, his laced hat in his hand, that I could scarcely bear it.

"I do not know, I do not know!" I cried, scattering tears even as I fumbled for my handkerchief. "I should be—be *happy*!"

"Of course you should," he said, and folded me into his arms. "You are here with me, and I am here with you. What more could you wish?"

I thought of how Father had asked me much the same question, and to my shame and frustration my tears welled up again.

"I—I will be happy," I declared, angry with myself for weeping. "I will, and—and, oh, a pox on these stupid, stupid tears! What is *wrong* with me?"

"Not one blessed thing," he said, and turning my face up toward his, he kissed me.

Now, if this had been one of the French novels I did so love to read, our kiss would have been a gentle pledge of devotion. Perhaps it began that way; I cannot recall for certain. What I do remember is that instead of taking tender solace in his embrace, I hungrily poured all my own longing and uncertainty into kissing him in return. If my response surprised him, he did not show it, though sweet faith, what man would?

Instead within moments we were kissing with such mindless fervor that I fell back against the stone wall behind me, needing its support as I reeled from a surfeit of passion and emotion. As many times as I'd been kissed—and I had more times than I could recall—I'd never felt what James was inspiring in me now. His scabbard bumped awkwardly against my thigh while the brass buttons on his uniform tangled in the lace of my kerchief, and behind me the rough stone snagged at the silk and crushed the elaborate pleats of my mantua's skirts, and I did not care. Why should I? Here was the proof that James wanted me, desired me, just as I did him, and that my earlier misgivings with my father were unwarranted. Perhaps I was ready to test love's waters in earnest, and offer my heart. Perhaps even more important, James could be ready as well.

When at last we parted, we were both flushed and as short of breath as if we'd run all the steps to the top of the castle. I heard a woman's laugh at the far end of the cloister, and a man's rumbling deep reply. Doubtless we'd been seen, or maybe we'd only shared this place with another couple. If there were no secrets at Court, then there was even less discretion.

James grinned, I think more from his pleasurable bewilderment over what had just occurred than from any real amusement. He rested his arm against the wall over my head, leaning over me in a possessive manner that I found wildly exciting.

"Katherine," he said. "You are happy now?"

I smiled, so giddy I vow I could have floated into the sky with the rising new moon.

"I am happy," I whispered, and reached up to kiss him quickly once again. "I *am*."

And truly, by every oath I could swear, I was.

Chapter Nine

WINDSOR CASTLE, BERKSHIRE
August 1674

"The little war should begin soon, shouldn't it?" asked the duchess, her voice vibrating with excitement. "His Highness said at nightfall. Oh, I cannot wait!"

She was not alone. Our six weeks here at Windsor had been one amusement after another: walking in the Great Forest, dining informally in the meadow, watching the racecourse at the nearby village of Datchet and the troupe of players from Oxford, hawking and riding and fishing and dancing and drinking, and even a lavish wedding between the king's bastard daughter by Lady Cleveland to the Earl of Sussex. The ancient castle itself offered us further entertainment, having been newly refurbished to make it fit for royalty with rich paintings by the master painter Verrio, lavish rooms of state resplendent with gilt, carvings, looking glasses, and fanciful plasterwork, and staircases that were a builder's marvel. Much to His Majesty's delight, Father pronounced Windsor to be a rival of Versailles itself, and he was able to judge, too, having been a guest at Louis's great country estate.

But now all this would be made to pale before the greatest royal diversion in anyone's memory, for tonight the Court was to be treated to a complete re-creation of the siege of the Dutch fortress at Maastricht.

We'd watched the preparations for weeks. Under the supervision of the Duke of Monmouth, who had fought in the actual siege last summer as a part of Louis XIV's French forces (as had my James, too), an elaborate false fortress had slowly risen on the meadows between the river and the north side of the castle. Everything had been arranged with as much accuracy as was possible. Thanks to the Peace of Westminster, England now regarded the Dutch again as allies rather than enemies, but that was no reason for His Majesty and the rest of us not to watch and cheer at a reenactment of the worst Dutch loss of the last war.

Walking with me this last week, James had proudly pointed out every detail of the preparations, from the earthworks to bastions and bulwarks and a score of other things I didn't understand. Dozens of soldiers would be employed in staging the siege, with every aspect of a real battle replicated, including cannons and gunfire. Spectators had been arriving from London and the surrounding countryside all day, and we could see them by their lanterns as they gathered over the meadows, like another invading force.

We ladies who now sat in a specially constructed viewing box waited with a mixture of excitement and dread. God willing, this would be the closest that any of us would ever come to a true war, yet still we worried that matters might become too genuine, and gentlemen dear to us might be injured.

"Please God His Highness will be safe," Mary Beatrice said to no one of us in particular. Though the evening was clear and still warm from the day, she would take no chances with a chill, and kept a lacy woolen shawl over her shoulders. She was four months with child, the soft swell of her growing belly now apparent beneath her petticoats. She rested her hand over her unborn child now, as if by protecting him (for all England prayed it *was* a him) she was likewise protecting her husband. "I pray he'll take no unnecessary risks."

"Gentlemen as brave as Father don't need to take risks," declared the Lady Mary of York, sitting beside the duchess in another armchair that showed that she, too, was a royal princess. Lady Mary was the twelve-year-old daughter of His Highness's first marriage, second in line for the crown after her father. Unlike many girls confronted with a new stepmother, the two were so close in age that they had discovered an instant affection for each other, and were often together. "You need not worry for Father."

"No one will hurt Father," agreed the Lady Anne of York from the other side of the duchess. Lady Anne was three years younger, and freed from the nursery tonight to watch the siege. Where Lady Mary was already a lively beauty, tall and fair-skinned with chestnut curls, Lady Anne was sullen and doughy with dun-colored hair and an unfortunate squint brought on by a weakness of the eyes. She leaned forward, swinging her legs beneath her skirts. "No one would *dare* hurt Father."

"You are right, of course," Mary Beatrice said, then sighed in a way that showed she didn't think Lady Anne was right at all. "He is the leader of the attacking regiments. No ill would dare come to him."

I agreed with Lady Anne. For now, the duke was heir to the king. He might be in command of one group of forces attacking the castle, just as Lord Monmouth would lead the other, but His Highness likely wouldn't ever be in any real danger, as much as he might wish to be daring or brave. The king simply wouldn't permit it. The three princesses in their tall-backed armchairs needn't fear.

But for me crowded together with other lesser ladies on a bench toward the back of the box, the worry was genuine enough. James had vowed to be in the thick of the fighting, just as he had during the actual siege, and the more he described the realism that was planned for tonight, the more I feared for his safety. He had laughed at my dread, and promised to come find me as soon as he could at the late supper that would follow the divertissement.

Trumpets sounded, and the attack began. Several officers too old to participate stood nearby to explain to us ladies what exactly was occurring, but their words were soon drowned out in the crackle of musket fire and the thundering of the cannon, and the stirring, near-constant tattoo of the drums. Nor, truly, did we need much explanation. The finer points of the siege might have been lost, but it was impossible not to be swept into the excitement of the spectacle of bright-coated soldiers and waving banners beneath rolling white clouds of gunpowder smoke lit by burning brands. By the time it was done and the "fortress" duly captured, my heart still raced with excitement and my voice was hoarse from cheering. So genuine had the siege appeared that I couldn't believe that there'd been no casualties, as His Majesty proudly announced.

As soon as the last rockets had burst in the night sky, we hurried to the courtyard to be reunited with our warriors for supper and refreshments. Fiddlers played merrily, their tunes bouncing back and forth against the castle walls, while the acrid scent of gunpowder still filled the air. Already the yard was thick with folk, courtiers in their usual finery mingling freely with roaring officers in coats muddy and worn from the battle, and the usual servants bearing flacons of ale and bottles of wine as well as dogs yipping and darting between the legs of the unsuspecting.

The king had soon found the duke and Lord Monmouth, and was noisily congratulating them on their so-called victory. I stood to one side on a stone step, as clear as I could be from the crowd, and continued to search vainly for my James among the sea of bobbing plumed hats. Perhaps there had been some mishap, I thought anxiously, some dreadful accident not yet revealed.

"Katherine, here!" James called finally, finding me before I'd seen him. Without any further ceremony, he caught me about the waist and swung me down from the step, my petticoats flying about my ankles. This was an advantage of being so slender; to James I was but a featherweight in his arms, and he could feel as strong as Atlas himself as he lifted me up.

"You damned rogue!" I laughed with relief and happy delight. "Where have you been, to make me worry over you? I feared you'd been killed, and for no useful reason at all."

"Killed by that little romp?" He laughed with me, and kissed me loudly. His handsome face was smudged with soot and dirt, his linen crushed, and his scarlet coat begrimed, yet in an inexplicable way I found him far more attractive like this than when he was pressed and primed for Court. "That was nothing, Katherine, only mere idle sport to make you ladies shiver. You should have been with us at Maastricht to have seen true valor."

"I'm thankful I wasn't," I said, and kissed him again, my arms wrapped tight around his shoulders as he held me, my slippers not touching the stone steps. I guessed he'd already been drinking with his fellow officers, for he tasted of wine, and smelled of sweat and gunpowder, ripe, manly scents that were more enthralling to me than the sweetest perfumed ambergris. The mock siege had left him with a rare energy I'd not seen from him before, as if the intense ferocity of battle still burned within him; I could feel it as he held me, radiating from him like the rays of the sun.

Now, if I'd more experience in the world, I would have known that such fires in men can burn others as well as themselves, and I'd have been advised to keep my wits and my defenses sharp, even with a gentleman I regarded as my dearest friend. But I was only sixteen, and though I believed I was as world-weary as anyone else at Court, I still had much to learn.

And learn it, alas, I would.

Finally, slowly, James set me down. "If you leave, will you be missed?"

I glanced across the crowd to where the duchess and the duke were seated at a table with His Majesty. "Her Highness scarce knows I am here at all, let alone to miss me."

"Then come with me." Already he'd taken my hand and begun to lead me through the others.

"Don't you wish to sup?" I asked. "Surely you must be hungry."

"There's time enough later." He grabbed a bottle of wine from a passing footman. "I've things to tell you."

"Things?" I repeated. "That's very vague of you, sir, if you please."

He laughed. "Good things, Katherine. You must trust me. Excellent things."

I did trust him, as I'd come to trust him throughout the weeks at Windsor. That first kiss the day I'd arrived had signaled a change between us. Oh, we still called each other friend and no more, but in the beckoning, shadowy corners of the great castle as well as beneath the spreading trees in the surrounding forests, I'd gradually granted him more and more favors, until only the last remained undone between us. Though we never spoke of it, we both knew where such teasing play would eventually end; in our world, the only mystery was when, not if.

But as James and I left the castle and headed for our favorite spot overlooking the river, my one thought was what good and excellent things he'd to tell me. He refused, of course, no matter how much I coaxed him to do otherwise, and by way of distracting me from my questions, he urged me to join him in enjoying the wine he'd brought with us. It was no trial; the evening was warm, and the wine was a prize from His Majesty's cellars. We drank it directly from the bottle's neck, a coarse informality that made us laugh more, and pause again and again to savor the same vintage on one another's lips.

By the time we reached our place by the river, I'd come to rely on his arm to steady my steps, and with a happy sigh, I sank to the soft and fragrant grass, looping my arms around my knees as I gazed up at James. It *was* a beautiful night, I decided, with the nightingales singing sweetly and the branches over our heads like ever-changing lace. I'd heard that the king himself retreated to this riverbank with his French mistress Lady Portsmouth, and I could well believe it, it was that perfectly romantic.

"Now you must tell me your great secret," I ordered. "You have no excuse not to. There is no one to overhear us, and nothing to distract me from giving you my absolute attention."

"Pray, Katherine, don't mock me," he said, pulling off his coat, sword, and hat before he dropped to the grass beside me. "There's no sin in wishing to share such news with a dear friend, is there?"

"I am sorry." Contritely I leaned close, pressing my breasts into his arm, and kissed him again, all by way of apology. "Please tell me."

"Dear Katherine." He threaded his fingers through my hair, holding my face close to his. "Then I will have you know that I am done with antechambers and drawing rooms."

"Done?" I said, giggling silly with the wine, and not following because of it, either. "No more drawing rooms?"

"Not a one, you goose," he said, punctuating his words with quick, nipping, small kisses. "Because through the supreme generosity of His Highness, I have been appointed captain to the Earl of Carlisle's Foot."

"Oh, James, I am so happy for you," I whispered. The significance of his news wasn't clear to my wine-fuddled head, but I knew it had made him happy, very happy, and thus I would be, too, as any friend would for another.

Yet it was not as a friend that he kissed me then, nor did my own answering eagerness show any signs of reluctance or hesitation. Instead I only sighed with willing acquiescence as he rolled me back upon the grass, expecting that this would be another pleasant evening of kisses and caresses and gentle laughter, fairly exchanged.

Whether he sensed in me more willingness than I realized myself, or his blood remained heated from his earlier martial exercises, or we'd simply between us drunk more wine than was wise, I do not know. But I soon understood he intended to make another conquest that night, and that this siege was going to be brief. His kisses had grown fiercely determined, his caresses more demanding. As he moved atop me, I felt at once he'd another sword ready to put to brave use, and my blood quickened with anticipation. I'd heard and spoken bawdry for so long that I believed I knew what to expect next, but no foolish words prepared me for the reality of a man's desire.

In an instant (or so it seemed), he'd thrown back my petticoats and unbuttoned his breeches to free his cock. With little ceremony, he pushed my legs apart and entered me. A few brisk shoves, and he was seated, and I was undone, there beside the river beneath the rising moon.

"Ahh, Katherine, my sweet," he said, groaning with evident pleasure. "I knew it would be like this between us."

I could not say what I'd thought. I felt no pain, only the unfamiliarity of being filled in a place I'd not realized was empty. Nor did I feel much joy, either, lying crushed and small beneath him. Where was the pleasure that inspired poets? What was there in this awkward intimacy that made others willing to risk so much?

"Let me look at you," he said, rearing back on his knees and drawing me with him. His breathing was harsh, his handsome face contorted. "Little jade."

How ungainly, I thought, and blushed to have him look at my most private self by the moonlight. But it was better not to have his weight upon me, and when to my surprise he slipped his arms beneath my knees, I discovered his movements had become more agreeable, even pleasing. Faith, he was a beautiful man, and I could scarce believe I'd been the one to inspire him to this glorious, rampant state. I gasped, a sweet, shuddering sigh, and he made a grimace of a smile.

"Show your spirit, Katherine," he said, his voice ragged as he began to move more forcefully. "Fuck me properly."

I wasn't certain what was proper and what was not. I did recall, however, that liveliness was prized, and tentatively I began to rock with him, and we both gasped at the improvement.

"If—if I am your jade," I said breathlessly, writhing my limbs about him to follow the pace that he set. "Then—then you're my wicked rogue."

He chuckled, as much a laugh as he could manage in the circumstances, then groaned, and at last it seemed we were in agreement. It did not take long after that for us to finish the race, and though James did seem to think all was exactly as it should be, I was dazzled by my first spend, and the rare gift he'd given me. Though I was too shy to tell him, I do not think he even knew he'd claimed my maidenhead, and wistfully I wished it had been otherwise. Afterward I wished nothing more than to talk sweetly to him, to kiss and dandle as true lovers should when they lie side by side, yet to my consternation, all he could speak of was his new appointment.

"I cannot believe the good fortune in it, Katherine," he said, lying sprawled beside me as if I'd been the one who'd ravished him. With his clothing mussed and askew and his long body at ease, he was a fine, manly sight, one that roused my newborn passions again just to gaze upon him. "This peace is the most damnable thing, with regiments being dismissed every day. To be made a captain for Lord Carlisle is a sizable honor."

"But you're already a captain," I said, pillowing my head upon his chest. "How can you be made what you already are?"

"Because it's a better regiment, sweet," he explained patiently, absently stroking his fingers across my tousled hair. "I'll be able to return to France now, and see action again with Louis's forces."

"Back to France?" I said, troubled, and sat upright to see his face. "How can that be, when England's at peace?"

"England is, yes," he said. "But Louis has still more he wishes to claim from the Dutch in the Low Countries, and my regiment will be in his service."

"But not soon," I said, willing it to be so. "It's nearly September."

"That's why there's not a moment to be lost," he said. "I leave to join my regiment tomorrow."

"Tomorrow!" I exclaimed, my earlier joy shattered as thoroughly as a goblet of crystal dropped on a stone floor. "How can it be so?"

"It's so because my orders say it is, and orders must always be obeyed." He raised my fingers to his lips to kiss. "You don't know how grateful I am for this night, Katherine. To have you bid me the best farewell that any soldier could wish."

"But I do not wish you to be grateful!" I cried, anguished. "I wish you to *stay*!"

"My dearest friend," he said, pulling me back down into his arms. "No wonder I will think of you every day, every minute that I am away."

There was no persuading him, for it wasn't his choice to leave. Even I knew that in the army, orders were orders, and must always be obeyed. And I knew, too, that this new post was indeed a great show of favor for him.

And yet, and yet . . . how could he leave me when I'd only just become his? What if he were killed in those wretched Low Countries, and never returned to me at all?

"My own wanton Katherine," he whispered as he kissed me again. "How I will remember you!"

Even as my heart was breaking, I lay with James again beneath the nodding boughs, determined to claim as much of him as I could in these last hours together. I stayed in his company nearly all the night through, until at last we said our final farewell and he left me for his lodgings to make the last preparations for his journey.

I was not brave. I wept as if I'd never stop, and though I remained at Windsor another fortnight with the rest of the Court, then duly followed it back to Whitehall, I was numb to its pleasures and blind to its delights. How else could I feel, without James to share them with me?

For the next month, I made the same calculations that women have always made, counting days and whispering prayers against their own ruin. Finally, on the last Monday of September, my courses came, and I wept again from both relief from not bearing a bastard, and from perverse sorrow as well, to have lost that phantom connection to James.

I wrote volumes of letters, and received few in return. This paucity was easy enough to explain, for what officer in the perilous thick of war has the leisure to sit with his pen like a poet? Surely that was the nature of his letters when they did reach me, hastily scrawled missives without much content beyond how much he missed my companionship. Though hardly the impassioned love letters for which I yearned, I treasured them still, tying them with ribbons and always sleeping with the most recent one tucked in my pillow bier at night.

When James had first gone away, Father had commiserated with my sorrow, and had the kindness not to recall how often he'd warned me against officers. But when my melancholy persisted through the winter and into the spring of 1675, he began to urge me to rouse myself from pining after James and look about at other gentlemen within the palace. He argued that no lady of seventeen should be reserving herself for some faraway gentleman who'd never pledged himself, nor asked for that kind of devotion from me. Now I know that he was right, but at the time I refused to see his wisdom as anything but cruel cynicism, and instead clung stubbornly to my ribbon-tied letters, and the memory of that one night at Windsor.

When James wrote that he'd been rewarded again, and that through the favor of the duke, he was now a captain in the Coldstream Guards, a sizable promotion, I rejoiced with him, and proudly waved the letter before Father as proof of James's merits. But when in June of 1675 he was permitted a brief leave home to England, he repaired not to London to see me, but to the house of his elder brother, Sir Richard Grahme, far away in Cumberland.

My first inclination was to surprise him there, a notion which Father quickly denounced as foolish, as well as a rude imposition upon Sir Richard's wife. Sadly I agreed, and was tormented by James's single letter recounting how much he'd enjoyed Cumberland, and the company of Lady Grahme's numerous family, she being a Howard and daughter to the Earl of Carlisle. I suppose I was to be impressed by this mention of the Howards, that ancient stew of schemers, but I would much rather have heard that James had had a day to spare for me instead.

To distract me (and likely keep me from more rashness), Father obtained an excuse from Court for me from the duchess, and took me with him on a leisurely inspection of his own holdings in Southfleet, near Gravesend in Kent. He was deep in writing another play based on the ancient story of Anthony and Queen Cleopatra, and claimed he needed the solace of the country to collect his muse; a pretty excuse to hide his concern for me. It was pleasant enough to walk beside the sea with Father, who remained the best company in the world, especially given that Lady Sedley was left behind in London. But what pleased me even more was the letter that was awaiting me when Father and I returned in early September.

At last James had completed his tour with the French army, and was returning to England for a lengthy stay. Best of all, he wished to see me on the very day he arrived.

"BUT YOU CANNOT HAVE HEARD THE latest tale of the Lady Portsmouth!" I said, taking another drink of my claret as I made wide, knowing eyes at James over my goblet. "It involves her sister's husband, the Earl of Pembroke, and since it only occurred this week past, I'm sure it will be new to you."

"The Duchess of Portsmouth!" James exclaimed, his eyes bright with anticipation as he settled back in his chair, his own goblet in his hand. "S'blood, what has she done now? One would believe she'd be content in her place in His Majesty's bed without causing more vexation for him."

"Oh, it's not what she has *done*, but rather what the earl threatened to *do* to her." I grinned wickedly. This truly was like the old times. I'd not seen James in over a year, yet we'd fallen into our usual ways as if it had been hours, not days, since last we'd met. He'd brought me here to dine at Chatelin's in Covent Garden, for after having spent so much time among Frenchmen, he'd developed a taste for their food as well. While Chatelin's was the only London tavern of quality with a French cook (and the outrageous bill would show it, too), I was pleased to come here on account of the private dining rooms. We'd a handsome small chamber to ourselves, with our own fireplace and a potboy to bring us the supper that James had bespoken for us, a fine, snug place for our reunion. I'd dressed myself in the French fashion as well, in a rich green silk sack gown with point lace at my cuffs, pearls at my ears and around my throat, and a bright garnet drop to add a bit more color to the paleness of my skin.

"Pembroke is a madman," James said with more relish than disapproval, "and rages so when he drinks that no sane gentleman will keep his company. I can't fathom why Portsmouth was so quick to wed her sister to him."

"They say the lady herself desired him above all others," I said, "though faith, one vows she must be mad herself to choose such a husband."

James held his glass for the potboy to refill. "I doubt he would've chosen her, either, were it not for the dowry the king gave her. Unless she's improved with time, I recall her as being as unlovely as her sister the duchess is beautiful."

I shrugged, making no judgment on the younger de Keroualle. Even with James, I remained uneasy discussing any other lady's lack of beauty; it was a poisonous dart that could too easily be turned back against me.

"Then considering how that royal largesse comes by way of Lady Portsmouth, one would think His Lordship would show more kindness toward her," I said instead, and leaned forward to confide the most luscious facts of the tale. "Pembroke has forbidden her to enter his house, saying he wished no whores consorting with his wife, despite the whore in question being his wife's sister. On discovering her beneath his roof—for so the two women did disobey him, from natural fondness for each other—Pembroke fell into a great rage and, brandishing his sheathed sword, chased the shrieking Lady Portsmouth from the house in view of savants and others passing in the street."

"Oh, the poor lady-whore!" James said, jeering at the mistress's plight. Any other lady would have earned his sympathy for such rough treatment, but because Lady Portsmouth believed she was the highest bred creature at the Court except the queen, it somehow seemed almost merited. "She fancies herself to be so surpassing genteel, that his frank talk must have vexed her no end."

"I heard she was less vexed than terrified, fearing for her very life," I said, gesturing to give the story the dramatic ending it deserved. "You know how Pembroke bellows, roaring so all of London might hear him. As he chased her down the street, he threatened to hang her by her ankles from a nearby tree and bind her skirts over her head, so that the world might view all her secrets, and know exactly what ruled our king."

"Hah, how fast she must have scurried away at that!" James exclaimed, roaring with laughter at the discomfiture of the haughty French mistress. "Oh, Katherine, I vow that no one tells the newest bawdy story as well as you."

"More like the latest bawdy scandals," I said, laughing heartily with him. How good it felt to share this with him again! "Faith, I'd wager our Whitehall can conjure more scandal in a fortnight than you heard in France in the entire time you were away."

"It wouldn't matter if there'd been French scandal or not, considering it would have meant nothing to me without you to tell it." His amusement faded, and he reached across the table to take my hand. "I cannot begin to tell you how much I've missed you, Katherine."

"Nor I you, James," I said softly. In his Coldstream uniform, he surely must have been the most handsome gentleman I'd ever seen, and the warmth in his gaze as he regarded me was better than a thousand kisses from other men. In that moment, every too-short letter was forgiven, and every absent endearment forgotten.

"Without question you are my dearest friend in London." He raised my hand to his lips in tender salute. "I do not believe I would have survived being at Court last year without you. You showed me kindness when no one else would see me, and you made me laugh at every folly, and for that I shall always hold you in the dearest and highest regard, a friend among friends."

"And I you, James," I whispered, overcome with the sweetness of his words. "And I you."

"Dear Katherine," he said softly. "You understand why I was determined to see you first when I returned. I've something to tell you, a confidence that you above all others will understand, and share in my joy."

My heart fluttered with hope, squeezing so tightly in my breast I scarce could breathe. Here at last would be the declaration of love that I'd so longed to hear!

He took a deep breath, and grinned. "I'm to be married."

"Married?" I repeated, so stunned I wondered that I could speak the word. "Married?"

"Yes, married," he said, and chuckled as if he'd just told me the best jest imaginable. "There, I knew I'd surprise you!"

"Married," I said again, the word now like a well-honed dagger through my heart and my hopes. I drew my hand away from his, folding it tightly into its mate before me. "What lady?"

"Dorothy Howard," he said, so enraptured by his own thoughts that he'd not noticed I'd taken away my hand. "She's a distant cousin of my brother's wife, and she was with them this summer when I was there. Her grandfather's Lord Berkshire. She's a most excellent lady, virtuous and quiet in her manner, and yet of the rarest beauty, too."

Virtuous and quiet in her manner, and of the rarest beauty; in short, my opposite in every possible way, and with the Earl of Berkshire for her grandfather.

"Likely you have seen her at Court, though I had not," he continued happily. "She serves as maid of honor to Her Majesty."

Oh, yes, I knew her, by sight if not by reputation, for as far as I knew, she had none. Dorothy Howard was enchantingly plump and as fair as a porcelain shepherdess, her hair golden blond, her eyes pale blue, and her mouth the tiniest of pink rosebuds. If she'd any cleverness, I wouldn't know it, for I do not believe I'd ever heard her speak so much as a single word beyond those required to answer the queen.

He smiled his contentment, clearly envisioning her before him. "Mrs. Howard is everything any gentleman could wish in a wife. I knew that from the instant we met. I first asked for her hand before I left my brother's house, but because her parents thought my prospects were beneath her, they refused to give their consent. But now she has told me that, after prayer and reflection, she had decided to accept me, whether with her father's consent or without. The courage of a lion in the shape of the sweetest lamb!"

"When will you wed?" My voice sounded distant and hollow, as if I stood at the far end of an echoing cave.

"Next week," he said proudly. "Now that she has agreed, there is no reason for delay. I'll be called back to France soon enough."

"Oh, no." I looked down at my clasped hands, afraid my eyes would betray too much. The choice before me was at once impossibly easy, yet painfully hard. He regarded me not as the lover I'd hoped, but as a friend. I could fall into a wounded rage born of my pain, hurl the bitterest curses upon him and his bride, and storm away from the eating-house, never to speak to him again. Yet if I were to do that here in Chatelin's, the entire Court would hear of it with their morning chocolate. I wasn't the Duchess of Portsmouth, entitled by my beauty and rank to tempestuous displays. Instead I'd be mocked for having aspired to such a handsome man, ridiculed for believing I could claim him as my own, and greeted by knowing smirks wherever I went. I'd long ago learned from Father and his friends that at Court it was far better to be spoken of for scandal than to be ignored in virtuous silence. But not like this; not like this.

And what, truly, would it gain me?

But if instead I could make myself mask my hurt behind a happy smile and good wishes, my secret would forever be buried. I might never have possessed James as my lover, not really, but I could at least keep him as a friend. I still loved him too well for it to be otherwise.

"Katherine?" He was waiting, unsure.

Slowly I looked up. I held my goblet up toward him, and forced myself to smile.

"To you, James," I said softly. "To you, and Mistress Howard, and much joy to you both."

But that night in my bedchamber, I sat before my fire and carefully untied the ribbons from his letters. One by one by one, I dropped the pages into the flames, watching them burst bright before they curled and blackened and fell to bits.

If a part of my heart did the same, then no one but I would ever know.

Chapter Ten

THE DUKE'S THEATRE, DORSET GARDEN, LONDON
March 1676

It should come as no surprise that after the debacle with James Grahme, I once again threw myself into life at the Court. For a brief time, he had anchored me and kept me from drifting into deeper, more perilous waters, but no more. I was again on my own. Not only did I hope that the feverish pace of palace life would make me forget the sorrow of my misbegotten first love, but the cynicism of this king's Court held a fresh appeal to me now that it hadn't before.

Five days before Christmas, I had passed my eighteenth birthday. The first tender flower of my youth had passed now, lost forever along with my innocence. I no longer saw the boundless hope in life that I once had, nor did I dream of love as an achievable ideal. Instead I resolved to keep what was left of my lonely heart locked away against further pain, and guard it close with the sharpness of my tongue. This wasn't difficult, for I'd always spoken freely. I was my father's daughter, and could not be otherwise.

Yet in the strange manner of men, what I had conceived to keep them away seemed only to draw them closer. In our palace-world where ladies were either easily breeched playthings or distant saints, I'd become an unpredictable challenge, and all the more desirable among the jaded gentlemen at Court because of it. I seldom longed for male company, and it seemed I'd always some gentleman or other hovering like a buzzing dragonfly at my side.

Of course, there was more virulent talk about me, too, doubtless spread by those who found me too acerbic for their tastes. I simply shrugged, and paid it no heed.

With that in mind, it seemed fitting that the most anticipated play of the winter season was *Man of Mode; or, Sir Fopling Flutter*, by Mr. George Etherege. Mr. Etherege was another of Father's circle, though of such a quiet and unobtrusive nature that he was fondly called "Gentle George" by the others. What Mr. Etherege was rumored to have done, however, was to have taken his friends piecemeal and stitched them entire into his play.

Little wonder, then, that on this March afternoon, every seat was taken in the playhouse, and little wonder, too, that Her Highness had made space for me to sit beside her in the royal box. This was as crowded as the rest of the playhouse, with the king and the duke together in the center, as was usual, and the duchess among her train.

"Sir Charles would have told you, Miss Sedley, being his daughter," she said to me eagerly over her fluttering fan. "Now you must tell me, if you please. Will what we see in the play today truly represent Mr. Etherege's friends?"

"Forgive me, Your Highness, but I know as much, and as little, as do you." I smiled warmly, happy to share even an empty conspiracy with her. Truly, it was impossible not to like her. She had been married a little more than two years, and had done the best she could to make her way in a country that despised both her and her faithless husband. In that time she had miscarried twice, borne one daughter who had died an infant from convulsions, and was now with child again. She'd earned the sadness that marked her young face, a wealth of burdens for a lady of seventeen.

Yet Her Highness's single fault was a grave one, for she viewed the duke's conversion to her faith as a personal holy crusade, even though it could well ruin him and England, too. Like most Papists, she simply refused to see the peril. Even now she could not have chosen a worse necklace to wear to a public playhouse, a strand of pearls with a large silver crucifix set with sapphires, and I marveled that His Highness had not cautioned her against it.

Unaware of my thoughts, she puckered her mouth with disappointment. "You are certain you cannot tell me, Miss Sedley?"

"I vow I would if I could, Your Highness," I said, "but though I believe Father has seen the rehearsals for the play, he will not tell me a thing, lest I spoil the first effect of Mr. Etherege's words."

"Likely Sir Charles is wise to do so, but I cannot say I care for it." She sighed her disappointment, and leaned over the rail to look down upon the crowded pit. "That is your father to the front, yes?"

I leaned forward, too, the thick dark curls over my forehead trembling on their fashionable wire supports. "On the front bench, Your Highness, to the right," I said, pointing with the ivory blades of my furled fan. "The stoutish gentleman in the dark green brocade coat, between Lord Rochester and Lord Middlesex. I would guess the empty space is being saved for Mr. Etherege, who must still be with the players."

"Oh, yes, of course," she murmured, studying the three gentlemen's backs with such intent that I wondered what she saw in them.

For me, of course, it was entirely different. The sight of my father between his two dearest friends (Lord Buckhurst having inherited his maternal grandfather's estates and now styled Earl of Middlesex) was a rare one now. Father devoted more time to Lady Sedley and his son, his writing, and his seat in the House, while Lord Middlesex was often with his own new wife in the country. Lord Rochester, too, frequently repaired to the country, both to be with his growing family and to nurse his faltering health. Yet when I gazed at the three of them together on the first bench, my round, small father with his lavish neckcloth and large black wig between the two taller earls, I'd only the merriest of memories of sitting on that same bench with them.

"His Highness the duke says they are the wittiest gentlemen in the realm," the duchess continued. "He said that any play that employed their conversation would surely be the most amusing we could ever hope to see."

"His Highness is quite right, ma'am," I said proudly. "I've spent much time in their company, and I can vouch for their wit. If all that Mr. Etherege did was copy their speech word for word, then he'd have a play that would run until Easter."

"Please, please forgive me for interrupting, Your Royal Highness," said a gentleman on the far side of the duchess, leaning between two other ladies to address her. "But I have read the play in its entirety to have been able to write its prologue, including being consulted upon Mr. Etherege's most heartfelt dedication to you, Your Highness, and I do believe Miss Sedley is showing a daughter's devotion to undervalue the poetical genius of Mr. Etherege."

"Indeed, Sir Carr," the duchess said, the weary irritation in her voice unmistakable. "We have already told you how we enjoyed the prologue."

"The honor was entirely mine, ma'am," Sir Carr said, with the horrible grimace that passed for his smile. As unlovely as his name, Sir Carr Scroope was a short, brash, scrabbling baronet of questionable birth from Lincolnshire, with a hunched back and worse manners who pretended to be a wit, a poet, and a gallant, without the qualities or the talent to support any of it. "But if Miss Sedley would only admit that—"

"I invited Miss Sedley's opinion, and she granted it," the duchess said. "She need admit nothing beyond that."

"Oh, but forgive me, ma'am, but she does, she does." To my dismay he'd pushed his way past the other ladies and had squeezed close to my side. "If she would but hear my prologue, ma'am, then she would see that—"

"I have read it, Sir Carr," I said, which was true; Father and I had skewered it royally between us last evening as a mighty poor effort. If Sir Carr wished to engage me in a conversation such as this, then I hoped he was well prepared. "I have read it, and in my opinion, you have dishonored Her Highness greatly by it."

"I have? How? How?" Sir Carr managed to look both stricken and peeved. "Where could I have erred, with Her Highness to inspire me?"

I smiled, perfectly aware of how everyone within hearing was waiting for my response. Tomorrow the Court might speak of what the other ladies wore, but they'd repeat whatever I said next to Sir Carr.

"With Her Highness to inspire you, you should have at least attempted the poet's art," I said, affecting the wry bemusement that I'd learned from Father. "Her Highness does not deserve to have 'scum' and 'home' forced to rhyme in her honor, as you have writ in your blessed prologue."

"Miss Sedley, I—"

"Nor 'face' and 'glass,'" I said, recalling another ill-sounded pairing that had made Father howl. "Most awkward."

"Not if spoken well!"

"But true poetry must be read as well as craftily spoken," I said, waving my fan gently before my face. "While the ear may discover no fault, the eye will spy it at once. As I recall, you employed both 'Giddy Fools' and 'Wanton Fool' within a dozen lines of one another. Surely such an excess of foolishness connotes a lack of creative genius, or simple idle laziness. Or perhaps I misspeak, and the conceit is meant as a tribute to the Poet Fool?"

Beside me the duchess smothered her laughter behind her fan, and the other ladies around her likewise laughed at the baronet's expense, and beyond them I could see more than a few gentlemen leaning in their seats to hear as well.

Sir Carr's scowl deepened, his face turning a murderous plum as he waggled his hideous features before me. "Stay your sword, Miss Sedley. I'd not have you poison my audience ere they've heard my offering."

"I warn them, Sir Carr, that is all." I smiled pleasantly, for this was all sport to me. "What manner of friend would I be to stand aside and say nothing, and let them be felled by the poisonous tedium of your so-called wit?"

"You are *villainous*, Miss Sedley, an ill-favored, villainous creature," he sputtered, his composure entirely undone. "It would seem that even a great poet such as Sir Charles can sire a low, base critic, just as the finest bred stallion might still father a mule."

"Sir Carr." Her Highness's voice bore enough frost to freeze the Thames. "We do not wish to hear more from you at present."

At that he'd no choice but to scuttle away, glaring fiercely at me as if I were to blame for his being dismissed. I was certain the thing wasn't done between us, and that he'd try to best me again. I cared not. I knew my gifts, and they would always outdo his.

But as he left us, the fiddlers finished their overture, the conversations in the audience fell silent, and as one we all turned expectantly toward the stage. It *was* indeed painful to suffer through Sir Carr's prologue, but it was soon done, and the play proper began, with Mr. Betterton (the very best actor of the Duke's Company) as Dorimant, the sparkish hero of the piece. He'd scarce begun before I saw how closely Betterton followed Lord Rochester for inspiration in every languid gesture and drawl, just as Mr. Etherege had copied the exact amusing pattern of his speech as Dorimant grumbled about the start of his day. All of us from the Court saw and heard it, too, and roared our appreciation, led by the king himself.

"Oh, Mr. Betterton is very like Lord Rochester, isn't he?" the duchess whispered with delight. "How deliciously clever!"

But as clever a character as Dorimant might be, I gasped aloud as his friend appeared next, come to call on him with the freshest news of the day. This friend was called Mr. Medley, only the slightest distance from my father's name, and why not? Truly, I felt as if I were watching Father transformed upon the stage before me; Mr. Medley was that close to Sir Charles Sedley in every aspect of his speech and drollery, even to the perfect description of his becoming "rhetorically drunk." I understood now why Father had kept the script such a secret from me, to heighten the surprise and pleasure I had in seeing it now performed, and from the reaction of Father and his friends in the pit, the play was every bit as enjoyable to them as it was to the rest of the house.

To be sure, there were certain dramatic strictures that were obeyed by the play that were not quite true to life. Dorimant might have been tamed by the wily Harriet, but Lord Rochester himself had as yet never come close to that degree of affectionate subservience to any lady, least of all his wife. But the play as a whole was such a delight that the king led all of us from the royal box to call upon the players in the tiring room and congratulate them and Mr. Etherege on the performance.

For me the tiring room behind the stage was as friendly and familiar a place as could be, with many kisses and embraces to be shared with those I'd known since I was a child. Of course, Nell was there to celebrate the opening of the new play. With Dorimant's extravagant plumed hat on her head, she held Court like the boisterous small queen that she was in that particular backstage kingdom, and lifted her petticoats high to show the king her newest pair of jeweled slippers (only proper, considering he'd paid for them) and a good deal of her legs besides.

"Come with me, Little Kid," Lord Rochester said, finding me in amongst the revelry. He took me by the arm and bent to speak directly into my ear. "I need a word or two with you."

"With me, my lord?" I asked, my voice raised above the din of laughter and racketing flirtation. "Why would you wish to leave with me, when you are the very center of all attention?"

"Not I, Katherine, but Dorimant," he said shrewdly, wagging his finger at me. "Pray do not confuse the two, however similar we may appear.

But he is useful; I'll not deny that. You can come converse with me, and we'll leave Dorimant behind in my stead."

I laughed, and willingly let him lead me from the tiring room and down the close-packed hall. Again I thought of the old times, to be in his company like this again; he had always been my favorite of Father's acquaintances. But if I'd grown from a child to a woman, he'd changed, too, and not for the better. He was not yet thirty, but the pox, debauchery, and an excess of drink had left their unfortunate mark on him. His once-handsome face was bloated and ashen, his eyes shadowed, and the ugly sore at the corner of his mouth was like an ominous veil over every smile.

Throughout, his wit had remained, yet ever-sharper and more bitter as his body faltered. I was thankful to be considered among his friends, and so be spared his bite. Which was not to say I didn't enjoy seeing it directed toward others, for he could toss and tumble his words in the air with the agility of the most skilled juggler at Southwalk Fair.

Now His Lordship took me to a quieter corner in the playhouse, where the cheerful confusion of the celebration was not so loud but that we could converse. He pretended to assume a stern face fit for the pulpit, folding his arms over the breast of his plum brocade coat.

"I will bid you tell me the truth, Katherine," he said, so severe I had to struggle not to giggle. "As true as if you were one of my own daughters. Whatever did you do to Sir Carr Scroope to reduce him to the condition of a blithering, impotent turnip?"

"Oh, my lord!" I laughed aloud, unable not to. "Were you watching?"

"Most of the house was watching," he said. "Though we couldn't make out your words from our bench, we could see the results. Middlesex believed Scroope would suffer an apoplexy there where he stood, and topple into the pit."

"It wasn't as bad as that," I protested, laughing still. "I swear to you, it wasn't."

"Then you have made a conquest of the vile baronet?"

"Faith, no!" I exclaimed solemnly. "I would not dare make such a claim, not when Sir Carr has eyes only for Mistress Frazier."

Now the earl laughed with me. Sir Carr was widely known to be penniless, and had proclaimed to all the Court his need for a rich heiress. If I'd shown him any kindness, he doubtless would have pounced on me; but because I hadn't—oh, preserve me!—he'd set his heart on Mrs. Carey Frazier, the most beautiful (and ambitiously wanton) of Her Majesty's maids of honor. She had been raised at Court, her father being the king's chief physician and much favored for curing the pox and ending unwanted pregnancies. Now everyone knew that Miss Frazier had briefly embraced Sir Carr, and found him so sadly wanting as a lover that she refused to suffer any more of his addresses. But that had not stopped Sir Carr from writing mooncalf songs in verse to her that he proudly passed around Whitehall.

As if reading my thoughts, Lord Rochester heaved a sigh so deep it seemed drawn from the soles of his feet, and with his hand pressed over his heart, he began to recite one of these songs in perfect imitation of Sir Carr:

I cannot change as others do
Though you unjustly scorn
Since that poor Swayne that sighs for you
For you alone is born.
No Phyllis, no, your heart to move,
A surer way I'll try
And to revenge my slighted love
Will still love on, will still love on, and die.

"Stop, my lord, stop, I beg you!" I cried, laughing so hard I was forced to hold my aching sides.

"Then tell me what you said to him before Her Highness."

"Oh, my lord, it was nothing," I said, taking out my handkerchief to wipe the tears from my eyes. "I chided him for the ill-formed rhymes in his prologue, and he damned me for a villainous creature."

"That's wicked cruel of him," Lord Rochester said with mock outrage. "He's already vexed me sorely by his outlandish pretensions, and I'd let it pass. But my grace is done. He can't be permitted to abuse dear Miss Sedley in this ungallant fashion."

I shrugged. "Her Highness dismissed him for his rudeness, which was likely punishment enough considering how he was so convinced of earning her favor. Besides, he'd suffered by my hand."

"No, no, it's not to be borne, little miss," he declared, and from the gleam in his eye I suspected he was already planning to be my champion. "Such insult cannot be allowed to pass unavenged."

"Oh, it won't pass, my lord, not for long," I said. "I'm certain Sir Carr believes himself to be the one who was insulted. What of it? It's not as if he can challenge me to defend his honor with swords drawn at dawn on some misty field."

"Hah, how I'd like to see that!" he said, laughing at the ridiculousness of the image. "But we can't let the rascal escape entirely, not after defaming you. I'll pink him lightly on your behalf, Katherine, just enough to make him bleed a bit so others take notice, and send him off to rage again. He did make a fine purple-faced turnip, didn't he?"

"Rochester, there you are!"

At once the earl's conspiratorial laughter vanished, his expression instantly composed into genteel diffidence. I turned swiftly to see who the newcomer might be who'd followed us here, and nearly bumped into His Highness the duke.

"Your Highness," I murmured, mortified, and sank into a deep curtsy.

Despite how often I was in the duchess's apartments and in her company, I seldom saw the duke, who was much occupied with his own troubles with Parliament. When I did, I was always among so many other ladies that I doubt he took any notice of me at all. It was a strange irony that while Father had feared I'd been invited to Court only because His Highness had formed a lascivious interest in me, in truth when I'd arrived practically beneath his nose, I'd become invisible. At first I'd been dismayed—what lady wishes to be ignored?—but then I'd met James Grahme, who'd made me forget my disappointment at being overlooked by James Stuart.

"So what's it like to see yourself trotted out on the stage, Rochester?" the duke said. "I vowed I'd seen your twin, that Dorimant was so like you."

With a glass of wine from the tiring room in his hand, he looked far more at his ease than when I'd seen him at Whitehall, but then, there was no one here at the playhouse to hector him about his religion, either. I always forgot how tall he was, and how much presence he had. In the murky light of this wandering hallway, two things about him still shone brightly: the glinting gold threads of the Garter-star embroidered on the chest of his coat, the constant emblem of his royalty, and the intense blue of his eyes.

Lord Rochester, of course, was likely thinking no such dizzying thoughts. "I should think the world a much improved place, Your Highness," he said blithely. "How could it not be, with two of me in it?"

The duke laughed. "Indeed, it is," he said. "There aren't many men I'd like to see doubled, but you, sir, are one."

"Perhaps Mr. Etherege can be persuaded to work his spell in reverse, sir," Lord Rochester said easily. "If he can double me, then surely he can take those odious rascals and halve them into nothingness."

The duke laughed again. Though he'd not given me leave, I finally dared to rise from my curtsy, and daring further, glanced up at him.

He wasn't looking at Lord Rochester. He was looking at me.

"Miss Sedley," he said, smiling warmly. "You amused us today, too."

"I, Your Highness?" I asked, so startled by his interest that my cheeks burned hot.

"Yes, you," he said. "Her Highness told me of how you defended her against Scroope's sour rhymes. It was most cleverly done."

"Thank you, sir," I said, and finally smiled. "I'm grateful that Her Highness in turn defended me against Sir Carr."

"Don't be modest, Miss Sedley," he said, teasing. "From what my wife told me, you defended yourself well enough without her help. I like a clever lady, you know."

"Oh, our Katherine's clever as can be," Lord Rochester said, happily playing the pander in a way that would have made Father furious. "She's certainly the cleverest lady at Court, maybe in all London. She can't help it, you know. 'Tis in her very blood."

"True, true," the duke said. He was studying me closely, as if he'd never seen me before. I knew enough of gentlemen by now to tell when they were pleased or not, and to me it was clear enough that the duke was indeed very pleased with me. "I can't recall the last time I heard a clever word spoken by a lady in my brother's Court."

I knew that wasn't true, for the king liked his ladies to be quick-witted and amusing. No one could tell a lewd story as well as the Duchess of Cleveland, and as sweet-faced as Nell Gwyn might be, it was her wit that had made her the king's jester as well as his mistress. But if the duke wished to single me out as a rarity, then I'd hardly argue.

Suddenly his face lit with recognition. "I recall you now," he said. "Long ago you stumbled before my horse, and when I came to see if you were unharmed, you gave me an apple, bold as Eve in the Garden."

"Yes, sir, that was me." I grinned wickedly from beneath my lashes. "It must have been the serpent that frightened your horse."

"I don't doubt that it was." He chuckled, his eyes wandering freely over my person, and I guessed he was remembering how much of my legs he'd glimpsed when I'd fallen, too. It was rare for me to garner the interest of so grand a gentleman as His Highness for the sake of my person, and I fair glowed beneath his attention.

"I trust we'll see more of you, Miss Sedley," he said. "I like apples."

"Yes, sir," I said. "I'll take care to remember that."

"I'm sure you will." He lingered another moment, then nodded to Lord Rochester, and left to return to his brother and the others. I watched him walk away, his tall figure silhouetted by the brighter light of the tiring room, and thought of what a handsome, fine-made man he was.

"There's a fine afternoon's work for you, Katherine," Lord Rochester said dryly. "You've wounded Sir Carr and slain the duke."

"I haven't slain him at all," I scoffed, then grinned. "Leastways, not yet."

He laughed. "Take care with that dragon, my dear. He breathes fire readily enough where ladies are concerned." He raised a thoughtful brow. "I doubt your father will be pleased if you go traipsing into that particular cave."

"No," I said, and with real regret, too. "Not at all. Please, you won't—"

"What, come between you and Little Sid?" He rolled his eyes, then smiled at me with such a genuine kindness as to astonish those who knew him only by his libertine reputation. "Be easy, sweet Katherine. He'll hear none of it from me."

I smiled my thanks, and meant it, too, for the indulgence he was granting was important to me. I loved my father dearly, as he loved me. I knew exactly what he'd say if he'd witnessed this little scene with the duke, because he'd said it many times over: "That's not what I wished for you." In a way, he'd been even more crushed than I over my disappointment with James Grahme.

I could understand Father's concern, too, now that I'd seen more closely the trials that a royal mistress faced, and how perilous their situation could be. As the best-loved mistress to His Majesty, the Duchess of Portsmouth was regarded as the most powerful lady at Court. Just the same, she'd recently been infected with the pox by the king himself. She'd been banished from Court for months while she took the cure, forbidden the solace and company of the king and even of their son. Her position, her wealth, and most especially the place she held in the king's affections had all been in jeopardy, with scores of enemies gathered like jackals to rip everything away. It had taken her considerable skills at politics and seduction, as well as considerable luck, to regain them when she'd returned. I wasn't sure I'd wish such a life for myself, no matter how great the rewards or how charming the royal brothers might be.

Yet I will not lie and claim that the challenge of it did not tempt me. When the duke gazed at me as he just had, my heart quickened at a pace that no other gentleman had been able to inspire. To tame such a dragon by my cleverness would be an accomplishment indeed.

Besides, I'd a taste for apples myself.

THOUGH MOST AT COURT REGARDED Sir Carr Scroope as little more than a bad jest in the form of a misshapen man, Lord Rochester seized upon him as the ripest target for his satire. I don't know what there was about the lowly baronet that inspired other gentlemen so negatively. Father had sputtered a wealth of epithets when I'd told him what Sir Carr had said to me, though Father was too kind a poet to write them down for circulation among his friends. The Duke of Buckingham had shown no such consideration when he'd written that Sir Carr was so vastly ugly that:

He dare not stir abroad for fear he meet
Curses of teeming women in the street.

The least could happen from this hideous sight
Is that they should miscarry from the fright.

But Lord Rochester had been more richly inspired by Sir Carr's ill usage of me, and his own verse was more finely wrought, and more scathing. He'd seized upon the lovesick song that Sir Carr had written to Carey Frazier (the same one he'd recited to me at the playhouse) and turned it into something quite different.

I swive as well as others do,
I'm young, not yet deformed,
My tender heart, sincere, and true,
Deserves not to be scorned.

Why Phyllis then, why will you swive,
With forty lovers more?
Can I (said she) with Nature strive,
Alas I am, alas I am a whore.

As can be imagined, I laughed long and heartily over this little pasquinade, and even read it aloud with Lord Rochester before a small party at Locket's tavern late one night. Copies were passed about the Court with lightning swiftness, until there were a great many others beside me who could recite Phyllis's part. I couldn't resist adding a few cleverly satiric and cutting lines of my own to the public circus as well, demonstrating the woefulness of Sir Carr's so-called poetry. My part in all this made me much celebrated, and everyone was wonderfully amused by the earl's cleverness at Sir Carr's expense—except, of course, Lord Carr himself, who challenged me directly one evening while I waited for my coach at the palace gate.

"*You* are the cause of the outrage against me, Miss Sedley," he said, his outsized nostrils flaring and his fists clenched at his sides as he charged up the steps toward me. "*You* hide behind Lord Rochester and urge him on to say villainous things of me, whilst I know it is all your evil, vengeful doing!"

The other ladies with me shrieked and scattered as if we'd been charged by a mad dog—which, in a way, I supposed we had been. Bravely I held my ground, though inside I was quaking as much as the others who'd fled. If I were willing to unleash Lord Rochester to wage slanderous battles on my behalf, then I'd have to be ready to answer if one of His Lordship's salvos blew back into my own face. What use was being a cowardly wit?

"Consider who was the first to slander, Sir Carr," I said, struggling to contain my fear. Instead I tried to draw myself into the very picture of a wounded lady, though in truth I doubt I succeeded. "Before Her Highness and a score of others, you used words no gentleman should to a lady."

"I'll not deny it," Sir Carr sputtered on the step below me, "for every word I used against you was well deserved, and here's more for your trouble. Harpy! Shrew! Damnable, cursed jade!"

To my endless relief, two of the guards from the palace came running forward to my aid, drawn by Sir Carr's intemperate shouts. He heard them, and quickly stepped away from me before they'd joined us.

"This is not done between us, Miss Sedley," he said, practically spitting out the words as he turned away. "It is not *done*."

Shaken, I made my way home. I found Father reading before his fire in his library, and indignantly I told him what had happened, expecting sympathy. I received none.

"What else can you hope for, Katherine?" he asked me after I'd told him of Sir Carr's fury. "He is only a man. A disagreeable and ugly man, to be sure, but a mortal like the rest of us. He has a right to be angry at what has been written of him."

"But he began it!" I protested.

"You provoked him for your own amusement," Father said mildly. "If you jab a dog's rump long enough with a stick, you have no grounds for protest when he jumps up to bite you."

"But Lord Rochester wrote the song, not I!"

Father sighed, tapping his fingers against the arm of his chair. "The stick did not poke the dog of its own volition, Katherine. You should know by now that my acquaintance is much given to mischief of this sort, as is Lord Buckingham, and yet they almost never suffer for it. Once, long ago, Lord Middlesex and I were involved together in a foolish public prank that we believed to be extraordinarily entertaining, though I doubt the crowd who witnessed our drunken idiocy on the Cock's balcony agreed."

Of course I'd heard of this escapade from Father's past, not from him, but from others. He might dismiss it now as a foolish prank, but it remained powerfully notorious, and had involved Father and his friends standing roaring drunk and naked on the balcony of a Bow Street tavern. Father had delivered a blasphemous parody of a Puritan sermon, followed by a lewd pantomime, and when the outraged crowd that had gathered in the street below had begun hurling stones at them, Father and his friends had answered by pissing a golden rain upon them.

"I should hardly equate a poem with what you did," I said wryly. "Nor did I speak it naked in Bow Street."

He grimaced. "I should hope not, Katherine. That would be a bit strong for any lady. But the point of this tale is that for our folly, I was punished with a week in gaol and a fine of one thousand marks, while Lord Buckhurst was not charged at all."

"That's hardly fair," I said, shocked by the sum. "A thousand marks is a prodigious fine for a frolic."

"I believe the judge called it 'profane actions committed against the public decency and misdemeanors against the king.'" He smiled at the memory. "Buckhurst was equally guilty, but he was heir to a peerage, and I was only a baronet. Thus I was punished, and he was not."

"It's still not fair."

"It will not change." He shook his head, not with the bitterness that I felt, but with his usual benign resignation. "One can see insults everywhere and go about with a drawn sword like a madman, but hot tempers and duels accomplish little. Far better to keep one's frustrations to one's self, and present a pleasing smile to the world instead. I know that lessons don't sit well with you, Katherine, but that is one worth heeding, especially if you wish to continue at Court."

It was an old iniquity, one I must have realized in the cradle, though knowing it was so didn't make it any easier to accept. Yet instead of making me more resigned, like Father, his tale only inspired me to rise higher myself. If I could only become a peeress, then I'd be as safe as Lord Middlesex had been.

"You know I do not like lessons, Father," I said crossly, fussing with my bracelets. "I never have."

He sighed. "I didn't enjoy learning that one, either. But here is another for you, Daughter, that no matter how many times I've tried to teach it to you, you refuse to hear."

His expression surprised me by its seriousness, and so did the tender way he covered my hand with his own.

"Do not make enemies for the sport of it," he said softly, "whether they're His Majesty or Sir Carr Scroope or even the lowest maidservant who fans your bedchamber coals in the morning. It's a dangerous habit to fall into, and one best avoided."

"It's wicked hard to avoid." More likely it was nigh impossible, I thought glumly, remembering how sweet the laughter of others had been when Lord Rochester and I had recited our little satire.

Father grunted, knowing me all too well. "I know it's hard, especially for a lady as clever as you. But there are people everywhere eager to see you falter and fall. It's the way of the Court. The fewer enemies you acquire and the more friends you can hold, the easier your life will be. It's as simple as that."

Sitting so peaceably beside the fire with him, far removed from the temptation of fame and admiration, it was easy to see the wisdom of his advice.

"I'm sorry, Father," I said contritely. "I won't do it again."

"I'll pray that you mean that, my dear Kattypillar," he said. "I'll pray that you do."

Yet he smiled sadly, as much as admitting he'd pray in vain. It grieved me that he'd so little faith in me, loving him as I did, yet I could scarcely fault him for it. How could I? He was my father, and knew me all too well. As much as he might wish otherwise, he doubted I could do as I promised.

And so, God help me, did I.

Chapter Eleven

Peter Lely's Studio, Long Acre, London
June 1676

"So which would you have me wear, Master Lely?" I looked at the assortment of loose-fitting gowns and cloaks in rich cloth hanging on pegs before me. An open casket on the floor held a fool's fortune of false pearls and brooches of glass rubies and sapphires set in brass gold, all waiting to become part of my new costume. "Faith, I do not know where to begin!"

Master Lely lifted one bright swath of cloud out from its peg, then another, as he critically considered which color would suit me best. As the principal painter to the king, Peter Lely was by far the most desired artist for portraits of fashion in London, and when Father had finally badgered me into agreeing to sit for one, there'd been no question who would paint it. I'd already been here once to the Dutchman's studio, to sit for drawings as he decided on a pose.

Things had not gone well at first. I was too ill at ease to sit with any natural grace, and so unsure of how I could possibly be presented as a beauty that I'd been stiff and miserable while Master Lely's chalk had moved swiftly over his page. But gradually he had calmed me by remarking on the qualities of my person that I secretly liked myself—my dark eyes and my gracefully shaped arms and hands—instead of the practiced, empty flattery that always put me on my guard. By the time I left, I'd decided I could trust him neither to mock me, nor to make me look like a sad twin to a true beauty like Lady Portsmouth.

Now, here again in his studio, that trust continued, even as he lifted down a brilliant salmon-colored silk gown.

"What of this, Mrs. Sedley?" he asked, holding it beneath my chin. "It's a cheery color."

"Perhaps too cheery for me," I said, skittishly turning away. One did not sit for Master Lely in one's ordinary dress, but let him compose fanciful costumes from these pieces in his collection. The most pious lady in the Court might be painted in the same contrived gown as the most notorious, with no ill reflection on either. But I'd seen that salmon-colored silk before in a portrait of one of the great Court beauties, and I didn't wish the unfortunate comparisons that were sure to be made between us. Instead I seized upon a deep bronze-colored gown with little notched tabs for sleeves like an antique doublet, with a slate blue cape with a gold fringe tied to one shoulder.

"I like this one," I said. "If I'm to be shown in the woods, then this seems more fitting."

Master Lely hesitated. "I have used that arrangement only once before, Mrs. Sedley. It might not please Sir Charles to have you wear the same."

I grinned at his reticence. "What, was it some great whore?"

He gave a careful little shift to his shoulders, expressing everything and nothing; clearly diplomacy was another art he practiced well. "It was worn by the actress Mrs. Gwyn."

"Nell wore it first?" My grin widened. "Then I shall be honored to wear the same, and so should my father."

Thus I came to be painted in the same attire as Nelly, even to the same brooch clasping the cape to my shoulder. When I climbed onto the small stage to pose on a bench (later to be transformed by Master Lely's art into a mossy bower), I thought of her clad in the same costume, and was at my ease. The conceit of it amused me no end, and my delight must have showed in my face. Driven by inspiration, Master Lely's brush now flew happily across the canvas, and by the time he declared our session to be over for the day, he had roughed in the outline of my figure and already made a good start to my face.

I was still in my costume, admiring the painter's work, when one of his assistants came hurrying in to announce the arrival of Lord Middlesex. The earl followed directly after him, sauntering in as if Master Lely's studio were only one more of his many properties, using his tall walking stick not for support, but as if to stake his claim to whatever he chose.

"Katherine, my dear," he said, smiling at me with what seemed genuine pleasure. "I didn't expect to find you here playing masquerade with old Lely."

Master Lely bowed, unperturbed at being called old. "Sir Charles has honored me by asking for a portrait of his daughter. Mrs. Sedley has just completed her first sitting with me."

"Hah, I guessed as much." He turned his cheek toward me, bending down for me to kiss him. I did so from long habit as one of Father's dearest friends rather than from my own affection. I do not know why I'd never warmed to him the same as I had to Lord Rochester; he'd always been pleasant enough to me. But I'd often wondered if it came from having long ago glimpsed him intimately tangled with Nell, and the uneasiness the sight had provoked in my childish innocence. He and Nell had parted bitterly after that, and the open resentment he still bore toward her did not recommend him to me, either.

He was smiling at me now, fortunately unaware of my thoughts. "I like how you dress the ladies, Lely," he said, studying my costume. "Cunning disarray, yes?"

Master Lely nodded. "It's meant to be more romantic than cunning, my lord, to show the ladies to their best advantage."

"It does do that," he said with unexpected approval. "You should always dress like this, Katherine. It becomes you. And consider how much you'd save your poor father's pocket!"

He laughed, but to have his gaze lingering so long on my form was making me uneasy. The costume might look well when painted, but in reality there was little to it. While Master Lely might call it romantic, in truth it was more undress than otherwise. The loose-fitting gown had been pinned behind to fit my narrow figure, while beneath it I wore only a billowing smock without stays. My bosom might not be as richly endowed as other ladies', but what there was of it was wantonly displayed, and I self-consciously tugged it higher.

"It is one thing to dress like this for Master Lely, my lord," I said, "but entirely another to traipse about trailing enough satin for a ship's sail."

"I never said it would be convenient," Lord Middlesex said, chuckling. "Only beguiling."

"Only because you, my lord, are not made to dress the same." I kicked the satin puddled around my feet by way of demonstration. "I'm sorry to disappoint you, but Her Highness is expecting me at St. James's, and by your leave I must shift into more appropriate clothes."

"Ah, I am bound for the palace as well." He waved his hand, the lace on his cuff ruffling around his wrist. "It shall be my pleasure and my honor to take you there with me, Katherine."

"You're most kind, my lord, but I must refuse," I said quickly. "My own carriage and people are waiting for me."

"Then we'll send them away," he said with lordly disdain. "The streets around the palaces are crowded enough without us adding two coaches where one will do. You'll come with me, Katherine, and that's an end to it."

It was, too. I couldn't think of a way to excuse myself from Lord Middlesex's offer without offending him and likely angering Father as well. As little as I wished for more of His Lordship's company, I could make myself bear it for the short drive to the palace. With a grudging sigh, I went off to change, dragging my overlong skirts with me, while Lord Middlesex concluded whatever business had brought him to Master Lely's studio in the first place.

I'd grant that Lord Middlesex's carriage was a good deal more elegant than Father's. It was smaller in the new French style, and sensibly made more for navigating narrow London streets than broad country highways. With the body of the carriage studded with polished brass nail heads and the red-spoked wheels lavishly trimmed in gold, I'd no doubt that we would receive a much better reception when we passed through the palace gates.

But as soon as we both climbed inside I realized that the fashionably smaller carriage would also mean that I'd be squeezed snug beside Lord Middlesex. His Lordship was a large man, grown larger still over the years since I'd first met him, and while I tried to shrink my smaller self into the corner of the seat, his hamlike thigh still pressed unavoidably against my leg and his brocade-covered arm pressed into mine. The sensation of over-closeness only increased when His Lordship complained of the sun in his eyes, and ordered the footman to unlash and lower the leather shades over the carriage's windows.

"Is Her Ladyship well?" I asked, knowing I'd be expected to make conversation.

"She's well as can be," he said blandly, "and perfectly content with her daughters in Essex."

I couldn't help but raise my brows at that. His wife, Mary, had once been among the most flirtatious and seductive ladies of the Court and had always been a close friend to Lady Cleveland; I doubted very much she'd ever be content set aside alone in the country with only two young daughters for company.

Clearly her husband, however, would rather discuss me. "I wonder that a young lady like yourself has waited so long to be painted by Lely."

I opened my fan, the air in the carriage already too still. "I'd likely be waiting still if Father had not wished it so."

"He was wise to insist," he said with more seriousness than I felt the subject deserved. "Every father would wish his daughter's beauty preserved and recorded, especially by the same artist who paints His Majesty."

I glanced at him sideways, not sure whether he was teasing me or not. He'd never been among those who'd lavished me with false-hearted praise for beauty I knew I did not possess, or at least he hadn't before this.

"'Preserving' sounds as if you mean to put me up in an earthen pot with oil and sweet herbs, to hold against next winter," I said. "What I rather believe is that Father hopes some hapless bachelor gentleman will see my portrait and fall rapturously in love with the image that Master Lely will create, and then make Father an offer for my hand before my unlovely self appears to fox the proposal."

He laughed as I'd hoped he would, tipping his head back so I could see how the soft flesh beneath his chin shook with his amusement. "I cannot say whether you or your father fares worse from that duplicitous little prediction."

I laughed with him over the top of my fan. "And what of Master Lely, my lord? You must include him in your judgment. His picture will be the cause of the entire deceit."

"Indeed!" he exclaimed, his face filled with approval. "You have always been of a forthright wit, Katherine, even as a child. I'm glad of it, too."

"You are, my lord?" I asked, surprised again.

"Yes," he said, his laughter subsiding as his gaze remained uncomfortably intent upon me. "Yes."

"Yes," I repeated warily, for I'd no notion of what else to say.

He nodded firmly, as if to signify some momentous decision. "Your father says you've no wish to wed," he said. "Is that true?"

I'd not expected that at all. "What is true, my lord," I said carefully, "is that I've yet to find a gentleman worth my love and freedom."

"Or your money," he added, ever the cynic. "You don't follow after Lady Hobart, do you?"

"Lady Hobart?" I repeated, incredulous, and snapped my fan shut. Lady Frances Hobart was known to be a disciple of Sappho, and worse, to have preyed upon the younger maids of honor in her care when she oversaw their lodgings in Whitehall. "Faith, my lord, of all the slanders that have been hurled at me, surely that is the most outrageous!"

He smiled slowly, a wolfish smile that did little to reassure me. "Then you prefer to trust your pleasure to a gentleman's cock?"

"You amaze me, my lord," I said as evenly as I could. "My father would have your head if he heard you speak so to me."

"This does not concern your father, Katherine." He leaned close to me, and covered my knee with one thick-fingered hand. "I believe in being direct, my dear. My wife has grown wearisome and dull to me. You would be quite the opposite. You are not encumbered with an inconvenient husband or foolish dreams of love, and I suspect we would amuse each other quite thoroughly for a time."

"If you are direct, my lord, then I shall be so as well!" I cried, aghast. The old image of him with Nell rose again unbidden in my thoughts, how he'd grabbed at her and tore at her shift, his face contorted with lust, his hips bucking to drive into her. "For you to suggest this—this misalliance between us—"

"Don't refuse me." He turned on the carriage seat to face me, his hand tightly grasping my knee. "I can give you all you desire."

I tried to wriggle free, but he'd trapped me against the corner of the carriage seat.

"No, my lord," I said, turning my head away from him. "*No*."

"And I say yes." He caught my jaw in his hand and held it fast to kiss me, his mouth laboring hard across mine. My stomach churned with revulsion at the wrongness of it, and though I thrashed mightily beneath him, I could not escape, pinned beneath his far greater weight and size. When at last he released me, I scrambled as far away from him as I could.

"There," he said, breathing hard. "Hah, I cannot wait to tame you! I knew you'd be full of fire."

"Full of disgust is more true, my lord," I said furiously, wiping my hand across my mouth as if I could wipe away the indignity of what he'd done to me. "How could you treat me so, knowing me and my father as you do? How could you?"

"Pray recall who I am, Katherine," he said with an ominous smile, as if my wishes were nothing, which they likely were to him. "I want you. You'd please me."

The coach was slowing, and from the calls of the driver and the footmen I realized we'd reached St. James's. Lord Middlesex must have realized it, too, to have stopped his assault when he had. God only knew how far he would have pressed his advantage if he hadn't feared the door opening on him with his breeches around his knees.

But then, perhaps it wouldn't matter to a peer, as His Lordship had just so kindly reminded me that he was, and I wasn't. It was likely just as well that he'd reminded me, too, because in my fury, my one thought was that he was a low, despicable man who wished me to become his whore.

"I can be generous," he continued, reaching for me again. "I promise you, you won't be disappointed."

"I won't be disappointed, my lord, not as you shall be," I said, each word sharp on my tongue. "Pray forgive me if I decline the honor of being your whore."

He scowled, his outstretched hand halted in the air between us. "Consider this well, Katherine. With your face, you can ill afford to be haughty, and I don't like to be denied."

I knew I was no beauty, but to have it flung back at me like any other base insult stung me even through my anger. Fleetingly I thought again of how Lord Middlesex had treated Nell, and how vituperative he'd been after she'd left his bed for the king's. Everyone in London had heard his slanders about her; they'd been impossible to ignore. Since my last exchange with Sir Carr, I'd tried to follow Father's counsel against making enemies, and Lord Middlesex would be a formidable enemy to make. But that was not reason enough to lie with a man I did not desire, or even like, especially given the pain it would bring my father.

Beside me the carriage door abruptly swung open, unlatched by an unwitting, startled footman, and I barely caught myself from tumbling out.

"Katherine, here," Lord Middlesex said, brusquely beckoning for me to rejoin him as if I were some wayward hunting dog. "Refuse me, and I'll make certain you'll suffer for it."

"And if I accepted, my lord," I said, "I would forever loathe myself. Good day, my lord."

With my skirts bunched in my hands, I clambered down from the carriage, ignoring the footman's offered assistance. With my back straight and my head high, I walked swiftly through the familiar brick arch of St. James's. I am sure the guards at the gate had witnessed my ungainly departure from Lord Middlesex's carriage, including our last exchange, and I was just as convinced they'd be describing it to their fellows as soon as they could. It couldn't be helped. At least Lord Middlesex had brought me here to the duke's household as he'd promised. Considering the circumstances, he could well have abandoned me unceremoniously somewhere in the middle of the park, or worse.

I hurried through the palace's old-fashioned halls, praying my gown didn't look as obviously crumpled and crushed as it felt to me. There was no time for repairs; I'd been expected to join Her Highness and her ladies for card play, and I was already late. I made myself think only of that, shoving aside the memory of what had happened to me with Lord Middlesex. At least St. James's, being used only by the Yorks in the summer, wasn't crowded the way that Whitehall was, and there was no one to see how I was nearly running, my petticoats flying about my ankles.

But by the time I'd climbed the last staircase, my anger had faded and my earlier bravado had begun to crumble. Like a leaf tumbled and tossed by the wind across the grasses, I'd no say at all in what Lord Middlesex had done to me. I had never encouraged his attentions in any fashion, or even so much as smiled at him flirtatiously, yet now I'd be the one who would be made to suffer. People would listen to him, and whatever tattle he said of me would be believed.

Even worse was knowing he'd believed I would fair leap at his offer because I was too ill endowed to expect better for myself. What woman wishes to hear that any man thinks her so woefully desperate? He'd wanted to possess me and tame me, as if I were no more than some dumb creature, as if my cleverness was something to be destroyed for his pleasure, rather than relished. And this, too, from a gentleman I'd known most of my life.

Yet what could I say in defense? I *was* plain. He was already married to a beautiful wife, with no need for a lady such as me. No one would believe it if I announced he'd tried to force his attentions on me, but they would happily accept that I'd been the attempted seducer.

With your face, you can ill afford to be haughty.

I swallowed back a small sob of frustration at my powerlessness. Who would question the word of a peer? He could invent whatever he pleased about me for the amusement of the Court, and be praised as a wit for it. I'd no real recourse at all. Father might urge me to be meek and accepting, but that was not my temper, and never had been.

Alas, my choices were few. I could leave Court entirely, and live a quiet, dull, tedious life in the country. Or I could persevere and be strong, and try my best to ignore what was said of me, no matter how hurtful it might be. But I wouldn't forget, and if fate ever offered me the ripe chance to pay Lord Middlesex back in kind, I would take it.

At last I reached the door to the duchess's quarters and announced myself to the guard. The door opened. I shook away my unhappiness and smiled, and entered to make my curtsy before Her Highness.

And I *would* be strong.

To my considerable relief, Lord Middlesex was soon after called away from London to Essex, where his father, Lord Dorset, had been taken grievous ill. Though I was sorry that this venerable gentleman was unwell, I was not at all unhappy that Lord Middlesex was now far removed from Court and unable to cause me mischief. It was not quite the avenging act that I'd longed for, but it would suffice for now.

I was heartened enough to tell Father, too, once Lord Middlesex was safely away. Though I know it may seem strange that I'd not confided the earl's unseemly proposal to my father at once, I'd guessed what his reaction would be, and as soon as I finally did tell him, I learned my guess had been right.

"What would you have me do, Katherine?" he said, more exasperated than sympathetic. I'd followed him into his library after supper, where he'd shed his heavy coat and waistcoat in favor of a light silk dressing gown, and traded his wig for an embroidered cap over his shaven head. "Rise before dawn to defend your honor on some damp and foggy field? Demand blood be spilled from one of my oldest friends because you behaved like an impudent little chit?"

"What of him?" I cried defensively. "Have you no fault to lay upon him for asking your daughter to be his whore?"

He looked at me as if I were daft, and impatiently shoved his cap back on his head. "What else do you expect, Katherine? If Middlesex weren't at fault, then there'd surely be some other rogue in his place. You're nearly twenty years of age, with seemingly no interest in marriage."

"Because I've yet to find a gentleman worthy of my interest!"

"If ever such a paragon exists in this world," he said. "Husbands are flesh-and-blood creatures, Katherine. Even the immortal gods on Olympus had their flaws."

"Oh, yes, the same lustful, cuntstruck flaws as His Lordship," I retorted, "though at least Jupiter had the decency to transform himself into a more pleasing creature than Lord Middlesex—a swan, perhaps, or a bull—before he fell upon his hapless lady."

Father flung his hands heavenward in despair, a despair surely born of the arid years he'd spent with only Lady Sedley to warm his bed.

"There now, there is your answer," he declared. "'Cuntstruck'! So long as you insist on speaking as if you were born in a brothel, Katherine, you'll have gentlemen believing you reside in one."

Now I was the one who threw my hands up with sorrowful dismay.

"Who taught me to speak so, Father, not in a brothel, but in this very house? Who took me to the playhouse and bid me keep to the tiring room whilst you were in the back hall, serving some actress or another against the wall? Who amused his friends by teaching me as a girl to speak lewd rhymes and songs?"

He frowned and looked down, shaking his head with a stony solemnity at odds with the gay pink carnations stitched into his hat, and now sitting on his grim-cast brow. I waited for his answer, and waited more, for it was a question that I'd always longed to have explained to me, though until now I hadn't dared to ask it.

"Please, Father," I asked, more gently. "Why did you make me what I am if I am not now to your liking?"

But if I'd long wished his answer, I was sadly bound to wish longer still. As grieved as he was—and I knew him well enough to see and recognize the genuine unhappiness that marked his face—he could not bring himself to reply to my question, not with the truth I sought.

"You've always been strong-willed, Katherine," he said finally, without daring to raise his gaze to mine. "The only way you'll ever change is to find a man who is your match."

Bitter tears stung my eyes. "Am I such a disappointment to you as I am, Father?" I asked forlornly. "You, too, would wish me tamed, the same as Lord Middlesex?"

"No, Katherine, no," he said softly, drawing me gently into his arms. "Not tamed, but loved. Only loved as you deserve."

I FOLLOWED THE COURT TO WINDSOR when it retreated there, as the king chose to do every summer to avoid the London heat. From afar, it seemed as if everything was much as it had always been, with the usual rounds of country amusements and scandals. The queen kept her distance from the rest of the Court, and the Duchess of York was brought to bed of another frail, disappointing daughter. The king had made gossip more interesting by taking yet another new mistress, Hortense Mancini, Duchesse de Mazarin. This outrageous older lady (she was nearly thirty years in age) affected men's dress and swordplay, and had come from Italy to escape a mad husband by way of visiting her cousin Mary Beatrice. In addition to enjoying His Majesty's favors, Lady Mazarin was also whispered to be engaged in tribadism with Lady Sussex, the king's illegitimate daughter by Lady Castlemaine. It was all deliciously entertaining, and having Lady Portsmouth pouting over being neglected only added to the sport for the rest of us.

But to anyone with wit enough to look, things were not always as they'd once been for the Court, not even to me who was so young. That the duke now was a complete and practicing Papist was widely known, and the pretense of masking it from the rest of the world dropped. He and Her Highness and their Catholic attendants worshiped openly in the little chapel in St. James's, and their separate trains were now filled with priests and others of Romish orders. Further, the duke was now viewed by the French as an avid supporter of their causes, and the French ambassador was often seen in close and cunning discussions with him, without a breath of subterfuge.

So much popery did not sit well with most Englishmen. The duke remained the king's heir, and the king steadfastly refused either to set aside his barren queen for a fertile replacement, or to remove the duke from the succession in favor of one of his Protestant princesses, or even to send His Highness with his priests and incense away from England. As a result, the fear and suspicion of Papists rose everywhere, and the blind hatred I'd witnessed on Guy Fawkes Night grew into rampant violence. Anyone so much as rumored to be Romish dared not walk about London for fear of being attacked and beaten, or even killed. Even Lady Portsmouth's carriage was besieged, and there were cat-calling riots in the playhouse when she attended with her friends. For their own safety, the duke and duchess themselves were seldom seen as publicly as they'd once been, and even the king was no longer cheered with the same enthusiasm on account of his tolerance.

Because my mother and her family had worshiped as Catholics, I had no fear of Rome or priests, and though I believed that many of their rites and rituals were overwrought and foolish, I didn't feel myself in any danger from them. But even I became uneasy when I read the pamphlets and newssheets that were so popular. Full of lurid hysteria, the anonymous writers warned of Jesuit plots to seize London and the English throne for the Pope, of invading armies of French and Italian Papists determined to destroy everything the common Englishman held most dear. Churches would be burned, and all Protestants would be forced to convert, and any who resisted would be tortured, raped, and murdered in the most gruesome ways possible. At the helm of all this villainous mayhem was perceived to be the Duke of York, lurking in wait behind his brother's throne. Was it any wonder that the prayers for the continued health of His Majesty were read with enthusiastic fervor each Sunday in Protestant churches across his kingdom?

Some of this discontent had risen up in the few years whilst England and Catholic France had briefly been allies against the Protestant Dutch led by their stadtholder (and yet another relative to the English royal family as the king's nephew), William of Orange, an alliance that had found few supporters beyond the palace. It was one thing for the king and his brother to have kind feelings for the French King Louis, seeing as how they were cousins with shared blood, but the rest of us English had been born regarding the French as our mortal enemies, and so it had been for more generations than I could count.

But gradually, Parliament had prevailed, and forced the king and his ministers to back away from supporting Catholic France and return to a Protestant alliance with the Dutch, beginning with the signing of the Peace of Westminster. England now sat in the unfamiliar situation of peacemaker between the other two countries, with the duke pressing for the French interests and the king inclining toward the Dutch and his nephew William. And that, truly, was how it stood, a choice between the two royal brothers: the Protestant king and the Catholic duke who would succeed him. For most Englishmen, it would have been an easy enough choice to make.

From my place in the circle around Her Highness, the duke did not appear the Romish fanatic that the broadsides painted him to be. Instead I saw a man who had chosen to follow his conscience to worship as he felt best for him, and who would risk even a crown for it. I couldn't agree with his choice, but I did admire the way he stood fast in his convictions, an admirable trait indeed considering how most other gentlemen at Court (including the king) concerned themselves with their own idle pleasures and little more.

This is not to say that the duke abstained from dalliance; though he showed respect and regard for the duchess, he also was still visiting Arabella Churchill and several other ladies in passing. Of course, he'd far too many concerns of his own to take more notice of me, but that didn't stop me from imagining all the amusing things I might say or do to ease his burden and raise his spirits. Long ago he'd said he liked clever women; if he'd but notice me, he'd soon discover I was exactly that.

Thus by the fall of 1676, our little world around the duke and duchess felt curiously unsteady. It was like walking on ice: around us everything might seem bright and full of beauty, yet the surface beneath us was slippery, and threatened further by the occasional ominous crack to remind us that nothing was as secure as it seemed. For me, too, there was even more to unsettle me. Two gentlemen who'd been away from Court came back, each to disturb my peace in very different ways.

The first to return was Lord Middlesex, his father having sufficiently recovered. At first he paid scant attention to me, acknowledging me with a brusque nod and no more. I suspected Father had spoken to His Lordship to be kind to me, though he'd never admit it. Inwardly I rejoiced to have been spared; but my celebration was premature, as I later was sadly to learn.

But as for the other gentleman—ah, that was an entirely different matter.

On a bright morning in November, I sat in a carriage with several other ladies of the Court on the edge of the parade ground in Hyde Park, there to watch the muster of the Guards. The day was chill, with a sharp breeze to steal away the last golden leaves from the trees and swirl them across the dulling grass. Clouds burdened the sky overhead, yet still from above streamed that rare, silvery, clear light of late autumn. Many of the ladies had decided not to venture out at so early an hour, preferring their own hearths or downy beds to a chilly parade, but I never could resist the spectacle of gentlemen in scarlet coats. Besides, though England was not at war at present, many of our officers continued to serve in foreign regiments, and as I watched the well-executed exercises before us now, I thought wistfully of James Grahme. Despite his marriage, he'd soon returned to fight with the French against the Dutch, and I still prayed for his safety in battle.

"Such a brave show," Lady Orton said beside me, leaning from the window to watch. "I vow there are few things finer than a martial display."

"I should like it a good deal better without the gunfire and shouting," said her friend Mrs. Boynton with a sigh. "Gentlemen do enjoy their racketing, don't they?"

But something else had caught Lady Orton's eye. "Mark you, there's Lieutenant-Colonel Churchill, there on horse. I'd not seen him since he's returned from France. What a pretty fellow he is!"

I looked, and smiled, too. John Churchill *was* a pretty fellow, and an ambitious one as well. He'd not only succeeded in his military career—to be made lieutenant-colonel at twenty-six was a rare accomplishment—but equally at Court. Part of this came from being Arabella Churchill's younger brother (for surely she'd asked for favors on his behalf), and more from his own natural gifts and good fortune. He was one of His Highness's gentlemen of the bedchamber and had been sent on several diplomatic missions to France. Yet what we ladies noted more was his manly grace in the saddle with his golden hair ruffling over his shoulders, and how well his red coat fit across his shoulders, and how, to our joyful surprise, he was riding to our coach.

"My lady," he said, raising his laced hat. "Mrs. Boynton, Mrs. Sedley. Your servant, ladies. His Highness sends his compliments, and his appreciation for such a showing by you this morning. If there is anything I might explain about the muster, I pray you shall ask me."

"You are most generous, sir," Lady Orton said, giving him a mighty lascivious look. "I'm sure you'll be most obliging."

Because the colonel had been one of Lady Castlemaine's lovers (and likely the father of her last bastard) and had shown himself to appreciate ladies of an age greater than his own, the older ladies like Lady Orton were in turn quick to show their appreciation of him.

But to my surprise, he smiled not at her, but at me. "Mrs. Sedley," he said, his gaze warm. "While I was last in Paris, I had the honor of speaking with Captain Grahme, who asked to be remembered to you."

"Thank you, sir," I said. It was a fine thing to be remembered by James, but also a bittersweet one, and I realized I'd much rather smile at John Churchill than to think overmuch about James Grahme. "What news do you have of Paris?"

"Oh, a thousand things, Mrs. Sedley, great and small," he said lightly, his manner most charming. When he smiled, he'd dimples, quite unexpected in a warrior of his reputation. "Do you like Paris?"

"I cannot say, sir, having never visited it myself," I admitted. "But I've heard so much praise of the city from others that I long to see it."

"If you'd but grant me to sit by you tonight at the palace, Miss Sedley," he said, "then I promise I'll tell you even more."

"I should like nothing better, sir." I smiled, pleased beyond measure by his attention.

"I shall count the minutes," he said with such burning gallantry that, after he'd bid us farewell and left us for the next coach on his errand, the other two ladies regarded me with new (and grudging) regard.

"It would seem the colonel has an interest not in Paris, but in you, Mrs. Sedley," said Lady Orton archly.

I blushed. "I venture the colonel is interested in many things, my lady."

"Many things, but only one other lady," Mrs. Boynton said. "I've heard he's a powerful interest in little Mrs. Jennings."

I'd heard rumor of that, too. Three years younger than I, Sarah Jennings was one of the duchess's maids of honor and close friends to the Lady Anne. She was fair enough, but she had a righteous fine opinion of herself coupled with such a lack of humor that I found her company tedious.

Lady Orton must have felt the same. "Oh, Sarah Jennings," she said with a disdainful sniff of dismissal. "A foolish snip, that one. I've heard that though the colonel pressed his attentions, she would not oblige, putting marriage as the price on her maidenhead, and told all who would listen of it, too."

"Mrs. Jennings did that to a gentleman like the colonel?" asked Mrs. Boynton, titillated. "She dared refuse him, a gentleman so amorous that he could satisfy Lady Castlemaine?"

"It doesn't matter whether Mrs. Jennings did or she didn't," Lady Orton said severely. "Her father is nothing, and she hasn't a farthing to her name."

I listened, and inwardly I rejoiced. Everyone knew my father, and I'd a good deal more than a farthing to my name. That, and my ability to make most any gentleman laugh at will, could go far to overcome Mrs. Jennings's golden ringlets.

"Colonel Churchill is well rid of the Jennings girl," Lady Orton continued, "and if he now desires to speak of Paris with Mrs. Sedley, then that is his perfect right."

Whether it was his right or not, John Churchill did speak to me of Paris that night, and a thousand other things besides. He'd so much to say, in fact, that he sought my company the next evening when we were all gathered in the Banqueting House at Whitehall to hear a singer visiting from Venice, and he found me again the following night, and the night after that. He was an ambitious gentleman with heady plans for his future, and the sizable gifts to make those plans possible. But John was no dry, dull soldier. He was also intelligent, with a dry wit, and so pleasing that when at last he kissed me, I welcomed it.

Still and all, I had learned the pain of loving too swiftly with James Grahme, and as much as I enjoyed John's company, I was determined to give my mended heart away again with only the greatest care.

Yet when, in December, Father told me with great excitement that John's parents, Sir Winston and Lady Churchill, had written to make overtures for a match, I dared to consider my future with John in it. Finally I gave Father my consent to begin negotiations, with his old friend Henry Savile acting as the intermediary between Father and Sir Winston. I knew they'd be arduous, since Father would insist on the terms being as favorable to me as possible, while the Churchills, being impoverished gentry, would do their best to wrestle the most they could from Father for their son. I agreed with John not to announce our betrothal until this dry work was done. I wasn't offended; this was how matches were arranged, and it was time. I'd pass my nineteenth birthday before the year ended, more than of a marriageable age.

"It's clear enough that we suit each other, Katherine," John said to me one frosty night. He'd taken me to the privy garden where we'd be alone except for the ghostly stone statues that seemed to shiver above the empty beds. "At least I pray it's as clear to you as it is to me."

I laughed softly. We stood close together with our arms inside each other's cloaks, warm and snug in our embrace, and when I looked up at John, I saw the heavens full of stars above him.

"Of course you suit me, you wicked devil," I said, my words in the icy air showing as little clouds before my face. "Surely you must know that."

He chuckled. "I'd be a considerable fool not to, my darling."

"Then do you love me, too?" I demanded, daring greatly. "Do you?"

He smiled, full of tenderness. "How could I not love you?"

I closed my eyes and pressed my face against his breast, my heart overflowing with joy. To be loved, to be loved; truly, that was all I'd ever wanted.

"My own dear Katherine," he said tenderly, and when he turned his face up to kiss me, ah, I believed it. Every word, every kiss, every lie: I believed it all.

Chapter Twelve

WHITEHALL PALACE, LONDON
January 1677

As soon as Twelfth Night and the Christmas season was done, the duchess startled everyone by announcing she would host a grand ball in the Banqueting House at Whitehall at the end of the month. I say that we were startled, for the second half of January was usually a time for quiet and recovery from the boisterous celebrations of earlier in the month, and not for further entertainments. Which was not to say the Court faulted Her Highness for her plans; rather, we embraced them with a near-feverish gratitude, relieved that we'd now have one more large festivity to anticipate amidst the long, dark nights of winter.

In Her Highness's quarters, there was endless chatter of who would wear what, and who would dance with whom, as was always the case before a ball. Among those helping Mary Beatrice make her plans was her cousin (and the king's new mistress), the Duchess of Mazarin. Together the two Italian ladies sat as close to the enormous fire as they could, never having accustomed themselves to our English cold. But where our duchess swaddled herself in furs and quilted petticoats to keep warm, Lady Mazarin wore a man's plush breeches and high flopping boots for riding, even to the thick stockings and spurs. She was a tall, immodest woman, anyway, with a strong Roman beauty, and in these clothes she appeared more manly than a number of gentlemen I could name in our Court. Yet for being so outspoken, she was also very charming, and could coax those around her to laugh even after she'd sworn at them in a half dozen different languages.

"You will wear a gown to my ball, Hortense, won't you?" Mary Beatrice asked anxiously, pulling her fur-lined cloak more closely around her shoulders. "You will promise me to dress like a lady?"

Lady Mazarin laughed, idly tapping her fingers against her goblet of wine. "And what if I do not, Cousin?"

Her Highness's eyes widened. "If you don't, why, then no one will know how to regard you. Should ladies dance with you, or gentlemen?"

"I should dance with them all," Lady Mazarin declared, "and enjoy myself twice more than anyone else, for I shall have twice as many partners."

As if to demonstrate, she tipped back her head and began to sing some droll little tune; she did have a lovely voice, and often accompanied herself on the Spanish guitar. "Dorinda, *ma bellissima* Dorinda—but wait, Dorinda is here, is she not?"

"Dorinda?" asked Mary Beatrice. "There is no lady by that name here."

I guessed something was amiss when I heard the smothered, sniggering laugh from one of the maids of honor who were playing cards at a table near the window, though I scarce could have known who they meant.

"Oh, she is, *cara*, she is," Lady Mazarin said with a throaty chuckle. She swung her long legs around, the rowels on her spurs jingling, and turned to face the group of us ladies who sat on low cushioned stools around them. "There she is, there. The most famous Dorinda!"

To my thorough surprise, she was pointing at me.

"I, Your Grace?" I said. "Forgive me, but I fear you have confused me with another. My name is not Dorinda, but Katherine. Katherine Sedley."

But she only nodded, her mane of unpinned black curls bouncing around her face. "Then you *are* one and the same with this Dorinda. Lord Middlesex himself told me so, that though he'd employed a classical name as a poetical conceit, it was meant to be you. He said you were the inspiration for his latest little satire."

"A satire by Lord Middlesex, Your Grace?" I said warily, already dreading the very worst. "He said I was his inspiration?"

"Yes, yes, I know it was your name that he said," she insisted. "Katherine Sedley. All who were there recognized it at once. Oh, how His Majesty did laugh and laugh to hear it last night, when His Lordship recited it for our amusement!"

Mary Beatrice sighed with disappointment. "I wish I had been there to hear it as well. Lord Middlesex is a very clever, witty gentleman."

"His Lordship can also be a very malicious gentleman, ma'am," I said, unable to help myself as my cheeks grew hot in woeful anticipation. "His words can be sharp as piercing barbs."

"But that is the nature of a good satire, Mrs. Sedley, isn't it?" Lady Mazarin said, searching through the pockets of her gentleman's waistcoat. "I'm sure I have a copy of it somewhere about my person, writ out for me by Middlesex. I know you are a lady of some wit yourself, and thus able to recognize the genius in another's work. Ah, here it is."

Triumphantly she unfolded the small crumpled sheet, and behind me another lady giggled. Had the entire Court already heard this "little satire"? Was I the last?

Lady Mazarin cleared her throat and began to read aloud.

Dorinda's sparkling Wit and Eyes,
United, cast too fierce a light,
Which blazes high but quickly dies,
Warms not the heart but hurts the sight.

Love is a calmer, gentler Joy,
Smooth are his looks, and soft his pace;
Her Cupid is a Black-Guard boy
That runs his Link full in your face.

To no surprise, every lady in the room laughed at the poem, and at my expense, too. How could I have believed Lord Middlesex would not avenge himself toward me? I was too perfect a target for him to let pass. For His Lordship to discredit the brightness of my dark eyes, to say I was so ugly that he couldn't bear to gaze at me, to claim I was too harsh to be favored with love—oh, yes, he was determined to make me suffer for refusing him. Lord Rochester had once described Lord Middlesex as having the worst-natured muse in England, and here surely was the proof. He must have spent all the time he was in the country with his father polishing these few withering lines so that every one of them would draw blood.

Yet somehow I found the strength to smile. To do otherwise would be exactly what Lord Middlesex wished, and to spite him I'd keep far more pain than this my secret. And if my wit were my one defense here at Court, then, as Father had warned me, I must be prepared to accept my battle-scars in return.

Besides, I'd find no allies here. I wasn't exactly scorned by Her Highness—she was too generous and well bred to give slights—but I'd never won her full favor as I'd hoped, either. In truth, it shouldn't have surprised me. The company of my own sex was seldom as pleasing to me as that of gentlemen, and in turn most other ladies often found my wit too sharp for their tender sensibilities. By way of snide retaliation, they'd try to wound me first, and clumsily fault my lack of womanly beauty as a lack of worth. There would be plenty in this room who would see my plainness as a fit reason enough for Lord Middlesex to mock me, and enjoy each poisonous word.

"You must agree that it's as pretty a satire as ever you've heard, Mrs. Sedley," Lady Mazarin said, amusement still ruffling through her voice. "Or should I call you Dorinda?"

"I believe I'll continue with my own name, ma'am," I said quickly. Once before His Lordship had inflicted a nickname upon me (the loathsome "Little Sid's Kid"), and I prayed desperately that this one would not stick to haunt me, too. "Surely it's better to be named for a blessed saint than by a satirical poet."

"I should think it rather an honor to have a poetic name, like Phyllis or Silvia," Mary Beatrice said almost wistfully. "Or Dorinda. But tell me, Mrs. Sedley. Have you scorned Lord Middlesex, to inspire him so, or is it only another conceit?"

"Oh, I would venture it's only a conceit," Lady Mazarin said before I could answer for myself. "Another lady asked that question last evening, which only made His Lordship sigh so hugely that we laughed again. But as His Majesty reminded us, Lady Middlesex is such a rapturous beauty that he'd never have reason to wander. It is clear that the poem is only a satire on a true lover's poem."

Still I smiled, my mouth as stiff as if it were carved from wood. It would seem that the notion of me tempting Lord Middlesex was so hideously laughable that he'd only to attach my name to his poem for the rest of the Court to understand the satire. If only John Churchill and I had already made our betrothal common knowledge, then no one would be laughing. If only he were here with me now as my intended husband, then they'd all see that I was desirable enough to win a handsome, gallant lover for myself.

"Then it must be true," Her Highness said thoughtfully, accepting the hateful explanation as all the others did, too. "But explain if you will one more thing. What, pray, is a 'Black-Guard boy'?"

"If you please, ma'am, there's little reason for you to know about the Black-Guard boys," said one of the maids of honor. From where I sat, I couldn't see which it was; not that it was of much interest to me, considering how they were all so much alike in their pathetic desperation to please.

"They're always lolling at the back of the palace and near the Horseguards' Parade, ma'am," the maid of honor continued. "Packs of unkempt, foulmouthed boys who, for a coin, will take a horse to be watered, or, after darkness has fallen, light the way with their vile, smoky links."

"True, ma'am, all true," murmured another lady, languidly stroking the long-eared spaniel in her lap. "Those rascally boys are the vilest creatures imaginable."

"Yes, my lady," continued the maid of honor in her cheerful, high voice, refusing to be deterred. It was almost as if she were making a school-room recitation, she was that determined to finish, whether we wished to hear it or not. I certainly didn't, serving as it did only to heap more insult upon me by way of this infamous Dorinda. My first surprise and shame was now matched with my rising indignation, and I labored to keep my face pleasant and my temper under control. I'd long ago learned that Her Highness had no tolerance for oaths, anger, or other wicked talk among the ladies in her company, and as tempting as it was now to give voice to my outrage, I knew it would be a disastrous mistake, and possibly an end to my welcome in her presence.

Not, of course, that the impudent young maid of honor cared.

"They're known as Black-Guard boys, ma'am," she continued, "on account of the dirtiness of their persons and their oaths. To have one serve as Dorinda's mercenary Cupid, brandishing his link like a pike, shows exactly how despicable and false a lover she must be."

"Indeed!" exclaimed Her Highness, impressed by this spiteful scrap of nothing. "It would seem that Lord Middlesex must have chosen his symbols with the greatest concern for their effect."

"Yes, ma'am," the maid said, milky-sweet. "His Lordship has much talent."

"He does," the duchess said, smiling with the oblivious indulgence that royalty showed to their favorites like this maid, a kind of favoritism that I'd never receive, no matter how hard I tried. But this lady had become as much a pet as the spaniels curled at the duchess's feet; there was no doubt of it. Her Highness would never have let her prattle on so long if she weren't. "We thank you for enlightening us as to this sordid aspect of the poem, Mrs. Jennings."

Mrs. Jennings, I thought with surprise: the maid of honor whose name had once been bound with my John's. I'd not expected that. Mary Beatrice rose, determined to go walking through the palace with her cousin, and continue their conversation with more privacy. Respectfully we all stood to curtsy, and one by one and according to our rank, we followed after Her Highness.

At last I could see Sarah Jennings, and what was more, I saw how she was looking at me. No, not looking, but staring, her gaze twisted into a fearsome scowl and her plump red lips pinched so tightly together that they'd nearly vanished. The ferocity of her expression shocked me, especially in a girl of seventeen, yet now I understood why she'd been so determined to explain Lord Middlesex's slander of me to Her Highness. No matter what John might believe of how he and Mrs. Jennings had parted, I saw at once that she still cared for him, and worse, that she considered me to be a fixed rival.

I'd only a moment to consider how best to cope with this astonishing revelation. The other ladies were moving swiftly before me, their silk skirts *shushing* against the frame of the open door. Because my father was a baronet and of a higher rank than Mrs. Jennings's, I would precede her through the door. I took my place, and as I passed her, I nodded in her direction, the smallest (and safest) acknowledgment I could make. But that wasn't sufficient for Mrs. Jennings.

"Mind your Black-Guard Cupid," she whispered as I passed. "*Dear* Dorinda."

I looked at her sharply, but she was smiling now as if nothing was amiss. I let it pass, and answered nothing. Yet what she'd said had troubled me mightily, and I could scarce wait to share my concerns later that evening with John. I waited until we were alone late that night, together in my carriage, where I was certain we'd not be overheard.

"You worry overmuch about Sarah," he said, his voice low and calming. "She is a passionate woman, and given to jealousy."

"She's also one of the duchess's little pets," I said, unable to help myself. "She as much as licks Her Highness's hand. Did you know that?"

"She has no fortune, and does what she must." John sighed. "Do not think of her, Katherine. Nothing more will come of it than this, I promise you."

"But if you had heard how she went on and on about that scurrilous poem, as if to poison Her Highness against me—"

"Hush, hush, sweet," he said, kissing me lightly by way of distraction. "I tell you, it matters not. Sarah is of no consequence to you. What concerns me far more is the great dislike Lord Middlesex bears you. Isn't he a friend of your father's? What would possess him to write such a piece about you?"

I sighed, wishing that in the darkened carriage, I could see more of John's face to judge his mood. I'd never told him about what Lord Middlesex had proposed and I'd rejected; not that I wished it to be a secret, for I was hardly at fault, but simply because I hadn't seen the purpose to describing an event that was so long in the past. Now I explained as best I could what had happened between Lord Middlesex and me, and how he'd taken my refusal as a great and personal affront. I'd feared that John might in turn take offense on my behalf and behave in a foolishly gallant way as gentlemen too often do, pledging his sword in the name of my honor, but this was not at all his response.

"Lord Middlesex has much influence with His Majesty, Katherine," he said. "I cannot believe you would anger him like this over nothing."

"Over nothing?" I exclaimed. "Faith, would you rather I'd let him rape me instead?"

"No, no," he said quickly. "But surely, Katherine, there must have been a way to decline his offer without causing such grave offense. I cannot imagine what words you must have used that His Lordship would take so much trouble now to reply to you this way."

I shifted away from him on the seat. "I used the words that were necessary to preserve my honor, John. When a man is determined to throw a lady's petticoats over her head, he is not inclined to hear a polite refusal. Even if he's a peer. *Especially* if he's a peer."

"I am serious, Katherine."

"I am, too, John." Disheartened, I sighed again, crossing my arms as I looked away from him and from the carriage window. I didn't wish to displease him, but his stand made no sense to me. "Here I feared I'd have to coax you from challenging His Lordship to a duel, and instead it seems as if you're faulting me for his ill-mannered behavior."

"I'm not faulting you at all," he said, drawing me back into his arms. "My dear Katherine! All I ask is that you take more care in what you say and do with gentlemen like Lord Middlesex. If you behave rashly, without forethought, then I will be affected by it as well. I wish for us to prosper at Court, my love. For us to succeed, as my wife you must add caution to your demeanor, and behave with more modesty, as befits your rank. There are expectations for a Churchill lady."

I glowered, far from happy with his response. "Oh, yes, the Churchill ladies. Likely your sister could advise me further on the proper manner in which to lift my skirts and spread my legs for whoring with the duke, as she has."

John made a low growl of displeasure. "Katherine, please. We are not speaking of Arabella."

"What a pity we are not," I said. "It would make for a far more interesting conversation than this one."

"Forgive me if I bore you, Katherine," John said. "But all I expect from you is that you act with more deliberation and grace than impulse. That's not so much to ask, is it?"

I sighed unhappily, torn between my own beliefs and my love for John.

"Is it?" he repeated. "Tell me if you think it so, for I'd rather know it now than learn it later."

Reluctantly I shook my head, not wanting to displease him further, and let him kiss and coax me into an agreeable reconciliation. I knew he had many ambitions for our future together—it was in truth much of his shining attraction for me—and I'd hate to be the cause of any misstep in his plans.

Yet even as I basked in the pleasure of his embrace, I couldn't entirely put aside my niggling fears. He'd faulted Sarah Jennings as being overly passionate, and now me for behaving rashly. Clearly if I wished to remain in his regard, I'd have to guard myself even more closely against impetuosity. If that was the price to secure John Churchill's love and my happiness, too, then I'd willingly pay it.

THE KING ALWAYS HELD HIS MOST important entertainments and balls in the Banqueting House, and it was a sign of how much he favored Her Highness (and, of course, of how much he enjoyed any manner of frolic) that he'd granted her the use of it for her ball tonight. As if to prove it further, His Majesty was seen to dance most every dance, with partners that included Her Highness, his elder niece the Lady Mary, his mistresses Lady Mazarin and Lady Portsmouth, and even Her Majesty.

The evening was barely half done, yet I myself had already considered it a success. Both Father and John had vowed I was the handsomest lady in attendance, and with their praise as well as a new mantua of deep blue French silk brocade with a pattern of pomegranates, I felt as close to being pretty as I likely ever would.

John and I danced often together, an elegant couple. Though there was still no formal settlement between my father and John's, word of our impending match had become known, and we received a heady share of compliments for our coming marriage. Even His Majesty had winked broadly, teasing me about how John and I would surely produce our own little troop of soldiers to bring glory to England, and promised us a generous wedding gift.

I was perhaps proudest of how I'd managed to avoid Lord Middlesex, exactly as I'd vowed to John I'd do, and though I did hear several "Dorindas" directed to me, they were sufficiently well meant and without malice that I could smile and accept them not as an insult, but with good-humored grace.

Sarah Jennings sat with the other maids of honor, clustered together around Her Highness's tall-backed chair. I knew she watched me dance with John, for I could feel her gaze burning upon us, as hot as the flames of the candles overhead. So determined was she to keep us in view that she didn't dance herself, though gentlemen asked her and were rebuffed. And I—I did not care a fig.

Now I stood to one side to catch my breath between dances, having released John to speak to several other officers in attendance. Though outside it was a chill January night, in the hall the air was warm and heated with the crush of so many people and so much flirtation. Lord Rochester had come to keep my company; though he claimed he was too weary to dance, his wit was as sharp as ever, and to hear his remarks on the others around us made me laugh like the old days.

"Your father has told me this night that you're to wed Colonel Churchill," he said, taking me by surprise. "Is that true, or only another of Little Sid's idle fancies?"

"It should be true, my lord," I said, laughing softly. "John has asked me, and I have accepted, and now it's only the settlements that must be arranged."

He made a long face, as if smelling something disagreeable. "Oh, aye, the settlements. They're the true heart of every marriage, aren't they? Who can lay more waste to whose fortunes, and love be hung and damned."

"Pray don't be such a cynic, my lord," I said, giving his arm a gentle shove. "It's not pleasing to a bride."

"Hah, mind the wine, my dear, mind the wine," he said, raising his arm to make a show of protecting his goblet. Father sadly claimed it was as much a surfeit of wine as the pox that was slowly killing his friend, and when I watched how greedily he emptied the goblet and then thrust it out for a passing footman to refill, I could well believe it. He drank again, and seemed to find some comfort in it, for all that his hand continued to shake as he winked at me.

"You can chide me all you wish as a bride, Katherine," he said, "but it's your groom who concerns me at present."

"John?" I asked, bemused. "Whatever is there to concern you about him?"

"What is there not?" He smiled, but without any humor. "I know your father regards him as a prize, but I've my doubts."

"You shouldn't," I said in ready defense. "He's already achieved so much for a gentleman his age, and he's only begun his career."

"I'll grant you that he's brilliant when it comes to his own gain," he answered. "It's the more noble qualities that are lacking in the rogue. Consider how he treated my cousin Barbara, no paragon herself. He wheedled five thousand gold crowns from her in return for warming her bed, then left her with a bastard brat that he still won't own as his. Thank God His Majesty showed himself the greater gentleman and let Barbara pin the babe on him, else she would have been thoroughly disgraced and ruined."

He smiled drolly, for his cousin Barbara was the Duchess of Cleveland, and she'd borne so many bastards to the king that one more or less would make no difference to anyone. But I understood his warning. Even now, John spoke openly of Her Grace's immense gift to him as somehow his by right, rather than by the lady's fond generosity, and shrugged away any question of accepting responsibility for the child he'd sired on her. Neither posture showed him well, but like any dazzled lover, I was willing to explain it all away.

"He has many fine qualities, my lord," I said. "If you knew him, you'd see for yourself. His Highness has just recommended him to King Louis as the most qualified to command an English royal regiment in French service."

But His Lordship remained unconvinced. "Has he made you any gifts, such as one does with a betrothed?"

"No," I admitted reluctantly. "Not as yet. But then, his father is so far in debt that John has little ready money of his own, and must employ nearly all he earns to restoring the estate."

"Yet I'd wager five guineas that you've remembered him after some fashion."

"Small tokens, yes." I blushed for myself, not John. The small tokens had not been small at all, but a pair of costly Italian pistols with silver-wire inlays that John had admired in the window of a gunsmith. I'd later bought them for him as a surprise, and though he'd been delighted to receive them, he'd yet to reciprocate with so much as a posy of flowers from Covent Garden.

"No matter how small your tokens were, I'd wager his were smaller still, so small that a mite would find shame in them." Over the rim of his goblet, His Lordship studied me with pity, clearly guessing all I hadn't said. "But then, that's handsome Colonel Jack, isn't it? Shameless, blameless, and full of avarice."

"You're unkind, my lord," I said, even as the flush on my cheeks deepened.

"No one's ever said otherwise," he agreed, and smiled, the same beatific smile I'd first seen at Epsom now beaming from his ravaged face. "But take care before you yoke yourself forever to Jack and ambitions, my dear. You're far too clever to play camp follower to anyone."

For no reason at all I felt tears sting my eyes. Before they betrayed me, I took my leave from the earl and began across the crowded hall to rejoin John. Being as slender as I was, it was not an easy progress for me, and I was forced to dodge this way and that among the scores of others, excusing myself over and over as I hunted for John's scarlet coat. I'd only reached the center of the hall, not far from the little dais where the royal party was seated, when I first heard the man's mocking, braying voice, purposefully raised high to be heard over the rest of the voices and revelry.

"May all the gods on mighty Olympus preserve my sight!" he cried, fit more for the stage than here in the palace. "Here passes that ill-famed Gorgon, the notorious Dorinda!"

As if by arrangement (and perhaps it was), the courtiers stopped their conversations and stepped back and away to clear a wide swath before me. At the far end, His Majesty sprawled in his gilded armchair with Lady Mazarin on one side and Lady Portsmouth on the other, and yet all his interest seemed turned toward me as he grinned with wolfish anticipation of what would come next.

Come it did, too, in the apish, squat figure of Sir Carr Scroope, continuing the same declaration he'd already begun.

"It *is* Dorinda I spy before me!" he exclaimed, covering his face and howling piteously. "Oh, pray let this not be my last sight!"

Now I noticed Lord Middlesex, standing slightly behind the king. No wonder Sir Carr dared so boldly, with His Lordship to tug his puppet strings. It was not right to do this to me, nor was it fair. Yet this time my anger overwhelmed my shame, and I realized how mighty weary I was of playing the indulgent victim and meekly waiting to be struck again. It was time—no, past time—that I finally struck back on my own, and in that determined moment I forgot my promise to John to cause no scandal, and my vow to be only another pleasing lady to Her Highness. Instead I would be only myself.

"Dorinda, please, please spare my eyes," Sir Carr wailed, relishing the unfamiliar joy of making others laugh. "Oh, Dorinda, oh!"

"Hush, Sir Carr, cease your crying," I scolded with exasperation, as if he were no more than a petulant child. "Hush, and spare the rest of us the pitiful sight of a gentleman begging."

Now the laughter was for me, but Sir Carr refused to cede the attention yet. "Oh, oh, Dorinda, have mercy! Better to turn me to stone outright like the Medusa you are, and spare me my suffering!"

I sighed impatiently for effect, for in truth this exchange was now amusing me no end. "Why should you aspire to be made into stone, sirrah, when your wit is already more weighty than lead?"

"You scorn me, Medusa!"

"Medusa, Medusa," I said wearily. "This night I've paid a prodigious amount to a prating, prancing Frenchman, a coiffeur, to dress my locks, and the best you can say of his work is that it calls to mind an ancient head covered in snakes?"

That drew more laughter still as well as a smattering of applause, as any reference that denigrated Frenchmen was bound to do. But it had served its purpose, and won my audience for me. Better yet, I'd seized Dorinda away from Lord Middlesex and made her my own, boldly turning the name from an insult into a kind of raucous banner for my own use.

His courage fading, Sir Carr glanced uncertainly back to Lord Middlesex, a wordless appeal that didn't escape me. He'd wandered away from His Lordship's original poem and lost his way by mentioning Medusa (or perhaps Cupid and Medusa and Gorgons really were jumbled together as one in his overweening mind). Now he returned to it, doubtless recalled to his original purpose by the stony glance of Lord Middlesex.

"Turn your blazing face from my sight, oh, Dorinda," he said, covering his eyes again. "Do not blind me, and deny me forever the sight of real beauty."

"Then best cover all the looking glasses in your own house, Scroope," drawled Lord Rochester from within the crowd. "Your own monkey's face is pretty fair blazing, too."

Even the king laughed at that, thumping his palm on the arm of his chair to show his approval, and in desperation, Sir Carr tried another gambit altogether.

"By real beauty, I mean such as that of the fair lady who possesses my heart." He'd spotted the lovely Carey Frazier in the crowd, and to her mortification he now covered his breast with his hand and bowed low in her direction. "To be deprived of a sight such as that fair one would steal away my very reason for being."

I saw how unhappy this tribute made poor Mrs. Frazier, now the teasing target of those around her, and I resolved to speak not only in my own defense, but hers as well.

"If beauty alone could steal away your being, Sir Carr," I said, "then surely beauty would, and thus be spared the nuisance of your possession."

"Possession, Dorinda?" Lord Rochester asked, his voice rising with studied incredulity. "Possession implies completion, which in turn requires less toil by the heart and more from the cock. Oh, I do not believe that beauty has been much troubled at all."

The king roared with laughter at that and the rest roared with him, while Sir Carr was left to stand helpless, his face livid.

"Well spoke, my lord Rochester," I agreed, adding a graceful curtsy of acknowledgment. "Perhaps Sir Carr would wish to borrow one or two of my Black-Guard Cupids to assist him about his love's work. They're sturdy, upright fellows, equal to any task."

The laughter rose again, nearly drowning out Sir Carr's reply.

"You go too far, Mrs. Sedley," he sputtered. "By all the heavens, you are as vicious as your father and as mad as your mother."

I drew in my breath sharply at that. My father could defend himself (and doubtless would), but my poor mad mother did not deserve to be drawn into such a contest. No one but I cared, of course, and the jeering laughter continued, with my mother lost in the general mockery of Sir

Carr's manhood. I couldn't expect it to be otherwise. Once unleashed and set free, witty satire for amusement's sake is an impossible beast to contain, especially before an audience that was well eased by drink. Our ravening Court was not known for its kindness. The best (and perhaps the only) defense was to attack again, and with a careless little shrug to show my contempt, I smiled slowly, knowing I'd every ear in the hall bent toward me.

"You say I'm as vicious as my father, Sir Carr?" I said, as if mulling his judgment. "And as mad as my mother?"

"Every bit, you damned jade," he said, his own anger raging onward, confounded all the more by my show of calm.

"Here now, Sir Carr," the king said, surprising me as my champion. "Recall that Dorinda here is a lady, else you'll have Sir Charles to answer to as well as his daughter."

"Thank you, sir," I said, curtsying toward His Majesty with as much grace as I could. The king deserved my thanks: he'd unwittingly just set one last arrow in my bow, and it was most excellently sharp. "But at least *I* know that my father, though vicious, and my mother, though mad, were lawfully wed at my birth. Can you say the same, Sir Carr?"

"To the devil with you," he muttered, and threw himself so sharply away from me that he nearly staggered from the force of it. It was rusty old gossip that claimed Sir Carr's father had not been his mother's husband, so old that had not Sir Carr reacted with such violence now no one would have cared. But, as I'd suspected, he could not show any humor regarding his own history, and borne by his fury, he pushed himself into the crowd, shoving aside any who stood in his path. It was a grievous lapse for him not to wait for His Majesty's leave first, and an even worse one for him to show his back as he fled.

But the king was not a monarch who would fuss over protocol, especially not whilst laughing at Sir Carr's distress. Instead he asked that the music begin once again, and was chuckling still as he led Lady Mazarin (who was dressed in a woman's gown, doubtless to please Her Highness) to the head of the next set.

I, meanwhile, was swept up in a sea of well-wishers determined to compliment me on my wit and composure. I smiled and laughed, relishing my time in the glow of attention. But when Father came toward me, I saw at once that though his mouth was curved in his habitual smile, there was no happy content to be found in his eyes.

"Why did you do that, Katherine?" he demanded as he took me by the arm to lead me from the crowd to a small corner of quiet against the wall. "What demon possessed you, Daughter, to perform such a wanton, bold display?"

"It was only a frolic, Father," I protested. "Sir Carr began it, and I finished it. That was all."

"A frolic," Father repeated with dismay. "Have you forgotten everything I have told you, every warning and advice I have given you?"

I pulled my arm free. "It was only Sir Carr, Father. It signified nothing."

"What it signified is a great deal of trouble for you," he said sternly. "Sir Carr spoke with Lord Middlesex's support."

"I know," I said. "I saw him there, behind the king."

" 'Behind the king'; how blithely you speak it!" he exclaimed, incredulous. "Does that mean nothing to you? Where you stood, and who was there to watch your antics?"

I sighed impatiently. "I was before His Majesty and the rest of the royal party, and everyone else that could squeeze into the Banqueting House this night. But it's not as if I displeased the king, Father. You heard him laugh, and defend me, too."

"His Majesty also laughs when Nelly Gwyn dances jigs before him, and spins on her toes so her skirts fly above her garters," he answered grimly. "You are not Nelly Gwyn."

"I know I'm not Nelly." I looked up at him with the old coaxing slyness, one rascally Sedley to another. "But I *am* your daughter. Now tell me true, Father. I'd wager that you laughed along with His Majesty."

I saw he had; the corners of his mouth twitched even now with merriment and shone bright in his eyes, and there was admiration there, too, enough to make me grin.

"I knew it!" I crowed happily. "Faith, Father, I knew you'd—"

"Hold now, Katherine, hold," he cautioned, and the merriment vanished again. "In this, I'm of little consequence. What of Colonel Churchill? Have you forgotten the duty you owe to him? I cannot believe he would wish his future wife to stand before the Court to trade lewd insults with another gentleman and make the king laugh."

"Oh, Father," I cried softly, swept by sudden, panicking remorse. If I'd been possessed, it had been not by demons, but by Dorinda herself. How could I have become so delighted by my own little performance that I'd forgotten John entirely? How could I have forgotten the promises I'd made? "I must go to him at once. I must find him and explain."

"What you must do is beg for his forgiveness, and pray that he grants it," he said with concern, and my fears rose. "At least I did not see him in the hall during your little exchange. Of course, he shall hear of it—by morning everyone in London will—but if he didn't witness it for himself, perhaps you'll be able to persuade him your intentions were innocent."

My heart sank. How could I profess even a hint of innocence when I'd been making bawdy jests about cockstands and upright fellows?

"Quickly now, Katherine, go find him," Father urged, giving me a hasty kiss on the forehead for luck. "It's best he hears it all from you first."

I hurried away, searching for John's golden hair and scarlet coat in the crowded hall. Now the compliments I received on my wit felt empty and ill deserved, and I brushed them aside with scant acknowledgment. The heady pleasure I'd felt earlier was gone, replaced by a sick and guilty dread of what might happen next. What if my few moments of giddy fame tonight cost me my betrothal? I was almost certain John would not understand, no matter how much I explained, and sadly Father was right. My only hope would be to pray for forgiveness, and pray I did.

Still I could not find John, and with growing concern I asked one of his fellow officers if he'd seen him leave. The young lieutenant smiled and pointed toward the passage that led to the hall. This was a common place for people to repair when they wished for quiet conversation away from the music and dancing, and quickly I made my way along the shadowy passage, searching for John among those clustered beneath the infrequent wall sconces. I'd nearly reached the end when I heard his familiar dry chuckle from beneath the far side of the staircase, and eagerly I turned to join him.

And stopped. There beneath the staircase was John, and with him was Sarah Jennings. Her arms were looped familiarly around his shoulders as she lay back in the crook of his arm, while he was kissing her ardently with his hand covering the full swell of her breast. I'd already guessed that she remained in love with him, but to discover them together like this, in such fond embrace, left me no doubt that he still loved her as well.

"Sarah, Sarah, my life," he muttered, kissing the slender column of her throat. "My own love."

I must have gasped aloud or made some other sound that caught her attention, for even as he was kissing her, she opened her eyes and looked over his shoulder. Her gaze met mine, and she smiled, slowly, her rich triumph complete.

"My life, my own love"; John had never once called me that. I turned and staggered away, my eyes full of tears, and my heart—ah, after that moment, my poor shattered heart would never be the same.

Chapter Thirteen

WHITEHALL PALACE, LONDON
April 1677

The best that could be said of the end of my betrothal to John Churchill was that it was not as public a humiliation as it could have been. There was no spectacular quarrel at a ball, no wailing or fainting or threats of duels by outraged family. While my attachment to John likely ended that night at the duchess's ball when I discovered him with Sarah Jennings, the thing straggled and dragged through the winter like a torn petticoat trailing through a muddy street.

John, the cur, at first tried to pretend that nothing was amiss and that we'd continue exactly as we had. For the next month I tried to believe him, but my trust in him was gone, and with it my love had died as well. Willful blindness is a sad, sorry affliction, but the cure can be sudden enough. Once I'd seen Mrs. Jennings in John's embrace, I began to see a great many other things as well. She may not have loved him more than I, but she did love him more fiercely, and she was determined to fight for him in ways that I would not. Public fits of temper, withholding favors, and threats of every kind were all part of her arsenal, and while I might have had the approval of Sir Winston and Lady Churchill, Mrs. Jennings had gone further and made an alliance with Her Highness to help win John away from me.

It also became achingly clear that my fortune alone had made me a prize in his eyes, and that there was little else about me that pleased him. When word came that Mrs. Jennings's brother had died and she'd come into possession of a small inheritance (though a pittance compared to mine), the final impediment to their match was removed and the last withering hope of ours gave way. Mr. Savile ended his matchmaking negotiations with Sir Winston, John gave himself openly to Mrs. Jennings, and I—I was once again cast aside.

I had always been skeptical of marriage for how it seemed to benefit the husband much more than the wife. Now I resolved against it entirely, and swore to Father I wouldn't wed at all. As can be imagined, he was not pleased, and urged me to keep to my hunt. I insisted I was only seeing matters as they were: that I was nearly twenty, twice passed over, and with little wish to risk my heart again in love's games. Perhaps Lord Middlesex had been right, and my Cupid did have all the luck of a Black-Guard boy.

By way of consoling me, Father relented in his stand against me as a maid of honor, and when a place fell open in the queen's household, he submitted my name for consideration and pressed hard for my acceptance. But the queen was a pious, genteel lady, and sent word through others that she feared my bold manner and humor would disrupt the peace of her household. She already had Carey Frazier to deal with as a maid of honor, a challenge enough to respectability. Thus my application was rejected, and another, quieter lady chosen. While Father was furious on my behalf, I was almost relieved. I doubted the queen would have suited me any more than I would have suited her.

Alas, my relief was misinterpreted by others who wished me ill, and I was said to have scorned the place as beneath me. Now haughtiness was added to my other dubious qualities, and if bitterness grew in me as well, who could fault me for it?

Another sour lesson in the emptiness of matches and marriage soon presented itself not just to me, but the entire country. While for many months England had stood by in peace, the French under Louis had relentlessly continued their attacks upon the United Provinces, led by the Dutch William of Orange. For most Englishmen, this was inevitably perceived more as a conflict between Papists and Protestants, with the English king once again leaning uncomfortably close to his French royal cousin rather than his Dutch nephew.

Fifteen months had passed since the king had permitted Parliament to sit, a sinfully long time for the people to be held without a voice in their governing. When at last Parliament reconvened in early 1677, funds were voted to reinforce both the army and navy. In both the House of Lords and the Commons, sentiment against the French ran ever stronger, and support for the Dutch cause grew with each French victory. In April, the House of Commons audaciously asked the king to form a new Protestant alliance with Holland that would lead to a declaration of war against the French. Gentlemen are always bellicose, and though the grim memory of the last dismal war had scarce faded away, Parliament was already mad with battle fever, as if those fat lords and other members would be the ones to fire the great guns themselves.

But the king would have none of it. Choosing foreign allies and declaring wars were both royal prerogatives, and to punish Parliament for being so obstreperous, the king promptly prorogued the session again until July.

From his seat in the House, Father was in the thick of these discussions, and while he wished to support the king, as one old friend would for another, he had grown more and more resolved to support a purely Protestant England. Now he, too, longed for an assured Protestant alliance, if not for out-and-out war with France. The way Father explained it to me was that the king refused to declare war on the French until Parliament voted sufficient funds to support it, while Parliament, increasingly suspicious of the king's intentions toward the French, refused to vote funds until the king in turn declared war. Much of this Father blamed on the treasurer, Lord Danby, whom Father regarded with the greatest suspicion as a cold, conniving villain, unworthy of the king's great confidence in him.

But by the fall, the king had found another, less costly way to appease his Parliament and his Protestant subjects. As was usual, the king and much of the male Court repaired to Newmarket for the autumn meetings. Joining him was Prince William, whose presence was gleefully viewed as a strong sign of a coming Dutch alliance. It certainly couldn't have been for mere entertainment's sake. Though William of Orange shared the same lineage and blood as our king and duke, there could not be more different gentlemen. William was short and bent and in perpetual poor health, his eyes red-rimmed and his wheezing cough constant. There was little pleasing in his gaunt, hook-nosed visage, and less in his humor, and surely a more dour gentleman could not have existed. He seemed far older than his years and came without the slightest whiff of gallantry, which sat very ill in our merry Court. When he spent only a day with us in Whitehall before he traipsed off to Newmarket with the other gentlemen, none of us ladies who remained in London with Mary Beatrice (who was again heavy with child) were in the least disappointed.

But when the gentlemen returned to us, we soon learned much more had occurred in Newmarket beyond the usual heavy drinking, hunting, and horse racing. Though the Protestant pact anticipated by Parliament had not occurred, another sort of alliance was agreed upon, arranged primarily through the artful perseverance of Lord Danby, the king's most trusted minister. The duke's elder daughter, the Lady Mary, was to wed William as soon as it could be arranged. The groom decided the lady was sufficiently beautiful to be his wife, while the poor fifteen-year-old bride wept inconsolably for days when told her fate.

Unhappy though the Lady Mary might be, London was overjoyed with the coming union. The princess was next in line for the throne after her father, and there was considerable relief that she'd been wed to a Protestant prince instead of yet another Papist royal. Church bells rang out in celebration, bonfires were lit and guns fired, and countless healths were drunk to the young couple in countless taverns and ale-shops all over the country.

Joy was hardly the response from France. Louis was furious, accusing the king and duke of delivering the princess to his most mortal enemy. He claimed the match was as good (or as bad) as a lost battle to him, and the long-faced French ambassadors reported that the French king had raged and fumed for days when he'd heard of it—news that only served to fuel the celebrations in England.

Arranged for November 4, William's twenty-seventh birthday, the wedding was shamefully quick for a royal match. Part of this speed came from the groom's wish to return home to his responsibilities, and part, too, came from a round of smallpox making its perilous way through the palace. Several of the ladies had already been stricken, including the bride's sister, the Lady Anne, and while none had died as yet, it was considered prudent to keep the wedding company small.

Conducted in the Lady Mary's own chambers before only the family and a handful of well-chosen witnesses, the ceremony was a sad little affair, overseen by Henry Compton, the Bishop of London, to make it as purely Protestant as possible. The misshapen groom wheezed his impatience beside his much taller and more handsome bride, who continued to weep at her fate. Also weeping were the duchess and the queen, who likely recalled their own miserable weddings to grooms they had not known, and the only one with a suitably jocular demeanor had been the king.

Yet even His Majesty had been unable to make any sport of the traditional bedding that followed. To the horrified amusement of the rest of the Court, the groom was suitably put to bed beside his lovely new wife, yet refused to part with his coarsely knit woolen drawers. There was endless, riotous speculation as to the gloomy, dutiful fumbling that must have marked the consummation, but I'd only sympathy for the newly wed Princess of Orange. I'd experienced myself the disastrous result of yearning for a love match, but how much infinitely worse to be shackled to a stranger for life for the sake of politics!

Four days after the wedding, Mary Beatrice was delivered of a healthy, well-formed boy, who was at once baptized as an Anglican at the insistence of the king and the distress of the parents, who would rather have consigned his mortal soul to the Pope. Named Charles to honor his royal uncle, he was likewise given the unlucky title of Duke of Cambridge, the same title granted to the duke's first three sons by his first duchess, all of whom had died before they'd had a chance to live.

A healthy son and heir to the throne had been so long desired that celebration of such a royal birth should have been expected. But again the hatred and suspicion of all things Catholic rose up to strangle anything so innocently joyous. There was no cheering or other affectionate displays in London, no public delight for a child who was certain to be raised by his parents to be sympathetic to Rome, a child who might one day rule them surrounded by Jesuits and incense. The tiny duke's birth was greeted only with ill wishes, even curses, from his future subjects, and disappointment that, by his very birth, the earlier Protestant wedding of the prince and princess had been reduced to little consequence in the royal succession.

My sympathy for Princess Mary only grew when I watched her later that month, at the birthday ball for Queen Catherine. Early in the evening, I stood beside Father in the crowd as the king danced a minuet alone with the queen.

"The poor Princess Mary!" I said softly, behind my fan. "How could Prince William abandon her for his Dutch friends so soon? Look at her there alone."

"She's hardly alone," Father said mildly, sipping at his wine. "She's with Her Highness, and could not be more content."

Likely he was right. In honor more of the princess than the queen, the duchess had risen from her lying-in to attend the ball as a spectator. The princess had drawn her chair as close to her stepmother's as was possible, and the two had not only linked their hands together, but the younger lady rested her head against the duchess's shoulder. Because the newlyweds were to leave for Holland in the morning, both women clung to each other, dreading the inevitable parting to come.

"The prince should be with her, not wherever he is," I insisted, which was also right. "Cursed Caliban."

"Caliban?" Father repeated, his brows raised.

"That's what the ladies are calling the prince," I said. "At first it was only on account of his manner, but now it's for his bestial treatment of the princess as well. He's danced with her only once this night. That's shameful, considering they're so newly wed."

"Dancing is hardly the only way to judge a husband's favor," Father said. "Those pearls around her throat and the ruby on her finger are worth a hundred pavanes and sarabands combined."

"If a hundred pavanes and sarabands are worth forty thousand pounds, then they are," I said, repeating the value I'd only just heard for the jewels William had brought as a wedding gift.

"Forty thousand?" Father whistled lowly in appreciation. "That's a sizable amount of husbandly favor."

But I was still watching the princess and the duchess. Mrs. Jennings had come to whisper something to Her Highness, bending familiarly close to her ear to be heard over the music. The duchess nodded, and all three of them smiled together.

"Did you know, Father, that Colonel Churchill and Mrs. Jennings were among the witnesses to the wedding?" I said. "Fah, it sickens me to watch how she mewls and fawns!"

Father glanced at me. "Does Churchill still vex you that much, Katherine?"

I sighed impatiently. "I am not vexed by having John Churchill choose that insipid jade over me, if that is what you ask."

"It is," he said. "That's the answer I wished to hear, too. I would much rather have you angry than weeping with pity for your lot."

"Weeping, hah," I scoffed. "I'll not squander any more tears over him."

"You won't if you've any sense." His expression turned sly, his dark eyes glittering. "Here's a fresh tale you'll enjoy. Seeing room for advancement, the colonel asked Prince William the price of a place in his household. In the frostiest of terms—and the prince can damned well be as frosty as a witch's tit—he informed Churchill that at *his* Court, the offices were earned, not sold."

I laughed so loudly that others around us turned to frown with disapproval, making me quick to twist my amusement into a false sneeze. But Father always could make me laugh, and the tale *was* a good one at John's expense. Though the sting of bitterness remained, I'd come to realize I was well rid of John Churchill and his ambitious avarice. I'd heard that he and Mrs. Jennings were planning to wed before year's end, and I wished them well of each other as the most fitting fate imaginable. Lord Rochester had been right: I did deserve more for myself than to be John's camp follower, careful of every word I spoke. I'd learned that that role was not for me, nor the dutiful obscurity that came with it.

Father had fallen silent, perhaps to grant me time to recover my composure. Then the next dance began, and as others joined the king and queen in the dancing, the respectful quiet ended and the chattering conversations soon strove once more to compete with the fiddles. Father raised his goblet slightly, using it to point across the hall.

"Do you see that gentleman across the hall?" he asked with such studied indifference that I knew he was about something. "The fellow in the plum-colored coat with the silver sash?"

"You mean the goatish old rogue with the ginger-colored periwig and the tuft of whiskers like the old king?" I asked, laughing again. "Faith, Father, speak plain! The plum-colored coat is the very least of that fellow."

Father screwed his face up in pain. "He's no old rogue, Katherine.

He's Sir Edward Hungerford, a respectable widower twice over and holder of thirty manors in Wiltshire. He sits with me in the House as the Member for Chippenham."

"He may sit wherever he pleases," I said, "but to me he still looks to be an old rogue. He's far older than you, Father."

"I do not know whether to thank you for that, Daughter, or to thrash you for your impertinence." He grunted crossly. "No matter. I'll have you know that Sir Edward has asked after you."

"After me?" I was slow to understand, or perhaps it was simply that the idea Father was voicing was so thoroughly outlandish I couldn't conceive of it. "Do you mean Sir Edward has asked you for my hand? Oh, Father, be serious."

"You've had wicked bad fortune with the younger gallants," he said, almost by way of apology. "Perhaps an older gentleman—"

"No, Father, please, I beg you!" To my dismay, I could see Sir Edward purposefully heading our way, his wafting ginger periwig bearing down upon us like a ship of war under full sail.

I didn't linger, instead fleeing in the opposite direction, fair racing through the crowd as I darted this way and that until I reached the nearest entry hall, and ran deeper still into the palace, dodging servants hurrying with covered dishes and laden salvers as well as other revelers who'd withdrawn from the ball for quieter conversations or assignations. With my skirts bunched to one side, I twisted around to make sure I wasn't being followed, skipping lightly on my toes.

"Here now, here now, sweetheart, what's this about?" The man caught me gently by the shoulders, steadying me. "That's a mighty great haste for any lady."

Breathing hard from my exertions, I raised my hand to strike him for his impertinence. To my shock I realized it was His Highness the duke who'd stopped me, and with him was the black-clad figure of Monsieur Barillon, Marquis de Branges, the French ambassador. At once I did my best to collect myself, stepping back and sinking into a curtsy, even as my thoughts raced ahead in delighted confusion.

"What were you about, eh?" he said, raising me back to my feet. "We can't have ladies bolting after hares through Whitehall, you know."

The duke nodded to the Frenchman to dismiss him, and in a moment we were as much alone as was anyone in that long, shadowy hall. Like a tiny moon that circles its more illustrious sun, I felt as if I'd spent much of my life in the duke's shadow, and strange though it seemed, this was the first time I'd ever had his company to myself. Strange, and yet strangely exciting, too, and if my heart was racing now, he was the cause. Was this finally some knotty twist of fate to my favor, or only another cruel coincidence meant to raise my hopes with empty expectation?

"No, Your Highness," I said. "Forgive me, but I wasn't chasing after hares. Rather I was being chased by a large goat."

"A goat," he said, the corners of his mouth twitching. "In the palace?"

"Oh, yes, sir," I said with relish. I suppose I should have been nervous in his company, or at least shy, but instead I found it as easy to tease and banter with him as with any other gentleman. "There are scores of them here, you know, ready to leap on the backs of any unwary ladies who aren't sufficiently nimble to keep themselves safe."

He was smiling widely now, amused by my foolishness. "You're not among the unwary?"

"Oh, no, sir. I'm most admirably nimble." I bowed over my bent leg in modest acknowledgment, and raised my skirts just enough to display one of those selfsame nimble feet, cunningly clad in green silk shoes and red stockings. "Try as they might, the goats never can catch me. Nor do the asses, sir, and there a great number of them in residence here as well."

"I'd wager they don't," he said, chuckling as he admired my proffered foot. I wondered if he recalled how I'd once stumbled before his horse, and how then he'd taken advantage of my tumbled dress to admire my legs. I hoped he did, for that was much of the point of showing them again now.

"Mrs. Sedley, isn't it?" he asked, taking his time before he looked again to my face. "The peerless Dorinda?"

I nodded and chuckled, smiling warmly. There was much to admire about him, too. He was dressed with royal magnificence for the ball in midnight blue brocade with drifts of Flemish lace at his cuffs and throat, and the ever-present Garter-star on his breast. I'd always loved the deep blue of his eyes, the straight length of his nose, the cleft that cleaved his chin, all parts of a man who both attracted and awed me. "Your servant, sir."

"In truth, I knew that already," he admitted. "You see how wretched I am at dissembling. Of course you're Mrs. Sedley. You're not a lady easily forgotten. Hah, that time you trimmed Scroope before the whole Court—who could forget that?"

"Thank you, sir." What more could I wish than to be a lady who was difficult to forget? "I was inspired."

"By Scroope?" He laughed, quick and sharp, as if he were surprising himself. "People like you astound me. Your father and Rochester are the same, quick with the perfect clever word. By the time I think of a rejoinder, a quarter hour has passed and no one would care to hear it."

"Oh, sir, that's not true." I was startled that he'd make such a confession to me, yet oddly touched by it as well. "You're the Duke of York. I cannot believe people wouldn't care what you'd have to say."

"If you were able to take your father's seat in the Commons, my dear, then you'd have no trouble imagining it," he said glumly. "At least now they can't say I don't put England first. I've sacrificed my first daughter by wedding her to that grim little Dutchman for the sake of their cause."

"I'm sure they realize it, sir." Every father hates to lose his daughter through marriage, but I hadn't expected the duke to speak so plainly to me. "The bells and bonfires and all were as much to your honor as to the wedding."

Yet if I were to be honest, I'd venture that most Englishmen were giving credit for the match to the king and believed that in one neat move, His Majesty had neatly confounded his brother, Rome, and France. There would be very little credit to spare for the duke. People were simply too suspicious of him on account of his faith, and the only thing he could do to win them back would likely be to leave Rome and return to the Anglicans—which, of course, he'd vowed his conscience would never let him do. Nor should any stout Englishmen be trusting him so long as he was meeting surreptitiously with the French ambassador while the rest of the Court was engaged at the queen's ball. Even I knew that.

All of which made for piss-poor grounds for flirtation, as barren a bed as can be imagined. I'd been much better served by the nimble goats, and if I wished to make any more of this plum opportunity, I needed to put aside popery and lead our conversation back to more beguiling possibilities.

"I hope they are happy with me now," he was saying with gloomy resignation. "For once, I hope they are happy."

"One must be happy one's self, sir, before one can be concerned with pleasing others." I smiled winsomely as if to demonstrate, and tipped my head to one side to make my curls fall over one eye. My mouth was wide, my teeth white, and though I hadn't been blessed with the dainty rosebud that was so much the fashion, I knew that my broad, open smile could cheer most any man from whatever doldrums might plague him. "True happiness can wear many faces."

"Seeing your face pleases me, my dear, especially after I've been surrounded by naught but dreary, weeping women." He smiled wearily, but it was a smile nonetheless. I wondered if he included Arabella Churchill among the dreary women; after many years as his mistress, they had recently parted, and she'd left with her bastards for Paris. In her wake lay a ripe opportunity for the lady bold enough to make it her own, as all in our circle speculated. If the ancient Aristotle claimed that nature abhorred a vacuum, then our Court abhorred a royal prince without a mistress, as pretty a philosophical certainty as could be.

"You're often in the palace and about the Court," the duke said. "Why have you never taken a place in our household?"

"You do not know, sir?" I whispered like a conspirator, though none were about to hear me.

He leaned closer, intrigued, and lowered his own voice, too. "Tell me."

"Oh, it's no great secret," I said, knowing that what I said was of less importance than how I spoke it. "My father will not permit it."

"Fathers often have little say in their daughters' lives," he said, and though his smile remained, I guessed he must have been thinking again of his own daughter Mary, and how the king, not he, had decided her new husband.

"True, sir, true," I said quickly, wishing to keep him from melancholy. "I try to obey my own father, sir, but too often I follow my own desires rather than his."

"Is that so?" he asked, his attention all mine again.

"It is, sir." I looked up at him slyly, not half so penitent as my words. "That is likely why he has never permitted me to leave his house and accept a place at Court."

He took a step closer toward me. "Court offers many temptations to a lady with desires."

"Indeed, sir," I said, and fluttered my eyes over his person just enough to show that I understood him to be one of the temptations. "Temptation is everywhere at Whitehall."

But he in turn was studying me, his gaze lingering on my bosom. With artful lacing and whalebone, I made as brave a showing as I could, though compared to the great beauties of the Court, it was a meager bounty indeed. To my relief, the duke seemed to find no fault, even ogling my slender form with appreciation.

"Temptation," he said again, with such relish I blushed with pleasure. "You gave me an apple once, after my horse had near trampled you."

"As bold as Eve in the Garden, sir," I said breathlessly. "That was what you said I was."

"That apple was among the sweetest I'd ever eaten," he said, remembering. "Sweet, and full of juice on my tongue. A lady like you would be welcome in my household."

Juice on his tongue, hah! That was worthy of Lord Rochester. For a gentleman who claimed to have no gift for wordplay, the duke was doing admirably well.

But still I shook my head, reaching up to smooth a stray lock of my hair behind my ear. "What Father says, sir, is that the positions are most often given to ladies without fortunes, and from pride he has never wished me among them."

"Nonsense," he said, dismissing my father's objections with a single word. "To be a member of a royal household is an honor. One of Her Highness's ladies is leaving us soon, and her place will be open."

I knew this already. One of the duchess's maids of honor, Anne Howard, daughter of the Earl of Berkshire, was leaving to wed Sir Gabriel Silvius, who'd been granted an appointment under the Prince of Orange—one of those rare appointments so desired by John Churchill.

But to appear too eager was never wise, and instead of leaping at the offer, I only shook my head with sad resignation. "My father will never agree, sir."

Gently, almost tenderly, he turned my face up toward his. I could not look away even if I'd wished it, and I wondered if he could feel how my blood quickened at his touch.

"That is only your father's wish," he said, lightly stroking his thumbs over my cheeks. "What is yours?"

"My wish, sir?" I smiled again and licked my lips. With the slightest motion, I turned my cheek and pressed it against his hand, as if to beg for his caress. "Why, to serve you, sir, as any loyal subject would."

"'To serve me.'" He chuckled. "You are a clever creature, aren't you?"

"I am, sir," I said, my voice low and trembling with anticipation. "I *am*."

He kissed me then, as I'd known from the first that he would. He was demanding, full of fire, and he pressed me hard against the wall so I might feel exactly how much he desired me. I did not succumb there, of course, though doubtless he would have been happy enough to have unbuttoned his breeches and taken me at once, there in the hall. Such things often happened in the palace. Instead I deftly slipped free as soon as I could with a pretty, breathless show of resistance, enough to make him smile as he let me return to the ball. Seduction was better played in several acts, and we both knew it.

But that single kiss had excited me mightily. I'd tasted the power of royalty in it, and of a man who was accustomed to having whatever he wanted. Yet I'd power, too, because what he wanted was me, exactly as I was and without any regard for my fortune. Was there any more heady realization than that?

THE PRINCE AND PRINCESS OF ORANGE left London the next morning, with the king and the duke sailing with them on the Thames to Erith. The farewells were poignant, with the princess still inconsolable at leaving England and her family. Her departure cast a shadow over the Court, made darker still by concern for her sister the Lady Anne and the deaths from the disease of several of her favorite ladies, including the princess's much-loved governess, Lady Frances Villiers. Smallpox struck without regard for youth or rank, and a party of doctors hovered at Anne's bedside. Because Princess Mary had never been afflicted herself, she'd been forbidden a last farewell with her sister, which had made their separation all the more onerous.

Yet worse lay ahead. As soon as the Lady Anne was declared recovered, she visited the nursery to welcome her new half brother, kissing and holding him as any proud older sister might. Within days, the tiny Duke of Cambridge showed the first ruddy eruptions of the smallpox, and by week's end, he, too, perished. His Highness grieved deeply, as can be imagined of a father for his son. Yet he also was old enough himself to understand, if not accept, the fragility of infant life, and had traveled the melancholy path of loss too many times before. Likewise he realized that his wife was still very young and in the first flower of her fertility, and likely able to bear him many more sons.

But his duchess was devastated, her sorrow so deep that she closed herself away in her bedchamber and refused any company beyond her confessor and several other priests. Those closest to her feared for her very wits, while others in the palace feared more practically that she and the duke were somehow cursed, and would no more produce a live child than Queen Catherine had with the king.

Out of regard for this loss, the Court was more somber than usual as we celebrated the holidays from Christmas through Twelfth Night, with the new year of 1678 in the middle. My birthday, coming as it did four days before Christmas, was always bound close to the holidays for me, but this year I received a gift that was so remarkable, so unexpected, that everything else in a season of feasting and excess paled and faded by comparison.

"What is it, Katherine?" Father asked, frowning as he set down his knife beside his plate. Supper had grown increasingly important to him as he'd settled more fully into domestic life with Mrs. Sedley, and there were very few acceptable reasons for a servant to interrupt us when we were at table at Bloomsbury Square. A packet from the palace, however, delivered by a royal messenger, was one of them. When that same packet was brought to me, not Father, his indignation at the interruption swiftly changed to concern. "What has happened?"

I broke the seal and quickly read the sheets within. It didn't take long; it was easy enough to comprehend, and more than enough to make my heart race with excitement.

"Please, Katherine, answer your father," Lady Sedley said. "Else you'll ruin his supper entirely."

"She already has," Father said. "Katherine, now, if you please."

"I have been granted a place in the household of Their Highnesses Duke and Duchess of York," I said slowly, reading the words once again to make sure I wasn't mistaken. "I am to be maid of honor to the duchess."

"Maid of honor!" exclaimed Father with disbelief. "How can this be? I never applied on your behalf, or asked after the place. How can you have received it?"

"I do not know, Father," I said, which was not entirely true, of course. I passed the letter across the table to him. "You may see for yourself."

He pursed his lips as he read, his gaze darting across the words.

"You're twenty years old, Katherine," Lady Sedley said. "Isn't that too advanced to be a maid of honor? Most of them are little lasses of twelve or thirteen."

Father sighed. "There are some who are older. The only requirement is that she not be wed, the assumption being that an unmarried lady remains a maid."

Lady Sedley ventured only a disgusted snort, a wordless estimation of my maidenly virginity.

"It's exactly as you say, Katherine, though it makes little sense to me," Father said, shaking his head over the paper. "I'd heard there were several places falling open, but they're usually so coveted that I cannot imagine one being simply given away. Perhaps the appointment to the duchess comes on account of being turned down by the queen."

"Faith, but that's flattering!" I exclaimed. "We didn't want you to sully Whitehall, but perhaps you'll do with the next in line. I suppose I should consider myself fortunate not to be asked to empty chamber pots for little Lady Anne."

"What else am I to make of it?" Father refolded the letters, mindful of the heavy seal that made them official, and handed them back to me. "If you've no explanation, then neither do I."

I took the letters from him, closing my hands reverently around them as if they were some lucky talisman. Though Father had always said what he wished most for me was happiness, it pained me still not to be entirely honest about this post. Fearing his certain disapproval, I'd never confessed to him how I'd met the duke at the queen's birthday ball, nor that we'd kissed, nor, most of all, how much the duke wished me to trade my father's protection for his. Though I hadn't sought this place as a maid of honor, I wasn't entirely surprised that it had fallen my way, either, not after the interest that His Highness had shown in me.

"Will you allow me to accept, then?" I asked, holding my breath. "Do you give your leave?"

"Could I stop you, Katherine?" Father asked, and as his gaze met mine across the table, I could not tell if he'd guessed the truth. "You're not a child any longer. You've made your share of missteps, but still and all, you've survived well enough. No husband, yet no bastards, either. Besides, if you've decided to cast the rest of your lot with the Yorks, then you'll do it with my permission or without."

"That's a fine answer from a father to his only daughter," Lady Sedley said, once again scandalized, but Father ignored her.

"All I ask, my dear," he continued, "is that you keep to your own church and far from their priests, and don't let yourself be persuaded to join them at their masses. Her Highness has suffered much these last months, and the household you're entering is not a happy place at present. I trust you'll do what you can to lighten their sorrows, and be as agreeable as your nature will permit."

I nodded eagerly, though my thoughts ran toward the duke rather than the duchess, and the exact manner in which I meant to cheer him.

Father sighed again as he glanced down at the now-cold fish on his plate, and forlornly motioned for the servant to take it away and fetch a fresher dish.

"It's an ill wind that blows no one good, Katherine," he said with doleful resignation. "If anyone is to prosper amidst the misfortunes of the Yorks, it might as well be you."

From Father, this was the same as any ordinary blessing. With tears of joy in my eyes, I smiled my thanks with the precious letters still clutched tight in my hands, and began to plan exactly how I'd turn that wind to my own advantage.

Chapter Fourteen

WHITEHALL PALACE, LONDON
January 1678

I began as a maid of honor to the duchess soon after Twelfth Night. Unlike most others new to the post, who arrive in London for the first time from distant counties, it was not so great a change for me, nor was there much to dazzle or amaze me about my new station. I'd been free about Whitehall Palace for more than half my life, and I was as familiar with its twisting halls and galleries, chambers and closets, as any courtier three times my years. Likewise where most newcomers to Court were faced with the dizzying task of learning scores of new faces, names, and titles, I already knew most every personage who frequented the palace, and those few who I might not know well enough to greet, I did recognize with ease. I knew who among the peers and other grand folk never to counter, and who could be counted on to oblige for a favor, who would laugh at a sly jest and who would take instant and lasting offense.

I knew the lesser people, too, the servants and others without whom the grandeur of the place and its rituals would never exist. Before I'd brought so much as a single chest to my new lodgings, I'd already arranged which laundress would wash my linen and which footman would reliably provide the wood for my fire.

I'd also known enough to make sure I wasn't given lodgings on one of the inner halls, with rooms that had no windows or opened over the stables, and because I wasn't afraid to mention my acquaintance with His Highness, I received small but pleasing rooms overlooking the river. Unlike the other maids of honor, I was not forced to share a chamber with a group of giggling, coltish girls, either, though I wasn't certain whether this was to oblige my wishes, or to keep my wicked, experienced self safely away from the true innocents. While I hadn't shared a bedchamber with anyone since I'd left my governess behind in the nursery, I still laughed aloud at the bedstead I'd been given, a narrow little cot fit for the most chaste of virginal maids. Not that it mattered one way or the next. If my affairs progressed with the swiftness I suspected they would, then my time in these first lodgings would be brief, anyway.

My duties as maid of honor were hardly taxing. As I had before, I sat in Her Highness's presence, I made conversation, I followed her about her day and to entertainments in the evenings. I suppose if I'd become a confidante of the duchess, or one of her sweet-faced pets, I might have been given more to do by way of small personal errands and tasks, or even invited to sit up with her in her privy chambers to gossip.

But whatever impression the duchess had of me was formed long ago, and would not change. She regarded me with distant tolerance, as if I were an unavoidable inconvenience that could not be helped. She never spoke a sharp word to me, even though on many occasions she must have sorely longed to; she was much too well-bred for that. Yet I did wonder if she ever questioned how I'd come to be among her ladies, an ungainly, cawing magpie among her other golden swans.

Besides, during the winter when I first began to live in the duke's household, Her Highness was still grieving the loss of her most recent little prince. She was listless and melancholy, and wanted only the comfort that came from her confessor and other long-robed priests. Some of the older ladies of the bedchamber, intimate with her monthly courses, whispered that the duchess was with child again, which would be the best possible remedy for her sorrows.

But for now, the short winter days were dark and dreary for us ladies attached to Her Highness. If she were unwilling to attend some frolic or performance given by the king, then we could not go, either. Patience had never been my strongest quality, and I rankled under what seemed like captivity. What was the use of the lavish new gowns I'd had made for myself if no one were to see them? Why bother with choosing which jewels to wear or how to have my hair dressed if my day was spent sitting amongst other ladies?

Again and again I thought of how the duke had told me how weary he'd become of female weeping, and how he wished for my merriment to leaven his humor. So why, then, had he gone to the trouble of bringing me into his household, only to abandon me here and let my merriment turn dusty dry from disuse?

Surprisingly I learned the answers from my father. Politics increasingly occupied Father, a more productive outlet for his energies than his old familiar debaucheries. He was thirty-seven now, of an age for more serious pursuits, and his friend Lord Dorset (my same nemesis Lord Middlesex, now raised higher by his father's death and styled the sixth Earl of Dorset and first Earl of Middlesex) was already cutting a prominent figure within the government. Father heeded what Lord Dorset told him as well as what he himself heard in the Commons, and in turn relayed it all to me. I was grateful. The only lady among the duchess's attendants who cared a whit for more than ribbons and puppies was Mrs. Jennings (newly married to John, but in secret, so she could retain her place as a maid of honor), and as can be imagined, we kept from each other's paths.

According to Father, the duke was among those actively seeking a fresh war with France. While the king remained determinedly neutral and disinclined toward waging war, His Highness was devoting every hour and energy to convincing the gentlemen in Parliament to agree with him and vote more funds to enlarge the army.

"To me that seems a wise thing for His Highness to do," I said thoughtfully as we walked together through the long gallery of the palace. "To show support for the Prince of Orange and the Dutch surely will show he's a kindness for Protestants. His daughter the princess must be pleased, too, to have her father embrace her husband's cause."

"That's entirely what you're meant to believe," Father said. He'd met me here after playing several brisk games of tennis with His Majesty on the palace court, and despite the January chill, he'd refused to put his coat on just yet and his white linen shirt was wet with the sweat of his exertions, and a light steam rose from his shoulders in the cool air. "It's false as can be, however. Even Barillon is disgusted by it. The duke must believe us all empty-headed asses to swallow such a ludicrous tale."

"Then what is the truth?" I asked curiously.

"Something a great deal more ominous, I fear," Father said, glancing over his shoulder to make certain we were sufficiently far from others so as not to be overheard. "Clearly His Highness wants to increase the might of the army so that he can employ it not upon the Dutch, but to enforce the desires of his Romish beliefs here at home. Whoever controls the army controls the country, and controls which faith will be practiced, and the wishes of the people be damned. He learned that lesson from Cromwell. We all did."

"The king would never permit that!" I said, shocked, and unable to reconcile this power-mad duke with the one who'd kissed me.

"The king is inattentive where his brother is concerned," Father said. "It saddens me to say it, for I have always believed His Majesty is a good man at heart. If only he were stronger! But he can be too lenient with the duke, and ignore his brother's true intentions."

"I've never heard you speak so strongly against Catholics, Father," I said slowly, thinking of my long-gone mother still shut away in her convent in Ghent. "Faith, you sound like Lady Sedley, seeing Jesuits in the chimney pots."

He stopped before a window, the pale winter sun that shone through the leading casting a pattern of wavering diamonds across his face. "It's not Catholics I fear, Katherine. Don't think that for an instant. It's the duke himself that concerns me, and what he will do with the power he desires. Do the ladies ever speak of these matters in your quarters? Does the duchess discuss her husband's affairs, as most wives do?"

I shook my head. "Parliament might not exist for all the heed the other ladies take of it. As for Her Highness, she has always believed that she was sent here on a holy mission to return England to Rome, beginning with the duke, but that is nothing new."

"No," Father said. "But over time, if a man hears the same message whispered in his ear each night, he begins to accept it as his own. It's no coincidence that the king's leaning toward France strengthened once he took a French whore to his bed."

This was true enough. While the duchess confined her ambitious longings to saving English souls for the Pope, Lady Portsmouth never seemed to miss a chance to promote French interests to the king, and there were even rumors that she'd helped negotiate treaties on Louis's behalf. Everyone knew she was as good—or as bad—as a French spy, yet the king remained so thoroughly beguiled by her voluptuous secrets that he didn't seem to care.

"Like flies to a dish of oversweet marmalade," Father said with disgust. "That's how those two royal gentlemen are with Catholic ladies, and with the same sticky entrapment. If only the duke had been content with some stout Bavarian princess for his wife instead of insisting on an Italian beauty, and if the king had kept constant to Nelly, then all of England would be much the better for it."

I looked at him slyly. "What manner of jam would Nelly be, I wonder?"

He smiled at that. "Something with more lemon to it, I'd wager. Sweet at first, then tart the next, yet always delicious."

Even as we laughed together, I considered this new notion. What if I became the duke's Protestant mistress, the one to whisper proper Anglican thoughts in one ear to balance the murky Romish ones that came from his priests and wife? It was most amusing, the ancient allegory of sacred and profane love made real, and I laughed all the more just to think it.

Unaware of my thoughts, it was Father who turned serious again as we reached the end of the gallery where we would soon part.

"I didn't wish to alarm you, Kattypillar," he said softly, taking me by the shoulders to kiss me on my forehead. "For now, you're safe enough where you are. But if you serve in the duke's household, it's best that you be aware of what is said of him in Parliament and elsewhere, and keep your own wits about you."

Later I wondered what Father would say if he knew I'd ambitions of my own regarding the duke. There had been a time when Father had openly feared I'd be drawn into His Highness's bed, but now, when the possibility was most real, he seemed blind to it. The duke's predilection for his wife's attendants was famously known, and the simple fact that I'd been given a post had made his interest as clear as could be, or at least it had to me. Perhaps Father had lost faith in my dubious charms after I'd been passed over by two other gentlemen, or more appealingly, he believed I was now sufficiently old and wise to keep myself from danger.

Either way he'd be wrong. And as I walked back to my lodgings,

I amused myself by considering what exact flavor of Protestant jam I might be.

In my dreams and imaginings, the duke would finally take notice of me in the grandest possible manner. I'd be dressed in a fantastically lavish gown with jewels to match, and at the beginning of a royal ball, he'd take my hand and choose me to begin the dancing over scores of pouting beauties. A pretty fancy, I know, but I was still young, and though jaded to the world, I remained tender in my heart.

What truly happened was much more prosaic.

I had played cards in Her Highness's rooms until close to midnight. I was happy; luck had smiled on me, and I'd won handsomely, including a pair of fine-wrought pearl and amethyst earrings that the lady who'd rashly wagered them was very sorry to lose. Knowing well that this was the best time to leave the table, I'd retired, and now sat in my own rooms at my dressing table while my maid Thomson brushed out my hair. Born on one of Father's holdings in Kent, Thomson had been my lady's maid for years, and looked after me exactly to my tastes. My hair was thick and long, nearly to my waist, requiring much of her artistry and many jabbing pins as well as sugar water to coax it into the elaborate styles then in fashion, and I looked forward to this time at the end of the day when I was released from its heavy thrall. I closed my eyes, drowsing and relishing the simple pleasure of the brush drawing through the full length of my hair.

Thus the rapping at my door took both me and Thomson by surprise. Given the hour, I feared the worst, a mishap with Father or some other disaster. Swiftly I stood and tied my dressing gown more modestly over my smock, and nodded for her to answer.

But the messenger at the door hadn't come from Bloomsbury Square. Instead I recognized him as one of the older and most trusted of the duke's servants, dressed in the York livery. His weathered face was carefully impassive as he placed the letter on the small silver salver that Thomson offered. She in turn curtsied and presented it to me; a silly bit of protocol, I know, given that we all were within a dozen paces of one another, but then, where would we in the palace be without ceremony?

I didn't recognize the hand that had written my name so boldly across the front, but the seal with its lion and unicorn was one I saw every day: the House of Stuart. My hands shook with excitement as I slipped my finger beneath the seal and opened the single sheet to read.

As I did, Thomson began to close the door, but the man put his hand up to block it. "I'm to wait for Mrs. Sedley's reply."

I read, and understood. The letter wasn't long—it was scarce more than a note, really—but in those several lines lay my future.

My dear,

I would be honored by yr. Company. Come to me now with the bearer if you please.

York

"I will come," I said to the man. "A moment to compose myself, and I'll join you."

He nodded, turning away and folding his hands to wait, while Thomson closed the door. Given the tiny size of my lodgings, he'd no choice but to wait outside, where his presence before my door would be as easily read as a tavern sign to anyone who passed in the hall. I'd have to accustom myself to such scrutiny. After this night, my most private life would become public and common in scandalous tattle, and faith, I was ready.

"Your hair, ma'am," Thomson said, her little face with its pointed chin wreathed with worry. "It will take more than a moment to dress it again, ma'am, as well as to lace you into your gown."

"Neither is necessary, Thomson," I said. "I'll go as I am."

"As you are, ma'am?" Her eyes widened, her distress on my behalf increasing. "Forgive me, ma'am, but surely you cannot intend that!"

"Surely I can." I bent before the glass to make a quick survey of my face. "I'm certain His Highness will not take the least offense."

"His Highness? The duke?" she asked, then of a sudden understood all. She blushed for me, and dropped her gaze in confusion. "Forgive me, ma'am, I misspoke."

"There's naught to forgive," I said, my spirits almost giddy. "Leastwise not by you. Fetch my black cloak, the one with the deep hood. I'll wear that, and no one will be the wiser as to what's beneath."

As she ran to fetch it, I bent closer to the glass. I'd yet to wash my face for the night, and my paint still looked well enough. My long, loose hair fell forward about my face and shoulders like a shining silken curtain, a sight whose intimacy would beguile most men. My smock was fine Holland linen, and trimmed deep with more (and more costly) lace than most ladies wore on their person even during the day. That, too, would do, as would the dressing gown I wore over it, peach-colored silk that gave a glow to my pale skin and was edged with soft golden sable along the neckline and deep cuffs. As a final flourish, I dabbed scent on my throat and behind my ears.

At last I smiled, trying to see myself as the duke would, and was satisfied. On an impulse, I took up the amethyst earrings I'd won earlier and hooked them into my ears, the large pendant stones swinging gently against my cheeks. Purple had always been the color of royalty, and that, coupled with the luck that had already brought the earrings my way, should bode most excellently for the rest of the evening.

"Your cloak, ma'am," Thomson said, draping it over my shoulders. I tied the ribbons at the neck and pulled the hood over my head to shadow my face. If I wished infallible anonymity, I would wear a vizard-mask, too, but it was so very late that I doubted I'd meet anyone else in this part of the palace. Even if I did, they'd be bound on some illicit purpose as well, and we'd each be trying so hard to avoid the other that no harm could come from it. I stepped into my heeled slippers, took a deep breath, and nodded for Thomson to open the door.

"You needn't wait for me," I said. "I'll wake you when I return."

"Very well, ma'am," she said, and curtsied as I passed her. "Good night, ma'am, and may God watch over you."

As I followed the manservant down the hall, I thought of how I was not so much commending myself to God as to the duke: a blasphemous notion, yes, but nonetheless one that made me smile, and I was smiling still as the manservant ushered me past the guards and into His Highness's suite of apartments. At the last door, he knocked in a way that was clearly a signal, and at once came the muffled reply from within. The manservant opened the door for me himself, and I slipped inside.

Of all the places I'd visited in Whitehall, I'd never before been here, in His Highness's bedchamber, yet surely it must have been one of the most appealing rooms in the entire palace. While it was most handsomely appointed, with dark paneling and carvings on the walls, elaborate plasterwork overhead, carved marble chimneypieces, and paintings by Master Lely and others, what was most striking were the windows that ran the length of the room, offering a splendid wide view of the Thames and the hills of Richmond beyond. White ice had narrowed the river to a single crooked channel, with only a few hardy boatmen plying their trade by moonlight. Snow on the banks and over the ice glittered more brightly than the stars overhead, magical and unreal. But just as stunning in the room was the Romish prie-dieu with its small triptych showing the Virgin Mary and several lesser saints and candles before it, the kind of shrine for personal devotions that I remembered from my mother's rooms.

Yet all that I noticed later. What I saw first was His Highness himself, sitting at a long table strewn with books and charts and papers. His pen was in his hand, a half-written letter beneath it. He wore a quilted silk banyan over his shirt and breeches and fur-lined slippers on his stockinged feet, with his wig carelessly tossed onto the back of another chair to bare his close-cropped hair.

It was a scene of surprising, tempting intimacy for any man to reveal, even more so for a royal prince. But the best part was the smile that lit his weary face as soon as he saw me, warm and welcoming, and the obviousness pleasure that filled his blue eyes as he set down his pen to greet me.

I was so taken with seeing him that I'd forgotten the obsequiousness I owed him, and belatedly I shoved my hood back from my face and curtsied deeply. The inky black of my cloak billowed around me, and my unbound hair spilled forward.

"Rise, my dear, rise," he said, coming to lift me up himself. He'd done this before for me, and I understood what a sizable honor it was. As soon as I'd stood, he bent to close the rest of the distance between us and kissed me lightly, more a kiss such as exchanged between friends than one of passion.

Anxiously I wondered if he'd changed his mind. Had I already disappointed him somehow?

With fresh determination, I shook my hair back from my face and smiled up at him as winningly as I could. By the light of the fire and the moon outside, I must have been nothing but contrasts: the black cloak over the soft peach dressing gown, my dark hair against my pale skin.

My smile widened with relief when I saw in his eyes how much he approved.

"Did I rouse you from your bed?" he asked, an idea that he clearly found pleasing. "Were you asleep?"

"Not quite, Your Highness," I said, equally aware of his own bed looming nearby. "I came as soon as I received your message."

"You weren't a quarter hour," he said, again with approval. "Most ladies would have taken far longer than that."

"I'd no wish to loiter, sir," I said, my voice low and breathless. "I've waited long enough."

He tipped his head, surprised. "You've been waiting?"

"Oh, yes, sir," I said, smoothing my hair behind one ear, the hanging amethyst bumping my hand. "Fifteen days and twelve hours."

He frowned, curious but not understanding, and I went on to explain.

"Fifteen days, sir, twelve hours, and a handful of minutes," I said. "That's how long I've been longing for you, tucked away in the clucking henhouse with the other maids of honor."

I'd just granted him the perfect opportunity to display his wit, as fine a gift as any to a man who worried he wasn't as clever with a jest as others about him. No other gentleman I knew would have been able to resist proceeding from hens to roosters to cocks, or miss the chance to speak such teasing bawdry to me.

Yet the duke did. His face relaxed, and he laughed at what I'd said, but that was all.

"Those ladies do cluck," he agreed. "I've remarked it myself. But I marvel that you know the days so precisely."

"What, sir, do you marvel that a lady would know my numbers, and have a passable skill at reckoning?" I laughed, too, though more from uncertainty than from humor. Skittishly I walked from him toward the fire, shrugging away my cloak and tossing it over a nearby chair. The light brocade of my dressing gown drifted about me as I walked, doubtless revealing enough to show that I'd no gown, petticoats, or stays beneath.

"I shouldn't wonder that you'd marvel, sir," I continued, holding my palms over the fire. "Some of my fellows are remarkably ignorant, save in how to simper and dance. Most marvelous, indeed."

"That's not what I intended," he said, his voice gruff. "I meant that I marvel that you would judge it worth your efforts to count your days so closely."

"I could not help it, sir," I said softly. "If that in itself is a marvel, then so be it."

It was also the truth, a truth that was so raw that it seemed to hang in the air between us with unbecoming awkwardness. He said nothing, nor did I.

I flushed, realizing I'd overspoken, and stared down into the fire. Too late I now realized I shouldn't have come. Despite my reputation for boldness and speaking clever nonsense, I lacked the worldly experience to play this role. I wasn't Lady Castlemaine or Lady Portsmouth, grand infamous mistresses who could sail forward borne on the cresting wave of their unquestionable beauty. All I had to offer was my wit, and even that seemed to have deserted me. What else could I have to offer a duke?

I cannot say exactly how long I stood there, before the fire, wallowing in this impasse of doubt like a small vessel in heavy seas. All I know is that enough time passed for me to fair toast my palms, and to realize an instant too late for comfort how close I'd come to burning them outright.

"Hah, a pox on my luck," I said ruefully, holding my overwarmed hands up for him to see. "Here I'm caught red-handed like some low Scotsman, without any sin to show for it."

To my endless surprise, that sorry witticism was the tinder he needed to spark his passion, for suddenly he leapt toward me and seized me in his arms, kissing me with all the ardor and urgency he'd lacked before. It was only a few steps to his bed, yet in that short progress he managed to divest me of my dressing gown and the few other scraps of clothing I'd worn beneath. He toppled me on my back and I sank deep into the featherbed, and without much more prelude than that he was on me and in me, and with a few breathless cries of surprise I welcomed him as best I could. Though most who knew me would doubt it, I was still a novice at Venus's games, and I'd lain with only one other man before this, and my inexperience must have been woefully evident.

But the duke either didn't notice, or didn't care. The bed creaked and groaned, and he groaned and grunted with it in an outpouring of exclamations and endearments that I would never have expected from so reticent a man. The realization that I'd inspired this kind of display from him made my own pleasure grow, and while his attentions were more forceful than loving, that pleased and excited me, too, more proof that I must be worthy. By the time he'd given me his final effusion, I'd offered him a tribute of my own, shamelessly expiring beneath him.

Afterward he rolled to one side, yet still keeping me in a close embrace that amazed me with its tenderness.

"Well now, sir," I whispered, my voice low with happiness. "That was sin enough to make me red-handed, and likely flushed in other parts besides."

He chuckled with the contentment of a man well-swived. "You are everything I expected and more, Katherine."

"If you expected to bed a scarecrow, sir," I said, unable not to deprecate myself, "then doubtless you are pleased beyond measure."

"Don't speak so," he said sharply, twisting about so his face was direct above mine. "You please me as you are. You're different from the others, and I like you for it. If I don't wish you otherwise, then you should be pleased as well."

I gazed up at him, his expression so serious as to be almost grim. I had loved the first man who'd become my lover, only to discover afterward that he hadn't loved me. This time, I'd become the duke's lover without loving him in the least. Yet those few words of faith in me were kinder than any I'd ever had from another, and sufficient to make my careful heart flutter anew.

"Thank you, sir," I whispered. It was a strange thing, being with a prince, for though he'd just possessed me in the most intimate of terms, I wasn't sure if royal protocol still applied. Surely it didn't, under the circumstances, and feeling ridiculously daring, I reached up and held his face in my hands. "Thank you for it all."

"Hah, I should be thanking you." He smiled and turned his face against my hand to nip lightly at my palm. I relaxed, realizing my fearful daring was no daring indeed. "I wasn't even sure you'd come."

"But I did come, sir, didn't I?" I said, laughing wickedly beneath him.

"I vow you fetched me quite handsomely. At least now you'll have a pretty sin for confession. Forgive me, oh, for I have fucked a Protestant!"

He laughed in spite of himself. "There will be that," he said slowly and with so much guilt that I pitied him. "It will not sit well."

"You would truly make such a confession?" I asked, incredulous, yet troubled as well.

"I will," he said solemnly, even as he had his hand upon my naked breast. "I must."

I couldn't believe that he'd just done what he had with me, and yet as happy as that had made him, he was already worrying over what his sour-faced priests would tell him. None of the gentlemen I'd known would have shown such a confusing nicety under the circumstances, and I'd no notion of what I should say or do.

"Do you wish me to leave, sir?" I asked, already beginning to slide away from him. "I wouldn't wish to put your soul in peril if you—"

"No, stay," he said, reaching out to draw me back. "Stay. That is, if you wish to."

"You wish me to stay, sir, even if you must confess my presence as a sin?"

He heaved an enormous sigh—an outward sign, I guessed, of whatever war his conscience was battling. "I will address that in the morning. Now I would wish you to stay."

"Very well, sir." I was happy enough to oblige as I returned to his embrace, curling my slender body against his. "Whatever you wish."

"I do wish it," he said, and now when he sighed again, I was sure that his pleasure had won over his weary conscience. His pleasure, and me. "If I send for you tomorrow night, will you come to me again?"

"I am your servant, sir," I said softly, and though his face was turned from mine, I smiled still. "I will come to you. I will come."

IN THIS MANNER BEGAN ONE OF the most delicious periods of my life. By day I continued as I had been, in the service of Her Highness as a maid of honor. I received neither more nor less attention from the duchess than I had previously, with my hours spent in the same company of her other ladies and passed in the same banal amusements. Each evening I retired to my room at the same time as the other ladies, yet while they slept their maidenly sleep (or perhaps amused themselves in their lovers' arms as well), I would wrap myself in my hooded cloak and repair to the bed of my lover, James, Duke of York.

Just as Nelly Gwyn had jested of Lord Dorset becoming her Charles the Second and the king her Charles the Third, I now had my own James the Second to follow James Grahme. Of course, I never presumed to call him by his given name—not even I would dare such informality—but in my thoughts he ceased to be the duke, or His Highness, and became only James, my James.

Miraculously, for those first few months in the winter and spring of 1678, no one else seemed to know. Or rather, no one of consequence, for of course my maid Thomson knew, and James's secretary Mr. Coleman knew, from having once appeared unexpectedly early one morning before I'd left. Since James had felt the unfortunate need to unburden himself, I'd thought his confessor would know, too, but James assured me that he hadn't named me to the priests. This curious distinction made me laugh, and as I pointed out to James, I should at least be credited for my sins rather than being reduced to no more than an anonymous Protestant whore. He hadn't seen the humor to it, but had only said solemnly (as he did many things) that he hadn't wished to disgrace me. Charmingly thoughtful of him, yes, but unnecessary. I'd made my choice, and I was happy with it. I could have been an ungainly, forgotten spinster, or the cherished mistress to a prince; hah, what manner of decision was that to make?

I knew full well that much of the reason that no one suspected our intrigue was that few would have believed it possible because of my lack of beauty. A royal prince has the loveliest ladies of his kingdom on constant display before him at Court, luscious temptation on a scale that few ordinary men can ever imagine. Certainly James's brother Charles (for by now I'd come to call the king by his Christian name in my thoughts, too) had enjoyed this bounty, plucking enough damsels to make the most gorgeous bouquet imaginable in his bed. That James should choose me must have been inconceivable. Even the duchess (or perhaps especially the duchess, who was most proud of her own beauty and virtue) must never have dreamed I'd become the drab magpie in her marriage nest, stealing away her husband's favors.

No matter. For those few months we were as secret as any lovers could be, a balmy little world of our own making. Yet the coupling was only part of what we shared. Like all the Stuarts, James was a man of endless energy who required little sleep, giving us all the more time to converse and learn of each other, and, before long, to become friends. While many ladies regard men as such unfathomable creatures that friendship is impossible, I preferred their company to most ladies', and I was honored by the confidences that James made to me. I'd always been plainspoken, and he welcomed that as a bracing counterpoint to all the fawning courtly palaver and priestly driveling around him during the day. It especially interested me to hear how differently James interpreted the same actions that infuriated Father and his associates in Parliament.

One such concern of James's that spring was the need for a greater army. He toiled incessantly on this project with Lord Monmouth, his nephew and a gallant young gentleman who, having served under the best generals in the French army, was clever about military matters, if little else. He was also supported by Lord Danby, who likewise believed that a strong army was best for the king.

I'd listened to Father speak of the dangers a larger army might pose to the country, and of how no single man should have so great a power at his disposal. But to hear James, a large and strong army was a necessity for England, not a threat. He saw it as imperative for maintaining the country's defenses against foreign powers, for keeping England's name a formidable one in the minds of her adversaries on the Continent. Further, and most perplexing to me, he saw it as a way to preserve the monarchy, which he believed was sadly deteriorating in his brother's hands. In James's eyes, the members of Parliament (like my own father) who confounded him were no better than a pack of dreaded republicans, determined to topple the monarchy and rule themselves as Cromwell had done earlier.

"But that doesn't make sense, sir," I protested one night as he tried again to explain it to me. I was lolling in his bed against the mounded pillows, eating an orange, while he had returned to his paper-covered desk to set down one fleeting thought before it escaped him entirely. "Cromwell was a general in the army, and it was the army that overthrew your father. Yet you perceive a greater army as necessary to preserve the throne. How can there be merit in such a riddle?"

"Because while Cromwell was a general, he was also a fanatic bent on serving his own ill-formed church and imposing his wrongful beliefs." The light from the branched silk candlestick before him gave his angular face an impassioned fervor. "If my father had been better able to bring him and his followers more sharply to heel, then there would never have been an insurrection, and my father might have lived and still be ruling."

I listened, full of doubt; if his saintly father still lived, he would be an ancient gentleman of nearly eighty years, and no longer much use as a ruler, though I knew better than to point out such a fact to James.

"Yet there are many Englishmen who say the same of you, sir," I said, licking the orange juice from my fingers. "That you would wish a greater army so that you might impose your Pope and priests upon those who are already content in their faith."

"Oh, Katherine," he said with despair. "How many times must I explain this to you? To you, and to all the others? I do not wish to force anyone toward the True Church, and I never have."

"Then you should inform your duchess, too, sir," I said. "She tells anyone who'll listen that she came to England expressly to bring us dreadful ignorant Protestants back to Mother Rome, with you to lead the way to our salvation."

"She says that publicly?" he asked, clearly aghast. "To you in her household?"

"Oh, yes, to all of us, and any others who happen about," I said, biting into another segment of the sweet fruit, "with the entire chorus of her woeful priests chanting their 'amens' to every word of it. Not that us Protestants pay her ravings any more heed than they deserve."

"But that is not what I want, not what I believe." In disgust he threw down his pen, ink splattering from the nib across the letter he'd been composing. "You of anyone should know that, Katherine. All I wish is for those of us who believe in the True Church to have the same privileges as the Protestants. I wish us to be able to worship as we please, yet to serve our king and country the same as any other Englishman. Surely you understand that."

"It does not matter whether I do or not, sir," I said, slipping the last of the orange between my lips. "I am only a woman, not a Member of

Parliament. But I will venture that you won't get your standing army unless you can state your case for it more clearly than that, and without a flurry of Jesuits hovering about you."

He shoved his chair away from the desk and came to sit on the edge of the bed facing me.

"What can I do, Katherine?" he said wearily. "All I wish is the best for England and her people, and yet they will not accept that from me, no matter how I work for their behalf. I was fourteen when I last saw my father, fifteen when he was martyred by his own subjects and our country torn asunder by war. I haven't forgotten, and I pray each night for the strength to make certain such a calamity will not befall England again. What else can I possibly do for them, Katherine? What else can I do?"

I'd never seen such despair in his face before, or such suffering, and it grieved me so deeply that I'd do most anything to bring him ease.

"Oh, my dear sir," I said gently, looping my arms around his shoulders. "Know that you are a good man, a kind man. You must do what is right for yourself, and for England."

He closed his eyes, his head bowed. "If only they knew that as well as you."

"You must make them know it, sir," I said. "By your words and your actions. You must make them understand."

He groaned and drew me close, seeking solace in my arms. I did my best to comfort him, and did so until we heard the first stirrings of the servants in the palace, and I was forced to leave him alone with his dark thoughts. As I made my way back to my rooms, I wept for him, for us, for his late father, and for England, my handkerchief pressed to my mouth to keep my sobs from waking any others.

By your words and your actions, you must make them understand.

Could any advice be more simple, and yet more impossible for James to follow?

Chapter Fifteen

St. James's Palace, London
July 1678

As summer came, our household removed from Whitehall across the park to St. James's Palace, as was the habit of the Yorks. I had always liked the older, smaller brick palace to the rambling halls of Whitehall, and I liked it all the more now for the greater privacy it afforded James and me for our intrigue. With fewer courtiers to spy us, we could meet more often, in the palace's gardens and in other privy chambers.

James had need of the distraction. The threat of England joining with the Dutch had finally been enough incentive for Louis to end his war and sue for peace. The negotiations dragged on through the early summer, and as they did James and Lord Monmouth did their best to justify keeping the army that had been increased for the sake of the war that had not come. Parliament's uneasiness increased, fed by James's large and now-disappointed army waiting idle with no war to fight. As a result, relations between James and the king were strained, and once again the angry murmurings rose about James's true intentions for the forces.

The duchess was brought to bed early of a daughter, a weak and pitiful infant who survived only long enough to be baptized Elizabeth before she returned to her Maker. Only the duchess wept and grieved for her. The rest of the Court saw the death as one more lost attempt at a male heir to the throne, one more doomed failure to be blamed upon the Catholic duchess.

By August, the Court was past ready for its annual recess to the green pleasures of Windsor, far from the worries of London. The last night I spent in James's bedchamber in St. James's was hot and still, the windows thrown open for any hint of a breeze from the park, and moon and stars hidden by a gauzy haze. Lying crossways on the bed, I sprawled naked on my back atop the sheets with my heavy damp hair spread behind me, letting my body cool as best it could after the heat of our passion. Beside me lay James, his head propped on his hand as he gazed down upon me, lightly stroking my breasts and belly as was his fond habit after we'd made love. I smiled drowsily at his touch, enjoying the lightness of his caresses. It would be more difficult for us to continue our rendezvous at Windsor, where the duke's apartments were arranged beside the duchess's, but James and I had already resolved to meet beneath the trees and forests that were among the castle's attractions.

"Katherine, sweet," he said, resting his hand low on my belly. "Look at me."

"You ask a prodigious favor, sir." With great effort I dragged open my eyes, my smile lazy. His face was close to mine, his forehead and shoulders glazed with sweat by the moonlight. "There. I have looked. Now leave me in happy peace, I beg you."

With a sigh that was more a yawn, I began to close my eyes again.

"No, look at me, sweet," he said gently. "I wish to see your eyes. Tell me: when did you last have your courses?"

That made me open my eyes at once.

"My courses?" I asked, purposefully not answering, though of course I knew the answer. Had he guessed, then? Had he somehow realized the secret I'd not yet wished to admit to myself?

"You're too clever for that, my dear," he said. Thoughtfully he considered my body, pearly white in the moonlight before him. "Nor am I a fool, either. I've sired at least a dozen babes. I know the signs well enough. You've changed. You've ripened."

I pressed my hands over my eyes in shame and mortification. Of course I was too clever not to understand what had happened to me, the same plight as had been visited on all women since Eve fell from the Garden. I understood, yet I'd no wish to accept. How could I get with child so soon, after only two months with James? Other women could dandle and sport for months without quickening, but with me his seed had taken at once.

"I'm sorry, sir," I said, my voice muffled. "I'm—I'm sorry."

"But I am not." Gently he pried my hands away from my teary face. "To have you bear my child—how could I regret that?"

"But now everyone will—will know, sir," I said, hiccupping as I wept. "This won't—won't be our secret any longer."

"Ah, well," he said, his face full of kindness. "It wouldn't have kept for much longer, anyway. What is your reckoning?"

"February, sir," I said. "That is as close as I can guess."

"Months away." He lay his hand again across my belly, appraising it. I'd noted the changes myself: my breasts were larger than they'd ever been and tender at that, and already I'd seen the first swell below my waist. "You're tall. You'll carry well. I doubt anyone will guess until after we return from Windsor. Then you will be forced to leave your post."

"I know, sir," I said forlornly. By the very definition, a maid of honor could not be with child. I wouldn't regret the place itself, but I would very much miss the excuse it had given me to live in the royal household. I'd no doubt the duchess would be furious when she learned, and cast me out, and then—then I didn't know what would become of me. It wasn't a question of money, for I'd more than enough to support myself and a child in perfect comfort, and I was equally sure that James would be generous in supporting his child. It was more the loss of friends, position, even family, that could come as punishment to a lady in my circumstances. I didn't even know if Father would take me back at Bloomsbury Square. Given his unhappiness with the duke, I suspected Father might be every bit as furious as the duchess when at last I'd be forced to tell him.

"You will be taken care of, Katherine," James said, as if reading my thoughts. "You're far too dear to me to part with now, nor would I disown our child."

"Thank you, sir," I said, weeping, and held him as if we'd never part. In a way, I supposed we never would, now that there would be a child to bind us forever together. Unlike ordinary bastards, those with royal blood were not scorned or abandoned, but recognized and showered with every privilege and honor. I'd only to look at the half dozen or so by-blow dukes that the king treated almost as handsomely as if they'd been born his legitimate sons, and James had done the same with his other bastards by Arabella Churchill. The only difference would be that, unlike Mrs. Churchill, I'd insist that my child was baptized and raised as a Protestant, not a Papist.

But that—that I'd save to tell James some other time.

CHARLES WAS A MAN RULED BY his physical restlessness. Just as other men began their days with a dish of tea or chocolate, so the king each day required a lengthy walk through the park with his dogs at a pace so furious that only a few of his gentlemen had the fortitude to accompany him. Later in August, the day before the Court was to shift to Windsor, Charles was engaged on one of these morning walks when he was approached by a man on the edge of hysteria, warning Charles against continuing into the park. This madman (for so we all assumed he must be) vowed that he'd learned of a plot formed by the Jesuits whereby assassins would fall on Charles as he walked beneath the trees and murder him outright. His information had come from a clergyman with the peculiar name of Mr. Israel Tonge, who in turn was informed by another clergyman named Titus Oates.

As can be imagined, Charles was startled by this grave news, yet thanked the madman with his usual courtesy before continuing on his path undeterred. He emerged from the walk unharmed, and while jesting with his gentlemen, dismissed the warning as only one more slander against the Catholic faith. He barely remembered to put Lord Danby in charge of an official investigation before he left London, and then forgot it entirely.

But Lord Danby took the affair much more seriously, and addressed it with his usual thoroughness. He took testimony from both Tonge and Oates, and as the weeks wore on, their tales grew, naming more and more well-known names. When Lord Danby wrote to James that Oates had included James's own confessor in his stories, James addressed the investigating council, who agreed that the "proof" Oates had offered was all forged, and ineptly at that. Satisfied, James followed Charles to Newmarket for the October races.

I could not exactly tell whether James made his own plans for the fall to please me, or his duchess. Knowing Mary Beatrice had no patience for the bawdy excesses of Newmarket, he had arranged for her instead to travel to the Hague to visit his daughter Mary, the Princess of Orange. The visit was unofficial, with only a few of her closest ladies and their husbands for attendants. Mary Beatrice was delighted by this pleasure junket, as were both the prince and princess, and the three of them judged this to be a very kind display of regard from His Highness.

Yet while his wife was away, James took me with him to Newmarket, where I was sure our presence together as much as announced to the rest of the Court that I was now his mistress. The evidence was as clear as a new day to anyone with half a wit for scandal. There could be no honorable explanation for a maid of honor to go traipsing off among the gentlemen to Newmarket, and even less for me to be tending so closely to my mistress's husband while she was absent. I didn't care. I was given lodgings of my own near the cottage that Charles had taken for Nell's use, apart from Palace House but close enough to it for convenience, and I could not have been happier.

No matter that I was with child; at that time, my pregnancy didn't even seem quite real to me. Truly, I felt no different. Because of my height, my belly had yet to betray me, and my usual ruddy health carried me through. I hadn't turned wan or sickly, as some women did when with child, nor was I stricken with morning vomits. The only change that I could see was that, now that I'd been caught, my passions had increased, and I'd become randy as a she-stoat in perpetual heat, much to James's amusement, and his pleasure, too. I still could indulge in the suppers, the races, and the raucous parties that lasted through the night, relishing them all the more because I was at James's side.

Thus I sat at a table of inveterate carders late one evening at Nelly's house, the only lady at the table with three gentlemen. James had gone with his brother Charles and several others to watch fighting cocks in the stable, a sport I'd little taste for, especially when compared to cards. The wine was flowing pretty freely and the play was as fierce as the stakes were high. Yet Dame Fortune smiled on me, and over and over my hands were the best. Though I wasn't sure (it being vulgar and miserly to count whilst playing), I guessed my winnings to be at five hundred or so guineas. This was a sizable amount by any reckoning, more than sufficient to support a respectable household with a half dozen children for an entire year, and yet in the heat of the play, I regarded the growing pile of mother-of-pearl markers before me as only a sign of my luck and no more.

"God's blood, Mrs. Sedley, look at those cards," said the gentleman across the table from me. "You've nearly ruined me."

Laurence Hyde, or Lory, as we all called him, was James's brother-in-law through his first wife, and a great favorite of the king's for being a clever and excellent diplomat. He was new-returned to England from a successful appointment in the Low Countries, where, if his play this night was any indication, he must never have gone near a table of cards.

Now he sighed mournfully, holding out his open hands to demonstrate how empty I'd left them. "I'm as good as a pauper."

"You're as bad as a liar, Lory Hyde," I said cheerfully. "Everyone knows you're rich as Croesus. I couldn't ruin you if we played a week."

Still he showed me the most doleful face, made worse by the heavy pouches he had beneath his eyes from drink and gloomy enough that those who'd gathered around our table to watch laughed. "You've come damned close, madam. Permit me a final hand, so at least I'll leave with a coin or two in my pocket for the linkboy."

Now, any sensible carder would have retreated with his or her winnings and retired to bed content. But I wasn't sensible, and further, I'd spied James returned from the cockfights and watching me from along the wall. In all that crowd, his gaze was bound on me alone, a heady realization that made me flush with pleasure. I smiled at him across all the others, and he solemnly nodded back to me. I knew my boldness always amused him, and thus I was now determined to put on as a good show as I could.

I lowered my chin and grinned like a demon at Mr. Hyde, and spread my hands lovingly over my markers, as a miser would show his fondness for his hoard.

"You wish another hand, Mr. Hyde?" I asked, as if still considering, which of course I wasn't. "Are you so convinced your luck will turn?"

"It will," he said firmly. "You know the fickleness of chance, Mrs. Sedley. One moment all is sunshine, the next thunderous clouds and the bloody fires of hell itself. Play me again, and I'm certain I'll win."

I laughed. For all that Mr. Hyde was a diplomat of repute, he was equally famous for swearing hard as a tinker and sharp as a cutler, which must have sat very ill among the priggish Dutch.

"Then you shall prove your worth, sir." I shoved the pile of pearly markers into the center of the table. "One card for each of us, and the highest takes all."

Those around us exclaimed in amazement, yet I held fast, my heart racing with giddy excitement at being the centerpiece of so much attention. I knew Mr. Hyde would not disappoint me, and he didn't. Gentlemen never refused such an offer from a lady. He smiled slowly, and waved for a fresh deck.

Doubtless drawn by the growing crowd at the table, Nell herself pushed through to stand by my chair.

"Here now, what mischief is this?" she said, her coppery curls bouncing as she leaned over the table, and her breasts bouncing, too, in their usual fashion. She might have left the playhouse behind, but she still treated her life as another kind of stage where all her friends became players with her, whether we wished it or not. "What are you about, Mrs. Sedley? You know I keep a *most* respectable house."

That made everyone laugh again. There wasn't much that was respectable about Nell, as she knew perfectly and happily well, and that disrespectability was why evenings at her house were so popular with Charles and the rest of us.

"I'd never slander the good name of your house, Mrs. Gwyn," I declared. "But if Mr. Hyde wishes to force his luck, then I've no choice but to oblige him."

"No choice, hah," Nell scoffed, gently shoving my arm for emphasis. "No one knows how to play against a gentleman better'n you, Mrs. Sedley."

"Save you, madam," I said, and winked, which made her tip back her head and laugh uproariously.

"Go on, then, go on," she said. "But if she wins, Lory, I'll make certain you pay up what she's due."

The dealer shuffled the cards, squared them, and set the deck on the table between us. Mr. Hyde nodded for me to choose first, and without hesitation I cut the deck for my card, holding it facedown on the table as he, too, drew his card. There we both sat, our cards waiting beneath our palms and our gazes steady across the table.

At last with a flourish I turned my card for all to see. "A black queen!" I crowed, sure I'd won. "Where's your luck now, sir?"

He sighed and shrugged as if already admitting defeat and slowly turned his own card: a scarlet ace to trump my swarthy queen.

"You dog!" I cried as the crowd around us erupted. I shoved my chair back and rose, throwing my losing card back on the table. With both hands I shoved the entire pile of markers toward Mr. Hyde, my deep lace cuffs fluttering back over my arms.

"There now, sir, it's yours," I said with dramatic resignation worthy of Medea herself. "Take it all, and rejoice in your good fortune. I'll not have it said that I don't lose as well as I win. But a pox on my ill luck, and a filthy pox on that black-clad queen who played me false."

Nell reached down to pluck up the discarded card, surveying it with a dreadful scowl.

"Why, I do not believe that's a queen at all," she said, sniffing as if smelling something foul. "Look'ee, Katherine, look'ee close. I vow there's a fishy, Friday taint to her."

I understood her meaning at once and seized upon it with her as a true conspirator, likewise scowling at the card in her hand. "How wicked clever you are, Nell! Why did I not see it before? The jade has a wimple, not a crown, and a sooty habit in place of royal robes."

"Take care what you say, ladies, I beg you," warned poor Mr. Hyde, pointedly trying to dissuade us from finishing the jest on account of his master the duke behind him. Mr. Hyde was most loyal that way, while I—I'd other intentions.

"Here now, all of you, bear witness," I said gleefully, taking the card from Nell to hold it high, turning this way and that so no one would miss it. "Here I've been betrayed not by a goodly Protestant queen, but by a lurking, black-clad Romish nun!"

Most laughed with Nell and with me, but others did not, for fear of offending James and the other Catholics in the room. With the card still raised brazenly in my hand, I turned toward where James had been standing earlier to watch me. To my disappointment, the place was now empty. But as I began to lower my arm, James was suddenly there beside me, taking me by the arm.

"Come," he said curtly, already pulling me with him from the room. His voice was terse, his expression set, even rigid. I'd truly no choice then but to join him, leaving behind an audience that was both scandalized and titillated.

With no further word, he grimly drew me through the hall and past more startled revelers, into the small passage that led from the back chamber to the yard beyond. He shoved the door shut after us, but there was no bolt nor lock on the door to keep others out if they tried to follow, and the threat of discovery only added to my excitement now. There were no candles in here, with the only light coming from the quarter-moon through the window behind him, but enough to show his expression still grimly taut.

He drew me sharply around to face him, pushing me back against the wall as at last he released my arm. I looked up at him through my lashes, my heart racing so fast in my breast that my voice was quick and breathy.

"What is it you wished to say to me in such privacy, sir?" I said, fair taunting him. "What can you not say before the others?"

"You risk too much, Katherine," he said, the words clipped and curt. The tension in his body was palpable as he struggled to keep control of himself. "You know you do."

I'd learned much about control from him. I shrugged my shoulders, a luxurious undulation against the rough plaster wall behind me, and tipped my head backward to display the pale curve of my throat to him.

"It's my own money, sir," I said. "I've taken nothing from you. If I choose to wager against Lory on the turn of a single card, then—"

"That's not my meaning," he said roughly, pressing closer against me so that I felt his heated breath on my forehead. "You know that."

"Ahhh," I said, exhaling in a long sigh of acknowledgment. I still held my losing card in my hand, and I now raised it between us, tapping the pasteboard lightly against the corner of my wide mouth. "Did you mean this, sir?"

His glance flicked down to the card with the black-clad queen, then at once to my mouth. As he looked, I licked across my parted lips, my tongue wet with invitation.

"You're a bold, wanton lady, Katherine," he said, his voice shaking, and in it I heard the first tremble of desire fraying his careful restraint. "You mock me, even as you madden me with temptation. You dare, Katherine. You *dare*."

"Then dare with me, sir," I said, my voice husky with my longing. I trailed the stiffened edge of the card along his square-cut jaw, another teasing kind of caress. "You know you wish to as much as I. Dare with me."

James groaned, an anguished, tormented rumble drawn from deep within his chest, and then fell upon me like a man famished, kissing me with an ardor that was so fierce as to be desperate. He shoved aside my skirts as I helped him unbutton his breeches, lust making us both clumsy. He pushed me back against the wall, and in the next instant he'd found my mark, entering me with such vigor that I cried out with the dizzying pleasure of it. We were both of a height to enjoy this manner of sport, and by the time we'd reached our release, my hair had half fallen down over my shoulders and the silk of my gown was snagged by the plaster behind me. I'd wrapped one of my long legs around his waist, I'd been that eager for his possession, and he'd buried his hands beneath my skirts to fondle my charms.

Yet lovemaking was often like this with him, and I relished it. Once James decided to succumb to my temptation, he could not claim me fast enough, fair devouring me as if I were some forbidden sweetmeat. Perhaps I was, too: a wanton, forthright, Protestant sweetmeat, forbidden by his confessor and every other priest around him, and likely all the more desirable for being proscribed.

"You're mine, Katherine," he whispered hoarsely into my tousled hair, his greedy hands still laying claim to my most intimate charms. "You see what comes of daring me. You're mine, and I cannot give you up."

"Then don't," I whispered in return, and kissed his rough cheek with true fondness. "Don't ever part with me, sir, and I'll vow to be with you always."

I closed my eyes, too overcome for the humble truths of sight, and rested my cheek against his broad shoulder. It frightened me, how much

I'd come to need him. With other men, I'd yearned so for love that I'd tried to mold myself into whatever form they wished. I'd tried, and to my considerable misery, I'd failed, and been cast away as unworthy. But James loved me for what I was, and how I was, and the more outspoken and true to my own willful and rebellious spirit I became, the more he seemed to love it, and me. I who had never belonged to any man was now the treasure of a royal prince, and I couldn't conceive of any whispered words more dear than to hear him call me his.

"I will come to you tonight," he said as at last we separated. "Warn your servants, and be ready for me."

I nodded, hastily smoothing my petticoats and trying to jab my hairpins back into some semblance of their former place, enough at least to satisfy the loose company of Newmarket. He was doing the same, stuffing his shirt back into his breeches and fastening his buttons. Last of all, he bent to retrieve the playing card I'd dropped on the floor.

"You *are* wicked, Katherine," he said with a sigh, the card in his fingers. "Nor would I ever want you otherwise, may all the Gods and blessed saints in heaven forgive me for it."

I grinned, and looped my arms around his shoulders. "Return to your rightful church, sir," I said softly between kisses, "and you won't have nearly so many saints to worry over."

"And there you are, Katherine, exactly as I said, my temptation incarnate." But this time he smiled, and to my delight, he pressed his lips to the black queen before tucking her away into his coat as a souvenir.

He opened the door and slipped away first, to return to the others as if he'd never been away, while I waited a few moments before I followed. But as soon as I crept from the shadows, my cheeks still flushed as I blinked at the brightness of the candlelight, I saw Nell. She stood alone before me with her plump arms, covered with bracelets, crossed over her chest and a thoughtful expression upon her round face.

"So that is it, eh?" she asked, surprisingly philosophical, or perhaps not so surprising at all. "Little Sid's Kid an' the duke. Lah, who'd have guessed such a pretty coupling as that?"

Who would, indeed?

Yet by the time we all returned to London with Charles the following week, there was little left to be guessed, with everything spelled out with perfect conviction by every wagging tongue at Court. I had only been back in town and in my lodgings at St. James's for a single day before Father summoned me to call upon him in Bloomsbury Square.

I should have known he'd have heard the gossip himself by then; he'd always prided himself on having the freshest tattle of the Court, and mine was very fresh indeed. Even without that certainty, the dry, precise tone of his invitation should have warned me that he was not in the best humor. Instead I was so wrapped in my own oblivious bliss that I was sure Father would want only to share the joy of my new situation and wish me the same happiness in it that he always had heretofore.

Alas, I was sorrowfully mistaken. I recognized that the instant I was shown into Father's library, where he stood waiting before his desk, as stiff and unyielding as a sentry at his post.

"Good day, Father," I said, coming forward with my arms outstretched to embrace him, as was our usual custom. "I trust you are well?"

"Tolerably," he said curtly, "considering the grievous news I have been forced to bear."

When he made no move to return my affection, I let my arms drop to my sides and my intended embrace withered away unwanted. "What news is this, Father?"

"What news, you ask?" he repeated, each word as cold and brittle as a shard of ice. "Why, only that my dear daughter has decided that common whoring is more to her tastes than any respectable occupation, and that she has so little regard for her own honor and worth that she would lift her skirts and spread her legs wide for a Stuart cock to fill her."

I winced and flushed with shame, not for what I'd done with James, for I felt no shame in that, but for the pain I'd brought to my poor father.

"I'm sorry," I began helplessly. "I'm sorry."

"Oh, yes, Katherine, I am sure that you are," he said, "now that your name is as common as water in the Thames, and as riddled with filth, too."

He pointedly turned from me, instead dropping into his armchair. The merriness that usually wreathed his face was nowhere to be found, and his cheeks seemed sunken with misery and carved with lines that hadn't been there when last we'd met.

"It is bad enough that you're a whore, Katherine," he continued, "but I'd never marked you for a coward as well. Why did you not warn me of your intent? Why skulk off without a single word to me, off to Newmarket like some jockey's trull?"

I looked down at my oversized castor-fur muff, absently swinging it back and forth on my wrists. "Is that true, Father? Would it truly have made it any easier for you to bear if you'd known before?"

"I would rather have heard it from you, yes, than from a score of other spiteful tongues," he said wearily. "His Majesty himself spoke of it this morning to me, asking if I were pleased to see my daughter in his brother's bed, with the same good cheer he'd employ to inquire after the weather, *damn* him."

To hear Father curse the king shocked me more deeply than hearing him call me a whore.

"Then I was a coward," I admitted. "I did wish to tell you, but I never could find the words to begin, knowing how unhappy I was sure to make you."

"Then why do it at all?" he asked. "If you dreaded the words that would make me unhappy, then why didn't you likewise save me the pain that your actions have caused me? Unless it was not your choice at all. Unless His Grace—"

"It was as much my choice as his," I interrupted, quick to defend my lover. "There was no rape or ravishment, no matter what you might have heard. He never forced any advantage that I didn't freely grant."

"Then why, Katherine?" he asked with despair. "Why would you ruin yourself like this?"

"Because—because he makes me happy, Father," I said, as truthful a confession as I could make. "I tried to do as you wished, and find a husband who could do as much for me, and I never could find one who pleases me half as much as His Grace."

"But he is more than twice your age!" he cried. "He is wed to another, with daughters grown and wed!"

"It matters not to me," I insisted, "for he makes me happy. Isn't that what you've always said you wished for me?"

"But not like this," he said, shaking his head. "Never like this. To a dull-witted, stubborn prince who would destroy his country for the sake of a misbegotten faith!"

"He's not dull-witted, Father, and he loves England and her people too well to ever wish them harm," I said heatedly. "Besides, I'm still of our Church. I won't be led astray to Rome."

Father didn't seem to hear me, or pretended as much. "There is still a breath of hope, of course. Oh, you will be the seven-days' wonder, to be sure, but at least you limited your intrigue to Newmarket. If you can end it now, before Her Highness returns from the Hague, then your misstep will soon be forgotten. You could travel to Paris, or even to Venice, with time away from England so that the Court will forget you."

"But that isn't what *I* want," I protested, "nor does His Highness wish to part with me. It's too late for that, anyway."

He lowered his chin, likely already guessing the worst, and thus I bravely plunged ahead, armed only with the truth.

"Our 'intrigue,' as you call it, was begun long before Newmarket, and before the duchess journeyed abroad," I said. "The duke has pledged to keep me properly as his mistress as soon as I withdraw from the duchess's household and our affairs can be arranged. For me, Father, and for my child. *Our* child."

"Your bastard, you mean." He groaned, and closed his eyes. "Merciful heaven, what manner of vengeful punishment is this upon me?"

"It is no punishment at all, Father!" I cried, coming to kneel beside his chair. "You and Lady Sedley are proof enough that the bonds of marriage aren't necessary for those who wish to be together. The bastard son that you have sired with Lady Sedley—"

"He is my *son*, Katherine, as surely as you are my daughter," he said furiously. "I won't hear my boy tossed in with that sniveling low herd of royal bastards."

I sat back on my heels, stunned. "But it will be my child as well as the duke's, and your grandchild, of your own blood. Can you not bring yourself to give your blessing?"

He rose abruptly and crossed the room, as if he could not bear to be near to me. "You have already acted without my blessing, Katherine. I see no purpose to condoning what you have done by giving you an empty blessing now."

"Because you are my father," I said from my knees, my heart breaking to hear such cruel words from the man I'd always believed had loved me. "Because despite what I have done to displease you, I am still your daughter, by birth and blood."

Yet not even that plea could soften him toward me. Instead he opened the door, determined to abandon me for the first time in my life.

"You'll learn soon enough the consequences of what you have done, Katherine," he said, looking past me. "When you do, you'll have need of far greater forgiveness than mine, and may God in his infinite mercy grant it."

Chapter Sixteen

St. James's Palace, London
October 1678

When I'd left my father's house in Bloomsbury Square, I believed that the consequences that he had threatened to me were all of his own doing. But as the last of summer slipped into autumn, I realized that being tied to James was far more complicated than I'd realized, and far more dangerous as well.

I had, of course, heard of the presumed plot by the Jesuits to murder the king, and the man Titus Oates who vowed he knew every detail of it. In our first days at Newmarket, Oates and his tale were much discussed, though usually with mocking derision. He'd soon been forgotten in the more interesting rush of racing and frolics, and I do not believe that even James spoke of the man once in our time together.

But in London, Lord Danby had patiently continued his investigation of Oates's endless accusations and reports. Everything was sworn under oath before a well-respected magistrate, Sir Edmund Berry Godfrey, and the testimony swelled to more than eighty separate articles. The names, dates, and insinuations astonished the councilors in charge of reviewing them. In addition to the Jesuits (who were by tradition blamed for most every misfortune that occurred in town, from a falling tea cake to the Great Fire of fourteen years before), Oates accused several Catholic lords and even James's own secretary, Mr. Coleman, claiming that Coleman, a Catholic himself, maintained an extensive, treasonous correspondence with the French and the Papacy on James's behalf. Sir Edmund himself warned James, and suggested that if such questionable letters did exist, they should better be destroyed.

Again, no one would have paid much heed to this, let alone read Oates's endless testimony, but the day after Sir Edmund had finished his duties, he vanished. Several days later his battered and decaying corpse, run through with his own sword, was found in the brush on Primrose Hill. Though most likely the magistrate was murdered by unknown thieves, it did not take long for the rumors to take hold in London. Surely Jesuits must be to blame for the death, for just as surely Sir Edmund must have discovered the details of their murderous plot against the king.

Like a blistering boil that craves the lance for relief, the ever-present sentiments of Londoners against Papists gathered and grew into a hard, painful knot of fear and hatred. Instead of being disregarded, Oates's testimony was now viewed as purest prophecy. He was called the savior of England and courted by great lords who should have known better, and even given lodgings at Whitehall. With Oates to offer suitable embellishment, Sir Edmund's death was regarded to be only the first of an impending slaughter of Protestant innocents. Anyone with Catholic sympathies was suspected of being part of the conspiracy, and every Anglican took care to guard their homes and families against the coming invasion of Catholic forces. Gentlemen carried extra weapons in case of attack, and even ladies began tucking small pistols into their muffs and pockets.

In such a climate, Danby's councilors naturally requested all of Coleman's papers, and naturally he provided them, including the key for all his personal ciphers. But to the shock of everyone—and most of all to James—Coleman had foolishly neglected to destroy incriminating letters as he'd been warned. Suddenly the most private and delicate of diplomatic correspondence was made public, linking James not only to Rome, but to the French king's own confessors. Though James at once swore that Coleman had acted on his own and without his knowledge, the damage was done. As soon as Parliament reassembled in October, demands were made in both Houses that James be removed from all government affairs as well as from the succession, and in the Commons there were even preposterous calls that he be banished from the Court for the safety of the king.

To my personal sorrow, my own father was among those calling. His politics had allied him first with the Duke of Buckingham's old Country Party, and now with the Petitioners, or the Whigs, as they were newly called, a pugnacious term borrowed from the old Scottish Whiggamores. Father found a happy place among these impetuous men, whose leaders included the Earl of Shaftesbury as well as his old friend Lord Dorset. He had even been among those gentlemen trusted with the task of translating Coleman's French letters into English to be used at his trial.

I could not tell if Father spoke and acted so strongly against James on account of me, or if he might have viewed my fall from grace more kindly if I'd chosen another gentleman. Father didn't give me the opportunity to ask, keeping his distance from me even in the times when we were both in attendance at Whitehall. I was cut deep by his rejection, and sorely missed his counsel, his wit, and most of all his love.

Through Father's man of business, I was soon informed that he had also changed his will against me. My once-lavish portion of twenty thousand a year was reduced to six thousand, with an additional ten on Father's death. The remainder of his estate was divided between Lady Sedley and his son. Father could not be more direct in his displeasure; clearly he believed that since I'd cast my lot with James, I must now look to him for practical support as well as for love.

Such was my life when Mary Beatrice returned from her pleasure-tour abroad. As a Papist, an Italian, a very niece to the Pope, she, too, was instantly suspected and at risk, and the fact that Coleman had often served as her secretary as well did not help her cause. Perhaps because of these much larger concerns threatening her household, she was not informed of my connection with her husband, and to my considerable surprise continued to treat me as she had before, a maid of honor in her household that she seldom deigned to notice.

It was just as well that she didn't. By the time we'd returned from Newmarket, I'd quickened, and to my delight and wonder I'd felt the first flutterings of the babe within me. The swell of my belly showed now, though the same artful mantua-maker who had once toiled to provide me with a show of plumpness now contrived to mask the reality, and for the present my secret was still mine to keep.

Mine, and James's. Amidst the turmoil around him, beleaguered on all sides, my visits to his bedchamber late at night had become one of his few remaining comforts. It had also become a place for confidences, for James had taken my father's rejection as a sign of my true loyalty to him.

He now considered me worthy of his most intimate trust, a friend as well as his mistress. How could I not be honored?

"Coleman will become a martyr," he began gloomily one night in late November as we lay together. "Now that they've arrested and arraigned him for high treason, they'll have no choice but to find him guilty. Parliament won't accept any other verdict."

I sighed, bunching the pillow bier behind my head so I could more comfortably see his face and thereby judge his humor. He was not good at dissembling, my dear James, a sorry lack for a royal prince. No matter that he spoke the sentiments proper for a given occasion; his face would always betray his true feelings, which did little to help his popularity. Charles was blessed with so much charm and guile that he'd only to smile whilst juggling even the most blatant falsehood to be praised for his conviction and make his audience as eager as his lapping dogs for more. But James was cursed with innate honesty and a conscience to match, and it was a sad testament to our times that he was often faulted for both.

"You'll see I'm right, Katherine," he continued dolefully. "They'll believe every lie that Oates will swear and not one truth that Coleman will offer in defense of his own innocence. Anglicans may profess to loathe saints, but they'll make one of Coleman if they martyr him over his loyalty to the True Church."

"If they do, sir, then Coleman will be a martyr to his own stupidity, not his faith," I said. "That man was warned with sufficient time to destroy any evidence that will be used against him, and yet he did not do it."

"He believed in goodness to combat evil," James said sadly. "He trusted too much in truth."

"The one who's trusted too much is you, sir, to let such a fool handle your affairs," I said bluntly. "His empty-headed behavior has put you at risk, and for what? No, you have done the right thing by swearing you knew nothing of his infernal letters, and shaken Coleman's dirt from your shoes."

"But I did know," he said. "He was only acting upon my orders, for the good of England, and now—"

"Oh, please, please, put that from your thoughts forever!" I cried with genuine concern, sitting upright to confront him. "If you say that before the wrong persons, then you, too, will be put in the Tower for treason, and I—I could not bear that, sir. I could not."

He smiled crookedly. "You care that much what becomes of me, Katherine?"

"I do, sir," I said, placing my open hand on his chest for emphasis. I did mean it, too. With each day and night, I had become more and more attached to him as my lover and as my friend, too, until it seemed as if James and our coming child had claimed the entirety of my life. Without my father's affection, I would need James's support to weather the coming months and the peril of childbirth.

But for now I gazed at him only with purest affection. "We make for a curious pairing, I know," I said. "But you're that dear to me, sir, that I cannot imagine my life without you in it."

"Hah," he said softly. "So you are to me, Katherine."

"Then you understand why I won't part with you," I said tenderly. "My own dear sir! Sometimes I believe you're too good a man for me, let alone for this country, though your enemies will never see it. A small measure of deceit would serve you well."

That made him laugh. "Am I so honorable as that, that I must go begging like a mendicant for a portion of wickedness?"

"I'll gladly share some of mine, if it would help." I leaned forward to kiss him as lasciviously as I could, and he rolled me onto my back to kiss me in return.

"There," he said. "Am I improved?"

"It's a beginning," I said. "Taking an Anglican to your bed will do that. But I vow you may require more."

He chuckled, sliding his hand along my body, to come to rest upon the rising swell of my belly. By the reckoning of my midwife, I was nearly six months gone, and the babe's kicks were strong enough that James could feel them, too. Gently he moved his hand until he felt the child respond, his smile broadening with happy wonder. Unlike many gentlemen who showed no interest in children beyond their siring, he had always been a doting father to his three surviving daughters as well as his children with Mrs. Churchill, and he showed every promise of doing the same with our babe.

"You can't keep on as a maid of honor, Katherine," he said. "Not like this. It's past time you resigned your post and moved to more suitable quarters."

"Not yet, sir, please," I begged. "This way I can see you most every night. If I leave St. James's, then you'll forget me."

"Nothing will keep me from you," he declared with reassuring conviction. "I'm weary of feigning otherwise. Everyone knows we dallied in Newmarket."

"Her Highness does not, sir." I was not such a fool as to dream of taking his wife's place, the way that Lady Portsmouth had done when she'd first become Charles's mistress. But my thoughts were confused where Mary Beatrice was concerned. How could it be otherwise, when I loved her husband and carried his child, yet had pledged my loyalty to serve her as best I could?

"What Her Highness knows or does not know is my concern, not yours," he said firmly. "I would wish the world to know your place in my life, and in my heart."

"More justly in your bed, sir," I said wryly, even as tears of joy stung my eyes. "But best for you to keep matters as they are for now. You've trouble enough without adding me as well."

"You are never trouble to me, Katherine," he said solemnly, and as he began to kiss me, the babe shifted again beneath his wide-spread hand.

"Now, that's a brave kick," he said proudly. "The work of a strong, lusty babe."

I smiled, though I wondered if he was thinking of all the other lost children he'd sired who'd not been strong and had died before they'd had time to live. Protectively I placed my hand beside his, reassuring myself of my own babe's liveliness.

"She doesn't like being jostled by you," I said. "Faith, you should feel her jump and dance when we swive!"

" 'She'?" he asked curiously. "You're convinced it's a girl?"

"More likely wishing it so," I admitted. "You've no need of a son from me. Bastard sons grow to vex and bring mischief to their fathers. You've only to look at Monmouth for proof of that."

"Oh, Monmouth," he said, and his expression darkened. There had been a time when James had been happy to be the favorite uncle to his brother's oldest bastard. They'd shared a common interest in military affairs, and the younger duke had showed considerable promise. But Lord Monmouth was nearly thirty now, and so restless with ambition that he'd come to believe those Whigs who wanted him recognized as Charles's Protestant heir in place of James himself.

"Exactly so, sir," I said gently. "I'd not wish our child to be another Monmouth. A daughter would be much safer."

"Not if she favors her mother," he teased, but the sadness remained in his eyes.

I lay my palm against his cheek to soothe him. "Nothing will come of Monmouth's desires, sir. You know that. Your brother has made it clear enough that he'll never give way."

"But what if he does, Katherine?" he asked, his pale eyes bleak. "He already has warned me not to attend the admiralty board and to keep away from the committee for foreign affairs. I know, too, that to please Parliament, he is considering further sanctions against Catholics. What if we're all swallowed up by the poison of Oates and Danby and the others, and Charles has no choice but to abandon me?"

"He won't," I said fiercely. "He is your brother. He is the king. His will can overrule all the others combined."

Yet even as I spoke, I began to doubt my own certainty. The arrest and sacrifice of Coleman would not long appease Oates and his followers, nor stop the madness that was threatening the Court and the country. What if for their sake and for peace, Charles decided another, more meaningful sacrifice was necessary? What if he chose to placate Anglican England over his Catholic brother?

And what then would become of James, and our child, and me?

As all at Court had expected, yet dreaded, Edward Coleman was found guilty of plotting to murder His Majesty, and in the first week of December, he was carted to Tyburn Hill and executed, still protesting his innocence. He was right. The infamous letters had proved indiscreet, but not treasonous, and certainly not sufficient to merit conviction. It had been the testimony of the monstrous Oates that had killed Coleman more surely than his executioner.

But instead of quelling public fear, Coleman's conviction and death seemed only to feed it. Emboldened, Oates made ever more preposterous accusations, including attacking six venerable and aged peers, gentlemen whose lives had been conducted without any stain, as being conspirators simply because they were Catholic. Now, too, Oates acquired an accomplice in a new and equally disreputable witness, one Captain William Bedloe. While Oates himself had hesitated at naming any of the royal family or their households, Bedloe had no such qualms. Soon he'd accused the king's own physician, Dr. Wakefield, of accepting a Jesuit bribe to poison His Majesty. He claimed that not only had the queen herself been party to this ridiculous plot, but that James, too, had been a willing witness to the various meetings that had taken place.

It didn't matter that Charles himself did not believe a word of this nonsense, or that he swiftly and efficiently defended the terrified and thoroughly innocent queen. He couldn't do the same with his brother. In the minds of most Londoners, James was now irrevocably tied to the worst of the accusations as well as to the more nebulous fears of popery, the French, and a too-powerful monarchy. But instead of standing above the gossip and accusations, as those around him begged him to do (for in this I was hardly alone), James insisted on wallowing into the mud to try to defend himself, which only made the suspicions around him grow more believable, yet also impenetrable. Many Members of Parliament agreed: why would the Duke of York take such a difficult stance unless he was truly guilty, with onerous, traitorous secrets he feared would in time be revealed?

Yet it was my own secret, not any of James's, that finally was revealed shortly before Christmas Day, and the same week as my twenty-first birthday. Despite my careful dress, I was now too far advanced for my pregnancy to be unobserved, and I was likewise slow to rise from my curtsies. I volunteered nothing of my condition, and gave out no hints as to the gentleman responsible, which only increased the curiosity of the other ladies at Court. I knew they all guessed it must be James's and counted the months after Newmarket, though none dared speak his name aloud before Mary Beatrice.

One afternoon, however, I sensed that one lady or another must have finally confided her suspicions to the duchess. As was our household's habit, I was among her ladies gathered in her parlor for our usual occupations of stitching, reading, cards, music, and conversation. Yet when I went to take my customary place within the warmth of the fireplace—mine by rights on account of being, at nearly twenty-one, the oldest of the maids of honor—Mary Beatrice stopped me, and in a voice as chilly as the December day, bid me sit at a distance from her. Though surprised, I could hardly protest on account of her rank and mine below it, and I went to shiver on my remote stool beside the ice-covered window, as sure a sign of disfavor as any.

For many days, Mary Beatrice had been working a complicated needle-piece in the Italian manner, which required scores of tiny garnet beads to be threaded on the needle and stitched into place. Previously she had taken the greatest care with the basket of beads in her lap, for they were costly and impossible to replace. But today she had scarcely gathered up her frame when she knocked the basket from her knee, sending the tiny beads to bounce and scatter willy-nilly across the floor around her. The other ladies all exclaimed with concern, and at once dropped to their knees to begin retrieving the wayward beads. But just as swiftly, Mary Beatrice stopped them and requested they return to their stools and chairs.

"Mrs. Sedley," she called to me, her usually gentle eyes now hard against me. "Here is a task for you. Gather up these beads for me, so I might continue my work."

I rose, and curtsied my acquiescence, as again I'd no choice but to obey. Carefully I knelt on the floor, my silken skirts settling around me. Bending farther to gather the tiny beads was nearly impossible with my much-thickened waist to impede me, but slowly I began, determined to finish the odious task without faltering or complaint. No one spoke, a rare, uneasy silence among so many ladies, and I could feel every one of them watching me, some with sympathy, some gloating at my discomfort. I cannot venture how long it took me to gather the beads, nor what thoughts passed through Mary Beatrice's head as I crawled about at her feet. Perhaps she was ashamed of the humiliating cruelty of her order, or perhaps nothing but jealousy raged behind her masklike face the entire while. All I knew for certain was that her stony silence continued as I dropped the last bead into the basket and at last rose clumsily to my feet, more like a lumbering bear than a lady.

I curtsied as best I could with the basket in my hand, and as she took it from me, I had a terrible dread that she might purposefully drop it again, and again make me gather up the beads. Instead she set the basket on the table beside her and turned back to me, her mouth taut, her gaze fixed on mine. Then, with shocking speed, she struck her hand across my cheek with a ferocity that knocked my head to one side and shook my wits and very nearly toppled me from my feet.

"I dismiss you from my service and from this household," she said curtly, her words echoing through the thrumming in my ears. "You will leave your lodgings here by this night, and not return."

Somehow I curtsied. Somehow I rose again and backed from her presence and from the room. Somehow, too, I made my way through the palace's halls to my lodgings with my head high and my step measured, and past the other courtiers who stared curiously at the blossoming mark Mary Beatrice's blow had doubtless left on my cheek.

My maid Thomson was not so restrained.

"Oh, mistress, your face!" she cried with alarm, rushing to me as I entered my rooms for what would be the final time. "How has this happened, mistress? What has befallen you?"

At last I touched my hand to my cheek, wincing as I felt the pain and swelling. I was certain my pale face would be bruised, and I was equally certain that I'd not cover the mark with paint or powder, but wear it proudly when I entered the palace on the following day. Now I smiled through my pain, and even laughed with a light-headed relief that worried poor Thomson all the more.

But the ruse was done, and at last I'd earned what I'd longed for most. I was no longer a lowly maid of honor. I was instead the recognized mistress to His Highness the Duke of York and the mother of his coming child. Now I'd have my place, and I'd have power with it, but most of all, I'd have James. Was there any wonder, then, that even in that shaken, troubled Court, I felt my life had begun anew?

I TOOK A SMALL, NEAT HOUSE for myself in King Street close by the palace, a house that I later learned was only several places removed from the one where the Duchess of Cleveland had begun her similar career with Charles twenty years before. The irony of that was wonderfully delicious to me, as was the swiftness with which I was given new lodgings in Whitehall. To be sure, they were not nearly as grand as the suite of thirty rooms that Lady Portsmouth possessed, but they were an open acknowledgment of my new role, which pleased me as well.

To be true, these lodgings were nearly the only acknowledgment. James was not like his brother, who fair trumpeted the name of a new favorite. When the Lady Portsmouth, then but a lowly, untitled maid of honor herself, had finally capitulated to Charles's seduction, her ravishment had been nearly as public as Bartholomew Fair, complete with a mock wedding ceremony between her and Charles and scores of drunken courtiers as eager witnesses. James was far more reserved, and would likely prefer to perish than subject himself or any lady to so public or lascivious a performance. There would be none of Charles's public fondling or great smacking kisses before a gaping Court, nor would I ever expect James to drape me with crown jewels borrowed from the state treasure in the Tower, as Lady Cleveland had once demanded of her royal lover.

James's regard for me was much quieter, in part because I was now within weeks of my time. Though I was too large for dancing, I still attended the balls and other frolics that marked the Christmas holidays and the New Year of 1679. I dressed myself as extravagantly as I could, and no longer made any attempt to disguise my belly. Instead I flaunted it proudly as a mark of favor that outshone any mere jewel or other bauble, and when James came to sit beside me, I took care to amuse him with my conversation and make him laugh aloud at my observations and witticisms, enough that others around us remarked on the obvious pleasure he took in my company.

I knew we were a curiosity, worth much marveling and comment. Royal princes, even modest ones like James, were expected to choose as their mistresses the rarest beauties of their kingdoms. That I was plain confounded every expectation, and even Charles made a pointed, unkind jest about how James's mistresses (meaning me and Arabella Churchill) were so unattractive that his confessor must have chosen us for him as a form of penance.

My old nemesis Lord Dorset was quick to be inspired by my situation as well. This time he called me Sylvia, not Dorinda, but I was doubtless his target just the same, and with his pen managed to slander not only me, but James, too:

SYLVIA, methinks you are unfit
For your great Lord's embrace;
For tho' we all allow you Wit,
We can't a handsome Face.

Then where's the Pleasure, where's the Good,
Of spending Time and Cost?
For if your Wit be not understood,
Your Keeper's Bliss is lost.

Another couplet was even less flattering to James:

Poor Sedley's Fall, ev'n her own Sex deplore,
Who with so small Temptation turn'd thy Whore.

I didn't care. In James's eyes, I *was* beautiful, for my cleverness, my daring, my spirit. I'd only to look across the room to where Mary Beatrice, far my superior in loveliness and rank, sat neglected among her ladies. I was the one James desired more; I was the one whose company he sought, despite the mockery of the Court and the displeasure of his wife and priests. I was the one, and I'd never been happier.

Though I was not so greedy for material gain as other mistresses, James was as generous as he'd promised he'd be. For my birthday, he gave me a splendid pair of earrings, emeralds and pearls, and for Christmas, four days later, the pendant and necklace that matched. Once I'd taken my new house in my own name, he'd been quick to see that the holding was paid by his accounts, and he likewise let me know that I could spend whatever was necessary to make both the house and my new palace lodgings more pleasing and agreeable to my tastes, and to provide as I saw fit for my lying-in. I could, of course, have done this from my own funds, for though Father had diminished my inheritance, I was still a lady of wealth, and now, to my droll amusement, I'd also my pension from having retired as a maid of honor. But it delighted me to have James look after me and my expenses, another way he showed his devotion.

In the curious way of fate, I learned of his largesse by a most unexpected messenger. Colonel James Grahme, my first love, had once again returned to Court, and as a reward for his good service abroad in the duke's name, he and his wife and growing family had been granted lodgings in St. James's, and the plum post of keeper of the privy purse. As keeper, he oversaw the ducal household's private expenses, of which I was now one.

James Grahme came to me himself to share the details of my new prosperity, and I welcomed him with the warmth of an old friend. Strange to realize that six years had already passed since we'd first met and parted, six years in which I had left my innocence behind and become a woman grown and far wiser in the world. The wounds he'd once given my maidenly heart had long since healed, and I was now able to be glad that he'd found love and contentment with his wife, just as I had with James.

Yet our reunion, made as it was amidst the dust and refurbishing of my new house, was not without its awkwardness.

"Let me study you properly, Katherine," he said, standing apart after our first embrace in greeting. "I vow you've grown more handsome by the day."

"Which is to say I'm still but a shadow of handsomeness compared to you," I said. He was near to thirty years now, his earlier military gallantry replaced by a gravity befitting his station as a gentleman, a husband, and a father, yet his visage remained as ripe with manly charm as I'd recalled it. "Faith, but you've always been a lovely man to gaze upon."

He flushed beneath his soldier's weathered cheek and smiled in the way I'd not forgotten. "I see you've not changed either, Katherine, and will always speak your thoughts plain."

"I will indeed," I said, laughing. "Which is why I will ask you what is so clearly perplexing you at present."

His eyes flicked down over my belly, a gesture that had become all too familiar to me.

"What is it, my dear colonel?" I asked. "Can you perceive the imprint of a crown glowing like a beacon from within my womb?"

"I'm surprised, that is all," he admitted. "I'll speak as freely as you do, and confess I'd never thought such a fate for you."

"Faith, that's a fine judgment to make of me," I exclaimed, surprised by his candor. "That I'm too plain to be a royal mistress?"

"Not at all," he said quickly. "What I intended was not that you are too plain, but rather that you are too clever for His Highness. However does he keep pace with you?"

"He doesn't," I said, and grinned with amusement and a certain relief. I might be well done with loving James Grahme, but I still didn't wish to be unlovely in his memory. "But by some miracle, we please each other, and that is sufficient."

He nodded, and now I blushed at how thoroughly he was searching my face. "You are happy, then? You are content? I'd never wish otherwise for you."

"I am," I said softly, and without thinking placed my hand across my belly. "I am happy with His Highness."

He nodded again, though I'm not sure he entirely believed me. "Then I am happy, too," he said. "It's good to find you here. The Court is not a garden where true friends flourish."

"Faith, no," I agreed. "No matter how much golden dung is spread about, more weeds will grow here than in any other plot in England."

He laughed, but his smile soon faded. "I didn't intend a jest, Katherine. A friend is a precious thing to have in this place, and I pray that you will consider me one to you."

"I will, and thank you for it." Touched, I kissed him lightly on his cheek as a pledge of that friendship he offered. He was right: true friends were few at Court, a treasure not to be squandered, especially in the perilous times that bubbled and swirled around us.

LIKE ALL WOMEN CLOSE TO THEIR TIME, I had let my thoughts focus most closely on my coming babe and the trial of childbirth that lay before me, like some perilous dragon that must be vanquished before I could reach the happiness that I knew lay beyond. Just as men perished in war, women perished in childbed, and though I was healthy and as prepared as I could be, I was still more afraid than I would admit.

Thus I will perhaps be forgiven that I'd paid less attention than I should to the misfortune that continued to threaten the Court and James with it. If the venomous accusations of Oates and Bedloe were not bad enough, in late December came worse news, this time from France.

The English ambassador to the French Court, Ralph Montague, had shown the supreme stupidity of seducing the young daughter of Lady Cleveland and Charles, and the indiscretion had instantly cost Montague his post. Waspishly, he had decided to retaliate, and introduced before the Commons his own collection of foul letters, signed by the king, that proved Lord Danby had accepted large gifts of gold on behalf of His Majesty for proroguing Parliament to oblige French policies. These letters only fed the suspicions and madness that already existed in the House, and overnight Lord Danby was transformed from the gentleman who'd first given credence to Titus Oates to the most prominent victim of the plot. He was charged with treason, and convicted by an outraged Commons. To save him from a final conviction in the House of Lords, Charles was left with no choice but to dissolve Parliament in early January and call for a new election.

It was a momentous decision, indicative of the peril Charles believed he faced. This Parliament had been first elected in 1661 in the welcoming flush of Charles's restoration to the throne and had, until now, been largely his friend. Now only the tiniest morsel of that goodwill remained, with only suspicion and ill will in its place.

The new House was bound to be more contentious regarding James and the succession as well as Lord Danby and the ongoing investigation of the Popish Plot, and by the end of the Court's usual Christmas revels, Charles was again desperately pleading with James to place the future of England first and return to the Anglican Church.

"What would make my brother do this, Katherine?" James exclaimed in impassioned anguish when he came to me one night in early February. "This day he sent both the Archbishop of Canterbury and the Bishop of Winchester to lay siege to me, as if my soul could be claimed by the most obstinate bidder!"

I was so unwieldy now that I'd taken to my bed, and I struggled to sit upright, as determined as James on this subject.

"Did you listen to their learned arguments, sir?" I pleaded. "These bishops are wise, thoughtful gentlemen, who wish only what is best for you. Did you set aside your stubbornness long enough to consider what they said?"

He lowered his chin and scowled, the very picture of the stubbornness I'd just declaimed. "Forgive me, Katherine, but you speak so only because you are yourself an Anglican."

"I speak so because I love you, as does His Majesty your brother!" I cried. "You can be an English prince or an English Papist, but you can never be both. A handful of words, and you will be received joyfully back into the church of your father, the church of your country. Your people will once again love you, and all will be forgiven. But if you persist in binding yourself to Rome—"

"Because my conscience knows it is the right course!" he shouted, striking his fist against the mantelpiece. "The right one, Katherine."

"Right in what way, sir?" I demanded heatedly, for we'd had this same battle many times before. "Right to betray your brother and his wishes for you? Right to heave England into another war that would make what Cromwell wrought seem as nothing? Right that you might be forever ruined, and lost to me?"

Overcome, I burst into anguished tears that I did not try to hide. At once he rushed to my bedside, meaning to comfort me, but I shook him away, scattering my tears over his breast.

"How can you not see it, sir?" I wept, my hands clutching my belly as if to protect the babe from its father's willful delusions. "You will be ruined, and not even His Majesty will be able to save you."

But James only bowed his head, his face twisted with an anguish that matched my own, and I saw that he wept, too, heavy tears that slid slowly down his cheeks.

"Charles will send me away," he said, his voice breaking. "He has already told me that. If I do not comply to his wishes, then he will banish me, and he will lose his crown as surely as our sainted father lost his."

"My poor dear sir," I whispered. "Oh, my poor love!"

He was wrong, sadly, horribly wrong, yet nothing I could say would persuade him any more than a score of bishops had been able to do. Instead I held my arms open to him and he came to me, resting his head on my shoulder as we wept together; for what was right, what was wrong, and the tragedy that would surely swallow us whole.

THE FOLLOWING NIGHT, I WOKE WITH a sense of grave foreboding. I climbed from my bed and wrapped myself against the cold, and began to pace like a restless beast. Snow was falling, the sky and street the same muffled gray. There was no dawn, no true sunrise, only a lightening of the gray to white. My pains began in earnest then, and at last I called for Thomson and she in turn sent for the midwife. I wrote a letter to James, asking his forgiveness for all the ways I had failed him, my words jagged as pain made my pen sputter and jerk. I labored through the day and into the night again, making the midwife shake her head at my slow progress. I wrote another letter, a single line, begging James to come to me so that I might see him one last time before I died.

He neither came, nor replied, and now I longed for death to end all my sufferings. By the next dawn, I was so weak that as the pains racked my poor body, all I could do was mewl helplessly while the midwife's women held my quivering limbs.

"Have courage, madam," the midwife said. "Bear down one more time, and you shall have your child."

My child, James's child—and with that thought like a prayer to guide me, I bore down as she ordered. One final pain, so grave I felt sure I would be split asunder, and then blessed relief as it slipped away.

"A girl, madam!" the midwife declared, and the other women made happy wordless exclamations with her. "A brave, lusty daughter for you!"

"Is she well?" I begged pathetically. "Will she live?"

"Course she'll live, God willing," the woman said, cackling at my doubt. "Judge for yourself."

She placed the babe upon my bare and shriveled belly, the now-empty place that had been her shelter these past months. Eagerly I reached down, desperate to be rejoined with her. *Her*; of course she was a girl, as I'd always known. She was sticky with blood and the muck of her birth, her black hair bristling from her head. Furiously she protested as the women wiped her clean, likely swearing one oath after another in whatever infant language she spoke. My daughter, yes. My daughter, Katherine, the same as I was called, and my mother before me. Yet I vowed I would love my little Katherine always, and never forget her as my own mother had forgotten me.

"She's hungry, poor lamb," the midwife said. "Let's put her to your teat, madam."

With their help, I held her close, and winced as she suckled hard.

"A strong little lass," said the woman with approval. "She'll take what she wants from life, that one will."

They laughed, but I did not, for already I knew it to be true. She would be beautiful like the Stuarts, with the wit of the Sedleys, and nothing would stand in her way.

As soon as I was able, I wrote to James to tell him I was safe delivered of his daughter. This time he wrote back at once, blessing us both and promising to come as soon as he could. While I waited, I sent Thomson to find the nearest Anglican minister, and before I let myself slip into the sweet sleep of exhaustion, I watched my daughter baptized into the Anglican Church.

James came that evening. He held and kissed and praised his daughter, and laughed at every unpleasant squawk she uttered. I wept with joy to see her in his arms, the dearest sight ever I could imagine. Yet I also saw the fresh lines on James's face and the bleakness in his eyes even as he smiled down at the babe.

"What is wrong, sir?" I asked softly. "What has happened?"

His bitter smile was more a grimace. "My brother has ordered me to leave England. I am banished, for the sake of the country. Her Highness and I must sail for Holland in two days, and can return only at my brother's pleasure."

"How long?" I whispered.

"I do not know," he said heavily, and looked down at our daughter. "Forgive me, Katherine, but I do not know."

Chapter Seventeen

KING STREET, LONDON
February 1679

A lady's lying-in should by rights be a joyful event, a time where little is expected of her beyond that she recover from the trials of childbirth. She may loll as indolently as she pleases in her bed, indulged and dining on whatever she pleases for the sake of regaining her strength. Her friends and family call to offer their congratulations and to praise the new child and welcome it into the family. Gifts and gossip are exchanged, and the new mother much petted and cosseted, until, by the end of the month, she is refreshed and ready to return to her duties.

Given my own situation, however, I'd little expectations of much company. True, my new daughter was sound and ruddy, and with her round cheeks and full lips, I'd already deemed her a perfect Stuart beauty after only a week. She was also already a lady. Before James had sailed, he'd demonstrated gratifying haste in granting the letters patent that had given her both a title and a surname: Lady Katherine Darnley. I'd indulged myself in the best lace-trimmed childbed linen, ready to show myself and little Lady Katherine in finery fit to receive the queen herself.

But I'd neither sisters nor aunts to wish me well, nor brothers with wives to act in that stead. My grandmothers were long dead, and my own mother lost to me. The few friends I'd made whilst in Mary Beatrice's household had followed her lead and swiftly abandoned me, and others I'd known from Whitehall would likewise likely judge it prudent to keep themselves clear of James's disgrace.

Thus I was surprised and touched by the attention I did receive. Colonel Grahme's wife, Dorothy, was first among them, bringing with her several other lady-wives of the duke's household. Laurence Hyde's wife, Henrietta, also called, as much a pretty sign of loyalty to my absent lover as to me, and once she did, several other, lesser ladies likewise saw the merit in paying me court. Nell Gwyn came, too, full of such drollery that she made my poor sore belly ache from laughter. Given how long I'd known Nell, her visit was to be expected, but the arrival of the Duchess of Portsmouth's elegant coach in King Street sent Thomson and the rest of my little household tumbling over one another for the privilege of waiting upon her. I'll grant that I was awed by her French magnificence, too, her famous beauty enriched by enough jewels to light a Court ball, and pleasantly startled by the unexpected friendship she offered.

"We must be allies, yes?" Her Grace said as she sat beside my bed, her fur-trimmed skirts arranged exactly so around her legs and her fingers arched to perfection as she sipped at her dish of tea. Her costly perfume was almost dizzying, like the most seductive incense. No wonder Charles was in her thrall. "When you are recovered, you must come to me in Whitehall. We are together in the same little boat, you know. How many other women can say they are loved by great princes?"

"Given the proclivities of the Stuarts, Your Grace," I said, unable to keep myself from the truth even in her exquisite company, "I should say a great many ladies might make that claim."

She raised her fine-plucked brows with genteel surprise, then laughed with a heartiness I'd not expected.

"You are sadly right, *madame*," she said, every word sounding more sweet for being sugared by her accent. "But there is the love that is given for a single night, and then there is the love that is more lasting, the love we have been favored to know. His Majesty and His Highness: they are special to us, aren't they?"

She turned to smile down on Lady Katherine, cooing in her cradle beside us. "Now you have this precious proof of His Highness's devotion to you. Ah, how fortunate you are, *madame*! How blessed!"

I was indeed, and though I longed for James to return, I thought of him each time I held our darling child, and was comforted.

But on a chill afternoon in the following week, long after my enjoyable company had departed, Lady Katherine became far less darling, and no comfort at all. She fussed and wailed as if her tiny heart were broken, and refused to be comforted. Her nurse said it was the usual fretfulness that can plague any infant, yet my thoughts were full of James's other fragile babes who'd perished over nothing. While I fussed myself and pleaded that a doctor should be summoned, the nurse assured me there was no cause.

It was clear I'd scandalized her, too, for ladies of my rank were supposed to be disinterested in the sordid concerns of their children. So that I might sleep, she took the babe away, yet Lady Katherine's plaintive cries still came to me from far away in her nursery, and I begged to have her returned to me. I insisted on taking her myself, walking her up and down before the fire and singing songs to her as if that might soothe her, and in a dark moment of disloyalty, I even wondered if her constant cry was a manifestation of James's habitual stubbornness. I was her mother, I told myself fiercely, and if I could not ease her suffering, then who could?

Such is the confidence of every new mother, I suppose, and such is the folly, too. Still my daughter cried, exhausting me if not herself, and when I gazed down at her in my arms it seemed to me in my frustration that her little face had become no more than a yawning, yowling, toothless mouth. When I heard the front door in the hall below open to admit another visitor, I shouted an order over my daughter's cries that whoever it was be turned away. I was in no humor to play the charming hostess now, especially not when my hair was frizzled, my eyes red and bleary from want of rest, and the shoulder of my dressing gown blotched with spit and sour milk.

But next I heard the door to my bedchamber open, and I turned about sharply, meaning to chastise whichever servant had disobeyed my order. To my shock, it was no servant standing there, but instead my own father. His face was rosy from the cold, and melting snowflakes glittered in the curls of his wig. He was, of course, as impeccably dressed as always, from his well-polished boots to his lace cravat, and all in glaring contrast to my own bedraggled appearance. I had not seen him alone since last autumn, when he had as much as disowned me, and though I would happily welcome a reconciliation, I did rather wish for different circumstances.

"I've come to see my grandchild," he announced, his voice raised over that same child's cries. "A girl, I'm told."

"She will not stop crying," I said, tears now filling my own eyes. "I'm sorry, Father."

"Oh, there's nothing to be sorry about," he said, setting aside his walking stick and holding his arms out. "She'll stop for me."

I paused, my weary gaze considering the perfection of his dress and how quickly my daughter would defile it. Then she wailed again, and helplessly I thrust her into Father's waiting arms.

"There now, mite, what can the trouble be?" he asked softly. "Whatever can be so wrong in your world to merit all this racketing? What can I do to bring you ease?"

Startled, the baby gazed up at him, while he in turn looked down at her. She shuddered and gulped, but most of all she stopped crying, her teary face turned in fascination toward his. He'd always had something of a baby's face himself, with his pursed lips and round, dimpled cheeks, grown rounder still with age, and I wondered if my daughter saw him as a kind of fellow.

"What did you do?" I asked, bewildered and more than a little jealous. What secret did he know that I didn't? I hadn't any recollection of him visiting my nursery when I'd been small, and he'd taken no real notice of me at all until I'd been older, the summer my mother had gone away. This newfound gift for children must have been discovered later, with his son by Lady Sedley. "How did you quiet her?"

"Oh, I treated her like any other grand lady," he said easily, still gazing down at the babe. "All she wished was to be reminded that she is the center of her world, and the rest of us merely exist in it to serve her."

"She's a good child," I said in her defense, wiping away my own tears with my fingers, for who knew what had become of my handkerchief?

"She's a brave, lusty child, which is more to her credit than any mere goodness," he declared proudly. "She's a Sedley, no mistake. No weakling would roar like that."

"Of course she's a Sedley," I said. "I bore her, didn't I?"

He grunted, noncommittal. "Has her father owned her?"

"At once," I said, and now doubly glad he had, too. "His Highness had the letters of patent drawn up directly and delivered within two days of her birth. She is called Lady Katherine Darnley."

"Darnley," he said, considering. "Scots, I suppose. Well, it's better than none. It took His Majesty three years before he gave a decent name to Portsmouth's brat. Has he seen to your other wants?"

"Oh, yes," I said, again proud of my lover's assiduousness. "He has been most generous in his allowances. Did you know that James Grahme now keeps His Highness's privy purse?"

"Oh, Katherine." He groaned. "Your life is more tangled than any Italian opera. I trust you'll not make the same mistake twice with that one."

"No, Father," I said contritely, wondering if he'd somehow guessed that the colonel had been the gentleman who'd taken my maidenhead. "But His Highness doesn't limit his regard for me to my allowance. He writes to me as often as he can, and sends his letters by way of the royal packets. He wrote to me from the Hague, where he visited his daughter, and then from Brussels, where he is now situated."

"And where he may now rot forever for what he has done to you," Father said with sudden vehemence, "and for what he wishes to do to England."

"Please don't begin about His Highness, Father," I begged. "For the sake of my daughter."

He sighed, and looked back down at the babe in his arms, who had at last fallen asleep. "Have you had her baptized in our Church, or did the duke prevail?"

"She was christened an Anglican on the day after she was born," I said quickly, knowing that would placate him. "I saw to that. His Highness was not pleased, but I acted first and he'd other matters to tend."

"Good lass." With the greatest of care, he laid my sleeping daughter in her cradle and drew the coverlet over her with a fond small pat. Then he led me to the pair of chairs close to the fire, where we could speak without disturbing the babe. "Lady Sedley and I would be honored if you would dine with us again, Katherine."

I wished for nothing better, but I also knew my father well enough that certain rules must be set, or we would be at each other's throats like thieves before the fish was brought to table.

"I would be much honored as well, Father," I said with care, "if we can together vow not to speak of His Highness."

He frowned and gnawed at his lip and shook his head, a jumble of little gestures that combined to show exactly how difficult a promise this would be to make.

"I know he is the father of your child, Katherine," he said with a care that equaled my own. "But I'll advise you as both your father and a fellow courtier that you would be wise to separate yourself from the duke as soon and as completely as is possible."

My heart sank. "Is that why you have come?"

"I came, Katherine, because I have missed you," he said, as if this were the most obvious thing in the world. "But it is because I love you as my only daughter that I ask you to part from this man who will surely ruin you."

If this were the price of my father's love, then it was too steep for me.

"I cannot do that, Father," I said softly, drumming the tips of my fingers along the chair's mahogany arm. "I can't abandon him, not now, when he is in such peril."

"At least that's truly spoke," he said with ominous certainty. "How much have you heard, Katherine?"

I looked at him with growing unease. In the past, Father and I had often discussed the doings of Parliament and the king's ministers, the same as we'd once spoken of the various scandals in the tiring rooms at the playhouses. Every fresh scandal had been ripe for spinning into a pretty thread for our amusement. But there was little amusement to be found in Parliament or the Court these days, and even less for me given my connection with James. Once, I would have greeted Father's simple question—*How much have you heard?*—with eager anticipation. Now it only filled me with dread and worry, and fear for the man I'd come to love.

"I have heard nothing," I confessed, and that, too, was true. "I've been removed from the world. When His Highness writes to me, it's of the sausages he's eaten or the horse he's ridden, and how much he misses England and wishes to return. For more than that, you must tell me, Father. I beg you, please. Tell me all."

He paused, a long, weighty, significant pause. Because of James, Father and I were on opposite sides now. He was firmly ensconced among the Whigs, while by circumstance I was associated with the Court Party, increasingly known as Tories, after a band of wild Irish brigands, though for no creditable reason that I could ever discern. Sadly I realized that, as Father stood before me, he was deciding if I could be trusted not to run back to my royal lover with whatever he told me: if, in short, I was more Sedley or Stuart.

"Very well," he said at last. "Though all of this is common now, or will be soon enough. When the new Parliament meets next month, Shaftesbury will introduce a new bill for exclusion, to officially remove the duke from the succession on account of being a Papist and in collusion with both the French and Rome."

"Such a bill will not pass," I said firmly. "It must not pass! Who would they place in the duke's stead?"

"Some would wish the king to declare for his son Lord Monmouth."

"Fah!" I said with a dismissive wave of my hand. "You know as well as I that he's an empty-headed fool. Pretty and full of charm, but no more brain than any other preening parrot."

Father smiled. "I would agree, Katherine. Yet Monmouth is a preening Protestant parrot, and enough like his father in appearance to soothe the qualms of many Englishmen. But there are other choices. The Princess of Orange would be agreeable, I think."

"Meaning her husband the Prince of Orange, for the lady has no will of her own." I sighed impatiently. "What would most Englishmen make of him? A wheezing Dutch dwarf who has been our sworn enemy through more than one war?"

"Again, a Protestant dwarf," Father said, maddeningly reasonable against my passion. "Like it or not, in the end it will all come to that and no more. Because of Oates and Bedloe, there are murderous Jesuits to be seen lurking in every dark corner. With this new Parliament, Shaftesbury could have a donkey made heir if it were only the will of the people."

"Thank God it is not," I said fervently. "The king has sworn to uphold his brother's right to the throne, and I must believe that he will stand by his oath."

"His Majesty will do what is best for England, and to preserve his father's throne," Father said. "If that means he must in time sacrifice his brother, he will do so."

I caught my breath, my fingers tightening into a knot in my lap. This was exactly James's greatest fear, that his brother would someday betray him to save himself.

"But what of the rightful succession?" I asked. "Isn't that best for England, too?"

Father smiled, and spread his hands wide in wordless appeal, his familiar gold ring with the carnelian stone turning red as blood by the fire's light.

"Much may happen, my dear," he said, "and equally much may not. No one can play Cassandra and see to the future. The king continues in such perfect health that he may outlive us all. He may take another queen, and yet sire a legitimate son. Or your duke may come to his senses, and return to the rightful church, and all of this will be of as little importance as ashes in the wind."

"I've told His Highness that, Father," I said, my voice trembling as I remembered the strong words I'd used. "I've told him, and told him, and *told* him, and yet he will not see either the sense or the danger in following Rome."

"Continue your telling, Daughter, and perhaps at last he'll listen. You can do no more than that for your daughter, or for England, either." He rose, and I stood with him. He drew his handkerchief from his pocket, an immaculate creased square of snowy Holland edged with lace, and pressed it into my hand.

"Keep it ready, Kattypillar," he said gently. "I fear you'll shed a good many more tears before you're done, but in the end, I pray it will all be for the best."

But as I used Father's handkerchief to daub my eyes, I was not nearly as certain as he was. No, when I thought of my dear James, I wasn't certain at all.

FATHER MIGHT HAVE CLAIMED NOT TO be another Cassandra, but his prediction of what would happen in London in the spring of 1679 proved as accurate as any ancient Trojan prophecy. The General Election of February in fact returned a House of Commons that was more Whiggish than Tory, flocking like sheep to Lord Shaftesbury's crook. His Lordship had several avowed goals for the new session to perform, and with that self-same crook, he wasted no time prodding his obedient herd to follow his bidding.

First, he wished to see the persecution of Lord Danby continued so as to have no rivals, and in this he succeeded. Based largely on Montague's letters, Danby was forced to resign his offices as the most powerful minister to the king. Not only that, but he was arrested and imprisoned in the Tower on a charge of treason. His place in the king's confidence was taken (though not officially) by another of the Privy Councilors, the Earl of Sunderland, a gentleman of the same Whiggish beliefs and persuasions as Lord Shaftesbury, but not as strident in them.

Second, because it suited his other purposes, Shaftesbury wished to keep the fires of suspicion and loathing against popery burning as brightly as a Guy Fawkes bonfire. This, too, he accomplished with seeming ease, by continuing to encourage Oates in his so-called testimonies; among the preposterous new revelations were claims that James I and Charles I had been murdered by the Jesuits, and that my James was somehow responsible for setting the Great Fire that had burned through London nearly fifteen years before. On the basis of such lies, five more Jesuits were convicted of plotting Charles's death and shamefully executed in July.

More quietly, yet with equal efficiency, His Lordship supported the dissemination of the most outlandish, hateful lies regarding Catholics among the members of the Commons and throughout the city by way of anonymous pamphlets filled with crude yet horrifying illustrations of an England destroyed by the Jesuits. To the new members representing neighborhoods distant from London, the pamphlets were particularly shocking, and taken for gospel instead of the fantastical lies that they were.

Thirdly, Shaftesbury wished to keep James away from London. This required more subtlety, more careful whispers in carefully chosen ears at Court, for his aim was to reach the most royal ears of all. Yet here, too, he succeeded, for though James asked his brother repeatedly to be permitted to return home, Charles refused. What I heard by way of Lady Portsmouth was that Charles feared an open rebellion if James were to appear, a rebellion much like the one that had destroyed their father nearly forty years before. But from Father I learned that this dreadful rebellion was only another invention of Lord Shaftesbury's, a few graying coals of innuendo puffed and fanned into full and dangerous flame.

Far removed in distant Brussels, James was duly informed by his brother of all of this, and spared none of the hostility or even the hatred that his name aroused. As can be imagined, his letters to me were sorrowful affairs, his exile so woeful that it seemed not even his faith could guide him. In England he had prided himself on working long hours on behalf the army and navy and a score of other projects. In Brussels, he'd nothing to occupy himself except calls from dull Flems he'd no wish to see and hunting through lands and forests that served only to remind him of how different they were from the lands and forests he'd been forced to leave behind.

I tried to make my letters in return as cheering as I could, and wrote not only of our daughter's progress, but also added my own observations of the events at Court, in Parliament, and in London, whether humble or grand. I sent my affection as well, and though he'd never know it, I pressed my lips to every page to help bring him back to me. I did not tell him how much I missed him, or how it seemed the cruelest twist of fortune that in the same week that Lady Katherine had entered my life, I had lost James from it.

The poets claim that separation from a loved one serves only to make that love stronger still, and so it was with my affection for James. It was a strange thing, I know, and one I could scarce understand myself. But the longer we were separated, the more fervently I missed him, and knowing that this same separation would likely continue with no foreseeable end only increased my devotion to him.

It should be of no surprise, then, that Lord Shaftesbury's final goal for that spring was the one that concerned me the most. As Father had predicted, this conniving lord introduced an odious proposal that instantly became known as the Exclusion Bill. By this bill, James would be removed from the succession, or excluded, not only on account of his faith, but also because of his too-close ties to France and Rome. Debate on the bill was minimal, and it seemed certain of passing. Lord Shaftesbury was already perceived to be flush with his success, and Lord

Monmouth, too, was heard to be making jests about how well the crown would sit upon his brow.

But neither of them had considered His Majesty's ire, or his true loyalties. It had been a difficult time for the king. His regard and popularity among his people were the lowest they had been at any time during his reign, and even many of his onetime friends and supporters, such as Lord Dorset and Lord Rochester, were writing scathing verses at his expense. Though outwardly supporting all measures to preserve the Protestant faith, Charles was privately determined to save his brother. In May, he prorogued Parliament to prevent further debate on the bill, and in July, he dissolved it entirely, sending the members off to their distant homes until another election was called. It was only a postponement of the question, not a solution, but after all the Court had suffered through over these last long months, it was a respite we all did need.

In August, Charles made his annual retreat to Windsor. With James still in exile, I'd no true reason to go, or to expect an invitation to be part of the traveling Court. But since Lady Katherine's birth, my acquaintance with Lady Portsmouth had blossomed and flourished, until I could now call her as much a friend as I did Nell, though surely there were no two ladies more different. I suppose it was natural, since as Louise—for so I now had come to think of her—had said to me, we three were indeed in the same little boat, albeit a golden boat rich with pearls and borne on the backs of Stuart lions and unicorns. In any event, Louise had requested my company with her at Windsor, and so in August I kissed my daughter as I left her with her nursemaids and made the journey up the river with the rest of the Court.

This time Father did not accompany me, choosing instead to retreat to his own estates in the country for the recess. He claimed he was too old and weary for the pleasures of Court, but I guessed it was more that his Whiggish politics made him uncomfortable at the palace, and that it was easier to avoid the company of his old friend Charles than to challenge it.

As Louise's guest, I had lodgings as part of her quarters in the great castle, which were nearly as extraordinary as the ones she'd been granted by Charles at Whitehall. She had a larger suite with more rooms than the queen, and it was furnished with better taste, too. Everything had been done in the most exquisite French manner, from enormous looking glasses on the walls that reflected every bit of sun or candlelight as well as the people within the rooms, to gold-framed paintings by the best artists on the Continent. As at Whitehall, Charles was in Louise's suite more than his own, and relied on her, not the queen, to act as hostess to his most important visitors. It was a remarkable thing to see, that a king who was under attack by his Parliament for being too closely aligned with the French would rely so heavily on his French mistress, and with such undisguised regard, too.

But what was most remarkable to me about Louise was the lady herself. Being plain, I had always believed that rare beauty, such as she possessed, would ease every hindrance and unpleasantry that ordinary women must suffer. I was myself seldom awed by even the fiercest gentlemen, but I will admit that there were times that I was nigh stunned by Louise's loveliness, overwhelmed by her dimpled white hands or the languorous grace of her gestures that were so different from my own sharp, angular figure and brisk motions. It was as if I were still in the schoolroom and dazzled with my admiration for an older girl. Oh, there was no denying that Louise's beauty had been the reason she'd first captured Charles's notice, but to my surprise it had not protected her from the endless attacks of others who wished to destroy her for her power, her foreignness, her Catholicism, and her influence, and for simple jealousy as well. Many at Court judged her to be haughty and aloof, but I saw her instead as guarded and cautious, a lady who'd been hurt too often to trust anyone but Charles himself.

To be sure, Louise de Keroualle never made such a confidence to me. While generous with her kindness, she took care not to share too much of herself with anyone. Yet I observed how she used her infinite grace and elegance not to welcome the world to her, but to deflect it—much in the same way that I did use my wit and cleverness. Perhaps this was necessary to survive as a royal mistress, and perhaps, too, Louise had recognized the same quality in me when she'd said we were in the same little boat.

Whatever the reason, I was happy to be included again in the frolics at Windsor, whether in Louise's elegant shadow in the castle or at Nell's more boisterous house in the adjoining town. My position was a strange one; I was acknowledged as a royal favorite without the presence of the prince who'd granted me that favoritism. Still, I made what I could of the situation, and through my usual candor and wit, was welcomed as an amusing addition to the party.

By the middle of August, everything had changed.

I woke one morning to Thomson drawing the curtains on my bed, the same way I began most every day. But the instant I saw her face, I could tell that she was fair bursting to tell me some rare news, and as I took my dish of chocolate from her, I finally gave her leave to speak.

"Well, what is it, Thomson?" I asked, sipping my sweet morning brew. "What fresh tattle have you heard about your betters down in the kitchens?"

But instead of the gleeful outburst of gossip I'd expected, Thomson's face crumpled. "Oh, ma'am, it is the worst possible news of all. His Majesty was stricken grievous ill in the night, and they say he is not expected to live!"

"His Majesty's ill?" I dropped my dish back into its saucer with a clatter of porcelain. Charles was one of the most robust gentlemen I'd ever known, still tall and lean and vital for all that he was fifty years of age. I couldn't recall the last time he'd been reported as ill. This was grievous news for all of England, most grievous indeed. "How? What ails him?"

Thomson shook her head. "Oh, ma'am, they say it was nothing, nothing at all! Yesterday His Majesty played tennis by the river—such as he's done a thousand times before—and they say he did not properly dry himself afterward, ma'am, and that he took a chill, and then the fever settled into him, and—"

"So that is it? A fever?" Summer fevers were sadly common here around the river, and I wondered that a gentleman who had spent so many of his summers around its banks would not have taken the necessary precautions against illness.

"Yes, yes, ma'am, a fever of the most fearful variety." Thomson snuffled loudly, wiping her tears with the corners of her apron. "The doctors and surgeons have been with His Majesty all the night long with this remedy and that, and yet he is said only to worsen. Oh, forgive me, ma'am, but I've known no other king in all my life, and I cannot bear to think of him gone from us!"

That was perhaps the most honest words my Thomson had ever spoken. Only the most aged of Englishmen could now recall before the wars to the reign of the old king, and to all of us gathered at Windsor, the king meant only Charles II. To have him perish so suddenly was beyond thinking.

I dressed as quickly as I could so I might seek the latest news, hoping that somehow Thomson was mistaken. But it was instantly evident from the shocked faces and hushed voices to be found in every room that indeed Charles was gravely ill, and that the doctors that filled his bedchamber despaired for his life.

Yet if Charles did in fact die—for as robust a gentleman as he was, he was in truth still mortal, and dependent on the awful will of God—who would assume his throne? No one dared ask the question aloud, even as no one could think of any other. By law and right, James was destined to follow his brother, Lord Shaftesbury's much-loved Exclusion Bill still only a bill and no more. But James was still in exile, and as every Englishman knew from past history, upon a royal death, the crown was often seized not by he who'd a right to it, but by the one who was nearest to claim it as his own. What if Lord Monmouth and his followers swept in to take the throne by force, or far worse, some other mad claimant suddenly appeared? While the Whigs might have spoken bravely in their debates in the House, when faced with this harsh reality, they realized they'd no real wish for rebellion or anarchy.

Instead, on the second night of Charles's illness, Lord Sunderland, the most trusted of the Privy Councilors, sent a messenger racing to Brussels to recall the Duke of York.

In the privacy of my rooms, I wildly rejoiced. Even in such somber circumstances, to be reunited with James so soon was beyond my most wistful dreams. Though I fervently prayed with the others for Charles's swift recovery, I still thought of little beyond seeing James again.

I was not alone in my imaginings, either. On the morning following the messenger's departure, I was surprised by a visit from Louise herself, come to call on me alone in my rooms. There are some women that rise to display their most noble qualities in a crisis such as was now facing Charles, who display such rare strength and fortitude as to give comfort not only to the afflicted, but to others who are likewise gathered at the sickbed.

I am sorry to say that Louise was not one of these women. As soon as the severity of Charles's illness had been recognized, she had panicked, weeping and wailing and throwing herself about, and making such a thorough nuisance of herself that Charles himself, though racked with fever, was forced to reassure her. After that, the king's physicians had decided they were in their rights to limit her access to his bedchamber, which was likely why she was now able to visit me in mine.

She was dressed simply, without her usual eye for fashionable excess: an unadorned dark silk gown, no lace or jewels, no paint on her face. The poor king must have taken one look at her and believed she was already mourning him.

I curtsied before her, as I would for any duchess, and waited until she motioned for me to sit.

"His Majesty has grown no worse," she announced, hardly a fortuitous beginning. "Nor has he ever lost consciousness, despite the seriousness of the fever, thanks be to God for that."

"Thanks be to God," I repeated in a murmuring echo that seemed safe enough for an Anglican to embrace. "I trust there is still hope, Your Grace?"

She sighed mightily, twisting her handkerchief into an anxious knot in her lap. "There is always hope, Mrs. Sedley. Charles himself has implored Dr. Lower to procure a certain remedy of which he has knowledge, an effusion made of powdered bark from the colonies. Dr. Lower is in such despair of a proper remedy that he is considering its use. His Majesty is not a man to be lightly denied, even in this."

"Oh, no," I said. Charles was seldom denied in anything, as was the privilege of kings; I couldn't imagine a mere physician beginning to do so now. Besides, Charles was known to delight in new discoveries in science and philosophy, and study them himself in his privy closet at Whitehall. What a ripe irony it would be if he could cure himself where the illustrious royal physicians failed!

Louise sighed again, her plump red lips trembling as she fought her tears. "The order for His Highness's recall remains in place. Lord Sunderland believes it for the best, and predicts that, with favorable seas and wind, His Highness should be able to join us within the next se'nnight."

I nodded, having already calculated myself that the journey from Brussels shouldn't take more than a week, especially given the urgency of the circumstances. "It is a mild season for travel, Your Grace, and I'm certain His Highness will make every haste."

But somewhere in my agreement, she'd stopped listening. She sat before me lost in her own fears, her shoulders huddled and quaking, her hands clasped together tightly around the sodden knot she'd made of her lace-edged handkerchief. A single tear slid down her cheek, hanging there for an instant before it dropped and spread on her wrist; she even wept with elegance, and rare poignancy, too.

"He cannot die," she whispered forlornly. "Not like this. He cannot leave me, not when I love him so well." She turned her lovely face toward me, her eyes swollen from weeping.

"You will recall the kindness I have shown to you, Mrs. Sedley?" she begged with pitiful eagerness. "You will make certain that His Highness will not forget me, or my little son His Grace the Duke of Richmond?"

"Faith, Your Grace, there is no need of this!" I exclaimed, taken completely by surprise. "His Majesty is not in his grave yet, nor is His Highness made king in his stead."

Louise only shook her head. "But if—if the worst occurs, you will have my place," she said with uncharacteristic (and unsettling) humility. "You will be as I am now, and I will be as nothing."

"Oh, you shall never be as nothing, Your Grace," I assured her. In addition to Charles's boundless indulgence toward her, she was also a peeress in France as well as in England, and wealthy, beautiful duchesses in either country were very rarely forgotten, nor were their sons if sired by kings.

It was the rest of what she'd said that startled me. I won't lie and claim I'd never thought of what it would be like to be mistress not to a prince, but to a king. How could I not, when the royal succession was the unending topic of the day? But those idle imaginings had always been centered on James himself, of openly belonging to him, of being at his side at balls at Court, of our daughter receiving the same honors as other royal bastards, and (perhaps selfishly) of how in time I'd come to replace

Mary Beatrice in most things, just as Louise had replaced Her Majesty. I'd even let myself consider inheriting Louise's lavish Whitehall apartments. But it all had been in relation to myself and James. I'd never considered being a woman with power at the Court and beyond, wielding influence through the king to determine who found favor and success at Court, and who would drop away forgotten.

Louise had such power, and a gift for intrigue of the highest sort. I'd heard whispers that she'd even helped negotiate treaties between the French and English kings. Clearly she believed I might soon have this power, too, through James—a serious, sobering, unsettling possibility. It remained in my thoughts after Louise had left me to return to the king's side, and it followed me to bed, to plague me all the night through, waiting to greet me the moment I finally woke.

But when Thomson appeared with my chocolate the next morning, she also brought the welcome news that Charles was much improved. The remedy that he'd insisted be tried had proven its efficacy, and not only was the fever much diminished, but his genial humor had returned as well. By the time that James and two attendants finally arrived at the castle on the second of September, expecting the worst and with mourning clothes in their traveling chests, the danger was well past. Charles greeted them merrily as he sat in his bed, dining on a great dish of savory partridges with Louise beside him and complaining impatiently about how Dr. Lower and the others had forbidden him his usual trip to Newmarket for the autumn meets. But Charles had saved the best jest of all for his brother: the true name of the miraculous powder that had preserved him, he explained with uproarious irony, was Jesuit's Bark.

In the end, the real irony had belonged to James himself. The lords who had brought him back had worried endlessly about whether their action would cause an uproar, or even another rebellion. Instead James had appeared at once as a veritable pillar of strength, quietly confident amidst the chattering disorder of an uneasy Court. He possessed a soldier's gift for order and the ability to act efficiently under pressure. True, the concerns surrounding Charles's health were not exactly the same as a battle with gunfire and explosions. But the hysteria that had plagued the Court over the last twelve months could indeed be likened to a war, and like the best of generals, James's very presence seemed at once to calm and reassure the entire Court, especially when compared to the vain, empty ambitions of Lord Monmouth. James had been painted as a monster for so long that people seemed most agreeably surprised when the actual, honorable gentleman appeared before them.

I could have told them that long before. I was among the throng that gathered along the castle's walls, above the gate, to welcome him to Windsor. From a distance, he appeared thinner than when he'd left, with a certain melancholy air that was sadly new. His smile was quick, almost shy, as if he seemed startled by so much attention, and who could fault him if he were? But his handsome face and quiet, steady demeanor were exactly as I remembered, and my heart ached at the very sight of him.

I'd written him while he was still in Brussels that I would be here at Windsor for the month, and as he glanced up at us on the parapets to wave in salute, I dared to believe he sought me among so many others. But no matter how much I ached to join him, I knew I must wait until a more proper, more private time. Even a lady as bold as I knew that there were few things more inconvenient and unseemly than a mistress in the middle of such a sober, serious crisis. Louise had already proven that, and she was a mistress of nearly ten years' standing.

But James hadn't forgotten me. Three days later, when the king was declared out of danger, a note in his familiar hand was brought to me, naming a room in one of the castle's towers. With touching humility, he invited me to meet him there.

And with unabashed eagerness, I agreed.

Chapter Eighteen

WINDSOR CASTLE, BERKSHIRE
September 1679

Windsor Castle had been built long ago as a fortress, and from its lofty heights it was possible to see many miles over the countryside, across distant towns and farms. Its stout walls had been intended to hold even the most daring attackers at bay, and for many centuries it had done exactly that. Now, in more peaceful times, Charles had made it over into a retreat of pleasure, filled with beautiful pictures, grand staircases, and fountains that jetted fancifully high into the sky, rather than a place of weapons and warhorses.

But for James and me, the old castle once again served its original purpose of keeping out the rest of the world. He had left behind in Brussels not only his duchess, but also his usual retinue of followers, priests, and other counselors crowding with demands. For two weeks we stole away to our distant room in the tower, with only a pair of guards beyond our door. While courtiers elsewhere in the castle must have speculated that we met, none knew for sure where or how often, our secrecy was that complete. James and I both understood how our assignations could be used by his enemies; to turn from what might have been a brother's deathbed to a lover's wanton embrace while his wife languished abroad could have been spun into an unsavory tale indeed for the pamphlets.

But it wasn't like that. I will not claim that we were chaste, for we weren't. We were both by our very natures too passionate for that, and our feverish desire for each other was much of what had first bound us together. To see how well and how often he loved me made me wonder exactly how seldom Mary Beatrice permitted him to her bed, for indeed he came to me like a man close to starving.

Yet what pleased me even more were our conversations afterward, when we lay curled together and the warm, sweet breezes from the open windows played over our heated bodies. I suppose this is the way of all mistresses and their gentlemen; a lady-wife and husband converse in their parlor over tea, but James and I had our conversations in tumbled beds.

We spoke freely at Windsor, too, as if we hadn't been apart at all, and with complete trust in each other. He told me of the tedium of Brussels, of how he'd hated the idleness of his position, and how he longed to be of use to England again. He spoke of how he'd feared for his brother, and how he was loath to become king when the crown would only be his at such a terrible cost. He confided how pleased and relieved he was to see that he'd not been forgotten whilst away, how gratifying he found it that he'd been welcomed so warmly. The much-dreaded Exclusion Act was still a chimera without fire or teeth; the lord mayor of London had been prepared to proclaim James king if his brother had died, and James proudly named to me each of the aldermen who'd knelt to kiss his hand.

"The lord mayor's favor is an excellent sign, sir, to be sure," I said, my head propped on my arm as I lay beside him to listen. "But you must be permitted to return to London so that more people may see you. So long as you're away from their sight, Shaftesbury and the others will paint you as black as coal."

"Including your father," he said wryly. "Don't deny it, Katherine. I hear things even in Brussels."

I groaned dramatically. "My father is but one voice of many in the Commons, sir," I said. "He's not Shaftesbury. You can hardly fault me for what my father says or does."

"Yet you say you take my side over his," he said thoughtfully. "Few daughters would do that."

"Few daughters are like me," I said. "I'm sure my father would say mercifully few. I think for myself, sir, and judge for myself, and at present your cause makes more sense to me than all the Whigs combined. As for my father, I can no more control his actions than he can control mine."

"Control you?" he said, teasing. "Is there any mortal man who has such powers, Katherine?"

"Don't vex me, sir, or it will go the worse for you." I shoved him hard, and he laughed, and drew me forward to kiss.

"But you should come back to London, sir," I whispered afterward, persisting. "I know His Majesty believes it for the best to have you away, but it's not. Do you know that in the playhouses, Monmouth is cheered as if he were the true heir?"

He frowned. "He has even less right to that than before. The boy has vexed my brother even further these last months by what he's doing in the north, rallying discontented fools around him as if he were another Messiah."

"That, and proclaiming to the world that his whoring mother was wed to His Majesty," I said. "He goes about with a locked black box that he swears contains the proof of their marriage, but he never opens the damned box for anyone to see inside. Faith, he's like a bad conjurer."

"Fool," James said with disgust. "A fool leading fools."

"But that is why you must come back to London, sir," I said. "Then everyone could see how strong and steady you are compared to Monmouth, and you could —"

"I can't, Katherine," he said gently. "Not without my brother's permission. You know that."

"But if you came to London, you could see more of me," I said, placing his hand over my bare breast. "You could see more of Lady Katherine, too."

"I should like that above all things," he said sadly. Not sad on account of my breast—I knew better than that—but because of our daughter. I'd contrived to have her brought to an inn nearby for James to see. She'd bloomed into a fine, sturdy little lass, able to sit on her own and stand on wobbling legs. To my pride and relief, she hadn't cried at all when James had held her, only staring up at him in perfect seriousness, as if she realized that this stranger was in fact her father. Tears had started in James's eyes, and though he loved my daughter for herself, I guessed, too, he was thinking of how much stronger Lady Katherine was than the doomed babes that Mary Beatrice had given him. Only one had survived, the impossibly frail Lady Isabella.

"To see our daughter grow and prosper, Katherine—what father could wish for otherwise?" he asked.

If it were his decision, then I knew he'd be in London with me. The sadness in his voice told me that, and warned me, too, not to continue to beg for something that was not in his power to do. Instead I only smiled, determined to cheer him as best I could.

"You say you've heard everything from afar, sir," I said, my words purposefully light. "Has anyone told you of Betty Mackerel's starling?"

"Bet Mackerel?" he asked, already intrigued. "That tall, lively wench at the playhouse?"

"The same, sir," I said, settling against his chest to tell my tale. "The one who speaks near as plain as I. In honor of His Majesty's birthday, she gave to him a starling that had been specially trained to talk bawdry. Charles was much pleased, as can be imagined, and kept the bird in his bedchamber for his amusement."

Already James was beginning to laugh, though I doubted he'd guess where this story would end. "A talking starling? Why did he not tell me this himself?"

"I do not know, sir," I said. "Perhaps he believed the bird would tell it you himself. One day His Majesty received the Archbishop of Canterbury in his bedchamber on some solemn business. But before they could begin, the bird did hop onto His Grace's shoulder, as neat as could be. 'Thou lecherous dog,' the bird said, 'wilt thou have a whore?' "

"The bird said that?" exclaimed James, roaring so with laughter that his chest quaked and bounced beneath me. "To the archbishop? Hah, how I would have liked to have seen that, after all that man has done to torment me!"

I laughed merrily with him, glad that I'd brought him that little pleasure. "So would I, sir. I do not know which would have been rarer to see: the archbishop's face or His Majesty's."

That set him to laughing afresh, until at last he drew me close.

"My own Katherine," he said with great affection, tangling his fingers in my hair. "How I've missed you, and how I'll miss you again."

"Then it is certain, sir?" I asked, striving to keep the crush of disappointment from my voice. "You are to return to Brussels?"

"Only long enough to conclude my affairs and gather Her Highness," he said. "Then I am to be sent to Edinburgh. At least I shall have some manner of employment. I'm to sit on the Scottish privy council, to listen and observe, and gain whatever is useful for my brother."

"Edinburgh," I said, unable to go farther beyond that. Edinburgh meant Scotland, cold and remote and primitive, and seemingly even farther from London than Brussels was. "I would not suppose there would be a place for me there as well?"

"Would that there were," he said with regret. At least I always knew the truth with James, for there wasn't a deceitful scrap in his being. "I would find it all far more bearable if you were along to cheer me. But I fear that—"

"You needn't say more, sir." I tried to smile. "I understand. Your character must be as unsullied as new snow until His Majesty decides you've suffered enough."

He stroked his hand along my hair, holding me close. "I'm sorry, dearest. If there were a way—"

"It's of no matter, sir," I said bravely. I didn't wish him to know how disappointed I was by his news, especially when it wasn't by his choice to leave me again. "Truth to tell, sir, I'm not certain I could survive such a journey. If I were forced to travel all the way to Scotland in the company of all those priests and Jesuits and confessors and repressors—"

" 'Repressors'?" he repeated, laughing again in spite of himself. "Oh, Katherine, you shouldn't speak such things."

"Why not, sir, when it makes you merry?" I'd learned early that despite his solemn devotion (perilously close to fanaticism in the eyes of an Anglican like me), he would still always laugh if I spoke about it in a humorous fashion, as if my irreverence somehow freed him. I was the only one permitted this liberty, and I took care not to employ it too often. Yet there were times where my frustration gave wings to my wit, and I could not help myself. "Or is it that your confessors *are* your repressors, and I've erred only in my usage?"

"Perhaps they are." His face twisted. "But I need those good gentlemen with me to help my conscience follow the path that it should."

"Do you, sir?" I asked, widening my eyes with feigned surprise. "Lah, and here I believed you a gentleman grown, free to follow your own will."

"It's not my will," he said, turning immensely serious. "It's God's hand, as it is in all things."

I rolled away from him. "It is very hard for me to believe that the same God that made possible your family's rightful return to the throne would likewise prefer that you squander that blessing by allowing a covey of black-clad priests to dictate your every step."

He reached for me as I slipped free, and groaned with disappointment.

"The Holy Fathers don't dictate anything to me, Katherine," he said. "They offer spiritual guidance, which I choose to follow. I promise you, that if I permitted them to dictate my actions, then I would have broken with you long ago."

"Truly, sir?" I asked, pausing where I stood, naked save for the sunlight falling over me. Though the rest of the Court might judge me hideously thin, James praised me for being elegantly slender, and loved my body for what it was. Thus I could stand before him now in shameless, tempting glory, and if I'd any doubt, I'd only to see the desire for me in his gaze as he studied me now from the bed. "The priests tell you I'm evil incarnate?"

"In so many words, yes," he said, his eyes hooded and hungry as he watched me.

"I'm honored, sir," I said, and though I laughed, in a peculiar way I *was* honored. To think that I was so alluring to James that the Pope in Rome was concerned—hah, who would have guessed I'd ever have such power over any man, let alone a prince? "I've been called Dorinda, but never sinful Eve."

"That's exactly what you are to me," he said, his voice low and rough. "You tempt me beyond reason, Katherine."

"I'm glad of it, sir," I said, "for you tempt me as well, which must by rights make it no true temptation at all."

Aware of how closely he was watching me, I walked slowly to my dressing table and gathered up the necklace of pearls and emerald that he'd given me at Christmas. The necklace was long, meant to be worn doubled around my throat, but now I let it fall forward in a single strand, the jewels sliding sinuously over my breasts. I shook my hair over my shoulders and down my back, and I hooked the earrings that he'd also given me into my ears, giving my head a small toss to make the stones dance and my hair shiver down across my back.

"There, sir," I said, smiling wickedly as I turned back toward him. "I've no apples plucked from the Garden with which to tempt you, but surely emeralds will do in their stead."

"You gave me an apple once before," he said, his gaze intent on the pearls swinging over my pale flesh. "On the Horseguards' Parade. Your stockings were the same color as those jewels, with orange clocks and garters. I should have realized then what you'd do to me."

"You recall all that?" I asked, bemused, as I came to stand beside the bed. "Faith, sir, I was but fifteen then, and a most petulant little chit, too."

"Old enough to beguile me," he said, despair now mixed with desire in his voice, an uneasy pairing. "More than old enough. They've warned me that you've bewitched me, you know. They've told me I must be strong against your powers, yet I am weak with you."

I chuckled, brazenly reaching to caress his cock. "You do not seem weak to me, sir," I whispered, leaning over him. "Rather you seem most wondrously strong, and most able."

He groaned, his eyes closed and his hips rising upward to meet my hand.

"Katherine, please," he gasped. "*Please.*"

"Do you wish me please to stop, sir?" I teased as I leaned close enough to whisper in his ear as my necklace thumped into his chest. "Or please to continue?"

In a flashing move, he seized me by the waist and flipped me onto my back to trap me there beneath his body, pushing my legs apart to torment me as I'd done him.

"What is your hold of me, Katherine?" he demanded, his breathing ragged as claimed me. "What spell do you cast, that makes me never wish to leave you?"

"It's—it's only fate that brings us together, sir," I whispered fiercely, clutching tight to his shoulders as he drove into me, over and over with growing force. "No magic. Fate, and love. Oh, sir, how I do love you!"

He did not hear me, or perhaps, when I considered it later, he did, but chose not to. He'd told me he wished never to leave me and I'd admitted I loved him, and truly, what could come from either confession?

He did leave me, of course. He'd no choice. The orders of kings, even brotherly kings, must be obeyed, and two days later I watched him ride out from Windsor. The sun had barely risen when they left, the sky still a pale autumn yellow. Wrapped in a dark cloak against the falling dew, I stood on the same castle parapets as I'd done to welcome him. Then I'd had much company, a cheering crowd of those who wished well to the Duke of York. Now, because of the early hour, I stood alone, where I was sure he'd see me. He turned back once on his horse, and though his face was hidden in the shadow of his wide-brimmed hat, I knew that he smiled.

For that, surely, was fate as well.

"Is it true, then?" Father asked, his manner caustic when next I saw him in his library in Bloomsbury Square. A fortnight had passed since James had returned to Brussels, more than enough for the rumors and speculation to begin anew. "That His Highness will put aside his wife so that you will be made queen?"

"Hush, Father, don't speak such idle foolishness," I scolded. "You know as well as I that there's not so much as an eyelash of truth to it."

He grunted, and filled my glass again with French sillery. "There's at least two eyelashes that say that when His Highness raced across the Channel to reach His Majesty's bed, it was in yours that he dallied the most."

"Not once in mine," I declared mildly, the sillery's tiny bubbles tart upon my tongue. "What lying dog told you that?"

"Rochester," Father said. "I'd like to see you call His Lordship a liar to his face, though I'll grant it does take one to know one."

"Lord Rochester was at Windsor?" I asked with surprise. I was sorry to have missed him. "I didn't see him there."

"It's difficult to see much when your petticoats are tossed over your head," he said pointedly. "But His Lordship's health is so perilous these days that he remained at Windsor only long enough to pay respects to His Majesty and hear the latest scandals. He says no one can fathom how much the duke's besotted with you, and I'll wager a guinea not even you will lie to me about that."

"I wasn't lying," I protested. "We never once employed my bed, not with Lady Portsmouth hovering with her ear to my door. We were more discreet than that."

"If you were discreet, Daughter, then it was the first time in your life that you were." Irritably, he jabbed at the fire with the poker, doubtless wishing he could do the same to James. "You didn't return with another brat in your belly, did you?"

"No," I said, though not without a certain regret. There was no doubt; the jostling carriage ride back to London had brought down my courses. As inconvenient as another babe might be, I loved both Lady Katherine and James so well that I wouldn't have minded if I he had gotten me with child again. "You can stand down from the pulpit on that particular sermon."

I should have known it would take far more than that mild rebuke to dissuade Father from what had become his favorite topic.

"You gain nothing by remaining with the duke, Katherine, and have much to lose," he said sternly. "Can't you see that simply by being with you, His Highness has already demonstrated his taste for infidelity? He's a Stuart, and half French. It's in his blood to be faithless."

I sighed, and let him ramble on. If the Stuart blood ran with faithlessness, then the Sedley stock wasn't much better.

"You're a clever woman, Katherine. You must know it as well as I," he continued. "No doubt he's already jumped from you to some fat Flemish creature."

"Or a Scottish one," I said, sipping my wine. "That's where the king has sent him next, you know. To Edinburgh. Or hadn't you heard that, too?"

Father wheeled around to face me. "Scotland?"

"Och, aye, Scotland," I said. "His Majesty wisely decided that if he must banish his brother, he should at least send him off to be usefully employed for the good of the Crown. He's to sit on the Scottish privy council, and they should consider themselves fortunate to have him."

"But Edinburgh, Katherine." Father shook his head. "He might as well be on the other side of the world. What could be next? Boston? The farther he is from you here in London, the farther you and your daughter will be from his thoughts. The man's as inconstant as a flea."

"But he is constant to me, Father, even in his inconstancy to His Highness," I said, determined not to quarrel. "It is, as Lord Rochester said, the greatest wonder of the world. At Windsor, Lord Sunderland himself has told me it was so, and Lory Hyde besides, both marveling that His Highness had no other low wench tucked somewhere about Brussels."

Father frowned, skeptical. "I suppose Sunderland would know, given the number of spies he employs."

"As would Lord Shaftesbury, given that he employs twice the number." I smiled, and emptied my glass. He was my father, yes, but on account of his Whiggish beliefs I would tell him no more: not of how I'd become a favorite of the Duchess of Portsmouth, or how she in turn had appealed to me when she'd feared for Charles, or how the Romish counselors of the Yorks' household feared what they perceived as my power over the duke. Most of all, I didn't tell him of how genuine that power might in time become, and with good reason, too. Because if I'd a hold over James, then he had just as great of a hold over me.

Instead all I did was smile and tell him next to nothing. "The truth is, Father, that I am as bewildered by this as anyone else. Yet so long as His Highness pleases me and I please him, I see no reason for not continuing as we are, and set the Romish Church on its ear."

That at least made Father laugh, and preserved enough of his good temper for us to sup in a semblance of peace and contentment. We spoke no more of James or Scotland or even Sunderland and Shaftesbury, and Lady Sedley's supper was much the better for it.

But while James and I might continue as we were, the rest of our Court-bound world did not. On the same day that James returned to Brussels, Charles decided he had had enough of Lord Monmouth's seditious mischief, and banished him, too, stripping him of his military commissions and sending him off into the Prince of Orange's keeping at the Hague. To reinforce the fact that Monmouth was no legitimate heir to the Crown, the king also wrote and signed a statement that swore that the only woman he'd ever wed was the queen herself—a step we all hoped would put an end to Lord Monmouth's mysterious black box.

In London, Lord Shaftesbury persisted in acting like a madman, and imperiously decided to call a meeting of the privy council himself to discuss the Duke of York being sent to Scotland. Only English kings have the right to call such meetings, and only kings, too, can dismiss a minister and strip him of his offices, and that is exactly what Charles did to Lord Shaftesbury. To further show his power remained, Charles also announced that while a new Parliament had been elected in the summer, he would not call it to London to meet for a year, not until November 1680. My father and the other Whigs found this arrogant and oppressive on Charles's part and smacking far too much of French absolutism, while Charles in turn believed that the firm hand of a strong monarch was necessary for the peace of the country. All of this served to reinforce James's position as the rightful heir, and I dared to hope that he'd soon be recalled to London.

I also learned that my sojourn at Windsor with James had become one of the least-kept secrets at Court. Though no one spoke of it directly to me, everyone knew of it, and decided now I was no fleeting and casual *amour*, but a mistress of standing. Others sought my favor, fawning and seeking to please me despite my royal lover being hundreds of miles away. I was included in most every entertainment at Whitehall, with a choice place close to my new patroness Lady Portsmouth and thereby to the king as well. It was almost as if my presence at Court represented James, a way to prove that though still banished, he hadn't been forgotten. As I wrote to James in distant Scotland, this seemed an amusingly ludicrous position for me to be in, fit for a farce or other comedy. I only hoped I'd survive to the end of the performance before the audience began to hurl spoiled oranges at me for my uselessness.

As 1679 ended and 1680 began, I was largely content, though restive. I sorely missed James, and because of his absence felt myself as much an oddity as a unicorn or other mythical beast. It did not help matters that Lord Dorset had decided to unleash another of his poetical lampoons upon me in my thin-veiled guise as Dorinda. Whatever rancor I'd caused him once by my rejection was long forgotten, and now he wrote for vengeance of another kind, his pen dipped anew in venom at my expense. It was a righteous, Whiggish pen, and I was a fit target for it, being the mistress of the loathed Duke of York. I doubted His Lordship would have dared so much had James been in London. This poem was the most astonishingly cruel yet, and also the one that most amused all those to whom he showed it:

Tell me, Dorinda, why so gay,
Why such embroid'ry, fringe, and lace?
Can any dresses find a way,
To stop th' approaches of decay,
And mend a ruin'd face?

Wilt thou still sparkle in the box,
Still ogle in the ring?
Canst thou forget thy age and pox?
Can all that shines on shells and rocks
Make thee a fine young Thing?

So have I seen in larder dark
Of veal a lucid loin;
Replete with many a brilliant spark,
As wise philosophers remark,
At once both stink and shine.

I wept with bitter fury when I read this, safely alone where no one could see the pain Lord Dorset had again caused me. I was not old, I was not poxed, I was not—ah, but no. The only possible defense was to shrug as if words had no power over me, and pretend to laugh at the myriad petty slanders contained in those few vicious lines. I burned the sheet, taking small satisfaction in watching the cruel words twist and curl and fall into the cinders. In my heart I knew the real curse was knowing how much truth the poem had contained.

At my twenty-second birthday, I was a mistress without a master, a woman defamed for wantonness who yet slept in a solitary bed, a lady scorned as old beyond my years and vulgar in my tastes, a disappointment to my father for remaining constant to the prince who'd sired my daughter. I was, in short, as great a contradiction as any to be found in London, but there was far more to question about my life than this, as I was soon forced to see to my considerable sorrow.

WHILE MY FATHER DID INDULGE IN politics to a degree likely grievous to his health, he had continued other, more beneficial practices from his youth such as tennis, swimming, and riding. He'd also continued writing, and was working on another play that he was fancifully calling *Bellamira*. As a result of so much activity, he was at forty still a gentleman in his prime, with none of the outward signs—gout, palsy, excessive corpulence and drunkenness, blindness, incontinence, running sores, and shortness of breath—of a former libertine's life that now plagued most of his old acquaintances. Though Father and I were too similar to entirely give up our occasional quarrels, I was still vastly proud of him, as a daughter should be of her father, and loved him dearly, too.

On an afternoon in late January, Father, his fellow playwright Sir George Etherege, and several others of his more agile companions were engaged in a vigorous game of tennis on a covered court in Peter Street, near Clare Market. In the middle of the sets, however, the wet snow that lay on the roof overhead proved too weighty for the supports, and the entire building collapsed, crushing and trapping those within.

I was in a goldsmith's shop on the Strand with Lady Portsmouth when the messenger found me, the two of us poring covetously over trays of baubles as if we each hadn't enough jewels in our chests at home already.

"There's been a terrible, terrible accident in Peter Street, Mrs. Sedley," the man declared, the sweat of his exertion streaming down his face for all it was January. "The tennis court there has collapsed, and all within were trapped."

"All?" I asked, staggering to my feet. "Pray God not my father, too?"

"I am very sorry, ma'am," the man said, "but Sir Charles and Sir George are both among those still missing, and presumed to be lost as well."

"No!" I wailed. "He cannot be lost! Not my father, not this way!"

"Go at once, Katherine," Lady Portsmouth said, embracing me swiftly by way of comfort and courage. "You must be there when they find Sir Charles, and pray to God that he lives still."

I urged my coachman to employ his whip, and raced as fast as was possible to Peter Street. With my footmen to make way through the crowd that had gathered, I pushed forward to where the fallen court and the tavern beside it had once stood. Now, like a tooth knocked out from among its fellows, only a gaping spot remained to mark its place, filled with the rubble of broken timbers and bricks, shingles and shattered windows. Over all was the blanket of snow that had caused the disaster, trampled and muddied by the men who struggled with shovels and bars to free those who lay buried beneath. Worst of all was the place to one side where the dead who'd already been recovered were laid in a hasty jumble upon the ground, their still, tormented faces and crushed and broken limbs exposed to those who'd come to gawk at their misfortune, the snow around their bodies stained crimson with their life's blood. Fresh widows wept, bowed and kneeling beside them.

I caught the arm of a man in a green cape who seemed to be ordering others about. "Has Sir Charles Sedley been found?" I demanded. "Is there any word of him yet?"

The man looked me up and down, finally deciding from the fur on my cloak and the pearls in my ears that I must be a lady, and deserving of the slight bow he granted to me.

"Are you Sir Charles's lady?" he asked, with so little preamble that I feared the worst.

"I am Sir Charles's daughter, Mrs. Sedley." I clutched my gloved hands together, beseeching. "I'll give a guinea to the man who finds him!"

"We've found no gentlemen as yet, ma'am, neither alive nor dead," he said brusquely. "Them's all from the tavern. But I should warn you that there is little hope—"

"Parker, here!" called another man excitedly, one of a group that had been working to clear away more wreckage. "We've found th' gentlemen!"

I ran to the spot beside Parker, my heeled shoes sliding across the wet rubble while my heart beat with the hope I'd been ordered not to feel. I arrived in time to see them pull aside another beam and uncover the lifeless bodies of my father and Sir George. They'd been trapped together by the same timber, taken by such complete surprise that their rackets were still in their hands. Their faces were as pale as their white linen shirts, bruised and smudged with dirt, and far worse, covered with their own sweet blood. I shrieked and tried to reach my father, but Parker held me back, rightly realizing I'd bring only more confusion. One of the other men knelt beside my sire's body, carefully freeing him from more rubbish. My father's head lolled to one side and slipped free from his wig.

Then I saw the great gash across his temple, and how the crimson blood marked his pallid face like some gruesome harlequin's mask.

Desperately I pulled against Parker's grasp as the other man pressed his cheek against my father's chest to listen for his heartbeat. He sat back on his heels, and smiled up at me.

"He lives, ma'am," he said. "Sir Charles lives!"

I gasped. But while I longed to feel relief and joy, I could not. He lived then, but from the sad and sorry sight of him, I could not assume he'd live much longer. With a flurry of orders, I had my father wrapped with every tenderness and placed within my coach, and sent for a surgeon to meet us at Bloomsbury Square. I ordered Sir George to be taken to his own lodgings and met by a surgeon as well, for he, too, clung to life, yet had neither wife nor daughters to look after his welfare.

The first surgeon I'd summoned tended Father as best he could, and then later the same day came a second, sent with concern by His Majesty himself. But neither of these learned gentlemen could offer much by way of answers. My father lay still and lost to us, at rest in the middle of his bed with his head neatly bound and his thoughts somewhere else entirely. He would shift and waken only enough to take water and broth, spooned between his lips, but that was all. No whispered words of endearment wrought response from him, and to see a man who was habitually so quick and full of snapping vigor be now so quiet was a frightening thing. All the surgeons could advise was peace, and time, and prayer.

Though in most ways Lady Sedley and I had little use for each other, we now joined together to preserve my father's life. I excused myself from the frivolities of Whitehall Palace, and moved myself and my daughter into my old rooms in Bloomsbury Square. Lady Sedley and I agreed that if Father were to wake from this malevolent sleep, the first face he saw should be a dearer one than that of a hired nurse, and so we kept our vigil, alternating our hours by day and by night so that he was never alone.

For the rest of January and into February, we saw little improvement. These were long hours for me, not only from fear for Father, but also for myself. There is nothing like so much solitude in the face of hovering death to inspire self-reflection, and to evaluate the quality of one's own life as well.

Now, though I considered myself a good member of the Church, I was not exactly an exemplary one. I attended services most every Sunday, and I kept awake during sermons, and I never left the poor box unattended, and surely I'd earn some special credit in Protestant heaven for all the times I'd told James he should abandon the Pope and return to the archbishop. But the private reckoning I made of my own mortal soul—of how I'd given my life over to idle pleasures, how I'd engaged in adultery with James and sinned against Mary Beatrice, his wedded wife before God, how I'd borne a child out of wedlock, how I dissembled, and swore, and employed a few special cheats at cards here and there—was not a very favorable one.

With my poor father laid before me in his darkened bedchamber, it was easy enough for my guilty conscience to recall every time I'd flagrantly disobeyed both him and the commandment to honor him. I even tormented myself with the sorrowful details of how I'd been employed while he'd suffered his accident, how I'd been sitting in the goldsmith's shop beside the Duchess of Portsmouth, a pair of royal whores greedily surveying their next worldly rewards, and wondered with despair if I'd somehow caused Father's suffering. Rubies and pearls and blood and snow were all now twisting and turning in my mind together in an agony of guilt and repentance, and fear for my father, myself, and even my little daughter.

James's letters from Edinburgh did little to comfort me. I missed him sorely in this time, and longed for him to be close enough to offer the solace of his embrace. While his written sympathy for Father's accident was genuine enough, the harsh words that he repeated from his Catholic advisers regarding death and final judgments were enough to terrify one of their own saints.

But in the end, the most fearful warning regarding the fragility of mortal life came from one I'd never expected to give it, and that was Lord Rochester.

Chapter Nineteen

Bloomsbury Square, London
February 1680

I had not seen Lord Rochester in many months. I'd first been occupied with the birth of Lady Katherine and then swept up in the business of the Court, while His Lordship had spent less time at Whitehall on account of his health, and increasingly more time with his family in the country, at Woodstock and Adderbury. When he came to call soon after Father's accident, I was shocked by the change in him, shocked and infinitely saddened, too. I recalled when I'd first met him at Epsom, how astonished I'd been by his manly beauty and grateful for his kindness to me, a small, shy, unlovely girl.

Now his formerly rapturous beauty was ravaged beyond recognition by drink and the pox, and his once-elegant figure twisted and shrunk like a scarecrow inside his rich clothes. He leaned heavily on his walking stick, needing its support as he entered the room, and his sight so clouded that he was forced to fumble and grope for the chair I'd placed beside Father's bed. The only thing that remained unchanged was his famously lazy smile, there for me like a ghost drawn from past days. He was only thirty-three, yet could have easily been twice that and more.

He gazed down at my father's sleeping form and smiled.

"So this is what it takes to make your father quiet," he said. "An entire tennis court must topple on his head. I've never been this long in his presence without having him gabbling away at me."

"He's been that way since the accident, my lord," I said softly. I don't know why I lowered my voice whenever I spoke around Father, when clearly he heard me not; I suppose from habit I continued as if he were only in the thrall of an ordinary sleep, and that he'd be irascible as ever if I woke him. "It is his silence that seems so wrong. The doctors warned that even if he does in time wake, he may not speak again, or be changed beyond knowing. But to think of him without his wit—oh, my lord, I could not bear it!"

"Nor could he, the fat little rogue, which is why it will not come to pass." He drew off his glove and took my father's hand with such gentleness that tears stung my eyes.

If ever a man's sins and excesses could have been made visible, then the proof was writ bold across the wreck of Lord Rochester. I'd committed many of the same sins as he, and I couldn't help but see his precipitous decline as a warning. Was this the unhappy future that waited for me? Would I, too, be made to suffer so dreadfully for my many sins if I failed to change my ways?

"You are good to come to him, my lord," I said. "Even as Father is now, it will do him well, I'm sure of it."

"Oh, there's little enough good in me," he said, and though I believe he meant it as his old raillery, there was a resignation to his words that saddened me further. "Little enough of bad, too, now that I think of it. A dry pea clattering in an empty tankard would have more substance than I. But mark your father. He hasn't dined properly in days, yet his cheeks are still fat as a suckling pig's."

I laughed in spite of myself. "You say that only because he can't answer, my lord."

"Oh, yes, perhaps I do." He sighed. "But Little Sid's not done yet. Every man has his time, my dear Dorinda, and God won't take any of us before He's ready. What does heaven need of another bad poet, I ask you?"

"Then you should be safe as well, my lord," I said, and lay my hand over his, and my father's with it. "May God keep you here among us, too."

His smile was melancholy rather than bitter. "God will do what He pleases with me, Katherine," he said, "and I will be ready when He does."

I've often suspected Father heard more than we realized, especially after Lord Rochester's visit. Perhaps his old friend's words reached him as none of ours did, or perhaps he realized how perilously close His Lordship was to death himself. I shall never know for certain, but on the following day Father began to sigh and frown, heartening signs, and soon after that he roused himself completely and returned to us. To be sure, he was so weak that he whispered rather than declaimed, and could barely keep awake more than a quarter hour before exhaustion claimed him again, but the worst was past, and each day brought cautious improvement.

By the end of March he was well enough to sit upright in his bed and jest with the unending parade of visitors who came to him. I knew that Father had many friends, but it seemed that half of London (at least the half that frequented playhouses and Parliament, with a good deal of the Court besides) must have come trooping through his bedchamber, all ready to rejoice in his recovery and make jests about how neatly he and Sir George Etherege cheated death.

"You would have marveled at it yourself, Mrs. Sedley," said Sir Fleetwood Shepherd, who had likewise been playing tennis at the time of the accident, but had escaped with much less injury to his person. "There was so much fire in your father's play that day that it blew up poet, house, and all."

Father had laughed. "No, Shepherd, you have it wrong, as you usually do. The play was so heavy that it broke down the house and buried the poor poet in the ruins."

But Father had changed. There was no doubt of that. I do not know what rare insight was granted to him while he slept, or what horrors were revealed when his own soul hovered in the balance as he lay trapped beneath the fallen roof, but as his convalescence continued, he requested books of sermons and other theological subjects rather than his old satires and novels. I often discovered him so deeply in thought that I feared he'd fallen ill again, it took so much to startle him from it. When Lord Rochester came again to him, the two conversed alone behind the closed door for several hours, so long and earnestly that both were exhausted by it.

Soon after, Dr. Gilbert Burnet called on Father. This worthy Scotsman was a divine of considerable energy, intelligence, and fervor, and as famous for his outspoken remarks as he was for his piety. Last year, in the midst of the worst of the Popish plot, he had won the favor of Charles by preaching moderation, and by defending James against his attackers. But he had undone that goodwill in January by writing a lengthy letter to the king that enumerated and addressed the royal sins, and Lady Portsmouth (doubtless herself one of the sins) had told me that the king's displeasure had been long and furiously indignant.

More purposefully, Dr. Burnet had been spending much time with Lord Rochester, addressing his questions and preparing his soul. I'd credited His Lordship's declaration that he'd be ready for death to Dr. Burnet, and I wondered if he saw in my father another soul in sore need of tending. As curious as I was to the nature of these meetings, Father kept them private and said nothing of them to me.

After one such visit, I stopped the minister in the hall to thank him for the comfort he brought to Father.

"It is to the credit and glory of God Almighty, Mrs. Sedley, and not to me," he said, his heavy dark brows coming sternly together. "Sir Charles is discovering his own way to salvation, and I am no more than the shepherd who guides him gently forward."

Gentleness was not a quality I'd necessarily ascribe to Dr. Burnet. With his rumbling voice and thick-set body, I'd always thought of him as more an avenging angel than a meek shepherd, especially if that angel were a booming Scotsman.

"Whatever the reason, sir, I am grateful for the result," I said. "My father is much the better for it."

"Thank the Lord," he said, nodding with satisfaction. "Perhaps there is a message for you, too, in Sir Charles's redemption. If you should ever wish to explore—"

"No, no, thank you, sir," I said quickly, shying from such a bold step. "I am happy as I am."

"Are you?" he asked, fixing me so surely with his fiery glance that I drew back, away from its powerful appeal. "God has placed you in a wondrous position, Mrs. Sedley. You have been granted the opportunity to do great good in this world, not only for His Highness the Duke of York, but for the rest of the kingdom, and all for the glory of our Merciful Lord. Consider well your every action and every word, Mrs. Sedley, consider them and act in accordance. There are consequences for everything, both in this mortal life and the next."

Startled by his boldness, I declined as graciously and swiftly as I could, and was relieved when the door closed after him. But his words stayed with me long after he'd left the house, and lingered with all the mighty power of a prophecy that I'd do well to heed.

But like any prophecy, the more I considered it, the more complicated and layered its meaning became, and the more confusing as well. At first I'd taken his meaning to be the most obvious, that I should set aside my royal lover and my lascivious sin with him, choose new and more godly companions than Nelly and Louise, employ my fortune to useful charities instead of frivolous indulgences, and devote myself to my daughter's upbringing. In short, to repent, and be a perfect Magdalene.

But for all his faith, Dr. Burnet was not some remote hermit, but a gentleman who moved freely in my very secular world, and understood the finest points of the Court. What if he'd intended me to remain with His Highness and try to influence him to return to the Protestant Church? Was that how I was meant to save England? Could this "wondrous position" that he'd mentioned be no more than the lascivious postures I'd already borrowed from Aretino? Was it only through more traditional sinning that I was to find my salvation? It was a troubling quandary, to be sure, one that claimed much sleep from me as I tossed and turned beneath its burden. Yet because I was far more accustomed to drollery than piety, I couldn't help but see the peculiar irony of Dr. Burnet's words, too, even as I tried to decipher their meaning.

"I understand that Dr. Burnet has addressed you, Katherine," Father said to me one evening with his new, uncharacteristic earnestness. "He's a very wise gentleman, you know. If he has favored you with his thoughts, then you'd do well to heed them."

But for the rest of the spring of 1680, Dr. Burnet devoted most of his energies to the final agonies of poor Lord Rochester. By the end of June, Father was well enough to travel by his own coach, and likewise made a final, sorrowful pilgrimage to Woodstock Lodge and his dying friend. To his regret, it was hardly the farewell both would have wished. His Lordship was so fuddled with the opium on account of his pain and convulsions that Father doubted he knew him.

When in July His Lordship's sufferings at last came to an end, Dr. Burnet was the one who helped ease the earl's soul heavenward from his tormented body. Father mourned his loss deeply, as did I, for it seemed with him had gone the last of my childhood, and the last of the happier days before plots and popery, Whigs and Tories, had strangled the joy from our lives.

Father believed that Lord Rochester had died a true Christian, and along with his own escape from death, took the nature of His Lordship's demise as a heartfelt lesson toward his own eventual redemption. But others of His Lordship's closest friends, including Nelly and Lord Dorset, believed the fervent deathbed conversion was more Dr. Burnet's contrivance than any true profession by His Lordship, and remained convinced that he'd died as he'd lived, an unrepentant, doubting sinner.

My own thoughts regarding Dr. Burnet's role at the earl's deathbed lay somewhere in between, unfixed and uncertain, as were my conclusions regarding his advice to me. Father had urged me to speak with Dr. Burnet again, but I didn't. With Father's health restored, my eventual salvation seemed less urgent and my soul in less need of tending. Besides, I didn't want to hear more of how he was guiding me with his shepherd's crook. I'd no wish to have the responsibility for the entire Protestant kingdom placed on my shoulders, nor did I wish to be regarded as an Anglican weapon against popery, any more than I desired James's Catholic priests and attendants to regard me as their keenest enemy. I would much rather be simply a tall, thin lady with a charming young daughter and a lover at present far removed in Scotland, and not even Dr. Burnet had the right to expect more from me than that.

Thus by the end of the summer, I'd returned to my own house in King Street, and to my place among the other habitual sinners at Court. For now, at least, it was where I belonged.

THE AUTUMN OF 1680 WAS NOT a good time for the King of England.

The Parliament that he'd put off for a year was at last meeting, and the main business on their agenda was the Second Exclusion Bill to remove the Duke of York once and for all from the succession. Most of Parliament, including my father, believed the bill would finally pass. To Charles's great disgust, even the formerly loyal Lord Sunderland had joined the Exclusionists, claiming it was the only sure way to save both

England and its monarchy. Charles did not agree, and furiously referred to Sunderland's defection as the kiss of Judas.

Nor were Charles's previous troubles at ease, either. Though removed from office, Lord Shaftesbury had continued busily sowing mischief in the House of Lords and elsewhere. Most recently he'd attempted to have Lady Portsmouth indicted as a common prostitute in the Whig stronghold of Middlesex, with a possible punishment that would include a public whipping and time in the stocks. Louise was terrified; Charles was, again, much angered. But Lord Shaftesbury had gone further still, once again encouraging Lord Monmouth's expectations, having him brought back to England against Charles's orders and set up on a kind of royal progress across the countryside to the cheers of his misguided supporters.

In October, Parliament met, and as expected, the House of Commons swiftly passed the Second Exclusion Bill with little discussion and on the third reading. The bill then was sent to the House of Lords, where no such welcome awaited it. Still, Lord Shaftesbury could taste victory for the Whigs, and confidently readied his arguments for the bill. The Lords had had enough of the obstreperous Commons, however, and enough, too, of Lord Shaftesbury. One grand lord after another rose to speak in defense of the king, the duke, and the succession as it existed. The king himself attended the sessions, listening closely and lobbying freely. The key to the attack, however, belonged to the Marquess of Halifax, who possessed the wit, the knowledge, and the boundless audacity to serve Lord Shaftesbury as he deserved. Every point that Shaftesbury attempted to make was deftly answered and then just as deftly deflated, even ridiculed. Not once in the ten-hour debate did Shaftesbury win a point, and at the end, the bill was soundly defeated, sixty-three votes to thirty.

Refusing to surrender, Lord Shaftesbury remained as nimble and busy as a body louse. The following day, he introduced an invidious bill to authorize a royal divorce and to separate the aging, barren queen from the king so he might marry again. But worse was to come. The six ancient Catholic lords who had been accused by Oates and Bedloe remained in the Tower, and now with a poisonous flourish, the Commons charged and swiftly convicted the most venerable of them, Viscount Stafford, based on the sworn lies of Titus Oates and others. At the end of December, Lord Stafford was executed, justly avowing his innocence moments before his severed head was raised to the crowd by his flowing white hair.

Sickened and disgusted, Charles again dissolved Parliament, and told them they next would meet in March, and not in London, but Oxford. That made the members grumble and fuss even more, and once again the Whigs prepared for battle throughout the winter of 1681. By the end of February, they'd already begun arriving in Oxford, blustering in the streets of that ancient town and singing crude songs against the king and the duke, and wearing pale blue ribbons in their hats to mark their cause. Some (like Father, proud to display both his party and his fashion), even wore ribbons with the slogan of NO POPERY! NO SLAVERY! woven into the satin. The ribbons had been supplied by Lord Shaftesbury, who had also stepped so far as to hire a band of armed men—his own small army—to march through Oxford, proclaiming his cause.

But His Majesty had a surprise of his own. The Commons was ordered to join the Lords, both houses to be crowded into a makeshift hall. When they arrived, they found the king himself in the full regalia of his throne: crown, ermine-trimmed robes of silk velvet, and scepter, an awe-inspiring sight to any Englishman, no matter his party. And with a single sentence, the king demonstrated the power that came with the show of ermine and gold:

> All the world may see to what a point we are come, that we are not like to have a good end when the divisions at the beginning are such.

That was all, a few short words that neatly summed the futility of the session. Before the members realized what was happening, the king bid the lord chancellor to dissolve Parliament, and that was the end. Then His Majesty left as swiftly as he'd arrived, riding away under an armed guard to Windsor. Those of us in the Court who'd expected a lengthy stay in Oxford and had taken lodgings were left to scramble willy-nilly after the royal party, which was doubtless what Charles wished us to do. Despite the trials of these last difficult years, Charles had still retained an excellent sense of humor.

Leaving Father behind to sulk and commiserate with the other disappointed Whigs, I set out as soon as I could in my own coach. I prided myself on having a fast team, and I reached Windsor in time to sup with Louise and Charles in her rooms, and with them a small party of courtiers who'd either been privy to the plan or had been able to coax or threaten their coachmen to show extra haste. We took our mood from Charles, and thus were a most jolly little party, toasting the completeness of the surprise and the astonished faces of the thwarted Whigs.

Yet as smug and pleased as we were, none of us save Charles himself realized the true significance of the day. It was only over time that the rest of us came to understand as well. Having dismissed this particular Parliament, he would never call another. Without confiding in any of his ministers, Charles had decided that he was done with Parliament, done with their interfering and their insults and their bigotry and their constant questioning of his authority, all reasons that were easily understood. This meant he was also done with listening to the will of his people through the representatives that they elected to serve them, which was a more troubling reason and far less agreeable.

But on that warm spring night, we knew nothing more than that the king had triumphed over his enemies once again. As the gentlemen sank deeper into their drink, Louise and I gathered our cloaks, and went to walk along the castle walls and breathe the air of the new season.

"When I was young in Brittany," Louise said, her face turned up to the skies, "I would make wishes on stars, and believed that if I could count them all, my wishes would come true."

"Even in France, Your Grace, that wouldn't have been possible," I said, ever logical. "There are far too many stars to begin to count them all."

"Thus none of those wishes came true." She smiled at the stars and shrugged. "But I am more practical now, you see, *madame*. I do not wish for what I cannot have, and I do not attempt what I cannot do."

"In everything, Your Grace?" I asked, curious, for it had always seemed to me that, one way or another, she'd gained whatever she'd wished for.

"In the right things," she said, absently touching the outsized pearl that swung from her ear as she looked back to the stars. "What do you wish, *madame*?"

That was simple enough to answer. "Only that His Majesty will relent, and permit His Highness to return to England, and to me."

"A good wish," Louise said. "An honest wish."

"A wish I wish would come true, Your Grace," I said sadly, and I'd drunk just enough wine to speak from my heart. "There are many days I wonder if he'll ever return to me, or if he has forgotten me."

"His Highness hasn't forgotten you," she said easily. "He writes to you, yes?"

"As often as he can, yes," I admitted, though his letters were hardly those of a romantic lover. James was not a natural writer, and it had always been clear to me that he was much more at ease composing military orders for his officers than a paean of endearments to me. He was further constricted in what he dared write of his daily affairs from fear of what could be misconstrued if his letters happened to fall into wrongful hands. While I wrote long, witty, entertaining letters, meant to amuse him with gossip and please him with my devotion, his in turn were short and brisk, and more devoted to the gloomy Scottish weather and his horses than I could have wished. But because he'd written these letters to me, I'd kept them all as rare treasures.

"And does he recall his child, and ask to be remembered to her?" she asked. "And your lodgings? Do his agents in London see that those are honored?"

"He does, yes," I said, now shamed for having complained to her. James recalled Lady Katherine in the most important way, with an allowance that had been unfailingly sent for her in addition to the one he'd settled on me. "He has been most generous."

She fluttered her fingers through the air. "I am certain he has not been as generous as you deserve. The more a gentleman grants a lady, the more he values her. The more he values her, the more pretty gifts he will offer. Even if the gentleman is His Highness."

Louise smiled proudly, as if she'd just parsed the greatest of mysteries, or leastwise the mystery of greed. It was well known the king had taken her maidenhead, but I did wonder what value she'd placed on her virtue, given how much she had extracted from him in return since then. Surely the commodity had long since fetched its price in "pretty gifts."

"I have never wanted for anything, Your Grace." Having always had a fortune of my own, I hadn't been inclined to pursue the royal plundering that Louise, Nell, and the other mistresses did.

She clucked her tongue. "You must consider your future, *madame*, and provide for your child as well as yourself. You would be wise to remind His Highness of his duty toward you in this."

I was feeling thoroughly guilty now, as if I'd somehow betrayed both James and Lady Katherine. "Forgive me, Your Grace. It was my own loneliness that made me speak so, and no fault of His Highness in any way."

"You must not doubt him, *madame*," she chided gently. "Do you believe you'd have kept your place here among us if one brother did not confide in another?"

She was right, of course. By 1681, I was an unmarried lady of twenty-three with a natural child. I'd neither youth nor beauty nor a title to recommend me as an ornament to the Court, nor was my diminished fortune sufficient in itself to draw favor. My father's strident politics alone would have been enough to make me unpleasant to the king, and I had been emphatically dismissed from my only official position at Court.

"You must have faith, *madame*," she continued. "With faith, everything is possible, yes?"

I looked at her sharply. Many at Court believed that Lady Portsmouth knew more of Charles's intentions than any of his ministers. "What have you heard, Your Grace? Please, please, what do you know?"

She smiled at me, her round, pale face as luminous as the moon. "I know that your wish is not so futile as you fear. I can tell you no more than that, *madame*. But there are things that are possible this night that were not when we rose this morning."

"Thank you, Your Grace," I whispered, my hopes rising as high as the stars above us. "Oh, thank you!"

"Be brave, *ma chère*, and be strong, and before long your faith will surely be rewarded." She nodded as if agreeing with herself, and made a pretty little sweep with one hand, the jeweled bracelets on her wrist clinking softly together. "I do believe His Majesty is not yet done amazing us, yes?"

I CANNOT SAY WHETHER THE DUCHESS of Portsmouth knew for certain what Charles planned, or if she'd simply grown adept at guessing after so many years in his company. But there was no doubt that His Majesty's actions over the next months did amaze a good many of his subjects, and outright shock a few more. It seemed his success in defeating the Second Exclusion Bill and in dismissing Parliament had given him fresh courage and confidence. He was no longer a young man—his last birthday had been his fiftieth—but he now acted against those who dared cross him not with the thoughtful caution of age, but rather with a young man's bold and swift decision.

In early July, Lord Shaftesbury was arrested for treason. He was charged with attempting to make war on the king; those bands of armed men he'd employed at Oxford with blue ribbons in their hats now seemed dangerously brazen rather than brave. Though he was acquitted by a Whig-loving jury drawn from the men in the city (a group famously resentful of the Crown), His Lordship understood how closely he'd come to the same fate he'd so blithely urged for others, and soon after he was released, he fled abroad.

Lord Monmouth was not so wise, which was, I suppose, much to be expected. Never one to display intelligence to match his charm and dash, he foolishly stood bail for his old supporter, Lord Shaftesbury. Charles in turn showed his anger by taking away several of Lord Monmouth's most lucrative offices, and gave them to the Duke of Grafton, one of his sons by the Duchess of Cleveland, and to Louise's son, the Duke of Richmond. Most men of any sense would have then retreated, but Lord Monmouth had no sense. Instead he decided that Lord Halifax—the marquess who had so ably defended the royal interests against the Second Exclusion Act—had come between him and his father, and challenged Lord Halifax to a duel. Lord Halifax declined, and worse, Charles took the marquess's side against his wayward son, and Lord Monmouth became an outcast at Court. The only one who still stood by him was Nelly, always loyal to her old friends, and her house was the last one left in London where he was still welcomed.

Not all Charles's actions were negative ones. Due largely to Louise's urgings, he began to make an uneasy peace with Lord Sunderland and put aside his past references to Judas, for he needed His Lordship's counsel and wise head. He also relied increasingly on Laurence Hyde, who was now First Lord of the Treasury.

But of greater importance was the less tangible shift of goodwill toward the king. The country was at peace, and prospering, with many English ships and merchants engaged in rich trade with the American colonies as well as the East and West Indies. The king had stood firm against popery, plots, the French, the Dutch, Lord Shaftesbury, and finally Parliament. He had defended himself and his Crown, and he'd even defended his queen, and his people approved. He was cheered whenever he appeared in public, and as the Whigs had lost their power, it had become fashionable to be a Tory, and support the Crown and the Stuarts.

To me, everything appeared to be arranging itself as neatly as could be for James's return. It wasn't merely the politics, though the less hindrance to be found in that area, the better. I saw it in more subtle ways, too, in how the same newssheets that had once depicted James as no more than a dangerous zealot in thrall to the Pope now wrote with favor of how well His Highness the Duke of York had conducted the king's affairs in Scotland, how deftly he'd balanced justice and fairness among the wild men of that savage place. I overheard gentlemen in shops and at playhouses discussing how fairly the duke had managed to resolve the difficult religious issues to the north, and without once imposing his own beliefs upon the conflicts, which augured well for the future. When I went to service with Father on Sunday, I realized that James's name had once again been included among those for whom we should pray, with as little fanfare as when it had been removed three years before.

All this I wrote to James, who in turn shared his ever-growing impatience to return to London, and to me. Together, across the distance, we dared to hope his exile would soon be done. Just as Louise had encouraged me, I urged James to have faith as well, and to be brave. And for the first time in years, it did seem as if that faith might finally be rewarded.

IT WAS THE WAGGING END OF the Christmas revels, after the New Year and Twelfth Night had been duly celebrated: an evening when everyone at Court was secretly weary of the long season of celebration. There had been some desultory sort of singers in the Banqueting House, and dancing afterward, but Louise and I had admitted we'd neither of us much patience for it, and as soon as Charles had left for billiards with several of his gentlemen, she and I had retreated with a few other ladies to her rooms to play loo and ombre.

But even the cards offered no real diversion, and as the hour grew late, the other ladies excused themselves, until only Louise and I remained, each of us sprawled with ungainly ease across a separate silk-covered settee as we gossiped. Louise lay back against a pile of cushions stuffed with swans' down, a silver dish of tiny square cakes resting on her belly as she delicately nibbled away the pale icing from each one in turn, while I sipped wine from a glass etched with centaurs and nymphs along its rim. We must have made a pretty picture of luxurious indolence, there amidst all the gold leaf and crimson brocade that Louise so favored. The fires still roared high in the chamber's four fireplaces and scores of candles were guttering in the chandeliers overheard, and all of it and us reflected over and over in the enormous gold-framed looking glasses that covered the walls.

That was how Charles found us. He entered quietly, through one of the hidden passages that riddled Whitehall, and when I drowsily looked up over the rim of my glass, there he stood, laughing at us.

At once I set down my glass and stumbled to my stockinged feet to curtsy, but Charles motioned for me to stop.

"No ceremony, Katherine, I beg you," he said, joining Louise on her settee. At once she curled against him and draped her legs familiarly over his as she offered him one of the little cakes from her plate. He smiled, and let her feed him, slowly licking the sugary icing from her fingers.

Uncomfortable, I looked away. Though she had been his mistress for nearly fifteen years, she still possessed the power to beguile him, and I'd no doubt that if I weren't there, they would have been on each other in an instant.

Truth be told, seeing them together made me almost unbearably lonely. But no matter how I longed to leave, I could not retreat without their permission, and so I stood, my gaze lowered in misery.

"You must be tired, *madame*, and wish for your bed," Louise said softly, understanding. "Might you give her leave, sir?"

"After a moment," he said easily. "I will not keep you beyond that, Mrs. Sedley."

"As you wish, sir." I looked to Charles. With his dark, melancholy eyes balanced by an ever-wry smile, he bore only a passing resemblance to his brother, and yet there was still something to his face that reminded me of James.

"I should think it's rather your wish, Mrs. Sedley, not mine," he said. "I will be leaving for the winter meetings at Newmarket in a fortnight. I know you ladies don't favor the cold, but I recommend that you join us. Your former lodgings have been taken for you again, and you will find the company to your taste."

I gasped; I could not help it. "Forgive me, sir, but—but you startle me, sir."

He laughed, clearly pleased beyond measure with himself. "Hah, that is what I wanted. You won't disappoint my brother now, Mrs. Sedley, will you?"

"No, sir—that is, not at all, sir," I managed to stammer, for once without words. "I would not disappoint him, not for all the world."

"I am glad of that," Charles said. "He needs wise counsel wherever he can find it."

But Louise only smiled. "I told you to have courage, *madame*," she said. "You listened, and now—now you shall have your reward, and so, too, shall His Highness."

Chapter Twenty

NEWMARKET, SUFFOLK
February 1682

In the long months that James and I had been apart, I'd often worried that he'd forget me, or worse, that when we met again, he'd wonder that he'd ever found me pleasing in the first place. It was no idle fear, either. We had been separated far longer than we'd been together, and though the ancient poet might claim that "always toward absent lovers does love's tide grow stronger," he had never known the fickleness of royal favor.

Yet as soon as James and I met again at Palace House, the king's lodgings in Newmarket, it was as if only a few hours had separated us instead of years. He had changed little: his expression more resolute, perhaps, his fair-eyed gaze more fiercely determined, but that was all. Lord Dorset and others who did not like me might claim I'd grown old and withered before my time, but James declared I'd only become more lovesome in his eyes. Thus it should be with lovers: that so long as we each pleased the other, then the rest of the world might be damned to the devil.

"There are those who will always dislike me, Katherine," he said, soon after his return to England. We'd gone out riding one sharp frosty morning before the rest of the Court was awake, crossing the fields outside of town. With no one to overhear us, he spoke plainly, our horses drawn close for conversation and his attendants and guards keeping their distance. "Halifax, for one. I could tell it as soon as I met him the other night."

"Lord Halifax?" I asked with surprise. "Faith, His Lordship was the one who defended you so strongly in the Lords!"

"He defended my brother, and he spoke against exclusion. He has never defended me." He nodded solemnly. "That's a world of difference, you know. Halifax believes Charles risked too much for me, and so resents me for it. I could see it in his eyes. If you want to know the truth of a man, mark his eyes."

"I could not tell you so much as the color of His Lordship's eyes, let alone what truth they betray."

"That is because you've no need to know, being a lady. A lady's eyes are an entirely different matter." He smiled crookedly, studying me from beneath the cocked brim of his hat, pulled low against the chill. "Your eyes are very beautiful, Katherine, and I could stare into them by the hour. I've always thought so, you know."

"Why, sir," I said, touched as I always was by his compliments. They were never very original, and often a little clumsy, as was this, but they were always so heartfelt in a way that a more practiced gallant would never be. "That is kind of you to say."

"It's not being kind," he said. "It's the truth. Just as it's the truth that Halifax doesn't like me."

I sighed, wishing there weren't such a fine line between being stalwart and stubborn. "Don't make an enemy of him, sir."

"Oh, I won't," he said. "But while I can't make him like me, I can make him respect me. You'll see, Katherine. I'm determined in this. I will keep myself clear of my brother's affairs here in England, and hold Scotland as my only purpose."

"You don't mean to return to Edinburgh, do you?" I asked with dismay.

"Not if it's in my power to remain," he said. "But I must earn my place here. Charles has made that plain. I must make myself agreeable, and be quiet in my worship, and then he will reconsider my future."

"You can convince him, sir," I said. "You will, so long as your priests stay tethered to their prie-dieus in your lodgings to keep them from appearing on the street and frightening the populace."

I'd meant that as a jest, but he'd taken it as an actual suggestion, the sort of misunderstanding that occasionally occurred between us.

"That's easily done," he said seriously. "Those good fathers have no desire to mingle with the jockeys and whores in this place."

Tempted though I was, I let it pass from affection for him, and also kept to myself all other observations that would have freely jumbled those same good fathers with the jockeys and whores. I could only hope that, for the sake of those poor priests, he wasn't really tethering them to anything.

"That will please your brother, sir," I said instead.

"I hope it does," he said, but there was a gloomy fatalism in his manner that showed he didn't believe it. "My brother will do what he wishes, as he always has, and tell no one of it until it's done."

"What he wishes is what is best for you, sir," I said, and so it was, at least by what Louise had told me. "Why else would he have sent for you now?"

"I can but pray that it's so," he said, his expression still dark. "Above all things, I know I must demonstrate that England would be better served by having me here than in godforsaken Edinburgh."

"I am certain *I* would be better served by having you here, sir." I drew my mare to a halt and grinned, determined to tease him into a better humor. "I believe I've made that plain, too."

"Have you now, madam?" He stopped, and guided his horse to stand beside me. He might not always be the gentleman with the quickest wit, but by his smile he'd understood perfectly what I was suggesting now. "Must I demonstrate myself to you as well?"

"Only if you can catch me first," I called over my shoulder, and led him a merry chase back to the stable. He did indeed demonstrate himself after that, and quite handsomely, too, not even pausing to remove his boots.

OVER THE NEXT WEEKS, JAMES MANAGED to prove himself so thoroughly to his brother that, after the races were done, he invited him to return to London with the rest of the Court. As James had predicted, Lord Halifax was the only one to protest this invitation, worrying that the time was still not right for the Duke of York to show himself in the city. But instead of inciting rebellion and mayhem, as the marquess had warned, James's return to Whitehall was marked only by cheering welcomes for "Our Jemmy." The tide had indeed turned back in favor of the Stuart brothers.

The spring of 1682 was a halcyon time for James and me as well. With no real responsibilities as yet—Charles was rightly cautious of that—he was free to indulge in my company and with as much amorous play as we pleased. From how he described the grimness of Scotland, I believed he well deserved whatever happy respite I could grant him. Not only had he been forced to deal with the violent madmen and religious fanatics to be found there, but he'd also suffered more personal trials: Mary Beatrice had been delivered of yet another stillborn son, and sadder still, the only surviving child of their marriage, the five-year-old Lady Isabella, had also perished. This was, I think, another piece of why people had become more tolerant of James, and a sorrowful piece it was, too: although Mary Beatrice had conceived at least one child a year, not one had survived to prosper. The threat of a Catholic heir beyond James seemed increasingly unlikely, even though the duchess was with child again, the reason she'd remained behind in Edinburgh.

To be honest, I had been glad Her Highness was still away, both to have James to myself and to be spared the fury of her jealousy. James came often to my lodgings in the palace and in King Street. He especially enjoyed Lady Katherine, now a busy small person of three years, and played with her as any ordinary father would with his child. We walked and rode in St. James's Park, took our daughter to feed the ducks on the canal, attended the playhouses, and a score of other simple amusements. This happy time would come to an end, of course, for in June James was traveling back to the north to fetch his wife, his daughter the Lady Anne, and the rest of his household back from Edinburgh to London, but for now we were blissfully content.

After a supper in James's honor shortly before he began this journey, I was surprised to find myself approached by my former suitor John Churchill. He was finding much success in his career, and had become one of James's closest advisers, occupying a position of great trust in the York household as the Master of the Robes. John had been one of the gentlemen to accompany James from Brussels to Windsor when Charles's life had been in jeopardy, and he had also accompanied James on this visit to Newmarket and London. He and his odious wife, Sarah, were said to be happy, though after their marriage he had ordered her not to serve in either royal household, which seemed passing strange to me.

For obvious reasons, I had kept from John's company, but on this night, he came toward me of a purpose, and I could not avoid him. He was still as handsome as when I'd fallen in love with him, though now in plain dress for evening instead of his officer's uniform. I thought he seemed more ordinary than I'd remembered, and shorter, too, now that I'd grown accustomed to James's height.

"Mrs. Sedley," he said, sweeping his hat in salute. "I trust you are well?"

"Well enough that you would come seek me out, it seems," I said wryly. "What makes you take notice of me now, John? Is there a spray of gold coins sprouting from the train of my gown that make me worthy of your attention?"

He winced, a pained look I confess I remembered all too well with him. "I see no reason why we cannot speak as old friends do."

"Very well," I said. "I shall walk with you once about the Privy Garden gallery, which should offer time for all the speaking we need do."

I took his offered arm, and together we began to walk the galleries that overlooked the garden, a square that likely would enclose the limits of what we could possibly have to say to each other. Below us in the moonlight, the statues in the garden looked pale and frozen, and likely no more at ease than I felt in John's company.

"What a pace you set, Katherine," he said. "I forget how swiftly you walk."

I didn't slow. "Forgive me, sir," I said, "but I forget your wife is short with limbs to match. These days I am more accustomed to the manly stride of His Highness."

"I'd venture you are," he said grudgingly. "Katherine, please. We were friends once, and I wish us to be friends again, serving the same master."

I raised my brows with amusement. "Faith, John, I trust you're not serving His Highness in the same fashion as I!"

He looked so shocked that I judged him again to be a dreadful prig. Then, to my delight, he laughed, and I laughed with him.

"I cannot make that claim, no," he admitted. "Nor do I wish to. But where is the harm in us being friends such as this, Katherine? We share the same loyalties."

"My first loyalty is not to my master, but to my country." This was no empty slogan on my part, but what I believed in perfect earnestness. I should have been a Whig by nature and a Tory by circumstance, but having observed the worst of both parties, I could in conscience choose neither, and instead simply stood by my native country in all her dear imperfection.

"Such a loyalty should be the same for you, too, John," I continued, "though I'll grant one is a good deal more generous than the other."

"I'll not disagree," he said, "and yes, I have sworn to serve England first above any other masters. His Highness would feel the same."

"On most days he does," I agreed. "But on some, I'm certain he feels that England has not shown him the same regard that it should."

He grew suddenly serious. "Has His Highness ever tried to persuade you to popery? Has he ever made his favor conditional on your conversion to Rome?"

"He has not persuaded, nor presumed, either," I said firmly. "But then, he knows better than to introduce such a notion to me."

When he didn't answer, I glanced to him, curious. "You're often with His Highness. Has he ever urged you to his faith?"

"No," John admitted. "He has never attempted it. But I have heard tales of others in his employ who have felt the weight of his proselytizing for Rome."

"He shouldn't do that, not if he wishes his brother to end his exile," I said, troubled by this news. "The Whigs already write too many falsehoods in that vein of him. If they could find even one servant who'd swear he'd tried to push them toward his priests, then he'll never be free of Edinburgh. I was sure His Highness understood that, too."

"Perhaps he does," John admitted, "and perhaps my information was misguided. But for His Highness's sake, it is good that we can speak like this, Katherine."

"I suppose it is." I stopped, slipping my hand free of his arm. "Here we are, sir, at the end of the gallery."

He bowed. "I thank you for the pleasure, Mrs. Sedley, and hope you will honor me with your company again soon."

I nodded in vague acknowledgment, and left him. I wondered how much worth there'd been in what he'd said, and how much was his own cunning and speculation. I did not trust him, of course. As a courtier and an officer, he would always vow that his first loyalty was to his country and his master, but I'd always suspected that his first loyalty above all others would be sworn to John Churchill. No matter. It would be safer and more useful to have such a gentleman regard me as a friend rather than otherwise, and perhaps more useful for James as well.

THE TRIP TO AND FROM SCOTLAND in May proved to be one more wretched example of the ill luck that plagued James through most of his life. Whereas his brother the king seemed able to dodge misfortune or even twist it about to his own use, James seemed doomed to plunge headfirst into it without respite, and often with the worst possible outcome as well.

So it was with this journey. To avoid the notoriously bad roads in the north during the rains of spring, James had decided to travel by sea. In the midst of a terrifying storm, the ship carrying them ran aground on the shoals off Yarmouth, with the loss of over a hundred lives. Later James told me that he'd expected to die, dashed by the raging waves against the rocks. He had tried his best to show the bravery of a leader, refusing to abandon the sinking vessel beneath him the way any captain or admiral would. More stubbornness, I thought sadly, even as I applauded his bravery.

But his fine show of courage ended when his gentlemen forced him not as a captain, but as heir to the throne, into a boat as the last to leave the wreck. Sailors and others who'd earlier been swept into the waves struggled to save themselves by clinging to this boat, threatening to swamp it entirely, and James's soldiers had been forced to beat them back to save their master. Those men left to drown clearly haunted James; he spoke of them often and prayed for them more, hoping they'd made peace with God before they'd died, even if none of them had been people of quality. Even to me, that had an unpleasant callousness to it, which I hoped was attributed to James's distress and no more.

The Whig papers viewed the tragedy through a more calumnious light, however, claiming that numerous witnesses had watched the Duke of York himself using his sword to slash away the hands of the drowning sailors. In the face of disaster, they wrote, James had cared for saving only three things: his priests, his dogs, and his strongbox.

But the worst version of all was the one I overheard told by John Churchill to another officer of his acquaintance. By John's reckoning, the grievous loss of life was entirely due to the obstinacy of His Highness, and that even in the fire of battle, he'd never witnessed such cruelty as the duke displayed toward others in peril. As a survivor himself of the wreck, John's word could not be questioned, but I doubted it still, and wondered at the motives behind it.

It took another gentleman from the York household to explain this more succinctly. As Keeper of the Duke's Privy Purse, Colonel Grahme was also close to James; like John Churchill, he was another soldier drawn into the Yorks' service, and one who'd also scarce escaped the shipwreck.

"People will see what they wish to see, Katherine," he said when I asked him his version of the tragedy. "You know that as well as I."

"Then tell me what you saw," I said. "What did you make of His Highness's demeanor?"

"I saw the duke behave with authority and command and great personal bravery," he said firmly. "He showed strength of character in a situation of enormous peril. He is everything we should want in a leader and a king."

"I am glad of it." I nodded, yet frowned, too. "If I told you what I heard Colonel Churchill tell—"

"I can guess too well," he said, and lay his hand on my arm as if to caution me. "Recall what I said first, Katherine, that people will see what they wish. Recall what you already know of John Churchill. That should be answer enough."

And for now, though I remained uneasy, it was.

THE MEMORY OF THE WRECK SOON subsided in people's minds, as did the reasons that James had been sent away in the first place. In many ways, he was more a guest at Court, and an extremely well-behaved one at that. He was careful to keep his opinions to himself, and was as pleasant as possible to everyone. I knew he was trying to reassure his brother and make certain he'd not be sent away again, like some low house servant from the country, on approval before a new master. I could see the little cracks that the strain of maintaining so careful a front required, and when he came to my house, I made sure that everything was done to please and amuse him, by way of a respite.

He'd find little of that in his own quarters. I'd been shocked by the change in Mary Beatrice when she'd returned. She was somber and ill, her cheeks pale and deep circles beneath her eyes. She was great with child again, yet because she already dreaded the outcome, she took no joy in her fecundity. She had suffered through at least one pregnancy for each of the ten years of her marriage, and several more besides, if miscarriages were counted as well, yet she'd no living children to show for so much suffering. The constant grief and travail had broken her health, and little remained of the beautiful young princess who had charmed us all as a bride. Always devout, she had withdrawn deeper and deeper into the murky solace of her priests and prayers, and I could only imagine how melancholy her household must now be.

While she had been away, I had come to think of Mary Beatrice as my rival for James's love, and I was fully prepared to defend myself against whatever attacks she might make against me. But after seeing her pitiful condition, I would have been mean and small indeed to consider her as a serious threat, or to plot against her in any way.

Too close to her reckoning for travel, she remained in London while the rest of us retreated to Windsor, as was Charles's habit in the late summer. Word came in the middle of August that she'd been safe delivered of a daughter, named Charlotte in honor of the king. James joined us soon after this daughter's birth and scarce spoke of the child. Two months later, she, too, was dead, perishing of convulsions in her mother's arms.

But as sad as this was, few of us at Windsor spared so much as a tear for the death of one more royal princess. We were far too occupied by the latest mischief committed by Lord Monmouth. With Shaftesbury to light a fresh contentious fire beneath his spoiled bottom, His Grace had once again taken to making a royal progress about the countryside, encouraging supporters to flock to him as a younger, more charming, Protestant alternative to James for the Crown. He was even touching invalids for the King's Evil, a right he most definitely did not possess. Making matters more ostentatious was the small legion of armed soldiers His Grace had with him as an escort, much the same sort of mercenary ruffians in gorgeous uniforms that Lord Shaftesbury had employed at Oxford. Indeed, they might even have been the same men, and no one would have been surprised if they were.

On the morning after this news had reached us at Windsor, I had gone walking with several other ladies by the river, while James had been closeted with his brother. Of course we ladies spoke of Lord Monmouth, and I guessed James and Charles did the same. I was curious to learn what Charles's reaction was going to be, and when I saw James coming up the staircase toward me I smiled, eager to hear what he'd learned from his brother.

But James's expression was as black as thunder, his face so ruddy with anger that I feared for him.

"What is it, sir?" I asked with concern. "Is there anything that I—"

"Come with me, Katherine," he said, grabbing me by the arm. "If I do not speak to someone of this, I am sure I will burst."

He pulled me into the nearest room, a small parlor used for card playing. Two serving maids were within, tidying the room from the night before, and at once they lowered their eyes and curtsied.

"Leave us," James said curtly. "At once. At once!"

The two maids fled, and James shoved the door shut after them.

"My brother is blind, Katherine, absolutely blind where Monmouth is concerned," he began, fair spitting the words at the door he'd just shut. "He refuses to see what is happening, what will happen, if Monmouth and Shaftesbury are not halted."

I took off the broad-brimmed hat I'd worn against the sun while walking. "Do you mean His Grace's progresses, sir?"

"Of course I mean the damned progresses!" he exclaimed, wheeling to face me. "Monmouth goes traipsing about the country like some costumed mountebank, kissing wenches and waving his sword and making a raree show of the monarchy as he pretends he has any true *right* to the throne!"

I had never seen James so angry before, his cheeks mottled and his eyes afire like a madman's, and the depth of his rage frightened me.

"Be easy, sir, I beg you," I urged, fearing he'd cause himself an apoplexy. "All his life, His Grace has been a spoiled, willful fool. You've seen it yourself, again and again. You must not let him vex you so."

"This is beyond vexation, Katherine," he declared, shaking his head. "Vexation I could bear, but not this. This is rebellion, anarchy, treason!

He will destroy us all without a care, and then who will be the fools, I ask you?"

"But surely His Majesty—"

"My brother refuses to see what's before his face, even when the proof is there in front of him." Unable to keep still, he stormed back and forth across the room, punctuating his words with sharp thrusts of his hands as if dueling with phantoms he could not see. "They plot in London and in the north, Katherine, planning our ruin. It will be worse than my father's time, worse than anything that England has seen before, and all because my brother refused to stop his bastard *son*."

Absently I turned the brim of my hat around and around in my hands. I didn't doubt that there were more plots, not with Shaftesbury behind them. James had spies everywhere, which was understandable when he had the most to lose.

"What would you have His Majesty do, sir?" I asked. "Would you have him send Lord Monmouth away again?"

"Why, when all he does is defy my brother's orders and return?" James stopped his pacing to stand before the fireplace, striking both his fists on the mantelpiece as he stared into the fire. "No, the time for obliging Monmouth is long done. You cannot reason with a spoiled fool, and a spoiled fool with an army could destroy everything. Better to put him in the Tower now, where he can do no harm, and try him for treason and punish him as he deserves, as a lesson to others."

"But the punishment for treason is death, sir," I said, appalled. It was impossible for me to think of a pretty, charming fool like Lord Monmouth as the same dangerous threat that James so clearly did. The real hazard lay in him being used as a pawn by a clever villain like Lord Shaftesbury, but even so, I saw no reason that Lord Monmouth should face execution for choosing false companions. "You cannot intend that, not for His Grace."

"It would have already been done long ago, if it had been any other man in the kingdom besides Monmouth." James turned away from the fire and back to me. His anger was spent, but the chilly resolve that had replaced it was more frightening still. "England must come first, Katherine, the strength of the kingdom and the peace of her people. How can one bastard duke matter more than that?"

"Because he's His Majesty's son, sir," I said, the truth that was obvious to everyone. "He loves His Grace, faults and all."

"Then what of me?" he demanded, his voice raw with a misery I'd never expected to see. "I'm his brother. I have always supported him and followed his wishes. Isn't that enough for him to love me as well as his bastard?"

"Oh, my dear sir," I said softly, holding my arms out to him as I did to Lady Katherine, and wearily he came to me, holding me tight.

"I have done everything he desired, Katherine," he said over my shoulder. "Everything, and yet it has never been enough."

There was no answer to that, not that I could give. "His Majesty will do what is right, sir," I said finally. "For you, and for England."

LATER THAT SAME DAY, WE LEARNED that Charles had in fact ordered Lord Monmouth arrested, as James had wished. The charge wasn't treason, however, but disturbing the peace at Stafford with his false royal progress—his "raree show," as James had called it—and His Grace was taken to London to be tried before the King's Bench. He posted bail, but he was absolutely forbidden to make any more of his progresses or to appear at Court, and forbidden, too, from appealing to his royal father in person to try to weasel free from his misdeeds. Though in the end he was acquitted and discharged, he found no agreeable choice open to him but to leave England again and go wandering about France and Holland, where James heartily wished him to remain forever.

While Lord Monmouth failed to heed his father's warnings and his uncle's wrath, Lord Shaftesbury understood exactly what it meant. His Lordship knew there'd be no paternal clemency for him as there had been for Monmouth, and fearing his own arrest, he fled in disguise to Holland. When word reached the Court in January that he had died, the sentiment was one not of rejoicing, but of a quiet relief.

There were no bonfires in London to mark the Guy Fawkes Day of 1682, no pope burnings or flaming effigies of any kind. Instead there was a new law against them, and a new crop of Tory sheriffs, carefully put into their offices by royal interests earlier in the summer, who patrolled the streets to make certain no one disobeyed. I heard much grumbling about this in Bloomsbury Square among my father and his friends, protesting that this was only one more Tory limitation on our freedom as Englishmen. When I remembered the hatred and bigotry that I'd witnessed myself at the bonfires so long ago, I could only applaud this particular limitation as a wise and useful caution.

By the beginning of 1683, London was outwardly a quieter place, and James, too, seemed more at peace with himself and his role within his brother's reign. In a rush of generosity, James increased my income and that of our daughter's as well. He'd gruffly said it was for the trouble he'd caused me and the devotion I'd offered him: dear, honest sentiments that made me love him more. A more visible proof was the large diamond ring he gave me for my twenty-fifth birthday, the stone sufficiently impressive to draw Louise's covetous admiration, to my considerable amusement.

The king, too, took care to look after those who had served him well. John Churchill was raised up to Lord Churchill of Eyemouth, Berwickshire, in the Scots peerage to acknowledge his loyalty to the Yorks in their exile. Colonel Grahme was likewise rewarded with a plum mission with Lord Ferversham to Versailles to present the English king's compliments to the French. Charles also decided that Laurence Hyde had labored long and well enough as first minister without a title, and made him the new Earl of Rochester.

While I didn't begrudge Lory Hyde the well-earned honor, both Father and I regretted how swiftly Charles had turned over the peerage of our old friend John Wilmot. His young son had only that year died, sent to his own untimely grave by the same grievous pox that had infected and killed both his father and mother before him. It was as true a tragedy as any in our time, to see a family with so much promise destroyed by that loathsome disease. It was also sadly a measure of our time that they were so quickly forgotten and replaced—a humbling lesson in the futility of striving for the honors of Court, and how soon their empty joy is revealed.

With such a lesson fresh before my conscience, my thoughts returned once again to what Dr. Burnet had said to me, and the path of righteousness he had seen set before my uncertain feet. I doubted that accepting diamond rings from James and acting the confidante of the Duchess of

Portsmouth were exactly what that good gentleman had intended, but by now I'd grown so accustomed to my place at Court and so secure in James's affections that I could not imagine my life otherwise—the excuse of all who consider reformation, but choose not to pursue it.

In this fashion, I once again watched one year slip into the next, content to remain as I was, and happily ignorant of how much around me was due to change, and not for the better, either.

THERE WAS NOTHING REMARKABLE ABOUT JAMES and Charles going to Newmarket at the end of February for the winter racing; it would have been more remarkable if they'd stayed away. They rode down with a small company of gentlemen and other attendants, making a merry party of it along the way, as was their habit. But one night not long after they'd settled comfortably into Palace House, a boy in a stable nearby left an open lantern too close to a measure of feed-straw, which soon took flame. A brisk breeze from the northeast did the rest, and before long not only that stable but a good deal of the rest of the town had burned to charred timbers. Grooms had been alerted soon enough to lead most of the horses clear, and there was little loss of either human or equine life.

But the damage to Newmarket was so severe and all in such disarray that the difficult decision was made to cancel the winter racing. Dutifully Charles and James offered funds for repairs, and then, with nothing further to keep them there, they rode back to London. One of the sights along their way was an ancient stone home in Hoddesdown, Hertfordshire, called Rye House after an earlier occupant who had been a maltster. A large, sprawling affair, the house was a picturesque landmark to travelers, with a commanding view of the narrowing road and all who passed by.

I welcomed James back to London, pleased to have him returned earlier than expected, and we all slipped back into our lives as before. But in June, a disgruntled Whig betrayed his comrades and revealed a treasonous plot to murder both royal brothers. It was simple enough: Rye House was to have been the point of ambush, when a cadre of rebels would have swept from the house onto the royal party and trapped it there on the narrowest part of the Newmarket Road. The king and the duke were both to have been murdered, and all others with them who resisted. The resulting chaos to the country would have been the spark to a general rebellion against both Stuarts and Tories, and have led to a new regime with sympathies to the Protestant Whigs. Everything had been in careful readiness, made easy by the king's predictable routines and his famous lack of concern for his personal safety.

But the fire in the Newmarket stables had changed everything, and when the king's party left the town earlier than expected, they'd unwittingly saved themselves from certain assassination. The realization that the king and duke might well have died and another civil war begun if not for the fire sent chills of dread throughout the country and across the Continent, and Whitehall was swept with relief and congratulations on the fortuitous escape.

James was horrified by how close he'd once again come to death, and for several weeks insisted on keeping a brace of loaded pistols beside my bed whenever he visited me. Louise told me that Charles, too, was much shaken.

Among those named in this plot were Lord Shaftesbury, now dead and beyond mortal punishment, as well as several other gentlemen, promptly arrested, known for their Whiggish politics: William, Lord Russell, son to the Earl of Bedford; Lord Grey of Werke; and Arthur Capel, Earl of Essex. Lord Grey escaped to France, while Lord Russell and Lord Essex were sent to the Tower. Lord Essex escaped trial in his own way by committing suicide, perhaps even more shocking than his part of the plot. There were a great many other conspirators named, too, lesser men of little interest.

But one conspirator's name in particular stood out among many, as boldly as if it had been writ on the list in scarlet ink. It was a name that shocked some, and caused others to swear they could have predicted it all along. But most of all, this name racked Charles himself with fury and despair.

That name was James Scott, His Grace the Duke of Monmouth.

Chapter Twenty-one

WHITEHALL PALACE, LONDON
July 1683

Most spectacles at Court were glorious affairs, meant to awe or entertain. Displays of fireworks and armory, masques and plays, mock battles, balls in honor of royal birthdays or noble visitors from foreign lands were all anticipated and discussed and reported as great events to the farthest reaches of the kingdom.

One of these was the wedding of James's remaining unmarried daughter, the Lady Anne, to Prince George of Denmark. It was a match made for politics, not love. Though the groom was Protestant, James gave his approval, since the prince had been suggested by the Catholic King Louis himself. The wedding took place on 28 July, St. Anne's Day, in the Chapel Royal of St. James's Palace. By Charles's decree, the ceremony was a quiet one for royalty, with few guests beyond the family. But at the ball that followed, I saw the jewels the groom had given his bride, including the pearl and diamond necklace valued at more than six thousand pounds, a pretty show of affection indeed. The couple themselves seemed bland and dull, but content enough with their fate, and hopes were high that together they could produce a Protestant child, something that the Prince and Princess of Orange had yet to do.

What interested me the most, however, was how John Churchill and his wife, Sarah, swiftly shifted themselves from the Yorks' household to that of the new Princess of Denmark. When I asked John why he had done this, he offered a roundabout explanation about Sarah's long friendship with the princess and the value of their new posts. I told him I didn't believe it, and with a sigh he then told me what must have been nearer the truth: that by joining the Denmarks' household, he could be more at ease as a Protestant, yet remain in the duke's favor. It was his usual form of loyalty tailored and stitched to serve his own needs, and that—that I believed.

But still I uneasily wondered about the deeper reason behind why John wished to distance himself from James in this fashion. To my mind, an ambitious man like John Churchill would stand to gain much more from remaining with the Duke of York. After the Rye House Plot had been discovered, James's popularity with the people had risen dramatically. There is no better way to increase the value of something than to threaten to take it away, and so it was with both Charles and James among their subjects.

Which leads me to the second great spectacle at Court that fall, one that was far more sordid, but likewise far more discussed than the Denmarks' wedding. During the summer, justice had been meted out briskly to all the Rye House conspirators. To no one's surprise, only Lord Monmouth remained at large and in hiding, despite the order for his arrest. James fussed and fumed about this, and with good reason, too. If Charles truly wished his natural son in the Tower, then he would have been found. No man could hide that completely in London, especially no one as gaudy as Monmouth.

One evening in late November, most of the Court were gathered in the king's chambers for Charles's *couchée*, his last informal audience of the day before he retired to his bed. I sat close to James in perfect contentment on a cushioned stool beside him; Mary Beatrice was not in attendance, still recovering from bringing forth yet another stillborn infant. Despite the presence of several foreign ambassadors, Charles was at his most comfortable ease, laughing and jesting with James and the other gentlemen around him while Louise played his hostess, making sure the wine flowed freely.

Without either warning or announcement, the chamber door flew open, and Lord Monmouth ran into the room, followed closely by a pair of guards. With his face contorted in deepest emotion, His Grace cast himself down at the feet of his father and uncle with such force that he slid toward them across the polished stone floor. Wherever he had been in hiding, he'd managed to find a barber and a tailor, for he was as gorgeously dressed and arrayed as ever, down to the jewels on his fingers—hardly a convincing presentation for true penitence.

"Forgive me, Father, I beg you, please!" he cried, wailing like a street crier as the guards stood over him with their pikes in readiness. "I have never wished harm, not to you or my uncle. May I die at this moment if I ever so much as thought otherwise!"

He raised his face from the floor long enough so show that he wept, large, rolling tears on his cheeks. It was a curiously unpleasant sight, a full-grown gentleman like the duke groveling and debasing himself before his father and uncle, and neither Charles nor James was touched by it.

Charles motioned for the guards to step back. "Why have you come here, Monmouth?" he asked sharply. "You were forbidden the Court even before there was a warrant on your head. I should let these men take you directly, so that you might be put with those villains who are your friends in the Tower."

"But they are not my friends, sir!" Lord Monmouth insisted. "They are false companions, traitors who inveigled me unwittingly into their plot. I beg you, sirs, you must believe me!"

Charles made a rumbling sound of disgust, a growl that Monmouth would have done well to heed.

"It was your own choice to keep such company," he said. "You should scarce be surprised to find yourself charged with complicity."

"How can I be faulted if they spoke their plan in my hearing, sir? How can my ears be blamed for what their false tongues did speak?" Beseeching, His Grace pressed his palms together, and when he saw no change in his father's face, he turned toward James, where I could have told him he'd find even less sympathy. "Please, kind sir, know my good wishes for your continued health, and be merciful!"

"Once you were a soldier, Monmouth, and fought with bravery," James said curtly. "Now you act as the lowest coward, without even the honor to stand by your own words or companions, however treasonous they are."

"But, sir, I meant no treason, nor harm!"

"Every act you have committed these last two years has been treasonous," Charles said wearily, "and we are done with it."

He nodded, and the two guards seized His Grace by his brocaded shoulders, dragging him to his feet. He groaned, stumbling as if he were too overcome for his legs to support him, and let himself be drawn away from the chamber and to the Tower.

It was a spectacle indeed, as were the stormy glances exchanged by Charles and James. Neither spoke, and none of the rest of us who'd stood witness dared speak, either. If the king had finally lost patience with his much-indulged son, what, truly, was there left to say?

But later, when James and I had retired to his rooms, he found a great deal more to speak regarding his wayward nephew, and none of it was good.

"I have never seen such a craven, despicable performance as that," he said as he jerked his arms from his coat. "Fah, that such a wretch shares my blood!"

I hurried to help him with his coat before he tore it in his anger. "As long as I've known His Grace he has been the same. There's far more of his mother's low blood in him than any Stuart."

"Oh, his mother," grumbled James, turning to let me play his manservant and unfasten the lace-trimmed stock around his neck. "If only my brother had not been led by his cock where that whoring wench was concerned."

I unbuttoned the cuffs of his shirt and tugged the hem free of his breeches. I liked undressing him in this way, as if discovering him anew each time, and he liked it, too, having me touch him in unexpected small ways. I slid my hands inside his shirt, up along his flat belly and over his chest, and was rewarded with a low grunt of pleasure.

"Monmouth's mother is long in her grave, sir, may she rest in eternal peace," I whispered, "and she needs be of no concern to you."

He closed his eyes. "Would that her bastard son were in his grave, too, so as not to vex me."

"Oh, sir, you cannot mean that," I said, even as my fingers bumped into the gold crucifix, replete with ruby stigmata, that he always wore around his neck, a secret mark of his Catholicism hidden by his shirt. "To wish your own nephew's death—"

"He has already wished mine, and my brother's as well," he said. "He has acted on that wish, too. Now my brother must do his duty, and punish Monmouth as he deserves. He must die, Katherine, as is meet. For all our sakes, he must be punished."

That made me shudder. I had gone to watch men die at Tyburn—who had not?—but I had never seen a peer lose his head on Tower Hill, let alone one that was known to me.

"His Lordship is a fool, sir, his vanity fed by the villains who would lead him," I said. "With Shaftesbury gone, how much further wrong can he do?"

"There will be others who'll rise up to take Shaftesbury's place," James said with gloomy conviction. "An ass never wants for someone to seize him by the halter and lead him. You'll see. Halifax could well be next."

"Lord Halifax likes his own place too well to risk it to Lord Monmouth." I'd observed the thorough dislike that James bore Lord Halifax, and decided that it came from James's unfortunate suspicion of any gentleman he perceived as being more clever than he was himself: a most unfortunate suspicion, considering how that would include at least half the peers and most of the Commons besides.

"Still and all, sir," I said. "I do not believe Lord Monmouth is clever enough to be as wicked as you paint him, nor wicked enough to merit his death."

"How much more wicked does he needs be, if not a murderer?"

"Some would argue, sir, that you are to blame for leaving the door open to him." I thought again of that gory, golden crucifix, glittering there beneath the vulnerable hollow of his throat. "If you were not a Papist, then he could not present himself to the people as the Protestant princeling."

He grunted again, reaching inside my dressing gown to find my breasts. "Some would say that you speak too plain of things that do not concern you."

I began to unbutton his breeches, slowly, knowing exactly how to tempt and inflame him. It was not by my touch alone, but by words, too, the right words. I didn't need worldly beauty for this, only wit, buoyed by love.

"Some would say that I do not speak plainly enough to you, sir," I said. "Some would say I must say more, for your own betterment."

"Some would be wrong," he said with a catch in his breath. "Ah, Katherine, please."

"Some being your fellow Papists, sir, your priests and confessors and learned Jesuits," I whispered, reaching up to breathe each word into his willing ear as I eased his breeches from his hips. "Some who tell you I'm Satan in a woman's guise. Some who warn you that each time you kiss me, and lie with me, and lose yourself in the willing flesh of my body, you put your soul in further peril. But some are wrong, sir, aren't they?"

"Yes," he gasped, pushing against my hand. "*Yes.*"

"Some can never know what binds you to me, and me to you." My whisper was ragged and tattered as he caressed me in turn, my delight rising with his. I'd long ago learned how it was with him: the more he felt that I was the seductress, then the more innocent he was of whatever carnal sins we committed, and the more eager, too, he was for them. "But how could they know, sir? How could they?"

He shoved me back onto the bed by way of his answer, and kissed me hard, and when he mounted me I claimed him with the same ferocity.

Some could say whatever they pleased. He would never give me up, nor, truly, would I ever wish it otherwise.

As much as James might long for Charles to sacrifice Lord Monmouth to the fullest punishment that he deserved, it was not to be. Though clearly Charles's patience was at an end, in his heart he still did love his wayward natural son too much to see him executed.

But Lord Monmouth would tax even the most devoted parent. First he offered a full confession to his part in the plot, which Charles joyfully accepted as a sign of his son finally showing a hint of responsibility. But no sooner had Charles accepted the confession than His Grace recanted and changed his story entirely in a shambling, stammering mess that was sadly more typical of his true character. When James furiously pressed for a full prosecution, Charles had no choice but to step in once again, and this time not merely send his son from England, but to banish him, making it clear that if he dared come wandering back, he'd face trial.

Even in banishment, His Lordship found mischief. Arriving in Holland, he somehow convinced the Prince of Orange that he'd come as an honored visitor, not as an outcast and outlaw, and so was welcomed by the Dutch accordingly. Both Charles and James interpreted this as a willful insult by the prince rather than a misunderstanding, and relations between the two Protestant countries were strained further on account of it.

Perhaps because Lord Monmouth had been so troublesome, the trials of the other gentleman-conspirators in the autumn of 1683 were quick, with Charles and James together participating in the interrogations. There was to be no gentle banishment for these defendants: Algernon Sydney was executed on Tower Hill in November, and William, Lord Russell, was beheaded in Lincoln's Inn Fields. Both became immediate martyrs for the Whigs, and Lord Russell's insistent declaration at his trial that there were times when it was a man's right and obligation to resist his government by force was called a brave rallying cry by the Whigs, and a dangerous threat by a deluded republican to the Tories.

As a prominent Whig, my father attended the executions, proudly standing where he could not be overlooked. With him were several of his closest friends from the last Parliament, including Lord Dorset, and together they hoped their presence would both comfort Lord Russell's distraught family and show the Tories that they were not afraid.

"I did not see you there, Katherine," Father said to me when I went to dine in Bloomsbury Square the following week. It was just the two of us, Lady Sedley having gone to visit her sister. "There were plenty of other Tory ladies gawking in their carriages, treating the death of an excellent gentleman as an idle amusement and no more."

"I do not like executions, Father," I said firmly, not wishing to quarrel over politics with him. "You know that. And if there were Tory ladies there to gawk, then several years ago there were also Whig ladies gathered around the entertainment of poor old Lord Stafford with his neck on the block. Whig martyr or Tory, I won't make a frolic from anyone's suffering like that."

Father glanced at me shrewdly, helping himself to another serving of the fish. "I'm surprised old Jemmy didn't force you to attend."

"Oh, Father, enough," I said. "Can't we speak of something else? The weather? Your new play? That ill-mannered dog you bought for your son?"

"We could, but we won't," he said cheerfully. "We see you so seldom these days, Daughter, that when you do honor us with a visit, I believe we should let your presence dictate our conversation. So why weren't you there beside old Jemmy, ready to glory in the bloodshed?"

"His Grace the duke had a reason for being there—to see justice served," I said, pointedly using James's title instead of Father's flippant "old Jemmy." "I know that if someone had tried to kill you, Father, you'd wish to be there when the table was turned."

"The table wasn't so much turned for Russell as overthrown," Father said. "But I've no doubt Jemmy found it all most gratifying. Which of us Whigs will be next, I wonder?"

"None, I should hope," I said firmly. "It would be very gratifying to His Majesty and the rest of us if we could have a spell of peace without any plots or conniving from either party."

"Oh, indeed," Father said expansively, sitting back in his chair so the servant could clear away his plates. "Peace is always desired foremost, even if it comes at the price of an Englishman's liberty and freedom to speak his thoughts aloud."

I set my wineglass down on the table with a thump. "Having a strong monarchy does not seem to have hindered the freedom of your speech, Father."

Father folded his arms over his chest. "Of course it wouldn't, Katherine," he said with bitterness I'd not expected. "Unlike my old brethren from the Commons, no harm shall ever come to me, not so long as my daughter whores for her Tory master."

"I didn't come here for this, Father." Briskly I began to rise from my chair, prepared to leave, when he caught my arm to stop me.

"Sit, Katherine," he ordered, and when I tried to pull away, he held fast. "Sit. *Sit*. Damnation, but I vow you would try the temper of one of your duke's saints."

"Or your wife's," I countered hotly, trapped by his grasp as we jerked each other back and forth. "Your *true* wife. My *mother*. Or in your rants against Tory popery, have you forgotten your *wife* languishes still in a Romish nunnery?"

He released my arm at once, sinking back into his chair with a low hiss of irritation. I stood for a moment longer, rubbing my forearm where he'd held it, the two of us glaring at each other like a pair of squabbling cats in the back alley.

To Father's credit, he was the first to back down. He rose from his seat, motioning gracefully toward my chair with a courtier's practiced flourish, and willed his expression into impassive blandness.

"Forgive me, madam, I beg you," he said with an evenness that astonished me. "I spoke in distress, and from passion. If you were not so *damned* dear to me, I would not be moved to speak so strongly."

"No, Father, I should be the one asking forgiveness, as is proper for a child to her father." I sighed wearily, my anger spent. "I should not have said what—what I said."

"But we each of us spoke the truth, Kattypillar, didn't we?" he said sadly. "We cannot help it, and where has it gotten either of us, I ask you?"

"It—it has gotten us here." Slowly I sat again in my chair, my heavy skirts settling stiffly around me. "Quarreling before the last remove. How wickedly ill-bred of us."

"Ill-bred, but Sedley bred, too." He motioned to the servant with the next dish who'd been hovering uncertainly in the doorway as we'd quarreled. "There is no help for that, whether Tory or Whig."

"Nor will it keep you from your dinner, Father," I said, unable to resist one more small jibe as a roasted duck was set before him—if in fact it was a jibe, or simply an observation. "Nothing keeps you from that."

"No," he admitted, gazing down with satisfaction at the fowl, glistening in its juices. "True enough. Which should prove to you the seriousness of what I say next."

To my shock, he pushed aside the plate with the waiting fowl, and instead reached across the corner of the table to lay his hand over mine.

"You've chosen a dangerous course for your life, Kattypillar," he said. "Oh, I know you claim the duke brings you happiness; that must be between you and His Highness. But to the greater world, he is a stern, perplexing gentleman, even a frightening one, and the more power His Majesty gives him, the more hazardous your own place at his side may become. Over these last years, His Highness has been in favor, and out of favor, and now is in it again. Like a clock's pendulum, England may well swing back against him, and where will that leave you?"

"I'll be well enough, Father," I said firmly, though I was touched beyond measure by his concern. "His Grace will see to that. Besides, my place is far better than that of most wives."

But Father only shook his head. "To be a royal mistress may seem a fine, glorious pastime now, but what when His Highness tires of you? He is only a man, and in time he will look to another for love and amusement, and what then? I would never wish you to become another Jane Shore, cast off to wither and die in shame."

"Ah, but isn't that another quality we Sedleys possess?" I said lightly, striving to coax him from this conversation. "That we feel no shame?"

But Father found no humor in this. "Katherine, please. Not even you can scoff at the power of the Church of Rome. You know His Highness's priests loathe you. What if they were to compel him to give you up?"

"They have not been able to do so as yet," I said with confidence. "You would laugh to see them scatter like frightened crows when I appear, Father. I, the evil Protestant bitch!"

"You should take care not to laugh too loudly, Daughter," Father insisted. "No lady in your position is invulnerable. I hear enough of the Court to know you have your enemies, and the duke has them by the score. Nothing at Whitehall lasts forever. Surely you must know that. What will become of you in the end, you and your daughter both? You must consider her, you know."

"I always will, Father, just as you do with me." I turned my hand to link my fingers into his, and smiled tenderly and with love. "Do not worry over me, I beg you. You'll see. I cannot say how or why, but when everything is reckoned in the end, I'll be happy. I *will* be happy. And what else could I wish for than that?"

WINTER FELL HARD ON LONDON SOON after Lord Russell's execution, fell as suddenly as any season I could ever recall. One day it seemed the last bright leaves of autumn still clung bravely to the trees in the park, and the next all was shrouded in sharpest cold. Some said it was a punishment, God's solemn judgment on those who had in turn presumed to judge and sentence Lord Russell and the others to their deaths. While a neat little parable, I could not believe it; the ones who suffered most from this sudden shift to winter were not the wealthy judges and other lords, wrapped in furs before their fires, but the poor and humble of London who had no fires at all.

By the end of December, the ground was frosted so solid that no burials could take place. Each morning brought a fresh toll of those who'd died in the night, with many bodies found frozen stiff and unyielding wherever they'd last stopped for refuge. Cattle perished from want of fodder, and wild birds and other small creatures died in untold numbers as well. The markets had little food to offer, and that at a price so steep that only the cost of wood and sea-coal surpassed it. Shipping came to a perilous halt, for not only was the river frozen solid, but the water around the seaports as well, and the vessels that had been trapped in the grasp of the ice had their hulls splinter from the force of the frost.

But Londoners are merry creatures at heart, and able to find pleasure in even the most grievous of circumstances. So it was now with this remarkable cold. As soon as the river froze solid—some said the ice was more than two feet deep—enterprising folk turned the river into a wide, white ground for play and entertainment, and in no time at all erected a great Frost Fair that stretched from bank to snowy bank.

There were makeshift shops set up in booths to offer a variety of wares, from costly clothes and jewels and Virginia tobacco to halfpenny trinkets to serve as mementos. By day and night, every imaginable kind of refreshment was offered, from brandy and beer to heated chocolate and tea, sweetmeats and pasties and pies. An entire ox was roasted and turned on a spit, the ice being so thick as to support the necessary fire, and the steaming meat was greedily devoured, with even His Majesty taking a slice direct from the spit. There was entertainment, too, horse and carriage races and rides on sleds, wrestling matches and bear-baiting, and even a brothel, though I would think that the novelty of such a letch might fade before the reality of a shivering cock.

As a frolic, I begged James to take me to the fair one night soon after Christmas. We set aside our rich Court clothing and dressed simply, so none would recognize us at first glance (though any who looked beyond our dress soon would see the nearby guards that James never went without). We wandered freely among the booths, drinking mulled wine and laughing at the boys who raced across the ice on Dutch skates with dogs skidding after them. It had been a long while since James had enjoyed himself so thoroughly, his face ruddy and easy from these simplest of pleasures.

"Are you happy, sir?" I asked, leaning close to whisper into his ear.

"With you, I am," he said quietly, his voice thrumming with warm affection. "How could I be otherwise with you beside me?"

I chuckled, well content in my love, and kissed his cold cheek, and then his lips, too. It wasn't until much later that we found other pleasures in my bed to keep each other warm, and I always believed that it was on that night that our second child was conceived.

The year of 1684 was in fact altogether one of my happiest. I had my place at Court and with James, and I was joyfully with child again, my growing belly proof of my royal lover's devotion to me. I was welcome in the highest and most intimate circles. In Louise's apartments, I became a favorite for my wit. Even the king, who in general had little use for plain women, came to appreciate me for my humor, and asked me to sit close so that I might amuse him. I couldn't help but think of how Father had performed much the same role earlier in the reign, and wistfully wished that his politics had not carried him so far from Court so that we might have entertained the king together.

The tension and fear of recent years, when plots and Parliament had so challenged the king and the Court, now seemed well past, exactly as Charles desired. James was finally again permitted to take his seat in the Privy Council—a place he'd been denied for nearly eleven years—and to return to his much-loved position in the Royal Admiralty, overseeing the navy. He took care to practice his faith quietly, with devotion but without ostentation, and that seemed well enough with most Englishmen.

One long-overdue justice came that summer when Titus Oates was finally arrested. He could have been charged with scores of villainous crimes, but his accusations of treason against James were sufficient to have him clapped in irons and imprisoned.

James was now not only restored to favor, but to popularity as well, and if 1684 was one of the happiest of years for me, then surely it must have been for him as well. When I was safely brought to bed of a handsome, lusty son (named, of course, after his father) in September, I truly believed our life could scarce be improved.

WHILE FATHER'S GREATEST WORRY FOR ME as a royal mistress was that James would at some point dismiss me without warning or support for my two children, I'd only to look at how James and his brother had treated their former mistresses and their offspring to see that I'd no cause for fear. Whatever other faults the Stuarts might possess where women were concerned, this was not one of them. They showed much care and affection for their natural children, and no lady who had served them well in this capacity had ever been forgotten.

I was reminded of this anew as I sat in Louise's apartments on the first Sunday night of February 1685. Not only was the usual company gathered, but by unusual coincidence all of Charles's most-loved favorites were in attendance as well: the Duchess of Cleveland, the Duchesse de Mazarin, and Nelly Gwyn, in addition to Louise herself. Most who'd observed these four ladies only from afar would be certain they'd squabble and fight among themselves, as men always expect (and wish) beautiful women will do. But such was the power of Charles's continued friendship for them that they sat instead in perfect harmony, laughing and drinking and chatting happily, and bound together by their love for the king.

Awed though I was to be included amongst so many great beauties, I still could appreciate the rare pleasure of that night, reflected over and over in Louise's famous looking glasses: the charm of the company, the elegant magnificence of the rooms, the genial happiness of Charles as he sat surrounded by so many friends, even the sweet-voiced French boy that Louise had employed to sing love songs, a bittersweet note to such a gathering.

When at last I bid farewell to James and the rest of the company, I retired to my house in King Street. There I kissed Lady Katherine and Lord James good night in their little beds, and slept well in my own. It was not until noon the following day that I learned the dreadful news from Whitehall: that Charles had been stricken by a grievous affliction or apoplexy while he slept. I dressed quickly and went to the palace, to learn the latest word and to be of what comfort I could to James. But I soon came away, not from disinterest, but because I did not belong. Deathbeds were for families, for children and wedded wives, and not mistresses. No matter how dear James was to me and I to him, by rights his wife must stand at his side as his brother lay dying.

Like everyone else in the Court—and truly, in all England—I could not believe that Charles's life could end so soon. He was not a young man, not at fifty-five, but one still so vital and quick that it seemed impossible that he'd falter. Already people wept openly in the streets. No one laughed, or sang, or even smiled, from respect for their dying king. Rumors raced through the city with lives of their own: His Majesty had been poisoned by the Jesuits, His Majesty was craftily staging his own illness to test the loyalties of those around him, His Majesty had declared the Duke of Richmond, his son by Louise, as his rightful heir. Ships were stopped at the port, and soldiers were everywhere in the city, their presence announced as a precaution, in case the French or other foreigners decided to take advantage of our sad, unsettled city. At Court we knew better, and guessed the true reason was that those in the palace—perhaps even Charles himself—feared some epic folly by Lord Monmouth, a bold move fostered by him with the Prince of Orange to seize the throne.

In the long week when the king lay a-dying, I heard but once from James, a hasty, anguished note. I was moved that he'd write at all, and did not expect more. Despite their differences, Charles and James were far closer than most brothers, and I could only imagine how deeply this last farewell would grieve him.

I was dining with Father at a tavern near Covent Garden when we heard the first church bells begin to toll. All conversation fell silent in the dining room as we listened to the somber, awful sound. One by one, people rose and bowed their heads in respect. Some cried, sobbing freely, while others prayed aloud. Beside me, Father slipped his fingers into mine and pressed my hand in shared, wordless sorrow.

The king was dead. Long live the king.

And God help me, I was now His Majesty's mistress.

Chapter Twenty-two

KING STREET, LONDON
February 1685

His Majesty King Charles II died on a Friday, the sixth day of February 1685. The last thing he was said to have seen from his bed was the pale winter sun rising over the Thames. Those who look for augers took this as a splendid sign for his brother James: as one king slipped from this mortal life, another rose bravely to take his place.

Surely after so much dread over James succeeding his brother to the throne, the actual event proceeded without the slightest conflict or drama. The transition was as easy as such matters could be. Charles was buried on the night of 14 February (cruel irony for a man who loved so well, to be buried on the day of St. Valentine!), with dignity and pomp. James's coronation was not to take place until April, after proper mourning for his brother and to provide sufficient time for foreign dignitaries to arrive and the whole lavish ceremony to be arranged. But as soon as Charles was dead, James was confirmed as the new king, and briskly began his duties.

He first set about reassuring any who doubted that he'd every intention of abiding by the laws of England regarding the Church and the state, and no desire for change. I wasn't surprised, since this was exactly what he'd always maintained, even when he'd been most under attack. This gratifying message, printed and sent and read around the kingdom, was reinforced by his actions.

He made few changes among his brother's ministers as well, keeping Lords Sunderland, Halifax, Godolphin, and Rochester as his primary advisers. He likewise declared that he'd maintain a more moral Whitehall than his brother's debauched Court had been, and that there'd be no welcome for drunkards, rogues, adulterers, or gamblers. Now, this was a bit disingenuous, considering how he himself was an adulterer, Sunderland a notorious carder and gambler, and Rochester drank so hard he'd slip through the neck of the bottle if he could. But the new king's intentions were greeted warmly and with favor—though what politician would dare say he'd preferred the old-style wickedness? James also raised several other followers from his household, most notably John Churchill, who was now made a gentleman of the bedchamber and Baron Sandridge in the English peerage. My old friend Colonel Grahme was named Keeper of the Privy Purse and Master of Buckhounds, appointments with sizable incomes. In general James treated the gentlemen with the greatest civility, and considering how dear I'd been to him for nearly ten years now, I'd no reason to expect anything less for me and our daughter.

Yet day stretched into day, and still James did not come to me. I saw him at a distance, of course, at his brother's funeral and before others in Whitehall, but not alone, not as it had been before Charles was taken ill. His wife the new queen was much with him now, and I observed how the frail duchess had suddenly burgeoned into a haughty, imperious queen. Emboldened by her new status, she brazenly surrounded herself with a large cadre of Italian-speaking priests and other Romish clerics, as if giving full lie to James's magnanimous promise to respect the Church of England.

I made excuses for James even as I worried over Mary Beatrice's ascendancy. I watched with sorrow his unkind treatment of his brother's former favorites, made so unwelcome at his upright new Court that both Nell and Lady Mazarin were forced to withdraw. Louise fled first to the shelter of the French ambassador's house and then to France, vowing never to return. I told myself how James must still be bowed with grief for his brother, and overwhelmed by the minutiae of beginning a new realm. But when Lady Katherine, now six, asked why her father had stopped coming to call upon us, I had no real answer to give.

Then, scarcely a fortnight after Charles's death, a messenger came to King Street in the royal livery. I didn't wait for his letter to be brought to me, but seized it myself, bearing it like a prize to my chamber to read alone. I read it, and read it again, my heart refusing to believe what my eyes saw.

Though the letter was in James's hand and above his mark, he was not the author. I saw that in an instant. Even if these hateful sentiments had flowed from him, they never would have taken the form of these words, not considering how arduous composition was to him.

With chill, precise formality, I was informed of His Majesty's new intentions. Having reflected on the frailty of mankind and the moral weakness as demonstrated by his late brother, His Majesty now resolved to lead a different manner of life than previously. To that end, His Majesty desired me either to go across the waters away from England, or to retire away from London to the country. Provisions would be made whichever course I chose, but I must understand that His Majesty was determined to see me no more.

By the second reading, I'd decided my course, and it would be neither going abroad nor into the country, but to Whitehall. Because I was not a member of the royal household, I wasn't obliged to follow mourning, and I dressed myself in full magnificence, including the largest of the jewels that James had given me. He *would* see me, I would make certain of that, and a pox on whichever foul priest had dictated that heartless, lying letter.

I had myself driven to the palace, and entered as I always had, cheerfully saluting the guards by their names as I made my way to James's apartments. Though some I passed gazed at me with surprise, no one dared stop me, which only infuriated me the further. Did they really believe I'd go so meekly that no orders had been necessary to keep me away?

By the time I reached James's new rooms, I was in a righteous temper, and without waiting to be announced I sailed through the doors. It was strange to find him here in place of his brother, but I saw he'd already made his mark: the voluptuously Italian painting of Venus and Mars that had always hung over the fireplace had been replaced by a murky weeping saint on her knees, her eyes rolling heavenward. As I'd expected by the hour, James had finished his first prayers of the day and was taking a dish of coffee amongst his gentlemen of the bedchamber, who at once rose as if to drive me away themselves.

"Your Majesty," I said, sinking into the most cursory of curtsies before James. I refused to debase myself before him as Lord Monmouth had done before the late king. Why should I, when my banishment from favor had never been earned? "Forgive me my intrusion, sir, but I'd no other choice if I *would* see you again."

James stared at me, his expression one of intense discomfort as a mottled flush of guilty surprise slowly crept up his cheeks. He looked thinner than when I'd seen him last, a misfortune in a man who was already spare, and though it was early in the morning, his eyes were shadowed with weariness. Any other time, and I would have rushed to him with concern, but not now. Now he was the king, and I'd already dared far too much.

I felt a gentle tap on my shoulder. "Mrs. Sedley," said John Churchill, Lord Sandridge. "If you please, His Majesty is engaged at present."

"Thank you, my lord," I said, my gaze not leaving James as he sat, engaged with his coffee. "But it is not His Majesty that I wished to see. Rather I've come to speak with the father of my children."

James's mouth twisted, and abruptly he stood. "I will speak to Mrs. Sedley alone."

With a shuffle of bows, the gentlemen left us, the door behind us shutting softly. Still we stood, facing each other as stiff as two sentries.

"Katherine," he said at last. "Why are you here? Were you not given the letter?"

"That letter, sir," I said, bitterness welling up within me. "That was not your work, was it?"

He swallowed, his pale eyes full of sadness. "It would have been better if you'd not come. It would have been better if you'd kept away."

"Better for whom, sir?" I asked, my voice brittle. "Better for your priests? Her Highness? Your dogs?"

"Better for England," he said heavily. "I wish to lead my life as an example for my people."

"What, sir, as a man who turns away from the one who has loved him so loyally and so well?" I cried. "As a man who scorns his son, his daughter?"

He cleared his throat, and I realized he was no longer meeting my eye, but gazing somewhere above my face. "You'll be well provided for. I know my duty toward you. You'll be rewarded for your service."

"Faith, my *service*?" I felt the tears sting my eyes and fought them, too proud to weep before him. "Is that all I've been to you, sir, a servant, like one more damned laundress in your employ? Is that reason enough to send me into exile?"

"It's not exile, Katherine," he said quickly. "It's—it's a reward, a remembrance."

"Then why not reward me here in London, sir?" I asked. "Why send me out of the country?"

"If that is what you wish," he said, seizing on the notion. "A grand house here in London, with everything exactly to your tastes and wishes. If you will only promise to keep away—"

"But I don't want a house, sir, however grand." My voice dropped to a plaintive whisper. "I want you."

He looked at me again, his expression bleak. "Before God Almighty, I have made a solemn vow to Her Majesty that I will give you up."

I drew in my breath sharply. How could I answer that? Yet for him to take such a severe measure could only mean he remained thoroughly attached to me. I saw it in his eyes, his face, his entire posture. No matter what he'd said, he loved and desired me still. It was a small comfort, but for now, it was all I had.

"A grand house in London, for as long as you live," he repeated. "I will order the arrangements this very day."

"As you wish, sir," I said forlornly. For now I must retreat, but I would take the offered house. I'd be an idealistic fool not to.

Especially, I realized, when I'd yet to agree to anything in return.

For the next three months, James kept to his vow. Oh, he saw me at Court, there among the crowds of others, but he never singled me out for any conversation alone or in confidence. He did not visit me or our children in King Street; his neglect of Lady Katherine and jolly little James perhaps wounded me the most. At Court it was assumed my days of power and place were done, and though I held my head high, I was scorned by many who'd once curried my favor.

There was no doubt that James had much to occupy him in those first months of his reign. In addition to the plans for his coming coronation, he'd also decided to call the first Parliamentary elections in years, and was rewarded with a staunchly Tory Commons. In return, he made his staunchly Tory brother-in-law Laurence Hyde, Lord Rochester, his lord treasurer and chief minister, choosing him over the Whig Lord Sunderland.

I watched it all, and waited, confident my turn would come again. James had kept his vow to his wife, but he'd also kept his word to me. He had bought me an extremely fine house in St. James's Square at the cost of more than ten thousand pounds, and granted me the indulgent freedom to refurbish it however I pleased. I hadn't forgotten my friend Louise's advice: that the more a gentleman is willing to invest in a lady, then the more he values her, and the more he will be inclined to invest again. To be sure, this was more a practical sentiment than a romantic one, but to see its truth, I'd only to look again at Louise, the dearest of Charles's mistresses, and all that he had given her—three merchant ships had been required to carry everything back to France with her—as commensurate to his great affection for her.

"I'll credit you with much grandeur, Katherine," Father said as I showed him the newest improvements in my house. "Surely everything that could have been carved has been so, and gilded besides."

I smiled proudly. "I've hired the same Italians that worked on Windsor. You can see their artistry everywhere, can't you?"

"Most likely the king sees it in his pocketbook," Father said, running his hand lightly over the polished marble top of a new sideboy. "Or rather, we miserable Englishmen do, since we're the ones who pay for all this in the end."

"It's paid for by the Privy Purse," I said in quick defense. "That's the king's money."

"And who do you think puts the money into that purse, Daughter?" he asked. "Your royal lover would do well to keep extravagance like this quiet until after Parliament meets and votes his new revenues, else he'll be sorely disappointed."

I folded my arms over my chest. Father was far too strong a Whig to have been reelected to James's new Tory Parliament—the first time in my memory that he'd been without a seat in the Commons—but I knew better than to believe that he'd be keeping his voice entirely silent in political circles.

"I trust you won't be the one who shares news of my 'extravagance,' " I warned. "There's no reason why Lord Dorset or any of your other cronies should be told."

"No, no, I won't betray you, though God knows I should." He sighed, gazing up at the new likeness of me in a golden gown that had just been delivered from Godfrey Kneller's studio. "Yet you say the king has yet to visit and view what he's paid for."

"He will in time," I said, certain beyond question. "I don't doubt him."

Father turned from my painted image back toward me. "Most believe the queen has won, and you have lost," he said gently. "Kings are notoriously inconstant, Kattypillar. You've done very well for yourself, with two handsome children and this house to show for it. If you were to follow the path of Arabella Churchill and marry—"

"Why do you always wish to see me saddled with a husband?" I asked, more bemused than irritated. Arabella had recently wed Colonel Charles Godfrey, one of her brother's fellow officers, and though she was said to be thoroughly content, that was not yet the future for me.

"It's the security of marriage I wish for you, Katherine," Father said firmly. "You're only twenty-seven, with an excellent fortune. No gentleman will find you less agreeable if His Majesty decides his time with you is done."

I smiled, serene in my confidence. "But it's not, Father. He's not done with me, not by half. He will come back, and when he does, not even the queen will be able to stop it. You will see. He will come back, and I will welcome him when he does."

But to my surprise, Father only shook his head, his expression grimmer still. "Then take care, Katherine. That is the best advice I can offer you. If he returns to you, take care, and pray, pray be wary."

THE CORONATION OF KING JAMES II and Queen Mary Beatrice of Modena was planned for the 23 April 1685. It was to be a celebration unrivaled by any that had preceded it for splendor and spectacle, and dignitaries and representatives from foreign courts had been streaming into London since the beginning of April. The actual crowning would take place in Westminster Abbey, and be performed by William Sancroft, the Archbishop of Canterbury, as solemn a rite as any in the Anglican Church, even though James, being a Catholic, was no longer a communicant in the Church of England. To avoid embarrassment, Holy Communion was omitted from the liturgy, an ominous change from long tradition that already had earned the disapproval of many Englishmen. Competition to attend the ceremony was keen. Those who'd been invited to participate or to be among the hundreds crowded into the Abbey boasted of it, while those who hadn't tried desperately to bribe their way into a place.

For obvious reasons, I was not among those invited. As the day drew closer, I learned it was just as well I wasn't. My infant son, Jamie, now eight months, was suffering mightily whilst cutting his milk teeth. His nurse had tried every remedy she knew to bring him ease, with no result, and when he became feverish, I summoned a physician for a bleeding, which brought no relief, either. Instead his fever rose higher and higher, his skin as hot as the desert and his lovely blue eyes dull and lost. I held him myself as the doctor bled him again, his poor little body quaking in my arms.

It did not help; nothing did. And on the same day as his father was crowned King of England, my little Jamie died, there in my arms.

I had never known what pain was until that moment, never understood the truth of the word "loss" until then. I wept over my son's tiny, still body as if my tears alone could carry his innocent soul to heaven. I buried him alone without James at my side to share my grief, for though he was my child's father, he was first a new-crowned king. Father was there to support me, and to my grateful surprise, so was Nelly Gwyn, who had likewise felt the anguish of having lost a tender son.

But on that same day I was brought a message from Whitehall: while only a few hastily written lines, it was enough to show that James shared my grief along with considerable remorse of his own. He begged me to come to him that night, and I did not hesitate to accept.

Yet because of that wicked oath he'd sworn to his wife, I was forced to travel to the palace in a plain carriage and wrapped in a dark cloak, so as not to be recognized. Worse, I was led up the back stairs to James's rooms by William Chiffinch, Page to His Majesty's Bedchamber and the man more commonly referred to as the royal pimp to the late king. On this night I was coming to James not as his mistress, but as one bereft parent to another, and I didn't deserve to be treated so shamefully.

But all that was forgotten as soon as I entered James's bedchamber and saw at once that his sorrow was a match to my own. He took me in his arms and embraced me with great love and regard, and bid me tell him every detail of our son's last days. When I could not keep back my tears in the telling, he wept freely with me, as any true father would. In time we did repair to his bed, but more from a need to comfort each other than from base desires, and afterward we lay together in each other's arms and conversed more, as we had done so many times in the past. Since we'd last been together, James's life had been tumultuous, and he'd so much to tell me now that it ran together into a disorganized jumble, great events mingling with small ones.

I heard of his brother's sad last hours and how strange it felt to be here now, in the same enormous black-oak bed that belonged to the king. I learned of his hopes for his own new reign, and how he feared he, too, might be stricken before his time like his brother had been. I listened to how he still suspected the Dutch and his nephew William of Orange, and how the Whitehall cooks insisted on making dishes that were too rich for his constitution, and how impatient he was with the French and King Louis, and how his brother's many dogs had grieved and whined so for their deceased master that James had been forced to send them away in a pack from Whitehall to live at Windsor.

I listened to it all, letting the torrent of words flow over me, soothing me with their very ordinariness. I was too exhausted and spent from our son's death to offer much in return, but James's wandering, one-sided conversation comforted me so much that I found myself drifting in and out of sleep, there with my head pillowed against his shoulder. He'd missed me, that was clear enough, and I'd missed him far more than I'd realized, and now—now the missing was done.

"It was Bancroft who turned clumsy with the crown," he was saying, having shifted to the coronation as his next subject. "How difficult could it have been to settle it upon my head? But Bancroft's hand slipped, and the crown slipped—just for a moment, mind you, yet quite sufficient for those who wished me foul luck, and now claim to see an auger for the future."

"That's foolish, sir," I said drowsily, drawing the purple velvet coverlet closer over my bare shoulders. "Surely the archbishop was anxious before the magnitude of the audience, and his hand shook from it. Such petty accidents are bound to happen in the course of any momentous event, and signify nothing."

"Not to you, Katherine, being a sensible lady," he said with a sigh. "But there are plenty of others who let themselves be guided by superstition and black thoughts. They'll see my downfall in a piece of burned toast, and tell the world as if they're a born oracle."

"You must pay them no heed, sir," I cautioned gently, resting my palm on his chest to calm him. I could feel his heart racing beneath my fingers, agitated with no real reason. Still, I understood. There was one far more ominous prediction that had been whispered about since the old king's death. Long ago, in the time of the Exclusion Bill, Charles himself had predicted that if James were to succeed him on the throne, he'd last only three years before England would have had its fill of him. Charles had said it in a teasing, jovial manner, but after his death, the prediction had taken on fresh significance, especially with my father and other Whigs.

"How can I not heed such warnings?" he said with resignation. "My father did not, and look how his people served him. I must be aware, and guard against those who would tear down the throne."

"The predictions of fools won't do that, sir," I said. "How can they hurt you or your throne?"

He sighed again, almost a groan. "Do you know the latest one that Sunderland told me this very day? That the death of our son on coronation day was a sign that my reign was blighted before it began."

"Someone said that?" I asked, stunned, and fresh tears at once filled my eyes. "Oh, sir, that's—that's damnably cruel."

"It is," he said. "Likely I shouldn't even have told you."

"I wish you hadn't, sir." I was more wounded by his thoughtlessness for my suffering than by the tattle. "To speak of my poor little Jamie like that!"

"It is better that you see what I must endure every day, Katherine," he said firmly, drawing me closer. "Everything in this life is the work of Divine Providence, even the tests of villainous tongues like that. God has brought me to the throne for His reasons, and I will not fail Him, no matter how I am challenged or tried. Though the reasons for His workings aren't always apparent to us, they are never without purpose in His Divine Plan. Even having you here now is part of His greater scheme. And as painful as our son's death might be, I am sure there was a purpose to it."

"What possible purpose could there be in the death of an innocent?" I cried miserably. James was a devout man, but I'd never heard him speak of it to this extravagant extent, leastwise not to me. "What good could come from it?"

"I do not know," he admitted heavily. "But it is through God's grace that I am king. With His guidance I will rule and follow His will for the betterment of England. If I am made to suffer, then I will bear it without complaint, as part of His Divine Providence. You'll see, Katherine. In time we all will understand His wisdom, and rejoice in it."

I was too exhausted to offer any argument. These notions weren't James's own; they smacked instead of the Jesuits, whispering every word into his too-willing ears. Even the most divine plan imaginable must rely on mortal men for its execution, and the duplicitous and conniving examples about the Court were scarce likely to serve any providence save their own, no matter how much James might trust them. But for England's sake, I'd pray that James was right, and that in time I'd be made to understand, too.

Because now, to me, it made no sense at all.

THOUGH MY VISITS UP THE BACK STAIRS at Whitehall were supposed to be secret, it wasn't long before much of the Court (excepting the queen) came to know of them, and of my renewed place in James's affections and passions. Likewise, they all knew he'd failed to keep his vow to his wife, and while many were amazed, even shocked, by my sudden resurgence, I wasn't. I'd known all along he'd choose me over Mary Beatrice. I won't say my return was a part of James's favorite divine plan, but I won't say it wasn't, either. I still loved him too well for it to be otherwise.

But the old wanton days of Charles's Court were already long past. James would never openly loll in lascivious indolence with me as Charles had with his mistresses. He'd made too public a show of sweeping Whitehall clean of sin, blasphemy, idle pleasure, and indulgence for that, and in their place he'd filled the elegant halls with excruciatingly proper Tories and Catholics and their grim, dull piety. The bawdy raillery of Nelly and the previous Lord Rochester had tumbled from fashion. Cromwell himself would have been proud—if Cromwell had been a Jesuit.

Sometimes it seemed as if I were the only spark of levity in that whole gloomy palace. I did not claim Louise's grand suite, still empty (and to me, haunted), nor did I wish it, preferring to keep my old lodgings and my fine new house, and a bit of distance from this gloomy Court instead. Nor did I crave the political power that Louise had wielded, either, entertaining foreign ambassadors and overseeing treaties. I would be twenty-eight by next Christmas, and my ambitions were much smaller. James granted me so many little favors, always seeking my company whenever he could, that I was content. I made him happy, and he in turn did the same for me. What more could either of us want?

But even if James were happy with me *au plus profond de son coeur* (as Louise would have said it), there was still much else in his life as king that remained unsettled. While he had a Parliament that smiled upon him, he had unwisely provoked them by reminding him that he was the king, and while he would consider their wishes, he was under no obligation to heed them. Perhaps this would have sat well with a party of Frenchmen, accustomed to absolute monarchs, but not with an English Commons, who bristled like a fox taken by surprise. When advised to heed their concerns, James refused, brushing aside the warnings as unnecessary.

In James's defense, he did have other more pressing concerns: at the end of his speech advising the House to take action on his income, James announced that the Duke of Argyll, a notorious plotter in exile in Holland, had landed an armed force in Scotland with the intent of launching a rebellion against James. Roused to patriotic action, Parliament immediately voted him the living he'd requested, plus several other bills for the funds to put down the rebellions and to refurbish the navy as well. Lord Argyll's force proved a puny, ill-formed affair, and the haste with which it was suppressed by the end of May 1685 only added to the luster of James's glory.

Yet three weeks later came word of another nascent rebellion, one of far more consequence and danger. Lord Monmouth was challenging his uncle's claim to the throne, and with a small army of supporters had sailed from Amsterdam to lead an invasion of England. He landed in Lyme Regis on 11 June, and at once he began gathering more sympathizers from the countryside. The news shocked London and sent James into paroxysms of anger and fear.

I wasn't surprised when he kept me waiting in his bedchamber. When he finally did join me, after one more meeting with his advisers, he remained so distraught that he could not sit still, but paced back and forth before the fire, his face contorted with angry distress.

"If only my brother had punished him when he'd the chance, then it never would have come to this," he fumed. "Monmouth shows his blood by this, behaving like the low bastard he was born."

"He will not succeed, sir." I sat curled in an armchair, in a dressing gown of pink linen shot through with silver. The evening was warm enough that the windows overlooking the river had been kept open to catch the sweet breezes of June. "Lord Monmouth has charm to win some supporters, true, but he'll be no match for your soldiers."

But it was as if I'd not spoken at all. "Do you know what Monmouth says, Katherine? What he claims? Not only that he is my brother's lawful son and his true Protestant heir, but that I am a *murderer* who poisoned my brother!"

I sighed. That sounded much like the Lord Monmouth of old, ready to believe any fabulous tale that was presented to him. "You must not take it so strongly, sir. You have been crowned king, whilst he has not."

"He is not king, no. But he is a soldier at heart, Katherine, a soldier I helped train, more fool I," he said bitterly. "And I'll stop him now, and do what my brother could not. I've chosen an officer to lead my troops who knows Monmouth as well as any other man and who'll hunt down every traitor in the countryside. I've sent Colonel Churchill."

"Colonel Churchill!" I exclaimed, shocked. With his experience, John was an excellent choice to put down the rebellion, but it was a cruel one as well. John and Lord Monmouth had served as young officers together, and once in battle John had risked his own life to save the duke's. If that were not enough, the Churchills were from Devon, near to where Monmouth had landed, and John would likely recognize all the other, lesser rebels he might capture. "What a trial that will be to him, sir!"

He stopped his pacing to stare at me, his expression frighteningly hard. "Colonel Churchill is a soldier, Katherine. He has sworn to serve his God, his king, and his country."

"But he and His Lordship have been friends for so long, sir," I protested, remembering the two so close as younger men. "To ask the colonel to now pursue him—"

"Colonel Churchill knows his duty, Katherine," he said sharply. "If he wavers in it, why, then I shall account him a rebel, too, and see that he meets the same fate as his traitorous 'friend.' "

"Your nephew, sir," I insisted. "Your brother's first son."

"My brother's bastard," he said. "Recall the difference, my dear. It is one I do not forget."

That was clear enough. At James's insistence, an Act of Attainder was passed against Lord Monmouth, authorizing his execution for treason without trial. Because James wisely did not trust local militias to put down the rebellion, the House immediately voted funds for increasing the army by twenty thousand men. As if to apologize for having harbored Lord Monmouth at the Dutch Court, William of Orange promptly returned the English regiments who had been serving in Holland.

But Lord Monmouth had not forgotten old friends, either. When Colonel Churchill approached with his by-now-superior force, the duke sent a message reminding the colonel of their long friendship and begging his assistance with the Protestant cause. John proved worthy of James's trust, leaving his former friend's appeal unanswered, and further, forwarding it to his king as a show of his loyalty. But even that wasn't enough for James. With an insulting lack of trust in John, James put a French officer, Colonel Feversham, over him and his English troops.

Whether insulted or not, it was John who relentlessly stalked and pursued the rebels across the West Country and oversaw the final, bloody rout at Sedgemoor of "King Monmouth" and his ill-equipped, makeshift army in early July. Feversham followed the less glorious route, hanging most every man he could find whether rebel or not. The duke himself was finally captured hiding in a ditch, dirty and disguised meanly as a shepherd. Hauled in irons back to London, James remained unmoved as his disgraced nephew groveled one last time for his life, pleading for mercy and forgiveness, and even offering to convert to Catholicism if it would save him. It would not. Thoroughly disgusted, the only mercy James granted to him was to be beheaded as a nobleman rather than hanged as a commoner.

For once Mary Beatrice and I were of a mind, each of us pleading separately with James to relent and preserve Lord Monmouth's life. We were hardly alone; there were many of us at Court who recalled the great love that Charles had showed his handsome, feckless son, and could not stomach the vengeance that James now demanded. But James held fast, and the execution was set for the fifteenth of July.

Though James asked me to attend and watch, I refused to go to Tower Hill, as did most every lady from respect for the duke. I was ever after grateful I hadn't; for though Lord Monmouth climbed the scaffold calmly, with the presence and composure that he'd never demonstrated before, his executioner, an inexperienced hangman unfamiliar with his ax, was anxious and unsure. Instead of a single merciful stroke, this butcher ineptly required a half dozen hacking blows to slaughter the duke in agony, finally resorting to his knife to sever his victim's head from his shoulders. It was so gruesome an end that many spectators fainted from the sight. Others watched James, who did not so much as flinch at the carnage, coldly observing every bloody moment of his enemy's demise. Near James was Lord Sunderland, that changeable chameleon, who had once encouraged Lord Monmouth's unreasonable hopes, now turned into his enemy to please the king.

By rarest chance I passed John Churchill, gorgeous in his uniform, on a palace staircase later that same day. Though as a soldier he'd been well trained to mask his true feelings, still I could see the pallor behind his sun-browned cheeks and a fresh grief in his eyes.

As we passed, I reached out to lay my hand on his arm on impulse, and in sympathy. "I am sorry for you, John," I said softly, "and for all you must have endured by way of your duty."

He nodded curtly in polite acknowledgment. "Thank you, madam," he said, deftly easing his arm free of my hand. "But I feel far more sorry for you, to be in His Majesty's company this night."

I understood. When I learned at supper that the queen had retired early to weep and mourn over the poor duke, I understood her grief, and when I overheard others discussing in horrified whispers the king's seeming heartlessness at the execution of his nephew, I understood that, too. We each of us had chosen loyalty to the king over our own sense of right, and there were many uneasy consciences in Whitehall that sorrowful day.

But though James requested my company that night, his mood was somber and melancholy, and as I lay beside him, he made no move to touch me. When I reached for him in the dark, lightly touching his cheek as was my habit, his face was wet with silent tears.

"It was divine vengeance, Katherine," he said. "It could not be helped. It was God's will for England, not mine."

And sadly, sorrowfully, I understood that, too.

Chapter Twenty-three

Windsor Castle, Berkshire
August 1685

After Monmouth's defeat and Parliament's late-summer recess, James led the Court to Windsor Castle as his brother had always done before him. The castle itself was as humblingly grand as ever, the surrounding fields and trees of Windsor Great Park remained lusciously green, the airs from the river as cool and refreshing and skies overhead as brilliant a blue. Yet because the nature of James's Court was so very different from his brother's, this retreat failed to have the same easy cheeriness to it. Instead of Charles's packs of lighthearted actors and actresses, jugglers and musicians to entertain us, James had somber flocks of priests, whose very presence as they walked along the parapets seemed to cast the old stone walls with monastic shadows. Catholic mass was said each morning in the chapel, and those dwindling few of us who preferred an Anglican service were forced to worship in the small church in the town below the castle. Even the nearby races at Newmarket felt changed, haunted as they were by the absence of Lord Monmouth, whose superior horsemanship was much missed.

Because the castle was smaller than Whitehall and lacked Chiffinch's convenient back stairs—and because, too, the queen and her servants had become more vigilant in spying on my whereabouts—I lodged instead at a house in town. James and I met away from the others, in one of the small hunting lodges in the old deer park. Our assignations were arranged by my old lover Colonel James Grahme as Master of the Buckhounds. Colonel Grahme met me in the castle's stables, and escorted me to the lodge, where James would soon appear under the guise of "hunting," all of which amused me no end.

"I've never forgotten how we first met, waiting for Mary Beatrice to acknowledge us," I said to the colonel on one of these rides. Like a child freed from a grim governess, my humor always rose when I left the castle, especially knowing that James awaited me. "Faith, who would have guessed we'd end like this?"

"Riding through the park together, madam?" He smiled blandly, but his eyes were full of the old laughter. "There's scarce anything surprising about that."

"Oh, no," I said drolly. "Nothing at all. The master of the buckhounds, taking one more bitch to his master."

He couldn't keep from laughing at that. "You haven't changed a whit, Katherine, have you?"

"I'm as wicked as ever," I replied cheerfully. "Though it's not so easy as it once was, not at this dreary Court."

His smile grew more questioning. "Are you happy, then? I think of my Dorothy at our home in Westmorland, her petticoats always rumpled from our little flock of children hanging on them, and filled with contentment. Then I see you, covered with pearls and rubies and His Majesty on your arm, as grand a lady as can be at Court."

"As grand a lady as a whore can be, you mean." I smiled, too, but with more bittersweetness than my raillery intended. "Am I happy? I am, I am. Nor could I imagine myself with your wife's grubby flock. My little Lady Katherine's enough for me."

"I'm sure she is, if she's in your image." But he was clearly now thinking of his own wife and children, and not of me: it showed in his eyes. "We each of us serve His Majesty however we can, don't we?"

"That we do," I said softly, thinking how far our fates had diverged. "That we do."

We'd come through the last of the woods and into the clearing where the lodge stood. To my surprise, James was already there and waiting, standing not far from his horse and impatiently flicking at weeds with his whip. His usual escort of soldiers must be watching nearby, shielded by the shadows of the trees; after the Rye House Plot, he never went anywhere without them. He heard us coming, and turned, his smile so wide and happy to see me that I felt the unbridled joy of it. Dorothy Grahme was welcome to her brood of grasping brats; I had a king.

The colonel dismounted and bowed before James, then came to play groom to me and help me down from my saddle. I thanked him formally, and he touched his hat in deference, all that was proper before the king. James took my hand to lead me into the house, and I heard the colonel ride away behind us.

"How well do you know Grahme?" James asked as we stepped inside. "You two seemed warm enough."

"We were friends long ago, sir." I paused to draw off my gloves and unpin my hat. "Long before I began with you."

He grunted and stamped his feet with male suspicion. "Friends, you say. Did you take him to your bed?"

"No, sir, not at all," I said in perfect truth; we'd lain together in the grass, never a bed. "He loved another lady too well for me to win him."

"He wants to fuck you still," James said bluntly. "I saw it in his face."

"What, sir, a brittle old stick like me?" I asked, bemused. Jealousy was not something I'd much experienced.

"Don't jest, Katherine," James said, his voice rough with the longing I recognized so well. "You have a way about you that makes men want you. I cannot explain it, but you do. Why else do I find it so impossible to break with you as I should?"

"Because, sir, you shouldn't." I turned to face him, smiling, and looped my arms around his shoulders. "Because if you truly wished to break with me, you would. But you don't, so you can't, and I thank every one of your Romish saints in heaven for it."

"You're a sinful, blasphemous creature, Katherine," he muttered as he pushed me back against the wall to kiss me. "But I cannot give you up. I cannot."

I closed my eyes, delighting in the rawness of his desire as he sought to claim me. So this was how it would be today: jealousy as a spice to his cock, with my petticoats rucked up around my waist and a swift possession like some sailor's wench against the wall. Yet by James's own beliefs, he was willing to risk his very soul to have me, and I would not trade that for anything, not for every last one of Colonel Grahme's children in Westmorland.

Later, we ate a lazy dinner at a small table on the grass behind the lodge, under an arbor of gnarled vines. The day was warm, and we were still half undressed, I in my smock and petticoat and no more, my ankles crossed comfortably on James's thigh, while he'd yet to resume his coat or waistcoat, with his shirt open at the throat and the sleeves shoved to his elbows. A single ancient servingwoman looked after us, while James spoke of how he planned to address the new session of Parliament.

"Now that the Sedgemoor Campaign is done, we can address other matters," he explained earnestly, leaning forward in his chair with his elbows on the table, the better to see my reaction. What he likely saw first was how distasteful I found this term for poor Lord Monmouth's last efforts—the Sedgemoor Campaign!—but I knew well enough that he considered the rebellion well in the past and of no concern to his plans for England's future.

"The members proved themselves mightily agreeable in the last session," he continued. "God willing, I should guide them through this one as well."

"It won't be the same, sir," I said, sipping the wine that I drank, and he, being righteously abstemious, did not. "They obliged you last session because you were new to your throne, and they obliged you with more soldiers because there was a genuine need. They won't oblige you again simply to be obliging."

"They'll oblige me in this," he said, leaning closer with eager enthusiasm. "Sunderland says they will, that it's the proper time for change."

"Oh, Sunderland," I said with disgust. "I don't know why you trust a word that spills from his mouth, sir."

"He's a very clever and ingenious gentleman, that's why," James said. "He is also receiving instruction in the True Church as a most earnest inquirer after God's truth, which makes him eminently worthy of my trust."

"Sunderland intends to convert?" I asked, astonished. "And you would trust him for it, sir? Why, that rascal would swear on the Scriptures that his own mother had been a whore in Tangiers if he thought it would raise him further in your eyes."

He sighed. "You are harsh, Katherine."

"I am truthful, sir, which Sunderland could not be if his life depended upon it." I smiled and winked and rubbed my bare foot lightly along his leg—something else that Lord Sunderland would never do. "But please proceed, sir, proceed. Tell me what manner of nonsense His Lordship is encouraging this time."

"It's not nonsense," he insisted, "and it's my idea, not his. The rebellion proved the need of a larger army to safeguard England. We cannot afford to go backward and dismiss the troops that have spent this summer in exercise and training. They must be kept, with their officers in place, to preserve the country against future disturbances."

I frowned, for this was not a subject for humor. "Parliament will not allow that, sir, nor will the rest of the country. No good can come from so large a standing army. Thousands of idle, armed men, trained for fighting yet with no enemy—hah, there lies the true danger, no matter what Sunderland tells you."

"There is no danger in a strong defense, Katherine," he said, his brows drawn sternly together. "You must trust me in this, as an old soldier myself."

"You may order me to trust all you wish, sir," I said, "but I won't, and neither will Parliament. Recall what became of your own lamented father when Cromwell's army grew too fat with their own power, and the civil war that followed. No one wishes that again."

But James only shook his head, refusing to see my logic. "Cromwell's army was led by Protestant fanatics," he said. "Wise Providence will not permit that to happen again, nor will I."

In a single horrified instant I realized all he wasn't saying outright. "You're going to try to make Parliament repeal the Test Act, aren't you, sir? You not only wish to keep the standing army, but you wish it with Catholic officers, too, don't you?"

"There is no useful reason why Catholic officers cannot be employed alongside Protestant ones," he insisted. "The Test Act is a vile, false creation, designed to make persecution lawful. These men served England well when the country had great need of their skill, and I will not shame them by casting them out now that the crisis is done."

"But what you ask, sir," I said. I'd heard that James had called more than a hundred Catholic officers—a sizable number—during the emergency of the rebellion, but I'd no notion that they remained with the army still, without having sworn the Test Act oath, nearly two months after Lord Monmouth's execution. "A standing army increased to twice its size, and led by Papists! No English Parliament will ever agree to that, nor should they."

"And why not, Katherine, when it clearly is God's will that they do so?" he asked, sweeping his hand up toward the heavens. "How else would I have been granted such a magnificent victory over those who threatened me, if not through the steadying hand of Divine Providence?"

"I'd rather believe it was the leadership of Colonel Churchill, sir," I said, always wary of James when he began to spout like a Papist preacher.

"Yes, yes, but the true leader was Feversham," he said doggedly, "a French gentleman, guided to victory by his true Lord."

I swung my feet from his leg, unwilling to continue in so affectionate a posture when he was so wrongly stubborn.

"Lord Feversham is not only a Frenchman by birth, sir," I said, "but he is also more an empty-headed courtier than a true soldier. Everyone knows he was still lying abed when Colonel Churchill was leading your troops into battle at Sedgemoor. If Feversham is the sort of officer you wish to employ in your army, then you will receive a cold reception indeed from Parliament."

He scowled at my now-covered legs. "Sunderland says otherwise."

"Then Lord Sunderland is kissing your ass, sir," I said bluntly, "for there is no other way to explain it."

Restlessly he tapped his hand on the edge of the table. "You speak to me as a Protestant, Katherine."

"I speak to you as a dear friend, sir, and one who loves you too well to see you falter." I pushed free of my chair and sank to my knees on the grass beside him, taking his hands in my own to beseech him. "You are the King of England, sir, and the men you rule are Englishmen. They are the best people in the world, but they are also firm in their convictions and their beliefs, and they will not follow you in this rash plan. No matter what Lord Sunderland, or your confessor, or Her Majesty, or even the Pope in Rome may tell you, I will tell you the truth: your people will not accept this from you, or any other English king who has sworn to uphold the Anglican Church."

As desperate as I'd made my plea, he did not answer. Instead he looked at me in a silence that was almost pitying, as if I were the one who did not understand.

Finally he smiled and raised my hand to his lips to kiss it. "My own Katherine," he said gruffly. "Time we returned to the others, eh?"

He smiled, and to my sorrow I realized that he'd not listened to a word that I'd said.

I WAS NOT THE ONLY ONE who worried over James and his determination regarding the Catholics officers. By the time the Court left Windsor and returned to London in early October, 1685, the three months' allowance permitted to Papists had expired, yet none had been forced either to swear that they were Anglicans, or to leave their commissions. The army remained as it had been in the summer, twice its ordinary size, with James refusing so much as to discuss disbanding. It was an ill-kept secret, too, if indeed James was inclined to keep it a secret at all, and every tavern and coffeehouse in London rumbled with anxious unhappiness over the king's imperious actions.

Nor was I the only one to caution James over his decisions. Lord Halifax, never a reticent gentleman, spoke with such vehemence that James dismissed him not only from his office, but from the council as well, sharply warning all others that he'd not tolerate any advisers whose opinions and beliefs differed from his own.

"Halifax is with us now," Father said with unabashed jubilation. Though holding no seat in the House, Father remained as busy as could be behind the scenes, and could scarce wait for the new session to begin in November. "You'll see, Katherine. You've heard Halifax before. Now that he's clear of that wretched office, he'll be free to address the king exactly as His Majesty deserves."

"What then, Father?" I asked with concern. While I'd no wish to see James hounded and harangued by Parliament, I didn't want my father to end in the Tower for speaking treason, either. "The king is not obligated to obey you or your friends. What will you do if he doesn't?"

"He will, Katherine, he will," Father said sagely. "Halifax will make him understand, and bring him round to a more moderate course."

But I knew James far too well to share Father's confidence. If James hadn't listened to Lord Halifax while he'd been one of the royal counselors, why should he heed him now, when the marquis would be no more than an articulate gadfly? Increasingly James was surrounding himself only with gentlemen who shared his faith, rather than ones who showed any gift for statesmanship or even common sense.

Instead of Lord Halifax's shrewd intelligence, James now preferred ranting zealots like the Irishman Richard Talbot, who had already been rewarded with the Earldom of Tyrconnel for filling the Irish army with Catholic officers in place of Protestants. Another who'd claimed his ear was Father Petre, an English-born Jesuit and the dean of James's Chapel Royal, who was constantly promoting ever-closer connections to Rome. Foremost, of course, was the duplicitous Lord Sunderland, whose influence only grew stronger the more he conveniently professed to turn Papist himself. The only Protestant ministers who still remained with any power were Lord Rochester and his older brother Lord Clarendon, and they only on account of being James's brothers-in-law from his first marriage.

In such an atmosphere, the new session of Parliament in early November was bound to be difficult. James wasted little time in declaring, even dictating, his intentions, using his first speech to the Commons to praise his army, briskly requesting both funds for its maintenance at its full size and to keep the Catholic officers for their merit. Even more disturbing was that, for the first time, James failed to make any mention of his role as defender of the Church of England, a most ominous sign to every Anglican member in the House. They responded by refusing to vote the full funds for a standing army, and more infuriating to James, they let him know, politely, respectfully, but firmly, that they believed the employment of Papist officers was against English law.

The House of Lords was even less pleasing. James himself attended their sessions, and was compelled to listen as, one by one, nearly every great peer of the realm bravely rose to defend the current laws against popery in every form, and to reinforce their belief in the Church of England.

James was still furious when I came to his bedchamber later that night, so angry that as soon as I joined him, I realized he wished a sympathetic ear more than any coaxing diversion I could offer in his bed. He still wore the same richly embroidered suit of clothes that he'd chosen to impress the Lords, magnificent dress of dark blue velvet and gold lacing with a formal, military air that should have reminded the peers that the king also commanded the army and navy as well as the country. But he'd also begun wearing a Romish crucifix publicly, there around his neck beside the Garter-star on his breast, an uneasy juxtaposition, and one that, however subtle, every peer in the Lords had noted at once.

"I've known many of those men all our lives, Katherine," James said, pacing before me, "and some so long that we were all in exile together as boys, thirty years ago. Yet this is how they humiliate me!"

"How, sir?" I asked cautiously. I drew my castor-lined cloak more closely around my shoulders, twisting my hands into the soft fur. The room seemed chill to me, the fire burned so low that I could only guess that James's raging fury had inflamed him so much that he didn't notice. "How could those worthy gentlemen humiliate you?"

"If you had been there, Katherine, you would have heard it for yourself," he said, slashing his arm through the air as if to smite his enemies there before the fireplace. "They doubted my motives; they questioned my very honor!"

"Was it the army question that plagued them most, sir?"

"My army, and my officers, and my own faith as well," he said, biting off each word with furious distaste. "I could not believe they would dare oppose their king in such strong language."

I sighed. Clearly matters had gone worse in the Lords than they had in the Commons, even worse than I'd feared, at least by James's reckoning. "I am sorry, sir. I'd suspected they'd show their unhappiness—"

"The unhappiness was the least of it," he continued. "Their disrespect, their contempt, their unbridled bigotry!"

"They are frightened and uncertain, sir," I said. "They do not see these things in the same manner as you do. If perhaps you were to explain with less forcefulness, or offer a few concessions—"

"It is not my place to concede to anything," he said sharply. "I am their king, not their puppet. It is by the hand of Divine Providence that I rule, and I *will* rule, and do what is right and proper for my people. I will be strong, Katherine, and I will survive this test as I have all the others intended to stop me."

Suddenly he stopped his pacing before me. His stern face crumpled and his shoulders bowed, as if the full weight of the day's events had crushed down upon him all at once.

"Before God, I will do my best for them, Katherine," he said, weary and bitter and sadly bewildered as well. "If they will but let me, I will lead them to salvation and glory."

"Oh, sir," I said softly, and when I opened my arms to him, he came to me with an exhausted sigh. "You will do what is right, and find a way to make peace with them in your fashion. You will, I am sure of it."

But by the following day, James had decided he'd had enough of the hostility he perceived so rampant in both Houses. Instead of offering reconciliation, he chose to demonstrate his power and authority. Though the session had scarcely begun, he prorogued Parliament and sent the members home. He never again called them back.

Amidst such momentous times, it is easy to forget that most of life continued at its usual pace. While the peers raged like tigers at the king's actions and my father's house in Bloomsbury Square was filled with angry, indignant conversations, farmers still brought their turnips and corn to market in Covent Garden, watermen still rowed their passengers along the Thames, and the goldsmiths' shops along the Strand still opened their shutters to customers each day.

My own ordinary life continued as well in my new house in St. James's Square, and it was on such a morning that I sat in my back parlor, listening as Lady Katherine recited her French. Because my daughter had royal blood and would someday be a lady of consequence (and, in truth, because my own education had been so haphazard), I took great care with her learning. I employed a Frenchwoman to speak that language to her in the best Parisian manner, and though Lady Katherine was only five years in age, she already could prattle on as prettily in that tongue as any child born to Versailles. Her skill delighted James no end, and it pleased him mightily to hear her converse in the language of his mother, the late Dowager Queen Henrietta Marie. Lady Katherine's task today was to learn three more verses of a fable by the French poet La Fontaine, and as I listened contentedly to her sweet, babyish voice, I did not realized I'd a visitor until the footman came to whisper the name in my ear.

"The Earl of Rochester?" I repeated with surprise. The lord treasurer had never once been a guest in my house. "His Lordship's here?"

I swiftly ushered Lady Katherine and her mademoiselle from the room and prepared to receive Lord Rochester, who was smiling still after passing my daughter in the hallway as she left the room.

"Lady Katherine is a lovely small lady," he said with approval as he took the chair I offered. "She favors you, madam."

"I should hope not, my lord!" I exclaimed, laughing at his having so shamelessly chosen politeness over truth. "She is far more beautiful than I have ever been, doubtless due to the Stuart half of her prevailing over the Sedley."

"I find that impossible to believe," he said with a doleful sigh. "But that is not why I have come to you, Mrs. Sedley. Instead I come in confidence, on an errand of considerable delicacy."

He cleared his throat, rubbing his open palm across the polished cherry arm of the chair. As ministers went, he was better known for his skill with the country's finances than with diplomatic words, as his uneasiness now proved.

"Mrs. Sedley," he began at last. "Mrs. Sedley, I am here to ask most humbly for a great favor, on behalf of England, her people, and even, in a way, of His Majesty himself. It's no secret that the king is mightily devoted to you, and turns to you even as he has abandoned his other Anglican advisers."

"Excepting you, my lord, of course," I said. "The last two Anglicans! That must make us like Noah and his consort, I suppose, the two of us the final pair of honest souls cast adrift in the whole rotten Romish Court."

"Madam, please, I beg you to be serious," he said so earnestly that I was forced to comply. "If you have any regard for the church of your fathers, for the Church of England, you will employ your influence over the king now."

"I, my lord?" I asked, incredulous. "Your confidence in me and my influence is most flattering, my lord."

"It's not flattery, Mrs. Sedley," he said solemnly, "but the fair observation of many."

I tried to be solemn, too, and not to think of how peculiar this all was: to have the most senior minister of the land telling me what to whisper across my pillow to the king when I lay with him. Yet still Lord Rochester regarded me with his long face stretched as somber as if for a funeral.

"You speak in perfect earnest, my lord, don't you?" I said slowly. "You would ask this of me?"

"I am as earnest as I can be, Mrs. Sedley," he said, and I did not doubt him. "The king regards the recent rebellion as a conquest of his might over wrongful forces. But most in England saw many men who would willingly fight and die to protect their church against popery, and how many, too, that would do the same for a Protestant king. His Majesty continues to gaze only toward Rome, and is blind to what is happening in England. Yet he must be made to see before it is too late, else all he and his brother suffered for will be lost."

No wonder he looked so somber, for this was a somber, serious conversation indeed, so serious that I'd no real notion of how to reply. It was one thing to overhear wild talk among Father's friends and their longing for the Prince of Orange as the future savior of the Church of England, but it was quite another to have Lord Rochester himself speaking thus in my own parlor.

"You speak frankly, my lord, and thus I must be frank in turn with you," I began at last, troubled beyond measure. "I have always spoken plain to His Majesty about our church and how he has put his crown at risk by his stubborn adherence to popery. Even in our most intimate exchanges, I have never varied from honesty or truth. Yet though he listens—hah, because I give him no choice!—he will never heed me, my lord. Never."

He listened, his expression unchanged. "He might if you were more in his company. If you once again attended your lodgings at Whitehall each night—"

"No, my lord," I said, shaking my head. "I like my own house and my bed here too well to return."

"Better than Lady Portsmouth's rooms?" he asked, a luxurious temptation. "They could be yours, if you wish it."

"The queen would never permit that," I said firmly, "nor do I wish to put myself in her path again."

"Her Majesty could be distracted," he said. "That, too, could be arranged with ease."

I shook my head again. It wasn't as easy to distract the queen as it once had been. As the Court had become more Catholic, Mary Beatrice had become more powerful, too, growing bolder with the flattering encouragement of Lord Sunderland.

"There would be other enticements," Lord Rochester continued. "Many things are possible."

"Pray recall that I've spent most of my life at Court, my lord," I said. "I'm far too old to be lured by a new bauble."

Lord Rochester frowned. "Then perhaps, madam, I should describe what will happen if His Majesty continues on his present course. Lord Monmouth could be only the first Protestant to lose his head. To be sure, there are risks. Nothing is assured. No matter what we do, Lord Sunderland may still have his way, and the Papists may still win, and we may all end in the Tower on false charges of treason."

"And if I push the king too hard, then I could lose his devotion forever." My smile was tight. "You see I am aware of the risks, my lord."

"Those are the risks if you agree, madam," he said, rising from his chair to take his leave. "But can any of us afford what will happen if we do nothing?"

He didn't need to say more. The next rebellion would not be so easy to suppress, and James could well find himself facing the same grim fate as his late father, the same that he'd ordered for Lord Monmouth. And what then would become of me and my darling Lady Katherine? There would be precious little mercy for the mistress of a fallen king, or for their natural daughter, either.

"It's your choice entirely, Mrs. Sedley," Lord Rochester said, taking his cloak and hat from my servant. "You must decide for yourself."

Yet in truth, what choice did I have?

BY THE CHRISTMAS SEASON OF 1685, I'd assumed a brave, brash place at Court. Through Lord Rochester's intervention, I was included in every entertainment, ball, and dinner at the palace, and he made so many requests on my behalf that there were a few foolish whispers that he shared my favors, too, though I couldn't guess when exactly these whisperers believed I'd find the time to dally with His Lordship, too.

The new role that had been urged upon me was no challenge, for it was much the same one I'd been playing all along. It was easy enough for me to aim my jibes at the various priests and Jesuits surrounding James and Mary Beatrice; there were so many black-clad figures in the palace now that it would be nigh impossible to avoid striking one even if I'd wished to. The jests themselves were easy, too. For a steadfast Anglican like me, there was much to mock about the convoluted practices and beliefs connected to popery.

What always surprised me, however, was how those same sly remarks so delighted a devoted Catholic like James. The more outrageous my remarks were, the more loudly he would laugh, even if all the other Papists around him pointedly did not. I told him that Lord Tyrconnel and Lord Arundel, the Catholic peers he'd chosen as counselors, were dull-witted, self-serving fools whose counsel would cost him his crown. I even made sport of Lord Sunderland, and how readily he'd changed his pew at morning prayer for a more comfortable one at mass. James had roared at that. While James's reaction had always pleased me in the past—for what born comedian doesn't relish an audience?—now it made me uneasy. I was like the jester of ancient courts, permitted to say what no one else dared. But how far could I take the privilege before I'd blunder too far and James would cease to be amused?

Lord Rochester only smiled and told me to be easy, that I was doing exactly as I should to please the king, even as I pointed out the foolishness of the Papists. With his approval, I continued as I was, and resolved to worry no more. But I could not entirely put aside the hazard of my situation: I was supported by Lord Rochester and the few other Protestants who remained at Court, while on the other side stood Lord Sunderland as Her Majesty's champion, with Father Petre and her army of other priests and Catholics besides.

Of course, with every mocking remark I made at the expense of rosaries or confessionals, the queen hated me a little more. But even her hatred had a curious feel to it, entirely directed as it was at what I said and not for being her husband's mistress. It was Lady Rochester who finally explained this mystery to me one night outside the palace's supper room, where we'd just observed the queen sweep past me as if I did not exist.

"It makes perfect sense," the countess said, her quiet solemnity a match for her husband's. "The queen doesn't fault you for lying with His

Majesty because she doesn't realize that you are. Instead she believes that His Majesty is intriguing with Mrs. Grafton."

"Mrs. Grafton?" Mrs. Grafton was one of the queen's current maids of honor, a sweet-faced girl of complete innocence, or so I'd believed, and I felt the sharpest pangs of nascent jealousy. But now I understood the vicious contempt that the queen had showed earlier toward this poor young lady, much as she had once done to me. "Does Mrs. Grafton have designs on His Majesty?"

"Oh, not at all," Lady Rochester said easily. "She's such an empty-headed ninny that I doubt she could make a design upon a kitten, let alone a king. That is why I chose her, you see."

Confusion must have shown on my face, for with a knowing smile she continued. "To divert the queen's suspicions from you, I whispered to her that His Majesty was bedding Mrs. Grafton. The more the pathetic little creature denies it, the more the queen believes it's so, and punishes her for it. A great convenience to us."

"Very great, my lady," I murmured, yet the unconscionable cruelty of this deception appalled me. Even after so many years at Court, I could still be stunned by what highborn people would do for power. I'd felt the sting of Mary Beatrice's vengeful hand against my cheek myself and I pitied the bewildered Mrs. Grafton.

"The girl has no family to speak of, of course," the countess continued, "and thus she will bring us no trouble. But then, what is the chit's honor compared to keeping you secured in the king's favor?"

"Indeed, my lady," I said, and smiled. "But I must wonder if you'll show me the same lack of regard if I fail to be as useful as you and His Lordship hope."

She smiled evenly, outwardly as unperturbed as I. But I didn't miss the slight twitch of her nose or the disdain in her eye, and I knew what she thought as clearly as if she'd spoken it aloud: that she was wife of one peer and the daughter of another while I was but a brash, vulgar whore, and in any other circumstances, she'd not deign to take any notice of me all.

"We all have our own usefulness, Mrs. Sedley," she said at last, "and we all serve the king to the best of our abilities."

"How true, my lady," I said, and smiled once again. "How fortunate for me that His Majesty can satisfy me so pleasurably even as I serve him!"

Her Ladyship's smile froze, and she swiftly excused herself, scuttling away to avoid contamination from my whorish self, I suppose.

But while I'd purposefully intended to shock Lady Rochester, what I'd said to her was also the truth. No matter the motives or machinations that had brought me back to the palace, James was delighted that I was there, and the more of my company that he had, the more he sought, as if he'd never enough. Over and over he told me so, and showed me his fondness in countless little ways as well, both before others and alone in his bedchamber. It was almost as if we were new lovers again, instead of an ancient couple of nearly seven years' standing.

Though I tried my best, I cannot say if by year's end I had managed to make James think more kindly toward the Church of England, or softened his heart toward his Protestant subjects. At least I could say I'd done no harm, and after the bloody rebellion in the summer and the disastrously aborted Parliamentary session in the fall, the winter seemed blessedly calm.

But I'd no doubt that James's hard royal heart had gentled even more toward me. For my twenty-eighth birthday, he presented me with a ruby ring surrounded with pearls and a new team of matched grays for my coach. For Christmas four days later came a pearl bracelet, and a much grander gift of several valuable estates in Ireland. Even more generous were the two additional incomes he'd settled on our daughter, Lady Katherine, giving her a fortune to match her title and blood. I recognized it for what it was, generosity born of devotion. Louise de Keroualle had been right about such tangible gifts signaling the degree of a king's devotion. I had never loved James more, and here was the proof that he cared for me as well. It did not matter then that more and more of his subjects were regarding him as a cold and heartless tyrant. When he lay in my arms, I knew otherwise. Together, James and I had love: true, lasting love, and peace.

Chapter Twenty-four

Whitehall Palace, London
January 1686

"Open it," James ordered, smiling with anticipation of my response. "You'll be pleased, I'm sure."

I grinned, and held the box in my hands another moment longer. It wasn't the usual shaped leather box that held jewels, his favorite gift for me. This box was wide and flat and made of polished wood with silver clasps and hinges, and when I shook it gently, I could hear nothing within.

"It's empty, sir," I teased. "You tell me you are giving me what I most deserve to have, and it's an empty box."

"It's not," he said. "I can promise you that. Open it, Katherine, please. I wish to see your face when you do."

No other man would wish the same, and suddenly my eyes swam with tears of happiness as I gazed at him on the bed beside me. "Thank you, sir," I whispered tenderly. "Thank you."

"Here now, no weeping." His brows rose with surprise. "And why thank me, when you've yet to see what's within?"

"Because what you give me cannot be put in any box, sir." I sniffed back my tears, knowing how they disturbed him, and looked back down at the box in my hands. I slipped the latch open and slowly opened the lid, then gasped—not with joy, but dismay. The thick parchment sheet was covered with writing so decoratively formal as to be unreadable, with heavy silk ribbons threaded through one side. All that was wanting was the thick wafer of wax, stamped with the Great Seal that would give importance to everything else, and if he'd proceeded as far as this, then that, too, would come soon enough.

"Oh, sir, no," I said, staring down into the box. "Please no."

"Yes, Katherine," he said proudly, ignoring my response. "I tell you, it's only what you deserve. Countess of Dorchester, Baroness Darlington. That's what those letters of patent make you, and past time, too. Now you can hold your head as high as any lady."

"I already do, sir," I said. "I don't need a scrap of parchment and sealing wax to do so."

"I say you do," he insisted. "You have been loyal to me through every weather and sea, Katherine, and have loved me without doubt or question. For those merits alone, there is no other lady who is more dear to me. Consider this as your reward."

"But I do not wish such a damnable reward, sir!" I cried. "Once, perhaps, I would have wanted to be recognized with such an honor, but not now. Can you not see that, sir? Can you not understand all the misfortune that will come of this?"

"No misfortune will come." He took the box with the patent and set it to one side on the bed, and instead took my hands in his and kissed me. "You are my dear friend, yes, and the mistress of my heart. But you should also be recognized and honored by others for your devotion to your king, and the regard that king holds for you. Even Rochester agrees with me."

"Lord Rochester agreed, sir?" My despair sank even lower. Likely His Lordship saw this title as only one more prize for the Protestants, a sign of glorious favor to be waved smugly before Lord Sunderland. He might even have suggested it. He would have thought nothing of what it could do to me.

"He did," James said. "He saw to the letters himself once I ordered it. But I should have done this for you long ago, sweet. My brother never waited so long with his ladies."

"That is because Madame de Keroualle and the others wished to be peeresses, sir, while I wish only to continue as we have." I shook my head, already imagining how swiftly this would topple the carefully built house of political cards on which I was balanced. "If you insist on this, sir, then I will instantly become a personage at Court who cannot be ignored.

Her Majesty has been able to pretend she knows nothing of me, of us, because I didn't signify. But if I am a countess, I must make my fealty to her, and she must acknowledge me and how I came by this title, and how by favoring me, you have broken that impossible oath you swore to her, and oh, sir, it will not go well for either of us."

"It will go exactly as I order it," he said firmly. "I am king, not my wife. If I say she must receive you as Lady Dorchester, then she will. It's your due, Katherine, and I won't have you scorned by anyone."

Alas, as was too often the case, my fears proved much better predictions than his certainty. In the next days, James must have gone to the queen and told her his purpose regarding me, and likewise how he expected her to accept it. Overnight it seemed as if everyone at Court knew of my impending title, though I mentioned it to no one. I suppose part of me still hoped that James would see reason and withdraw the letters before they were passed for the seal.

But once James decided on a course, no argument would ever dissuade him, and so, too, it was with this. Every Protestant congratulated me warmly on my coming good fortune, while every Catholic looked coldly on me with contempt. I was rumored now to be officially named James's mistress, much as Lady Portsmouth had been Charles's *maitresse de titre* after the fashion of the French Court, and that soon I'd be installed in her suite of rooms. I knew none of it was true, but the queen—ah, the queen must have believed every word of it, and more besides.

If James had believed that Mary Beatrice would be as meekly resigned to my ennoblement as Catherine of Braganza had been to titles that Charles had given to Lady Cleveland and Lady Portsmouth, then he was most grievously disappointed. I never learned what occurred between the two of them alone. Knowing her Italianate temper and her Romish fervor and his innate stubbornness, I can but imagine it was a fearful, raging discussion. What I did see, along with the rest of the Court, was Mary Beatrice's public performance that began on 19 January, the day my title was scheduled to pass the Great Seal.

Already diminished by the wasting illnesses that had plagued her for years, the queen made herself even less attractive by appearing at the royal table dressed as plainly as a novice of her own perverse faith, without any jewels or paint and her hair drawn severely back from her face. She did not greet James as she took her chair, nor did she speak to him or any of her ladies during the meal. The only one graced with her conversation was Father Petre, who stood behind her to whisper his poisonous words into her ear. She ate nothing that was presented to her, nor drank any wine, pointedly waving it all away untouched. As soon as she could, she rose and left the table, forcing her ladies and priests to leave hungry and hurry after her.

"Now, that was worthy of the tragic stage," Lord Rochester observed dryly beside me. "I suppose Her Majesty hopes to punish the king this way, but so public a display will not sit well with him, or any man, for that matter."

"That won't be the end of if, my lord," I said uneasily, not sharing his confidence. "You'll see. God only knows what she'll contrive next."

"Let her, then," Lord Rochester said. "She'll only displease the king more. Mark how grim he looks now."

James did in fact look grim, even sour, and mightily discomfited by his wife's untoward departure. But he also seemed determined to ignore it, turning toward the gentleman beside him to begin a fresh conversation. As the gentleman replied, James searched the room until he found me, standing beside Lord Rochester. His entire expression changed, softening, as likely mine did in return, and when he smiled at me, it was so clear a mark of favor that others in the room remarked it with a murmur of wonder. I flushed, feeling at once pleasure that he'd singled me out, and misery that he'd done so.

"There now, madam," Lord Rochester said with brisk satisfaction. "You see exactly where you stand."

But though I smiled back to James, I was not reassured. "I see nothing, my lord," I said to the earl, "nothing beyond that damnable, cursed patent."

He laughed. "You will feel otherwise once you hear yourself called Lady Dorchester."

I only shook my head. "Would that it were as simple as that, my lord," I said softly. "Would that everything were as simple."

BEING PROTESTANT, AS WELL AS THE subject for the queen's ire, I did not witness her next skirmish in the war against me, or rather, as the Papists perceived it, the war for the king's soul. But there were plenty of others who knew of it as soon as it occurred, two days after I had become Lady Dorchester, and I heard of Mary Beatrice's outrage in such detail that I felt as if I had indeed seen it for myself.

Gathering every priest and Jesuit to be found in the palace into her rooms, she summoned James. He told me he'd expected her to capitulate to his demands and to act with the obedience of the Christian wife she claimed herself to be. But as soon as James entered her chambers, he saw that no surrender would be forthcoming. Instead Mary Beatrice sat in her armchair, ringed round with her Papists, who at once fell to their knees at the sight of him, babbling as one in Latin. Father Petre dared to address James directly and without permission, speaking for all his brethren when he told the king sternly that I was not only a blight on his soul, but that I alone stood in the way of all their designs to promote their faith in England. He pointed dramatically to the queen, saying that James's seed would never find sweet purchase in her womb to produce a Catholic heir to the English throne as long as he dallied with me. The queen then sobbed as if she'd been struck, and wailed her accusations at him for being a cruel and faithless husband.

"You cannot imagine how I felt to hear that, Katherine," he told me later that night. He sat beside me on the bed, but without undressing, making it clear he wished to talk and nothing more. "To hear her shriek like that, with Father Petre explaining it all. I felt cursed. There is no other way to explain it. I felt cursed, and damned."

"Which you are most certainly not, sir," I said indignantly. "No Anglican among your subjects would accuse you of that."

He made an unhappy grunt. "You say that because you're one of them."

"I say it because it's the truth," I insisted. "If there is any fault for your lack of an heir, it should go to Her Majesty, not to you."

This *was* true. After conceiving at least once a year since her marriage, the queen had been too sickly to produce any further proof of her fertility for the past two years.

But James didn't answer, his expression far too thoughtful for my tastes, nor did I miss how his gaze wandered away from me toward the

Italian painting of a sad-eyed Madonna that he'd recently had hung not far from his bed.

"I do not know, Katherine," he said heavily. "If I have offended the Almighty Lord by my alliance with you, then He could well have challenged me by making my wife barren. Then she told me that if I did not send you from England, she would cease to be my wife and queen, and instead retire to a convent."

I slipped my fingers into his to reassure him, and myself, too. "What did you say, sir?"

He groaned. "I'd been caught by surprise, Katherine, and was willing to say most anything to ease her and silence their criticisms."

"Oh, sir." I could already guess the rest. "What did you tell them?"

He looked down at our clasped fingers, unable to meet my eye. "I told her that I'd granted you the title by way of breaking with you decently, and that I wouldn't see you again."

"Yet you bid me come to you again tonight, sir," I said softly. "You were true to me."

"I could not help being otherwise, Katherine," he said with unmistakable sorrow. "I have tried before to leave you, and I cannot do it, no matter how strongly I am urged by those who support me."

He tightened his fingers into mine, as if that gesture alone were enough to undo the knot I felt tightening about my slender hopes. He'd chosen me this time, but how many more times after that would he be able to withstand the arguments of so many against me? What was my lone voice against all the clamors of Rome?

"Then promise me this, sir, if you can," I said, my words a-tremble. "If the time does come that you must send me from you, then all I ask is that you tell me yourself and not by some cold messenger. Promise me that, and I will be content."

"You have my word, Katherine," he said at once, "because by my heart, that day will never come."

But as he kissed me to seal his promise, I was not nearly as sure.

TWO DAYS LATER, I MET LORD ROCHESTER by his arrangement, and together we set out to walk in St. James's Park. The sky was dull as pewter, the snow from the last fall trudged and gray, and the afternoon was cold enough that there were few others in the park besides us, exactly as we had hoped. There were far too many hostile ears in Whitehall these days to suit either of us, and the few desultory crows among the leafless trees were all the company we desired.

"Sunderland is showing his usual colors, my lady," Lord Rochester said, addressing me by my new, cursed title. With his black hat pulled low against the cold, he looked even more doleful than usual. "He has loudly declared himself to be a supporter of Her Majesty, and claims to fear so greatly for the king's morals that he has painted you as a manipulative, corrupting adulteress."

"Pox on Sunderland," I said warmly, the imprecation a frosty cloud before my face. I wore a black velvet vizard beneath the hood of my cloak, not only to protect my cheeks from the cold, but to keep my face from unwittingly betraying any fresh secrets to His Lordship. For now he was my most loyal ally at Court, but in truth I trusted him no more than anyone else. "He never dared call Lady Portsmouth an adulteress while he was so busily kissing her skirts."

"He would if he'd thought he'd profit by it," Lord Rochester said acidly. "You should know that he arranged for Father Giffard to speak with His Majesty today. They were closeted together for the better part of two hours."

"Likely the poor king never spoke more than a dozen words in all that time together," I said. Father Giffard was James's vicar-general, a learned but famously tedious Catholic prelate. "Giffard could preach a fish to tears."

"The king did seem weary when he emerged, my lady," Lord Rochester agreed, as close as he'd ever come to making a jest. "But while I'm sure His Majesty was soundly berated for his attachment to you, he did not yield to Giffard's pleas. Afterward, His Majesty seemed quite pleased with himself for standing firm."

"Hah, then a pox on Father Giffard, too." There were times when James's stubbornness and his reluctance to follow the will of others could be a wondrous thing indeed. "He and Sunderland can go take the mercury cures together."

"We are not clear yet, my lady," Lord Rochester warned. "Tomorrow Sunderland is joining Tyrconnel, Dover, and Arundel in an urgent private audience with the king. They will speak more frankly than Father Giffard, and more forcefully, too."

I frowned beneath my black velvet. The arguments of those Catholic lords, all of whom James trusted, would be more difficult for him to withstand. Earlier Lord Rochester had told me that each of these men had been promised rich prizes and posts through Sunderland's patronage if their pleas succeeded, and thus would be willing to say anything their knavish leader dictated. To be sure, only Sunderland of the four had any cleverness, but the other three could be counted on to bluster and rage, which would carry further with James than well-thought words.

"I also expect Father Petre to redouble his efforts," Lord Rochester continued. "He has been so much with the queen that I am sure he is planning another attack."

"I do not doubt it, my lord," I said, not hiding bitterness. "Do you know Father Petre has told the king that all Papist countries laugh at him for preferring an old and ugly Protestant bitch for a mistress over his young, beautiful Catholic wife? Fah, I am but a single year older than the queen!"

Embarrassed, Lord Rochester stared steadfastly before him. "I have also heard that Petre has suggested that the comfort of Holy Communion be withheld from the king until he agrees to their demands, but I doubt even a Jesuit would dare that."

"Then a pox on Father Petre, too," I said, though without the same enthusiasm that I'd showed earlier. Father Petre was a far different opponent from Father Giffard. Father Petre possessed all the cunning and ambition of a well-educated Jesuit, and not only did James respect him, but he was also so daunted by Petre's skill with an argument that he was, I think, a little afraid of him, too. After a smattering of Latin and a few *Aves* and *Paters*, Father Petre would need only to hint at withholding Communion, and James would capitulate. I knew James and his piety too well to believe otherwise.

A small gust of chill wind swirled at my skirts, and restlessly I twisted my gloved hands deep inside my fur muff, where His Lordship would not see this proof of my agitation. When I had been a child, Father had taken me with him in the summer months to his Southfleet estates in Kent, and from there we often went to walk along the sea. I'd shed my shoes and stockings like any common child to paddle in the water, shrieking with delight as I danced beneath the warm and glittering sun. But what fascinated me most was to stand as still as I could at the water's edge. I'd let the waves first rush over my toes and then swiftly retreat again into the sea, the water drawing the sand from beneath my feet with such force that I'd have to step backward, or fall.

That was how I felt now. No matter how I might try to hold fast to James, too many other forces were knocking me from my feet exactly as those long-ago waves once had done. Everything was sliding and rushing from under me, and I could sense how near I was to falling, falling, and no one could save me but myself.

"Pray do not be offended by what Lord Petre might say, my lady," Lord Rochester said, mistaking my silence. "He acts on orders from Rome. We must all pray to a righteous God to favor our cause and smile on England, and for Him to grant us victory over popery."

"Amen, my lord," I murmured, and said no more aloud. But did he truly believe I wouldn't notice that he sought no prayers for me?

THE NEXT DAY JAMES MET WITH the three Catholic lords and Lord Sunderland in great privacy, in Chiffinch's lodgings adjacent to the royal bedchamber. It was said they met for a considerable time, and that often their words became so heated that their voices could be heard through the doors. Yet when at last the gentlemen left the royal chambers, their faces were red with frustration, while the king—the king sent for me.

"Would that you'd heard them yourself, Katherine," James said, his spirits high and his expression still animated from his conversation. He poured himself a glass of the sweetened lemon water he preferred in place of wine, drinking it down rapidly in almost a single draught. "They tried to jump on poor Father Giffard's back and ride him to the same market. It was clear as the morning that Sunderland had spoken to the good father and relayed his arguments to the others, for they each repeated them in turn as if they'd been taught the same catechism."

"What exactly did they say, sir?" I asked, standing before him. As always, he'd given me leave to sit, but I was too agitated to do so. The best I could do was to stand before a chair, my hands clasped tightly before me. "What was this argument they repeated?"

He shrugged, refilling his glass. "I tell you, my dear, it was nothing new. They claim I give the enemies of the True Church an advantage by keeping you, a Protestant lady as my mistress, and they wish me to set a mark on those men who encourage you into my bed. Meaning, of course, the Hydes. I'm no simpleton, despite how Sunderland judges me."

"No one encouraged me into your bed, sir, except for you." I'd never been shy of being James's mistress, but I hated hearing myself stirred into this ominous Jesuit-flavored stew by Lord Sunderland, and I hated, too, to be considered no more than one of Lord Rochester's pawns. "Faith, how they will say anything!"

"They will, Katherine, they will," he continued. "But I turned their gambit back on them. I told them that I'd listened to Father Giffard because he was a very religious man, one who was by his function obliged to take notice and disapprove of me keeping a mistress. Then I said that this was the first time I'd taken them for divines, too, with a right to concern themselves with the state of my soul. Hah, they'd no answer to that!"

"Nor had they any right to one, sir, after hounding you like that." I felt hounded, too; how could I not? "Was that all?"

"Almost." He leaned forward eagerly. "I finally told them that they acted not from any religious concern, but from their own private piques and unhappiness, and I bid them for the future not to concern themselves with matters that did in no way relate to them. Wasn't that fine of me, Katherine?"

"Oh, dear sir, it was," I declared, surprised and honored, too, that he'd so willingly played my champion against these men. "They're wicked meddlesome knaves, every one of them, and I thank you with all my heart for defending me against them."

"You have been true and faithful to me, Katherine," he said. "How could I not do the same for you?"

He smiled then, a shy, crooked smile that belonged to the younger brother who'd always been second in cleverness. On impulse I rushed to his chair, intending to kiss him as a pledge that we would survive this together. Laughing, he pulled me onto his lap and into his arms, and I thought of how there was no other place I'd rather be. Perhaps he was stronger than I'd believed him; perhaps his love would be enough to save me. Perhaps—

"Forgive me, Your Majesty," Father Petre murmured, suddenly appearing like a demon beside us. "But Her Majesty and Lord Sunderland said I was to come to you here directly."

At once I slid from James's lap, collecting myself as best I could before this loathsome priest's gaze. I shouldn't have been startled to see him intrude like this; of course Sunderland would refuse to be defeated, and send his strongest ally. He stood before us now as if he'd every right to be there, studying me with the cold disgust and contempt that came so naturally to him.

But to my sorrow, James did not chastise Father Petre for intruding unbidden, or send him away as he deserved. Instead he rose at once and bowed his head to receive the priest's benediction. It sickened and saddened me to see the King of England bow his head before anyone with such unbecoming haste, especially before the likes of Father Petre.

"Excuse me for a moment or two, Father," he said, "and then I will join you directly in my own rooms."

"Conclude your business as you please, sir," the priest said. "I will be waiting."

Before he backed from the room, he made the sign of the cross, and again James bowed in subservient respect and crossed himself in return. As James bent his head, I saw Father Petre smile, a smile of pleased mastery that should have had no place in any English palace.

And in that instant, I saw my days in the king's favor were done.

"I must go to him, Katherine," James said at once. "I cannot make him wait."

"Of course you can, sir," I exclaimed with disbelief. The confidence he'd shown to me earlier was gone; the happy pride he'd expressed after dismissing the other lords had vanished and was now replaced with a guilty obedience and preoccupation that grieved me mightily. "You are the *king*, sir."

But James only shook his head. "I must go, my dear," he said, his thoughts clearly away from me and with the priest. "I must listen to what he says."

Tears filled my eyes. "Oh, sir, my own dear sir, do not let yourself be so ensnared by this man, I beg you! Pray recall who you are, and who you rule, and not let yourself be used in this way!"

"My dear Katherine." He smiled at me with kind indulgence, but the love he'd shown me earlier was gone. "If you care for me as you claim, then you will know that I must go to Father Petre, as the bearer of God's will for me."

"No, sir, please, do not twist my love against me that way," I cried with growing despair, seizing his hand to draw him back. "That evil Jesuit raven wishes me ill and will tell you whatever he must to bring my downfall from your affections. But heed me, please, my dearest sir and master, listen when I tell you that this man and his followers will bring you nothing but sore troubles and distress. They will ruin you, sir, and destroy you and your throne."

He smiled still as if I hadn't spoken at all, and raised my hand to his lips. "I must go, Katherine. Surely you understand."

I understood; oh, yes, I understood everything. My tears fell freely now, from my eyes and from my heart.

"Dear sir, my own dear sir!" I sobbed. "If I must be driven away and sacrificed like this, then please let it be because you bowed to your wife's wishes, and not for the jealous hatred of these damned cunning priests who would steal your kingdom from you!"

"Katherine, please," he said gently as he kissed me farewell. "Know that I love you, dearest, and let that be enough."

But it wouldn't be enough, and never would, and as he left me, I sank to my knees and wept; not for myself, but for James and for England.

AGAINST ALL REASON AND HOPE, I prayed that James would keep his promise to me and tell me to my face that he was done with me. That he didn't only proved to me that his decision was not his own, and though the knowledge didn't ease my sorrow, it did, in a way, make the parting easier to bear. I'd lost him not to disaffection, but to Rome, and how could I ever compete with that?

Three days later, Lord Middleton came to me on behalf of His Majesty and offered me the use of a royal yacht to carry me to exile in Holland. I thanked him, but refused, and told him that even if I were to be a Protestant martyr, I wouldn't be deported against my will. Next I was offered France, then Flanders. Those, too, I refused. My old acquaintance the Duchess Mazarin had once warned me never to go into any country on the Continent with Catholic convents, or risk being shut away among the nuns. I'd only to look at my own mother's fate to see the wisdom in her advice.

Finally, through Lord Middleton, I agreed to go to Ireland, with the excuse of visiting my estates there. I resolved to think of this as my choice to leave the Court, and not the banishment that it so clearly was.

I made my arrangements for my journey and closed up my grand house. I would leave servants behind, for I intended one day to return. But likewise I knew I could be away for many months, perhaps even years. Traveling such a distance was no small undertaking, requiring two coaches for my daughter and the servants who would accompany us, and wagons besides to carry our baggage.

By the middle of February, I was finally ready. We would leave London long before dawn, traveling by moonlight to take advantage of the empty roads. Despite the hour, Father came to bid me farewell, grumbling to have had to rise so early but there at my side nonetheless. Together we watched from the steps as the last trunks were lashed into place, with Father adding several well-meant suggestions as to the route and roads that doubtless my driver could have done without.

"You are certain your coachman has prepared the wheels properly?" Father asked. "With so much ice on the roads at this season, you don't wish to shatter a spoke."

"Everything is as it should be, Father," I reassured him. "I've no wish to tumble into a ditch, either."

"No, no." He was squinting a bit as he looked at me, as if striving to make certain he'd remember my face, or perhaps to keep from shedding a sentimental tear at our parting. "It's better for you to leave this way, you know. Take yourself away to meet new company where they don't know you. Perhaps even some decent gentleman who'll wed you."

"Oh, Father," I said, trying not to cry myself. "You always do wish me wed."

"I cannot help it, Kattypillar," he said wryly. "But you're well clear of Whitehall and the king."

"It is better this way," I said sadly. "Not for him, but for me."

"You're the only one who concerns me," Father said firmly. "I fear this reign will not end happily, and I'm glad you won't be tangled in the wreckage. Ahh, here's our Lady Katherine."

Grumpy with sleep, my daughter appeared with her governess to say her farewells, and soon was bundled into the carriage. I embraced my father one last time, and as we parted, a footman in royal livery came trotting to the carriage.

"My lady," he said breathlessly, bowing before me. "His Majesty sends his compliments, and asks your indulgence."

He stepped to one side and gestured with his arm. Another carriage stood at the end of the street, waiting. Though the carriage was plain, from the guards around it, I knew that James himself must be within.

"Will you go, Katherine?" Father asked softly.

For a long moment I hesitated between my past and my future. At last I looked back to the waiting footman and I smiled.

"Please thank His Majesty for his compliments," I said, "but pray tell him that he is too late, and regretfully I have gone."

I climbed into my coach and nodded to the footman. The driver cracked his whip and the horses stepped forward, pulling hard at their traces as the wheels began to turn. From the window, I waved to my father, and I did not look back to the other carriage.

Not once.

Author's Note

There are a good many royal mistresses scattered throughout the history of the English monarchy, but surely Katherine Sedley, Countess of Dorchester (1657–1717) is unique among them. She was neither beautiful nor voluptuous, and while remaining portraits of her don't show her to be as unattractive as her contemporaries claimed her to be, she definitely didn't fit the standard for beauty in Restoration England. Nor did she behave as a lady of her rank should; she spoke her mind, swore freely, and delighted in clever, sarcastic wordplay.

There is, however, no doubt that James Stuart loved her. While not as promiscuous as his brother Charles II, James had his share of extramarital lovers, but Katherine was both the last and the most lasting. His devotion to her mystified even Katherine herself: "He cannot love me for my beauty, for I have none," she once said, "and as for my wit, he has not enough of his own to judge it." But while James might not have been quick with a witty remark himself, he delighted in Katherine's irreverence, and their relationship remains one of the great contradictions of his life. Even as he grew increasingly more devout and attached to the Catholic Church, he continued to defend his bawdy, swearing, Protestant mistress as long as he could.

Katherine's "exile" in Ireland was short-lived. By the fall of 1686, she had returned to England, buying a large estate, Ham House, at Weybridge, Surrey. Here James was rumored to visit her occasionally, but the intensity of their affair was gone, and she never returned to her former power or place at Court. She continued her acquaintance with John Churchill, and was rumored to have taken a part behind the scenes in ousting her former lover. Still, when James was finally overthrown in the Glorious Revolution of 1688, Katherine was considered a Jacobite sympathizer, her actions watched with suspicion for the remainder of her life.

She certainly found no favor with the conservative new regime of William and Mary, who disapproved both of her and her former relationship to the old king. Katherine freely returned their hostility: "If I have broken one commandment, madam," she told Queen Mary, "then you have another [by dishonoring and overthrowing her father], and what I did was more natural."

Katherine finally did find respectable love and marriage. In 1696, just shy of her fortieth birthday, Katherine married Sir David Colyear (1656–1730), a one-eyed career soldier under William of Orange who was soon raised to Earl of Portmore in honor of his military success. It was enough to inspire her old gadfly, the Earl of Dorset, to write one final unpleasant poem at her expense:

Proud with the Spoils of her Royal Cully,
With false pretense to Wit and Parts,
She swaggers like a batter'd Bully,
To Try the tempers of Men's Hearts.
Tho she appear as glitt'ring fine,
As Gems, and Jet, and Paint can make her,
She ne'er can win a Heart like mine,
The Devil and Sir David take her.

But Katherine was thoroughly happy with her soldier and bore Lord Portmore two sons, famously imparting her brand of maternal advice before they left for school: "If anybody calls either of you the son of a whore, you must bear it, for it is so; but if they call you bastards, fight till you die, for you are an honest man's sons." Well content with her life, she died at Bath in 1717 at the age of sixty.

Her daughter with James, Lady Katherine Darnley (1680–1743), inherited both her mother's outspoken tongue and a propensity for scandal. First wed to the Earl of Anglesey, her marriage was dissolved by an act of Parliament on grounds of his cruelty. She next became the third wife of author, statesman, and libertine John Sheffield, Duke of Buckingham and Normanby, and lived with him in haughty splendor, always conscious of her royal blood. Their London home, Buckingham House, is today known as Buckingham Palace, one of the official residences of the current British royal family.

Katherine's royal lover, James II (1633–1701), did not fare nearly as well after their parting. He continued to promote his Catholicism to an unwilling nation and pursue a course of absolutism that made him increasingly unpopular. When Queen Mary Beatrice finally gave birth to a male heir in 1688, the child was widely believed to be an imposter, and despised as the Catholic successor to the throne. By the end of 1688, James's former supporters in the army led the rebellion to depose him in favor of his daughter Mary and her husband, William of Orange, in what became known as the Glorious Revolution. James, Mary Beatrice, and their infant son were permitted to escape to France, where they lived out their lives in unhappy, impoverished exile. Their son James (1688–1766) was known as the "Old Pretender" to the English throne, and became the centerpiece of the disastrous Jacobite rebellions in eighteenth-century Scotland.

Katherine's father, Sir Charles Sedley (1639–1701), was one of the Whig gentlemen who welcomed William and Mary to London in 1688. He certainly had the best remark to make at their coronation: "As the king [James] has made my daughter a countess, the least I can do, in common gratitude, is to make his daughter [Mary] a queen."

Laurence Hyde, Earl of Rochester (1641–1711), fell from James's favor soon after Katherine, and when he refused to convert to Catholicism at James's request, he was removed from office. He returned to the Privy Council under William and Mary, and continued in politics as a Tory leader until his death.

The careers of Katherine's two earlier lovers went in opposite directions after the Glorious Revolution. James Grahme (1650–1730) remained loyal to James II and figured in numerous Jacobite conspiracies throughout his life, finally dying in financial difficulties. John Churchill (1650–1722) abandoned James II and instead supported William of Orange. He became a noted statesman and legendary general, and, with his wife, Sarah, was often promoted as the special favorites of Queen Anne.

He died as Duke of Marlborough, and one of the wealthiest and most famous men of his times.

In telling Katherine Sedley's story, I have tried to remain true both to her irrepressible spirit and her times. By necessity, I've compressed the intricacies of Court politics and religious conflicts, but I have let Katherine and her circle speak for themselves in their own words whenever possible (even if those words come in the form of a scurrilous poem or two). As I've often said before, I'm a novelist, not a historian. I can only hope that Katherine would approve my version of her story.

Susan Holloway Scott
November 2009

The Countess and the King

A NOVEL OF
THE COUNTESS OF DORCHESTER AND KING JAMES II

SUSAN HOLLOWAY SCOTT

QUESTIONS FOR DISCUSSION

1. Most royal mistresses are famous for their great beauty, but Katherine Sedley was better known for her plain face and wit. What do you think her life would have been like had she been born a beauty instead?

2. James II has been traditionally portrayed as one of England's worst kings: a religious fanatic, a bigot, a sadist, and a tyrant. Recent historians, however, have been more sympathetic, viewing James as a man whose responsibilities exceeded his abilities, and whose strong personal beliefs and principles did not reflect those of his subjects. He also had the misfortune to follow his older brother, Charles II, a charming, charismatic ruler much loved by his people and endlessly skilled at the behind-the-scenes diplomacy so popular in Baroque courts. In other words, James wasn't so much a bad king, as the wrong king for seventeeth-century England. Do you agree?

3. Katherine and James made unlikely lovers. Katherine embodied so many things that James claimed to be against: she was a Protestant, the daughter of an outspoken Whig, and a ribald participant in Charles II's decadent court. Yet even after three hundred years, there's little doubt that he cared for her, and repeatedly defended her against his political and religious advisers. Why do you think he loved her? How do you think he reconciled their love with his own strict Catholic beliefs?

4. James's first wife, Anne Hyde, was born a commoner. While it

would have been politically disastrous (and very unlikely) for him to have chosen another wife who wasn't a foreign princess, would Katherine have fared better as James's wife than his mistress? Do you think James would have been a better king if Katherine had been his queen?

5. Sir Charles Sedley could hardly be called a responsible father to Katherine, yet throughout their lives, their relationship remained much closer than many other noble fathers and daughters of the seventeenth century. What do you think he did right—and wrong—as a father to a girl like Katherine?

6. Born shortly before Charles II's return to the throne in 1660, Katherine was very much a product of her times. Unlike the well-bred girls of the Elizabethan era who read Greek and Latin, few ladies of the 1660s were educated beyond the social "graces." Katherine, however, was exposed to much more literature and drama through her father and his friends. How do you think this shaped her personality?

7. Katherine often stated that she was more comfortable in the company of men than women, and certainly her intelligence and sense of humor were viewed in her time as more "male." How do you think posterity would regard her now if she'd been a man in Restoration England? Would she have been a politician in Parliament, a witty courtier, or a poet like her father?

8. Few seventeenth-century English ladies were heiresses in their own right like Katherine, and even fewer had fathers who permitted them to choose their own husbands. How did Katherine's fortune free her? How did it hamper her?

9. While no one now will know for certain, there is reason to question the extent of the "madness" of Katherine's mother. Some historians today view her as a truly tragic figure, an inconvenient wife who may have been pushed toward madness by the mercury-laden potions prescribed by physicians at her husband's urging. How do you think

this would have affected Katherine and her attitudes toward love and marriage?

10. While Katherine had a rich, full life that many would envy, she always remained self-conscious of her appearance and how it affected her interactions with others. Do you think she would have felt the same insecurities if she lived today?

Photo by Campli Photography

Susan Holloway Scott is the author of more than forty historical novels. A graduate of Brown University, she lives with her family in Pennsylvania. Visit her Web site at www.susan hollowayscott.com.